When Love Holidays

A Christmas Rom-Com!

S. J. Greene

To all who need a reminder to feel

joy, gratitude, and love.

Allow yourself. You deserve it.

Contents

Reader's Note:

If you're worried about landing on Santa's naughty list, proceed with caution. If you're already there, enjoy!

Part 1 – Enemies

"Whenever you are confronted with an opponent.
Conquer him with love."

— Mahatma Gandhi

1

54 days until Christmas

'Twas the unofficial start of the merriest time of year, and all the Christmas stars had aligned to lead her to the exact right place; that much was clear. The small town with "holiday" baked right into its name was more than perfect. It was destiny meets serendipity.

Destindipity.

Noelle sang along to Pentatonix's peppy rendition of "We Need a Little Christmas" as the road ahead unfurled like a spool of curling ribbon. *Yeah, we do. Right this very minute.* She'd resumed listening to holiday music around the same time she had decked her artificial Christmas tree.

In July.

Yes, she was *that* person. But Noelle didn't care what others thought when it came to her merriment. If not for her too-small beach bungalow, she would've blissfully left her tree up year-round, and there'd be no one to say a Who's poo about it. One advantage of being single, she supposed.

But all that was about to change.

Noelle had a plan.

As she neared her destination, four-thousand feet above sea level, it was as if she'd entered a cloud. The evergreens lining the shrouded road looked more like ever*grays*, and even the ever-present birds of prey circling overhead had vanished into the white abyss. A quick glance at the directions on her phone told her the property she'd leased was only a mile away.

Out of nowhere, a dark figure appeared on the road ahead. Noelle slammed on the brakes while swerving onto the shoulder. Was that a deer? No, it was too large to be a deer. A bear? *Were there bears here?* Heart pounding, she searched for it—whatever *it* was—once more in the dense fog.

Despite the lack of other vehicles on the road, a nagging sense that she might have traveled into another dimension had Noelle turning on her hazard lights. And then she saw it, slowly moving into view, right in front of her car. Evergreen—the trusty Volkswagen Beetle she'd driven for the last decade—was currently being eclipsed by a towering beast with…

Antlers?

Swirling white puffs of moist air distorted the visual, but there was definitely a branch-like structure on top of what was an enormous fur-covered head. Noelle sat in wonder as the majestic animal lumbered closer.

"Whoa there, Dasher," a husky voice called out from the fog.

Dasher? Realization flashed like the red glow of Rudolph's nose. The gentle giant now peering through her windshield was a reindeer. An actual reindeer!

Bubbling with excitement, Noelle nearly popped a cork when she saw the second figure emerge. Even through the haze, the burly man who approached was clearly attractive.

No, not attractive.

Gorgeous.

And wearing a freaking flannel! Long, blond waves fell across jacked shoulders decked in iconic red-and-black plaid. He looked like a cross between a Norse god and the modern Brawny paper towel guy—her holiday rom-com dream man.

She'd always known her plan would work, just not this quickly. Maybe her sister had been right all along: Noelle had the best luck.

Brawny Thor ran in front of the large reindeer, placing himself between it and Evergreen. Then he slipped a rope around its thick neck before it could advance any farther.

"Sorry!" he hollered.

"No problem," she said, opening her car door. She then circled around to get safely off the road. "Is it okay if I come say hello?"

"Sure. Dasher's friendly, even if a troublemaker. He's always breaking loose and wreaking havoc on the town. Our very own Deerzilla."

Noelle took a few steps closer, stopping when she could see a puff of warm air exit the reindeer's fur-trimmed nostrils. She marveled at Dasher's ombré coat—a flawless gradient of fawn to sable—which put her boots of similar color to shame. He was absolutely beautiful... as was his owner.

"If this is Dasher, does that make you Santa?" she asked, directing a flirtatious smirk at the flannel-clad man.

He laughed. "Not quite, but close. My family runs the Santa's Village Tree Farm up the hill here. I'm Noel Clauson—believe it or not—but I go by my middle name: Kris, with a K."

Noelle's jaw dropped. His name was also Noel? And he ran a Christmas tree farm? Someone had to be pranking her. Where were the cameras?

"Uh. Are you okay?"

"Yeah, it's just..." She blinked several times, then crossed her arms to block a gust of misty wind. "I'm Noelle. Noelle Serrano."

"Well, that's a happy coincidence. Nice to meet you, Noelle, Noelle Serrano."

Her dream man smiled and stuck out his hand, which she happily shook. It was warm, firm, and large—as she now imagined the rest of him to be. Despite the brisk weather, heat crept up her neck and reached her cheeks. Was she blushing? She couldn't be. With as many times as she'd been burned before, shouldn't she be immune to hunky men laying on the charm?

Then again, this wasn't some smooth-talking city boy. This was Noel Kris Clauson—her small-town hero.

"Were you born on Christmas too, as our name implies?" she asked, hoping they had yet another thing in common.

"No, I was a spring baby, but my mom loves the holidays… and liked the name, I suppose."

"Why do you go by Kris, then? Is Noel not a good enough name for you?" she asked with mock indignation.

"It's a perfectly fine name, especially for a beautiful woman such as yourself, but Noel feels a little too *on the nose* for a guy running a Christmas tree farm."

"And Kris Clauson isn't right up there on Rudolph's red nose?"

"Touché," he said, with a grin that melted her insides like a s'more. "Speaking of reindeer, would you like to formally meet Dasher? You can pet him, if you want. He may be an escape artist, but he's as sweet as Holiday Pines pie."

"I'd love to." Reaching up, she placed her hand on what appeared to be the reindeer's shoulder. "Hi, Dasher. Are you a troublemaker?"

The magnificent creature responded with a subtle bow of his antlers, and Noelle let out a delighted laugh.

"That makes two of us, then." She stroked Dasher's long torso. "He's so… fluffy."

"Yeah, reindeer have surprisingly soft fur. Two coats, actually. A dense, wooly coat underneath, and then these soft hollow hairs on top to trap additional heat. Would you like to feed him?"

Magically, a small bunch of carrots appeared and dangled in front of her face.

"Wow, where'd those come from?" Noelle scanned Kris, top to bottom. Besides the red flannel shirt, he wore relaxed-fit blue jeans and tan lumberjack boots covered in a light layer of mud. *Manly to the max.*

"I don't normally walk around with carrots in my pockets, if that's what you're wondering," he said with a laugh and adorably pink cheeks. "But I brought these to lure Dasher back to the stables."

"Stables? Do you have more than one reindeer?" she asked, taking a carrot and offering it to Dasher.

"A whole petting zoo full of them. You should stop by the farm sometime. How long are you visiting Holiday Pines?"

"I'm moving here, actually." She motioned toward the luggage and boxes that cluttered the backseat of her car. "My dad is bringing the rest of my stuff up in the morning, but I came this afternoon to get a head start. I'll be opening a year-round Christmas shop on Main Street, after some much-needed renovations to the storefront, which I plan to do myself."

There, Noelle thought. *Seed planted.* If he wanted, Kris could water it by offering his help. Love would certainly bloom during a fixer-upper project, the best excuse for forced proximity. She'd been in Holiday Pines for all of ten minutes, and her plan was already coming together perfectly.

Except it wasn't.

All the color had drained from his face. "The shop on the corner?"

"Yeah, why? It's not haunted or anything, is it?" she asked.

Kris gulped and took a few steps back, tugging Dasher along with him. "I should get headed back."

"Wait. Now you have me worried. What's wrong with the shop on the corner?"

"Nothing's wrong with it," he said, a little too quickly. "My wife ran a bookstore there for years. I should get Dasher back now. Good luck with your move."

Noelle stood dumbfounded as Kris hurried away. She had just met the man of her dreams—a gorgeous, charming, flannel-wearing,

Christmas tree farm owner—who, of course, had a wife. Yes, Alanis, it is *a little too ironic*. So much for her good luck.

Halloween was over, and ghosts weren't real. Noelle hoped not at least, as goosebumps crawled up her sweater-covered arms. She'd been joking when she'd asked if the store was haunted, but as she surveyed all the cobwebs and once-white sheets covering rows and rows of bookshelves, she wondered if it might be true.

The property, zoned for both commercial and residential use, had a second-story loft that would function as her bedroom-slash-shower. *Yes, only a shower*, and not even a large one. The rest of the bathroom was downstairs in the store area; as was the kitchen, which was more of an employee break room. Since Noelle intended to be the sole employee of her new store for the foreseeable future, it would have to do.

Lifting the nearest sheet, she choked on a plume of thick, gray dust that rose like the living dead. Her resulting coughing fit lasted a full minute before she thought to go outside to clear her lungs. After pulling on her faux-leather jacket, she stepped onto the sidewalk, her lingering coughs echoing in the wind.

Main Street mirrored the eerie quiet of her new store. A few cars sat parked in front of other businesses, but no one could be seen coming or going. Given it was a Wednesday afternoon, the ghost town vibe shouldn't have come as a surprise. Her real estate agent had informed her that most of Holiday Pines' business came from local tourists who frequented the charming town on weekends and holidays. Still, the emptiness unsettled her.

The dense fog from earlier had lifted, leaving a fine mist atop surfaces and a chill in its wake. She tugged her jacket shut to ward off the cold that accompanied her unease. The not-so-distant mountain peaks loomed all around, like castle walls. Sunshine battled its way through the clouds overhead as a single ray illuminated the hillside closest to her.

Unlike the pine-covered terrain she'd traversed on her way there, deciduous trees painted the backdrop to Main Street in brilliant shades of red, orange, and yellow—a vibrant reminder of the changing season. The fall scenery instantly elevated her mood, as most seasonal things tended to do, but it also reminded her of the tight timeline she'd given herself to liven up the store.

Deciding the face mask she'd packed for painting would suffice for dust protection, she grabbed it from her car and headed back inside. The work wasn't going to do itself.

@bookstafashionista

Transcript of social media video:

"Hiya, merry followers, Noelle here! I'll be posting the outfits inspired by last week's rom-com read here soon, so if you like what you see, be sure to click on those links!

"Same goes for the outfit I'm wearing today. This red cowl-neck sweater—which is ridiculously cozy, by the way—is paired with my trusty faux-leather jacket in faded mocha. Remember, faux or no-go when it comes to animal hides! And let me pan down to show you the best part of this ensemble… these oh-so-adorable booties! They're what I'm now calling my reindeer boots, thanks to the gradient that matches—you guessed it—a reindeer's coat!

"Oh, and I'm legally supposed to mention that I'm an affiliate, which means I make a small commission for purchases made using my links, blah, blah, blah. With that boring business out of the way, I also wanted to share a very special update: I've moved!

"That's why you see all the boxes in the background, and why you may unfortunately hear less from me in the coming days. But never fear. I will be back soon with updates you won't want to miss, including my new top-secret project!

"Until then, treat yourself to the new outfit you deserve and vote in the comments on the next book you'd like to see styled. And as always, stay merry, my friends!"

2

53 days until Christmas

"Thanks again for all your help today, sissy," Noelle said, sitting on the floor of her new living quarters.

The catchy melody of "Last Christmas" by Wham! played through the wireless speaker she'd paired to her phone—a makeshift solution until she could afford to install a sound system in the store.

"How many times do I need to tell you? You don't need to thank me. I'm sad you live so far away now, though," Jess said with an exaggerated pout.

"It's only an hour drive."

"Still. I can't pop by for quick visits anymore."

Not that there'd been much *popping by* over the past few months. Jessica Serrano was far too busy with her new relationship, two adorable children, sweet rescue dog, theater rehearsals, and concierge job.

Since saying so would be as pointless as a plain bulb ornament, Noelle shrugged. "I guess you'll have to plan longer visits, then."

"Done," Jess said, crushing Noelle with one of her signature bear hugs.

"Lucky me. I guess I better be careful what I wish for."

"Ha, ha. You better be careful all right, and you are extremely lucky, you little brat," Jess teased, squeezing Noelle even tighter as she did.

Noelle supposed there was some truth to that, as she often won things. *Contests. Jackpots in Vegas. Radio station giveaways. Game shows.* Silly things like that. But what her older sister didn't understand was that she would give up all her supposed luck to have what Jess had. *True love. Children. A family to call her own.*

Jess was the lucky one. But Noelle didn't need luck. She had a plan.

"Less hugging, more unpacking," Carlos Serrano said, as he carried another box from downstairs and dropped it onto the floor beside them with a bang. "Ay, Dios Mío! Are you moving bricks, Honeybee?"

"That box is full of books, Dad, and you shouldn't have lifted it by yourself! Mom will be even more mad at me than she already is if you throw your back out again."

Jess rested her hand on Noelle's shoulder. "Mom stayed home so she could pick up Chloe and Lucas from school for me, not because she's mad at you."

"That may be why she stayed home, but it doesn't mean she's not mad." Noelle turned to the one person who would never lie to her. "Right, Dad?"

The creases on her father's weathered face deepened in a rare moment of seriousness. "None of us are happy you moved way out here all by yourself, Honeybee. We worry about you. You know your mother, though. She takes things personally at first, but then she gets over it."

"You all act like I fled the country or something." Noelle threw her arms in the air. "I still live in the same county!"

"I know. I know," her father said, levity returning to his tone. "And honeybees *buzz buzz buzz* all around. It's why I call you that. I love your independent spirit, baby girl, but I don't have to like it." He grabbed at Noelle's nose with his knuckles, sticking his thumb between his index and middle fingers as if he'd pulled it off.

Jess harrumphed. "What about my independent spirit?"

"Yes, Kissin' Bug. I love both of my girls, pain in the necks as you two may be." Carlos then wrapped his arms around their necks in a wrestling move to make his point.

Noelle directed her best side-eye at Jess. As the stories went, her older sister apparently asked everyone for kisses as a toddler—a much sweeter nickname origin than Noelle's tendency to buzz around from place to place. But, whatever.

"Back to work!" Carlos shouted, releasing their necks before singing his way down the stairs. "Heigh ho, heigh ho, it's back to work you go."

"Dad, leave any more boxes of books downstairs, please," Noelle called after him. "I plan to put them on the bookshelves in the store anyway."

Jess clapped her hands. "That reminds me. You never finished sharing your plans for the store! What's it going to look like when it's all done?"

"Let's go help Dad, and I'll tell you."

They carried boxes from the truck to the store, taking the lighter ones upstairs, as Noelle did her best to put her vision into words.

"I plan to keep the bookshelves along both side walls, but I'll need to put the rest in storage to clear out the middle, where I'll have artificial trees set up to display the ornaments for sale. Each tree will be themed, with Christmas ornaments offered year-round, and some trees will be decorated for the current season or holiday, whether that be Halloween, Valentine's, or simply summer."

"And you'll sell books on the bookshelves?"

"The ones on the left side of the store, yes. It'll be mostly holiday romance novels, obviously," Noelle said.

"Obviously," Jess repeated.

"But also, Christmas cookbooks and other genres of fiction that take place around the holidays. Oh, and I'm reserving one shelving unit for Christmas movies, even though DVDs are obsolete. I figure it'll be a nostalgic item, and the holidays are all about nostalgia."

"Ooh, will you carry *While You Were Sleeping*?"

"Duh."

"What about *The Holiday*? And *Love, Actually*?"

"Double duh, and also, *You've Got Mail* and *Die Hard*." Noelle held up a hand before Jess could argue. "I stand firm that *Die Hard* is both a Christmas movie and a romance. He's trying to save his estranged wife—who he still loves—at a Christmas party. End of debate."

"Okay. Okay. If you feel that strongly about it," Jess said with an eye roll and a grin.

"That reminds me…" Noelle pulled out her phone to take a note. "I need to order a few copies of *Love Hard* as well. Catfishing with a twist; gotta love it."

"I'll give you *Die Hard*," Jess said, "but doesn't *You've Got Mail* technically take place over three seasons, fall to spring?"

"First, I love that you know that. If I didn't have a sister I could talk about rom-coms with, I don't know what I'd do."

A weak, pensive smile marred Jess's ordinarily cheerful face. "I love rom-coms. All movies, really. I'd always hoped to be on the big screen myself one day."

"You definitely could, sissy." Noelle gave her big sister's shoulder a squeeze, well aware of the regret Jess carried regarding her unpursued dreams.

Noelle had long ago vowed not to make the same mistake. She would follow her dreams wherever they led her, even if others disapproved.

"And secondly," Noelle continued, eager to lighten the suddenly heavy mood, "Christmastime is when the whole enemies-to-lovers plot takes root between Joe Fox and Kathleen Kelly. Ergo, holiday rom-com."

Jess quirked her brow. "Ergo?"

"What? I can't use fancy words to win arguments?"

"You can, but I wouldn't say you need to. I can't think of a single argument you've lost."

Noelle made a show of lifting her chin in triumph and dusting off her shoulders, which produced the laugh she'd been hoping for from Jess. She might be known as the brat in her family, but cheering them up was her favorite superpower.

"Will all the movies be rom-coms, then?" Jess asked.

"No, I'll also carry family classics like *A Christmas Story, It's A Wonderful Life, The Grinch Who Stole Christmas,* and so on. I'm still trying to decide if the movies should be for sale or offered as rentals. What do you think?"

"Hmm. I don't know. Video rentals might be too much of a throwback… and harder to track, too. I'd say sell them. They'll make good stocking stuffers."

Noelle nodded along. "Good points. Decision made. Thanks!"

"Happy to help. What else will the store have?"

"Well, the other wall of bookshelves on the right will display the home décor items, like snow globes and figurines. I'll also have a section for Christmas cards, wrapping paper, and things of that nature. And I eventually want to get a couple of racks for apparel, but that'll have to come later since I haven't locked in any fashion wholesalers yet and want to get it right."

"Wow. I'm so proud of you, Noelle! Thanksgiving's only a few weeks away, though. Do you think it'll all come together in time?"

"That's the plan. Most of the merchandise is already on its way here, and I'll be focused on the renovations in the meantime. The floor *def* needs to be replaced, so I'm thinking new tile in a black-and-white buffalo-plaid pattern."

"And you know how to do that?"

Noelle shrugged, doing her best to ignore her sister's skepticism. "I'll watch a YouTube video. It can't be that hard. I plan to use dark-gray tiles around the black and white ones to simulate the overlap. I saw some pics on Pinterest that looked *amazing*."

"That's great. But you know Brad is a general contractor and—"

"Ew! I'm not going to ask your cheating ex-husband to help tile my floor."

Jess picked up another box and followed Noelle upstairs. "First off, we're on good terms now. The divorce has been going smoothly. And secondly, Brad doesn't have to be the one to do it. He could give you some tips or recommend someone knowledgeable to do the job. Maybe even Kent—"

"No, thanks. I don't need any help from Brad or his awful brother. Besides, that would interfere with my master plan."

"Which is?" Jess asked, as if the answer wasn't already obvious.

"Find a handsome local to help with my renovations, complete the job together, fall in love by Christmas, and live happily ever after. Duh."

"Seriously, Noelle? You're still set on your small-town romance plan, even after that Brawny Thor guy you met yesterday had a wife?"

"Yes, Miss Judgy. One failed meet-cute isn't going to make me give up on my dream. Like I've told you before, I'm sick of waiting around for love to find me. I'm going to make things happen for myself. There will be other available MIFs." At her sister's confused expression, Noelle added, "Men in flannel."

"Ah, of course," Jess said. "And I'm not being judgy. I just don't understand why you had to move to some mountain town in the middle of nowhere to find love. Couldn't this plan of yours work in San Diego?"

"Again, I only moved an hour away. It's not the middle of nowhere. And no, it can't. My plan requires a wholesome, small-town hero. I'm done with *Man Diego* guys who only like me for my looks and then peace out once they get what they want."

Jess made a loud sound resembling water blasting from a whale's blowhole. "Well, I'd say they're not all the same, but my experience in that department isn't great. Give me a hug, you crazy girl," she added, throwing her arms wide.

Noelle stepped closer and leaned into the embrace. As frustrating as Jess could be at times, Noelle wouldn't trade her sister's love for anything in the world… not even ten Brawny Thors striptease dancing in Santa hats and flannel thongs.

Okay, wow, maybe she'd trade it for that.

"God bless America!" her dad shouted from the top of the stairs. "So much hugging going on up here. Come on, Kissin' Bug. We've got to head back now."

"Aww, do we have to leave already?" Jess whined.

"Yes, unfortunately. I told your mom we'd be there for dinner. Plus, I'd like to make it down the pass before it gets dark." Carlos turned to Noelle. "Did you save some hugs for me, Honeybee?"

"I suppose," Noelle said, already wrapping her arms around her father's solid yet trim shoulders. "Thanks again for everything, Dad, and tell Mom I miss her cooking already, even though she's mad at me."

"Your mom loves you, and so do I. Now, stay out of trouble. Do you hear me?" Carlos pointed his finger at her in a laughable attempt at sternness.

"I hear ya," Noelle said with an exaggerated eye roll.

"That's it. I'm gonna tell him!" Carlos shouted.

"Don't tell him, Carlos! Don't be cheeeee-ken!" Noelle and Jess both replied in unison, perhaps for the millionth time in their lives.

They all erupted in silly laughter before waving their goodbyes. *The perfect note to leave things on.*

As Noelle watched the large truck drive off, a shrinking silhouette against the rose-gold sky, the reality of her solitude hit anew. Her first night hadn't been easy—spent on an air mattress in the loft of a possibly haunted store—but it had felt temporary, like a camping trip. She knew the second night, and every night thereafter, would be different.

Her bed, furniture, and all of her belongings were there now. But her family was gone. She'd moved to Holiday Pines to find love and, as per usual, found herself completely alone.

Thank Christmas she had a plan.

@bookstafashionista

Photo caption:

Okay, merry followers, I'm horrible at keeping secrets, so I'm gonna spill some of the peppermint tea right now.

This is a "before" photo of what will soon be my new year-round Christmas and holiday joy shop! Ooh, I like that for a potential name. Help me decide on my official store name by voting in the comments.

A) Merry Every Day
B) Merry Holidays
C) Holiday Joy Shop, or
D) ??? - Tell me your ideas!

I'll be sure to post updates on my shop's progress, but in the meantime, stay merry! Logging off now to head to the hardware store (again!) #staymerry #holidaystore #christmas #romcom #masterplan #bookstafashionista

3

51 days until Christmas

It was her third trip to the hardware store. Who knew tiling a floor would require so many tools and supplies? The friendly, yet nowhere-near-attractive older gentleman working the counter pointed her to the back aisle for tile spacers, mortar, and something called a trowel.

"Thanks, Earl!" Noelle called out over her shoulder as she made her way past rows of light bulbs, paint, and gardening equipment.

Her first two visits to Screw It—*yes, that was the hardware store's name*—hadn't resulted in any chance encounters or meet-cutes, but Noelle had a good feeling that was about to change as she rounded the corner. A tall man with dark hair stood with his backside to her, and… *wow*. Ordinarily, she was not one to objectify men, but this dish seemed anything but ordinary.

She nearly salivated at the sight before her—an overall lean build augmented by broad shoulders, defined back muscles, and (most notably) a firm pair of Christmas hams on display under his slim-fit jeans. Never before had she been so tempted to sink her teeth into another human being. Whether luck or some other cosmic force was at play, he happened to be standing right in front of the tile spacers.

"Mind if I squeeze in there?" Noelle asked in her sultriest tone.

The mystery man whirled around, then pushed his glasses back into place before gaping at her. "Noelle?"

No, no, no. What was *he* doing here? Before her lips could ask, her treacherous feet stumbled backward, knocking her own curvy backside into the shelving unit behind her. This triggered a loud crash, followed by the sound of metal screws rolling across the cement floor. Stuck in a game of *Mouse Trap*, she wondered what chain reaction would be kicked off next. She got her answer when she leaned down to clean up the mess and was met with a hard smack in the forehead. *Cheese captured. Lights out.*

Something tapped her cheek. A hand maybe? She heard her name repeated, "Noelle, Noelle, Noelle," but each instance faded further into the background, like an echo trapped in a hollow bell—or, as was the case, in her throbbing head. Where was she?

With great agony, she cracked her eyes open and then snapped them shut again. The blinding fluorescent light sent a fresh dose of pain, this time piercing, right through her skull.

"Ow," she muttered, rubbing her tender forehead.

"Noelle, are you okay? I'm so sorry!" a male voice said.

Not any male voice. Even with closed eyes, she knew it was *him*. The too-smart-for-his-own-good, intolerable Kent F. Clark.

"Why are *you* here?" she asked with unrestrained annoyance.

"I was looking for you, actually."

"Why?"

"How's your head?" he asked, ignoring her question.

"It feels like I was knocked out."

"You were. I feel terrible. I reached down for a screw, and we bumped heads."

Fighting against the brightness, she forced her eyelids open once again and saw him crouched beside her. "Your big head is what hit me?"

"I'm afraid so." He gripped onto her elbow. "Let's get you on your feet."

Only then did she notice the icy hardness of the cold cement floor under her. As she shifted her weight forward, something sharp poked at the backs of her legs.

A few feet away, a teenage boy wearing clothes two sizes too large—and two decades behind the current fashion trends—stood sweeping screws into a pile. *Ah, that's right.* She'd spilled a bin full of screws onto the ground.

Like an idiot.

Kent rose, dead lifting her the way one would a dumbbell at the gym. That's how she must seem to him. Dumb.

"How come you didn't get knocked up too?" she asked once upright, though hardly stable.

She was in a carriage... on the treetop... when the wind blew. And when the bough broke... *Who in their right mind would put a baby on a treetop?*

"You mean knocked *out*," he said, disrupting her muddled thoughts, "and I suppose it's because my head is harder than yours."

"What did I say?"

"Knocked up, and I assure you I didn't do that. How do you feel?"

"Confused. What are you doing here, KFC? Besides *not* knocking me up with your big, hard head?"

When the young employee with the broom coughed to cover a laugh, Noelle put her still throbbing head in her hands and groaned. "I just heard how that sounded."

"Um, you might have a concussion," Kent said. "Let's get you to the hospital to get checked out. Do you think you can walk?"

"To the hospital?"

"No. To my car. Never mind." Without warning, he scooped Noelle off her feet and headed toward the exit.

"Hey, put me down!"

"Not a chance."

Three and a half hours later, Kent followed a vexingly resistant and unappreciative Noelle into her new building on Main Street. Had she really moved to Small Town USA on a whim? He'd heard that she'd "discovered" Holiday Pines by zooming in on Google Maps and liking the name, which sounded about right.

"For the millionth time, I don't need your help," she said, exaggerations aside, for at least the tenth time in the last ten minutes.

"Yes, you do. You have a concussion and need to be observed."

"And whose fault is that?"

He scanned the dimly lit room full of boxes. "Let's unpack one of the fifty mirrors I'm sure you own and find out."

"As if any of this could be *my* fault. You shouldn't even be here!" Noelle shot him the same look of disgust she wielded whenever someone paired socks with sandals. "And stop saying *let's*. It's annoying. *Let's* get you to the hospital. *Let's* unpack mirrors. Ugh."

Unbelievable. "Let me get this straight. This is all my fault, I shouldn't be here, and I'm no longer allowed to say the word *let's*. Is that correct?"

"First, it's not a word."

Kent cocked his head, unable to fathom what he must have said wrong this time.

"Let's is a contraction of two words. You should know that, Professor Smarty Pants. Secondly," she said, holding up a hand before he could interrupt. "Let's means let us, implying an *us* exists. It does not."

"Wow. There are no other words—or contractions—to describe… Just, wow."

"Why don't you 'wow' yourself out the front door and back to San Diego, where you belong?"

"Would a little gratitude kill you? I've spent the last three hours listening to how horrible I am, not to mention your premature Christmas music in the car, and yet I still plan to help tile this hideous floor. You're welcome."

"I am *not* welcome. I didn't ask for your help!"

"No, but your much more sensible sister did."

"Don't remind me. I plan to kill her later. Ugh. Right after my head stops pounding."

His anger dissipated in a flash. "Why don't we find somewhere for you to sit and rest?"

She only glared at him in return.

"What now?"

"*Why don't we* is a longer version of let's."

"Well, it's a shame that contraction is forbidden, then. I guess it'll take me longer to say things." He drew out each syllable toward the end to stress his point.

After a tense moment, she let out a sigh that signaled surrender. "I don't have any chairs down here yet, but my bed is upstairs."

Every muscle in his body tightened. Damn this woman's unique ability to make him feel the full Gaussian distribution of human emotions, even those many standard deviations outside of its curve. And then there were her curves…

"So, as previously stated, you can show yourself out, and I'll go take a nap," she said, interrupting his musings with yet another catty comment.

"You're supposed to rest, but not sleep yet. Did you listen to the doctor at all?"

"You mean during the five minutes he spent talking to you like I wasn't even there, after I'd waited three hours to be seen? Yeah, that was a colossal waste of time. I didn't need an ER doctor to tell me to take a Tylenol and get some rest. If I'd done that hours ago, I'd feel better by now."

She was *completely* and *utterly* insufferable. Redundancy justified. Never mind that he'd also spent three hours of his life at the ER, during which time she'd rattled on about being there against her will, calling him a kidnapper, a chauvinist pig, a brute with a superiority complex, and even a terrorist at one point, which earned them some looks in the waiting room.

He rubbed his pulsing temples. "Can we please stop fighting? It's not good for your head injury. The doctor said no mental, emotional, or physical exertion for two days, and no sleep until tonight. I'm supposed to observe you for signs of a more serious condition."

Noelle crossed her arms like a petulant child. "We weren't fighting. I was merely stating the facts. And I still haven't gotten a Tylenol or any rest."

"Here," he said, pulling the bottle of pills from the paper bag in his hand. "Let's get... I mean, let *me* help you upstairs, then you can take one of these."

"It seems I don't have a choice. I'm like a woman in 1843. Or present-day Texas."

Kent led her toward the back of the store by her elbow. "Your sharp wit requires mental energy, so try to dial it back. Up you go," he added, once they reached the base of the stairs.

"Yes, drill sergeant," she said, clearly unable to heed his advice. But he considered it a win when she ascended the narrow staircase as instructed. He'd play along if it got her to listen.

"Okay, soldier. Into bed," he ordered next.

She slowly turned and, like a jungle cat, peered up at him through a lush forest of lashes. "Only if you join me."

Kent froze. He couldn't move or even blink. His lungs had apparently stopped functioning as well, since his last breath was stuck somewhere in the middle of his throat. Speaking was impossible, so he simply stared, slack-jawed and stupefied.

"Oh Saint Nick!" Noelle laughed while lowering herself onto the bed. "You should see your face right now. Seriously, where is a mirror when you need one?"

At least his eyelids worked again, he thought as they instinctively shut.

Her childish prank shouldn't have come as a surprise, given he taught high school students with more maturity than Noelle Serrano ever cared to show—to him, anyway—and yet he'd been caught off-guard by her targeted antics more times than he could count. And as a math teacher, that was pretty darn high.

When Kent opened his eyes, he saw Noelle rocking back and forth at the edge of the bed, doubled over, most likely in stifled laughter at his expense.

"Are you okay?" he asked.

A long beat of silence passed. Too long. Was she in pain or still messing with him? For the first time in his life, he hoped for the latter.

"Noelle?"

When she didn't reply, Kent lunged forward and grabbed her by the shoulders. "Please, say something."

Finally, her head crept upright like a zombie rising from the grave. Her face, normally that of a beautiful mermaid, took on the pallid visage of a seasick sailor. She placed a delicate hand on his shoulder as he held onto both of hers.

"Noelle?" he asked again.

"I think I'm gonna be—"

Projectile vomit, lots and lots of it, directly onto his shirt, obviated her last word. On impulse, he raked his hand through her thick, shoulder-length hair, pinning it back against the nape of her neck. When the first wave of spewing ended, a second one started. There was nothing for him to do but to ride it out. And try not to look down.

"Sick," she croaked out, after he was covered in what he assumed to be the entire contents of her stomach. "I'm so sorry."

If her retching hadn't been proof enough, now Kent knew she was unwell. She was actually apologizing. *To him.*

"It's okay," he said, grabbing a pair of scissors he'd spied atop one of her moving boxes. "I didn't like this shirt anyway."

"Well, I wasn't going to say anything, but that boring T-shirt is not... What are you doing?"

"Carefully removing this boring, vomit-soaked shirt. I'd rather not lift it over my head, if that's okay with you." He cut down the center of his long-sleeved shirt, starting at the neck opening, then paused long enough to take in her horrified expression. "*Is* this okay with you?"

"Totally. It's just..." Noelle fell silent for *one, two, three* seconds. She had yet to blink when she blurted, "I'll buy you a new shirt. A better one. You know, something with actual style."

He had to fight back a smile. *There was the Noelle he knew.* She'd been mocking his fashion sense, or apparent lack thereof, for as long as he could remember. It felt oddly comforting for her to still be doing it while concussed.

Once the scissors reached the bottom hem, Kent peeled the wet fabric away from his skin, using great care to contain the mess within the shirt. "I'm going to run this downstairs, hopefully to a trash can, and I'll fetch you a glass of water while I'm at it. Do you have any cups unpacked yet?"

The look of horror returned to her face as she stared back at him with wide unblinking eyes, mouth agape.

"Noelle, cups?"

"Yes. Yes, please," she stammered, evidently not understanding his question.

"Never mind. I'll find them and come back with some water for you. Try to get some rest in the meantime."

He'd reached the top of the stairs when he heard, "Wait."

"Do you need something else?" he asked, turning around to see her countenance morph from one of shock to amusement.

Most of her color had returned, including a splash of pink across both of her well-defined cheekbones. Her ruby lips, no longer parted in disgust, curled into an all-too-familiar smirk.

"It's on your pants, too," she said.

A quick glance down confirmed her statement. His dark blue jeans were spattered with a pinkish, viscous substance, similar in appearance to Long Island clam chowder—a favorite dish he'd surely never eat again. The lion's share was concentrated in his crotch region, because *of course it was*.

"I'll use the sink downstairs to clean up," he said, before promptly descending the stairs as quickly as possible.

4

Noelle sank back onto her bed and stared at the ceiling. *What in the South Pole was happening?* It made zero sense that Kent was even in Holiday Pines, but now he was also in her new store-slash-apartment, shirtless and fetching her water... after she'd thrown up all over him.

Because *he* had given her a concussion.

It was important to remember that this was all KFC's fault. If he had stayed in San Diego like he should have, none of the day's terrible events would have happened. She wouldn't have been startled into knocking over the screw bin, nor would she have been knocked out by his thick skull—which likely damaged her already subpar brain.

Even worse, Kentucky Fried Clark would now be her prison warden for the next two days, forcing her to rest when she should be getting her store ready. If only her head would stop pounding long enough for her to figure out a way to get rid of him.

"Some water and a Tylenol," he said, magically appearing like a genie granting her wish. *A shirtless and surprisingly ripped genie.*

She'd always known Kent Frumpy Clark to have abysmal taste in clothing, but until that pivotal moment—the one where he'd cut the shirt right off his chest, revealing sculpted pecs and abs of steel—she hadn't realized just how unflattering his untailored attire had been to his physique.

The sight of him again, still bare chested and holding out a glass of water in one hand, pills in the other, did things to her insides. Weird things. Bad things. He was her archnemesis, not someone to be ogled.

"Thanks," she forced herself to say, taking the relief he offered.

The cool water soothed her burning throat as she tipped her head back once, and then twice, swallowing a much-needed pain killer each time.

"Better?" he asked.

"Yeah, that's exactly how fast pills work," she said with an eye roll that hurt way more than it was worth. "I still don't understand why I couldn't take the ibuprofen I had in my purse, way back when we were in the waiting room. Then I'd already be feeling better."

"As I explained at the time, ibuprofen increases the chance of bleeding, so it's not good to take for a concussion. I'm concerned about your memory," he said, sounding truly concerned. *Damn him.*

Kent then sat on the edge of the bed, of *her* bed, and reached behind her.

"What—What are you doing?"

"Calm down. I'm just adjusting your pillows to prop you up more. How's that?"

Calm down? Calm down? First off, any idiot knows not to tell someone who's riled up to *calm down*. It has the opposite effect. Secondly, how was she supposed to be calm with his bare chest mere inches from her face?

And then there were those arms.

She'd always been a sucker for a nice set of arms. Biceps were great, and his were above average, but those forearms… lean and tone with veins that bulged ever-so-slightly from his firm skin. Neither bulky nor scrawny, they were just right.

And those perfect forearms were framing either side of her head as he adjusted her pillow. If she were to lean an inch or two in either direction, she could lick one.

"Are you okay? You're drooling," he said.

Dear Baby Santa, he noticed her gawking at his arms. This was bad, very bad.

"What? Why?" she asked, not sure why herself. Maybe she wasn't okay. Checking out Kent Foul One Clark certainly wasn't normal behavior.

It didn't matter that his forearms were specimens of perfection. They were wasted on *him.*

He dabbed at her chin with the bedsheet. "There, I got it. I'm worried about you, though. Maybe we should head back to the ER for another scan."

Oh. She'd had actual drool on her chin. It wasn't a figure of speech. That was better, right? Or was it worse?

"No, no. I'm fine. I just need to rest."

If only that were possible in his presence. Her brain seemed to be sprinting a marathon in circles every time he spoke. For the millionth time that day, she knew exactly what she needed.

"Please leave," she mumbled, as her eyelids grew heavy.

When they opened again, Kent was nowhere in sight. Maybe he really was a genie. That was wish number two, if she were keeping count. She looked around the dark room. When had it gotten dark?

"Hey, you're awake," a voice said from the other side of the bed. A female voice.

"Jess?"

"Yeah. How are you feeling?"

"A little better, I think, but I'm confused. How are you here?"

"Kent called me. He explained what happened and thought he might be making things worse, so I offered to come up and keep you company. I'm so sorry you have a concussion!" Jess said.

"It's not your fault. Except, wait… it is! I can't believe you sent KFC up here! What were you thinking?"

"I was thinking you need help getting this place ready before Thanksgiving and that Kent, not KFC, is both handy and nice enough to make that happen. Please try to relax, Noelle. Getting upset is not good for your healing brain." Her tone was one hundred percent big sister. And one thousand percent annoying.

"It wouldn't need to heal if you hadn't meddled." Noelle crossed her arms with a *humph*, but in all honesty, it was hard to stay mad at her sister.

Jess had obviously dropped everything to rush to her aid, and Noelle knew her sister's intentions, even if misguided, came from a heart of pure gold.

"For what it's worth, I'm sorry," Jess said. "Is there anything I can get you?"

"Some more water would be nice. How long was I asleep?"

"A few hours, I think. I got here about an hour ago."

"So… Kent should be back in San Diego by now?" Noelle asked, feeling hopeful.

A male voice answered from the dark staircase. "No, Kent has been sanding your floor for the last hour. He also heard you talking and brought up another glass of water."

Seconds later, Kent appeared at the top of the stairs, holding said glass of water. Even if he hadn't annoyingly announced himself in the third person, Noelle would have recognized his shadowy outline. Thanks to his earlier strip tease, his cut figure would be forever etched into her wretched memory.

She groaned. "Ugh. You're still here."

"Be nice!" Jess scolded. "He's doing you a favor."

Kent set the water down on a box that was doubling as a temporary nightstand. "It's okay. I'm used to it. And I'm doing you a favor, Jess, not her. She's made that abundantly clear."

"*She's* lying right here," Noelle said, irritation brewing like steam in a teakettle. "And my sister is here now, so you can go home."

"Actually," Jess said, "I asked him to stay, because I have to leave in the morning. Avery is getting back from her trip early, and I need to pick her up from the airport before picking Lucas and Chloe up from Brad's on the way to church. I'm sorry. I could ask Brad to keep the kids an extra day, but I miss them, and I—"

"It's okay," Noelle said, placing a hand on her sister's arm. "Go see your family. I don't need a babysitter anyway."

"You're my family, too, and I want to make sure you'll be okay. And for the record, Kent is also technically family," Jess said, motioning to the large shadow on the other side of the bed.

"My sister's ex-brother-in-law is hardly my family," Noelle said, refusing to turn her head in his direction. "What about Mom and Dad? They could come up if I needed someone to look after me, which I *don't*."

"They're at that couples' retreat for Marriage Encounter this weekend," Jess said. "I already tried Mom's cell, but I think it's off."

"Oh. I forgot about that. It's fine. I wouldn't want to interrupt their romantic weekend. Or yours with Avery. Seriously, I'm fine alone."

She'd been alone for all her *nine and twenty years*, as they'd say in her Regency romance novels. A spinster by those standards. What was another weekend by herself?

"You're not fine alone," said the deep voice beside her. She'd have thought it her subconscious if not for the rich timbre reaching her toes.

Reluctantly, Noelle angled her head so that Kent was in her peripheral view. Her eyes, having adjusted to the dim lighting, could make out the tightness in his scruff-covered jaw, the defiance in his stance, and the intensity of his gaze through well-suited lenses.

Not for the first time, she imagined he'd make good money as an eyeglass model. Or at least score some free designer frames. That was, of course, if he didn't consider such a profession superficial and beneath him. *Cue mental eye roll.*

More importantly, Kent once again wore a shirt—a tight-fitting V-neck that most men would wear as an undergarment, but a shirt nonetheless. *Thank the North Pole.* Never mind those still exposed arms, which glistened with sweat and what appeared to be… wood dust? *Right.* He'd been sanding her floor.

"I'll keep an eye on her tomorrow, whether she likes it or not," he said to Jess. "I'm going to head out now. The inn down the street has a room available for the night."

"That's crazy. You don't have to rent a room, Kent," Jess said. "I brought up an extra air mattress you can use tonight. Between the loft and downstairs, there's plenty of room for all three of us."

"Thanks, but the inn is pretty affordable. It'll be worth it to have a hot shower, a real mattress, and no one wishing me harm." Kent turned his head in Noelle's direction on that last item.

She thought of her unused third wish and bit back a grin.

"Noelle," Jess snapped, "please tell Kent he's welcome to stay here tonight."

Noelle looked from Jess to Kent and then back to her sister, battling with what she already knew was the right thing to do. The words would hurt, but she had to say them. "KFC is welcome."

"Great!" Jess clasped her hands together. "Kent, please stay. You can shower here."

All three of them swiveled their heads toward the small shower stall in the corner of the room. It had frosted glass walls and zero other barriers between it and her bed. *Yeah, that wasn't happening.*

"Noelle and I can go downstairs to give you some privacy," Jess added.

"She needs her rest," Kent said. "Honestly, I don't mind going to the inn. It'll be a nice break for me."

"Ha!" Noelle exclaimed before she could stop herself. He needed a break *from her?* He'd been the one smothering her like a mother hen all day.

Both sets of eyes turned on her, and Noelle faked a cough. "I'm pretty hungry. Maybe we could grab some food while KFC takes a shower. He could definitely use one."

"There's an idea," Jess said, picking up her purse, "but you shouldn't be going anywhere. I'll go pick up some food for all three of us. In the meantime, Kent can help you down the stairs, and then he can shower this awful day off. Okay, see you soon!"

And then Jess was gone.

Her sister had always been good at getting her way, even if it was with the grace of a bulldozer.

"I didn't tell her," Kent said, "about the vomit incident, in case you were wondering. I would very much like to shower more than this day off, though."

"Oh. Of course," she said, the first half of the day already a distant memory. "I really am sorry about that."

"So… can I help you downstairs?"

"Sure," she said, accepting the hand he offered.

She swung one leg off the bed and then the other, bringing herself to a seated position on the edge before pressing weight into his palm. Her butt lifted about a foot off the bed, then crashed back down.

"Whoa. I've got you," he said, pulling her forward so she didn't completely fall onto her back. "Let's try that again."

"Let's?"

"Sorry, I guess you were right about me overusing that word… I mean, contraction."

At the sweetest three words his lips could utter—*you were right*—she found herself smiling up at him. Kent, of all people, had made her smile. The thought had her biting her lip. Maybe her head injury was more serious than she'd thought.

Kent gave her hand a gentle squeeze. "Noelle?"

"Right. I'll try to stand again."

She shifted all her weight forward, pressing into his hand once more, and made it onto her feet that time.

"Yay!" she cheered, before her head spun and her knees buckled.

But she didn't fall. Two strong arms squeezed into her sides, holding her up as a blanket of warmth wrapped around her body. Except there was no blanket, only Kent.

And those arms.

She'd braced herself by grabbing onto his shoulders, but as she stood there, swaying with the room, her eyes and hands slid, ever so slowly, down his finely chiseled biceps. Once below the inner bend of his elbow, her thumb leisurely stroked the fleshy slab of muscle otherwise known as *the perfect forearm.*

"Okay, you're definitely not fine. We're going back to the hospital," he said, in a throatier than normal voice.

"No, I promise I'm fine. The doctor said some dizziness is normal after a concussion."

His sharp eyes bore into her. "Now you remember what the doctor said?"

"It's coming back to me. See, I must be getting better."

When Kent continued staring at her, Noelle realized she was still stroking his forearm… and feeling as if she might swoon. *Comet, Cupid, Donner, and Blitzen*—she needed to lay off the historical romances.

"Well, there's no way I'm letting you walk down the stairs dizzy," he said, breaking her trance. "I suppose I could carry you."

"Absolutely not!" She released his arms and sat back down on the bed, crossing her own arms to demonstrate her resolve. "This is stupid. We're both adults and can be mature about this."

"That has yet to be seen," he muttered.

"What I'm saying is, I don't need to go downstairs. I'll just lie here with my back to the shower. Seriously, Kent, I'm not going to perv on you while you're naked." When he didn't respond right away, she added, "You better hurry, though. This town isn't very big. Jess will be back any minute with dinner."

When Kent signaled his reluctant acceptance with a single nod, Noelle reclined and then rolled onto her side to face the wall opposite the shower. *No big deal.*

After what seemed like forever, the sound of running water began, loud and forceful at first, followed by muted drips once he stepped in. Noelle lay perfectly still, listening, though not sure for what. The sound of him lathering his hard body with soap? Low moans of pleasure as the hot shower heated his core?

No, she certainly wouldn't be hearing any of that. This wasn't one of her steamy rom-com novels.

What she should be listening for was her sister's return. Jess would flip out if she walked upstairs and witnessed… whatever this was. Not to mention she'd see Kent naked. Noelle allowed herself to visualize, only for a split second, what that would be like. If his arms were any indication, the rest of him would be equally long and lean. Then there was that firm backside she'd admired at the hardware store.

And that was enough of that.

She could call Jess to give her a heads up… if Kent hadn't annoyingly taken her phone away after the hospital. He'd claimed she needed to limit her screen time—a fact her many followers would *not* be happy about. Getting her phone back thereby solved two problems. It was right there in her mind's eye, her lifeline to the outside world, sitting atop one of the many unpacked boxes at the other end of the room.

She could do this. The shower was still running. All she had to do was crawl backwards on her hands and knees to retrieve the phone, and then crawl forward and back into bed without him being the wiser. Easy peasy.

Without further delay, she wiggled toward the edge of the bed, slid her knees onto the ground, and then lowered onto all fours—all the while keeping her back to the shower. No problem at all.

Time to crawl.

Alternating her hands and legs backward felt a little like learning to walk again, but it didn't take long for her to get into a smooth rhythm. Right, left, right, left. Noelle yelped when her pinky toe snagged on a box, but she quickly recovered and steered around several more obstacles before arriving in the area she expected to find her phone. Back still to the shower, she lifted onto her knees and scanned the tops of all the nearby boxes.

Nothing.

That couldn't be right. Where was her phone? Since she couldn't look behind her, the distance to the end of the room was difficult to gauge. Maybe she hadn't gone far enough. She got back onto her hands and crawled farther away from her bed, hoping it was atop the next set of boxes. Again, she lifted onto her knees but didn't see her phone anywhere.

She repeated those steps—crawling backward, then stopping to search—several times before her foot finally hit the back wall. It was the end of the room, and her phone was nowhere in sight. *Well, gumdrops.* Maybe she had gone too far into the corner.

Mindful of keeping her back to the shower, she angled her body ninety degrees and crawled a few paces backward. Still nothing. A little farther. Nope, no phone.

She started again, then froze. The shower was no longer running. *O Holy Night!* When had it stopped? Panic and perhaps muscle memory set in, because the only thing she could think to do was to continue crawling backward.

A sudden kick to her side body was followed by an immediate swear and a loud crash. She collapsed onto her stomach at the punch of pain and then turned her head to the side. Directly in front of her lay a very wet, very male, naked body.

Kent Full-Frontal Clark's naked body.

5

Kent scrambled to get back onto his feet, all the while trying to ascertain what he'd tripped over. The answer let out a weak groan.

"Noelle! What the fuck?"

He didn't like to swear, especially in the presence of a lady, but what the serious fuck had just happened? One minute he was exiting the shower, the next he was on the ground, wet and completely naked in front of Noelle.

Noelle, who was supposed to be in bed with her back to him.

Noelle, who instead was lying on the ground in front of the shower, looking like roadkill. *Shit.*

"Are you okay?" he asked, crouching beside her.

"You're naked," she said with another groan.

Her ability to state the obvious in the middle of a crisis was mind-blowing. Still, she had a point. He needed to cover himself. *Where were her towels?* In his haste to get into the shower, he hadn't located them beforehand.

He spun around the room, searching for something, anything. Then he heard another voice coming from downstairs.

"Kent? Noelle? I'm back!"

Fuck, fuck, fuck. He would never live this down.

"We're upstairs, but don't come up here!" he yelled with urgency, before racing to Noelle's bed and yanking off the sheet.

"Both of you? Why can't I come up?" Jess hollered back.

At the same time, Noelle asked, "What are you doing?"

"Just don't, please!" he responded to Jess, while wrapping himself in the sheet. Then to Noelle, "Covering myself. What do you think I'm doing?"

"Violating my designer bedding," she said from her prone position on the ground.

"My destroyed shirt and your violated bedsheet. Let's call it even."

"Let's." She laughed—actually laughed—and then let out another groan that quickened his pulse.

"Noelle, are you injured?"

"I think so. Yes."

Clutching the bedsheet at his side, Kent sprinted across the room then squatted down next to her. "Where does it hurt?"

"What side of the body are kidneys on?" she asked.

"They're on both sides, near your lower back."

"In that case, I think my right kidney hurts."

"Here, let me help you up." Keeping one hand on the sheet, he slid the other one under her rib cage and lifted her onto her hands and knees. He then rotated behind her for better leverage.

"Is everything okay up there?" Jess called from downstairs.

"A few more minutes!" he shouted back, then turned to Noelle. "What were you even doing on the floor?"

And that's when he took in their position. Her plaid pajama bottoms had slid down her hips, exposing the "Y" of a red lacy thong above her curvy rear-end, which pointed squarely in his direction as he squatted behind her. A meager sheet and her revealing garments were all that stood between them and doggie-style.

Don't even think about it, he told the twitching appendage between his legs. Now was definitely not the time for that.

"I was looking for my phone," she said.

"A perfectly normal reason to trip someone coming out of the shower," he deadpanned.

"Where did you put it?"

Another twitch. *He knew where he'd like to put it.*

"You were supposed to be in bed. Do you think you can stand?" he asked, feeling more uncomfortable by the second.

"With your help, maybe. Can you lift me from under my armpits?"

Kent wasn't sure what was more surprising: her asking for his help, or her ass pressing into his loosely covered genitals. Both unprecedented events were doing things to his body that couldn't be put into words.

"Are you going to help me or not?" she asked, her voice laced with impatience as she once again pressed her backside into him.

He cleared his throat. "Yes, but…"

"But what?"

Your butt is in my junk, he screamed internally. Outwardly, and as calmly as possible, he said, "I can't use both of my arms and hold this sheet at the same time."

"Tie it, genius," she snarked, reminding him precisely why their situation should not be exciting him.

"Oh, why hadn't I thought of that?" he quipped with equal venom. Though, to be fair, he hadn't thought of it. He fumbled with the thin fabric. "How should I…"

"Like a toga. Julius Caesar style," she said.

"Okay, Brutus."

"Just hurry! All the blood is rushing to my head, which can't be good for the first injury you inflicted on me today."

Kent pulled one side of the sheet higher and quickly tied a knot near his shoulder. Was this how a toga was supposed to hang? Whatever. It worked.

He reached over Noelle from behind and placed a hand under each of her arms. "I'm going to lift on three."

"Careful there, KFC. You're groping the girls."

"The girls? Oh, sorry," he said, picking up on her meaning a beat too late. *As if he wasn't flustered enough by this woman.* After pulling his hands back into safe armpit territory, he once again prepped to lift. "Okay. One, two, three!"

On the third count, he tugged up with all his strength until he heard a loud, "Ow!"

"Are you okay?" he asked, scanning her for signs of further injury.

"Remember where my kidney is located? Maybe we shouldn't be doing this from behind."

"Ha!" he exclaimed before he could stop himself.

"And I'm the one who gets labeled immature," she scoffed. "I mean, try lifting me from the front. You're covered now, aren't you?"

"Yeah. Okay, hold on." He stood from his squat and walked around to stand in front of her head, which hung low between her shoulders. She was right. This couldn't be good for her concussion.

"On three," he said, placing his hands back under her arms.

Noelle groaned. "How about on one?"

"Right. One!" He heaved her upward with a grunt.

The rest happened in a flash—a concatenation of events, all conspiring against him. Noelle's upper body sprang up. Her hands gripped onto the sheet, tugging it downward as she lifted onto her knees. His haphazard knot didn't stand a chance. The bedsheet pooled around his ankles right as the room filled with a collective gasp.

"Oh my gosh!" a voice shouted from the top of the stairs.

His eyes flew to Jessica's horrified expression before dropping to see Noelle's slack-jawed face directly in front of his wooden soldier, standing at attention and saluting them both.

He immediately released Noelle and used his hands to cover as much of himself as he could. "It's not what it looks like!"

Jess was already heading back down the stairs. "Sorry! I shouldn't have come up there!"

Noelle, still kneeling in front of him, covered her mouth with her hands. And then she laughed. Because laughter is exactly what every guy wants to hear when standing naked in front of a woman.

"This is not funny!" he hissed.

"Oh, I beg to differ. Why are you…?" She pointed up toward the ceiling, laughing even harder.

He grabbed the useless sheet off the floor and wrapped it around his waist. "Why am I? Why are *you* even on the ground? None of this would have happened if you'd stayed in bed like you were supposed to!"

"No. None of this would have happened if you'd stayed in San Diego like *you* were supposed to," she retorted.

"Oh, that's right. Everything is my fault."

"Finally, we agree on something. Also, I don't think your shirt and my bedding both getting ruined by your big, hard head is an even trade. That sheet is Vera Wang," she said, crossing her arms and jutting out her chin.

Did she even hear herself when she spoke? This was the thanks he got for trying to do a nice thing. "Do you want to talk about the replacement cost of our damaged goods right now, or would you like help standing up?"

"Yes to both questions. I can do two things at once, especially while on my knees." She smirked up at him, and he thought he might burst.

Leave it to Noelle Serrano to torture him, even while injured. The unknown extent of her injuries was the only thing that had him reaching out for her hand.

"Stand," he ordered. "And try not to pull the sheet down this time."

She took his hand and applied pressure to it, slowly rising to her feet as she did. "Such a gentleman."

"I'll buy you new bedsheets," he said, ignoring her condescension. "Whatever kind you want."

"Whatever kind I want," Noelle repeated with a smile that threatened to make him regret those words.

"The food's ready whenever you two are," Jess called from below. "No rush!"

Kent buried his face in his free hand, still gripping the sheet in the other. "Great. Now your sister thinks we were… you know."

"And that's a bad thing, why exactly? You like my sister, don't you?"

"What? No! She's practically my sister, too. It's embarrassing, is all."

"Why would being with me be embarrassing? Because you're so much better?" Hands on hips, Noelle struck her signature pose. "Admit it. You like Jess."

"I like her as a person… more than you right now. But that's all. Besides, she's with Avery. Why are we even having this conversation?"

"Ha! I knew it! You're getting all weird about it. That means I'm right."

"You're the one getting weird about it," he said, feeling as juvenile as she was acting.

"It makes total sense now, why you're always hanging around at all our family functions, even though you're ex-family now."

"Think what you want. Let's get you back into bed."

"Let's," she mocked, as he led her across the room, then plopped her down.

"There. If it's okay with you, I'd like to get dressed now." He walked back toward the shower and grabbed the fresh set of clothes he'd gotten out of his car before *the incident from his worst nightmares.* "And since you can't be trusted, I'll go change downstairs and send Jess up with your food."

"Fine," she said.

"Fine," he returned, and it was like he'd regressed to a younger version of himself, fighting with teenaged Noelle.

Some things never changed.

Jessica hadn't stayed for dinner. She'd hightailed it out of there right after delivering Noelle's food upstairs, saying she'd rather get home that night to prepare for her early morning. *He seemed to have everything under control,* she'd said.

Under control was the last phrase Kent would use to describe the circus of circumstances. From the moment he'd arrived in Holiday Pines and bumped into Noelle—quite literally—everything had been spiraling toward chaos. To paint a visual: The plane was nosediving; he had zero flight training; there was no co-pilot; and, to top things off, the cockpit was on fire. His best chance at survival was to eject before crashing, but that option would leave a lone passenger to fend for herself.

Resolved to go down with the plane, Kent spread a thin layer of mortar with the trowel he'd brought with him. Leveling the warped wooden floor by sanding the rough spots earlier had been cathartic. He doubted laying the plastic membrane would be as gratifying, but it needed to be done to prep the floor for the tile work.

At least he knew what he was doing regarding handiwork. Kent often wondered if such skills could be inherited, and if so, what other traits he might share with his absent father.

Caleb Clark had been building a treehouse in the backyard before he unceremoniously left—a project Brad and Kent later finished themselves. A series of home improvement projects followed, including retiling the kitchen floor for their heartbroken mother. Brad had led the effort, but Kent enjoyed helping. It had made him feel useful.

"Kent, I need to speak with you, please," Noelle shouted from upstairs.

"What's wrong?" he hollered back. She was using his real name and the word *please.* Something had to be wrong.

"Nothing. I just need to talk to you."

"You're supposed to be resting." He grabbed his phone from his back pocket and checked the time. *10:37 p.m.* "Why aren't you sleeping?"

"Why aren't you sleeping?" she parroted back.

"I'm working on your floor."

He slid his phone back in his jeans and remembered hiding hers in the other pocket. Noelle's need to talk to him probably had something to do with wanting it back, but she was out of luck there.

No one was going to die if she didn't post about which shoes went with which outfit, nor would they miss ten selfies of her holding a book that happened to match her blouse. Though the matching part was surely no coincidence. Everything Noelle put out into the world was meticulously curated—from the green tips of her chestnut hair, which made her emerald eyes pop even more, to her red toenails covered in hand-painted snowflakes. *Not that he noticed such things.*

"Well?" she called down again. "Are you coming up here or not?"

"I'm a little busy. I need to lay this membrane before the thinset dries."

"I thought you were here to take care of me. What if I need something?"

"Do you need something?"

"Yes, to talk to you."

He pressed the side of the membrane covered in adhesive onto the floor and closed his eyes. This could easily go on all night. Circular arguments were Noelle's specialty.

"We're talking now, aren't we?" he asked, feeling mildly satisfied when his response elicited an exasperated huff loud enough to be heard downstairs.

"Yelling like this hurts my head," she moaned, a cunning strike to his Achilles' heel.

Though clearly a ploy, her weaponization of his concern for her wellbeing had him responding with, "Give me five minutes."

Five incredibly short minutes later, he crept up the staircase. "Are you decent up here?"

Noelle snorted. "You're one to ask."

He took that as a yes and stepped into the room, which only had a door at the bottom of the staircase to block it off from customers.

"That's actually what I wanted to talk to you about," she continued.

"About being decent?" he asked.

"Or indecent, in your case." She flashed him her signature smirk. "I think we need to talk about me seeing you naked."

Unbelievable. He turned on his heels and headed back toward the stairs.

"Wait! I'm serious," she said. "The longer we *don't* talk about it, the more awkward it'll get. Awkwarder? Is that a word? It should be."

"I don't think things could possibly get any *awkwarder*," he said, repeating the awkward sounding word. He then wondered if its meaning was due to its pronunciation.

"Do you think awkward means awkward because it's awkward to say?" she asked, on the same page for a change.

"And awkwarder is even more awkward to say," he added, "but we're getting way off topic here."

Wait. Maybe that was a good thing. He didn't want to be *on topic*—not the topic she had in mind, at least.

"Right. You naked," she said, as if such a discussion were entirely commonplace.

"Noelle."

"Hear me out. I saw you naked, what, five or six hours ago now? And during that time, you had a situation going on that one might consider embarrassing. But"—she held up a hand when he opened his mouth to interrupt—"I have an idea to help settle the score."

Score? He supposed he shouldn't be surprised that this was all a game to Noelle. To her, life was a game, and she, its fiercest competitor. Curious about what she had up her sleeve this time, Kent stepped closer, crossed his arms, and stared until she continued.

"Well, since you got embarrassed when I saw you naked," she said, reaching for the hem of her pajama top, "I figured it'd only be fair if you saw me naked, too. Would you like that?"

Kent pressed his glasses against the bridge of his nose and blinked to make sure he'd heard her correctly. *Was that a serious question?*

"I do have an ulterior motive," she confessed, dropping her voice low and motioning him forward.

"What's that?" he asked, temporarily rooted in place.

"Get on your knees first, like I was. Then I'll show you."

His brain yelled *it's a trap*, but his body urged him to comply. He was pathetic. He knew it, and worse yet, he knew that *she knew* he knew it. None of that stopped him from dropping to one knee in front of her bed and then lowering the other.

He steadied himself to sound more confident, then said, "I'm on my knees. Show me what you've got."

Her smile grew. First seductive, then devious.

"I've got this!" She held out a bejeweled hand mirror the size of a small tennis racket. "Seriously, your face never gets old!"

His own face stared back at him, not a touch amused. Meanwhile, she doubled over in raucous laughter.

He sprang to his feet. "One of these days, you're going to mess with the wrong guy, Noelle. That's what worries me most about your childish ways. Not all men would brush it off the way I do."

She continued cachinnating, like a rabid hyena, then finally calmed herself long enough to respond. "You're the only guy I mess with, KFC."

"Am I supposed to feel flattered by that? How old are you anyway?" he asked, his blood reaching three hundred and seventy-three Kelvin.

"It's not polite to ask a lady's age. What's your shoe size?"

"Twelve. Same as the age you're acting."

She merely nodded.

"You agree you're twelve?" he asked.

"No, but I was thinking about the correlation between shoe size and male endowment." Her devious smile returned. "I would have guessed maybe eight or nine for you."

He wanted to throw something at her—physically throw something. If he didn't leave right then, he might intentionally hurt a woman for the first time in his life. He stomped toward the stairs.

"Wait, don't be a baby! I was just teasing you."

Yes, she was.

"Good night, Noelle."

6

Merry vibe:

"My Only Wish (This Year)"

Britney Spears

50 days until Christmas

Bright morning light caused Noelle to squint. On the plus side, it no longer sent blinding pain through her head, so she assumed her concussion was healing. Today's mission would be to get her phone back. She was dying to check her socials and didn't even want to think about what the last day of inactivity would mean for her engagement stats.

Nearly one hundred thousand people depended on her for fashion tips, book reviews, holiday cheer, and general life updates. She couldn't let them down—especially not when she'd worked so hard to build up her following and the steady stream of passive income it brought.

Having already searched everywhere upstairs, she concluded that her phone must be with Kent. And after how mad he'd gotten the previous night, she doubted he would hand it over willingly. Seriously, when had he lost his sense of humor?

Noelle pulled the covers over her head and groaned. She supposed mocking the size of his manhood after seeing him naked might have been going a tad too far. In all honesty, though, he had nothing to be ashamed of in that department.

He was huge. *Like, world's tallest Christmas tree huge.* And as for shape and girth… perfection was the only word that came to mind. A lot like his damn forearms.

She'd admittedly had a flurry of thoughts that would get her on the naughty list for life when faced with… all of *that*. But then she reminded herself that such paradigms of male perfection belonged to a man who was her mortal enemy. The same man who considered himself far more mature than her and of a superior "caliber." Sure, she sometimes acted childish or petty in his presence, but it was only because Kent brought out the worst in her.

Noelle sat up in bed with another groan, dreading what needed to be done. Since it was only right, she would apologize to him, as a side quest to the mission of retrieving her phone, but first… time to pee.

Like Bambi learning to walk, she stood on wobbly legs and put one foot in front of the other. It might not have been graceful, but she'd risen without help, which was progress. No more crawling for her. She paused at the top of the stairs, knowing Kent would get mad if she attempted them without him.

"Kent?" she called out. "I need to come downstairs to use the restroom."

No response.

"Kent?"

More silence. Maybe he'd been more upset last night than she'd realized. Would he have left without telling her, though? If he had, her phone would be unguarded—an unexpected gift wrapped in a big, red bow.

Noelle gripped the handrail and carefully stepped down with one foot, then the other. She could do this. It was like people always said: one step at a time.

As she neared the bottom, there was a creak, followed by Kent rounding the corner. "Noelle! What are you doing on the stairs?"

His deep voice startled her forward, her hands flailing in front of her before hitting something solid. His chest, she realized, which was once again bare.

"You almost fell," he said, stating the obvious before helping her down the remaining step.

"Only because you scared me. I called for you first, but you didn't respond. Where's your shirt?"

"It's the only clean one I have, so I took it off to work on the floor. Also, I was in the bathroom for like two minutes. You couldn't have waited?"

"Oh, great," she said, scrunching her nose. "Is it going to smell in there?"

Kent's cheeks and ears reddened. "For the love of... No! That's not what I was doing in there."

"What *were* you doing in there, then? Two minutes is a long time for number one."

His expression, as always, was priceless.

"Hold that thought," she said, hobbling around the corner to relieve herself. "I really have to pee."

When she came back, Kent stood right where she'd left him. He reminded her of a sad puppy, abandoned on the side of the road, begging for scraps of kindness. If she didn't despise him so much, she might actually feel sorry for him.

"Fifty-eight seconds," she said.

"What?" he asked, adorably clueless.

"Fifty-eight seconds is exactly how long it took to pee and wash my hands. I counted."

"Congratulations. You have the counting skills of a seven-year-old," he said, turning his back to her and crouching down to reveal... *O Holy Night!*

"What have you done?" she exclaimed.

"What does it look like I've done?" Kent asked, clearly oblivious to his transgression. When he turned around again, his face dropped.

"What? Did I get the pattern wrong? Jess said you wanted buffalo plaid, which I had to research online, but it seemed pretty straightforward."

"No, the pattern looks fine… great, actually."

"Then what's the problem?"

"The *problem* is you're ruining everything!" She pulled at her hair while pacing in the small, untiled section near the bottom of the stairs.

"You're gonna have to walk me through that one, Noelle. You said it looked great."

She wanted to cry. *Like, literally cry.* "It's almost finished!"

"Yeah, I'm just waiting for the mortar to dry on this section, then I'll tile where you're standing. Another day or two after that, I can finish it off with the grout."

"You're missing the point! I don't want it to be finished yet!"

"Okaaay…" He dragged out. "Why not?"

Noelle lowered herself to sit on the stairs, her rage cooling to tepid dejection. "I had a plan. I was supposed to meet someone… here, in Holiday Pines, who would help with my renovations. We were supposed to work on the project together and fall in love before Christmas. But now,"—she motioned to her nearly finished floor—"it's all ruined."

Kent blinked at her, his expression that of a reindeer in headlights, for about a minute. *Easily fifty-eight seconds.*

"Are you going to say anything?" she finally asked.

"I don't know where to…" He brought his fist up to his mouth. "You do realize life isn't a Hallmark movie, right?"

"Laugh all you want," she said at the sound of poorly concealed snickers. "And to think, I came down here to apologize."

"I thought you came down to pee," he said, still chuckling.

"My endeavor had multiple goals. Speaking of which,"—she stood and held out her hand—"I need my phone back."

"No. In fact, you should be back upstairs resting. Let me help you," he said, closing the short distance between them.

Noelle planted her palms on his ridiculously firm chest and pushed. "I'm sick of your help!"

Unfortunately, Kent didn't budge, and she nearly fell backward. Only nearly, because he caught her. *Of course he did.*

"Be careful!" he scolded, gripping her shoulders and pulling her close.

So close, in fact, that she could practically taste his salty, woody scent. A deep inhale had her imagining them leisurely strolling through a coastal forest, holding hands while picking out names for their future children. *Damn him.*

"If you must know," she said, escaping his clutches, "I *am* looking for the kind of romance found in books and movies. What's so wrong with that?"

"Nothing. I—"

"You were embarrassed last night," she continued, "so here's my embarrassing truth: I'm sick of being alone. I'm also sick of dating guys who only want one thing, but—spoiler alert—I enjoy sex, so I find it difficult to say no. Then, as soon as I put out, poof, they're gone and I'm back to square one.

"So, make fun of me all you want, but I'm done simply watching and reading about love. I'm ready to experience it for myself. I figured if I moved to a small town, I could fall in love with a nice guy and finally start my own family. It's all I want for my birthday this year, and I have a plan to make it happen… even if that makes me pathetic." Swiping at her face, Noelle felt something wet drip from her jaw to her neck. "Great. Now I'm crying in front of you, which is a lot more embarrassing than being naked. Trust me."

"Noelle…"

"I'm going back upstairs to rest now," she said, pulling her arm out of his grasp, "and I don't need your help. You've already done more than enough."

"Wait, please," he said.

She reluctantly turned and saw him reach into his pocket.

"Here's your phone back. Just try to limit your screen time."

Noelle was tempted to scream that she didn't want his pity either, but wanting her phone more, she grabbed it from his hand, then headed up the stairs.

"There are other renovation projects needed to get your store ready," Kent said, stopping her in her tracks. "A couple of the shelving units are broken, and this whole place could use a fresh coat of paint, not to mention the sign outside. You could still meet a nice guy to help with some of that. I'm sure you will."

At perhaps the nicest words he'd ever said to her, she turned to face him. "Thanks… for everything. The floor really does look great. It's exactly how I'd envisioned it."

"Execution is only ever as good as the vision behind it," he said, meeting her eyes. "Get some rest. I'll go wrangle us some breakfast."

After an appreciative nod, she continued up the stairs, squeezing the railing with each step. Once at the top, she turned to see him walking away and realized she hadn't yet apologized. "Hey, Kent?"

He stopped near the store's exit. "Yeah?"

As she made her way back toward bed, she called out over her shoulder, "For what it's worth, size twelve suits you."

@bookstafashionista

Photo caption:

Winter white is the new black And it's the perfect base for accessorizing! Resting off a concussion doesn't mean you can't look cute… Check out my new "small-town girl" crop sweatshirt! I ordered mine online, and you can too! #concussed #selfie #fashion #smalltownstyle #winterwhite #staymerry

7

46 days until Christmas

"Thanks again for letting me borrow your kitchen," Noelle said, pulling the fourth tray of gingerbread cookies from the oven.

She searched for a place to set them down, settling for a small spot on the kitchen island—the only square-foot of counter space not already covered with little men made from molasses and ginger.

Jess chopped carrots at the kitchen table, while her adorably clingy dog, Prince Petey of Bay Ho, circled near her feet in a blur of white fluff. "You're always welcome here, but I don't know how you're going to live in that new place of yours without a proper kitchen."

"It's got the essentials: a microwave, a fridge, and an electric teakettle. Plus, I plan to rent a cute cabin off Main Street once the store is making money, so it's only temporary." Noelle picked up her phone out of habit and scrolled through the comments on her last post. "Ugh. People are so rude."

"What's wrong?"

"Someone commented on my"—Noelle framed the air with her fingers—"overuse of exclamation points. Like, do people have nothing better to do than criticize my grammar? And fifty-four people liked the comment!"

"What's this world coming to?" Jess asked in mock solidarity.

Noelle glared at her sister, then pasted on a smile when she saw her five-year-old niece hovering near the entrance of the kitchen.

Chloe's baby blues pleaded through her thick-lensed glasses. "Auntie Elle, I have cookie, peas?"

Guilt churned in Noelle's chest as she looked from Chloe to Jess, and then back to her niece's sweet face. *How could she have been so thoughtless?* "Sorry, sweetie, but your mommy is making another snack for you."

Chloe then looked at Jess. "Time for snack, Mommy?"

"Yes, baby. Go wash your hands in the bathroom, and then you can have your carrot sticks with some hummus." Jess mouthed a silent *thank you* to Noelle once Chloe went skipping down the hall.

"I'm so sorry. I should have thought about Chloe before asking to bake here."

"It's okay," Jess said. "Honestly, one cookie would have been fine to give her, but I'm glad she seems happy with the healthier snack option. Her doctor said her BMI dropped below the eighty-fifth percentile and to keep up what we've been doing."

"That's great news! You're such an amazing mother, Jess."

Having been born with Prader-Willi syndrome, Chloe always felt hungry and therefore needed her calorie intake strictly managed—a never-ending and often heart-wrenching task that her big sister was crushing.

"Aw, don't make me cry," Jess said, pulling her in for a hug. "You're going to make a great mom someday too, sissy."

The sentiment made Noelle want to cry as well, but one emotional display in a week was more than enough. She still couldn't believe she'd gotten teary-eyed in front of Kent, of all people. At least he hadn't brought it up for the remainder of that weekend.

They hadn't talked much once she'd gotten her phone back. She'd been busy catching up on her socials, checking emails, and confirming orders for the store. Kent had only interrupted to bring her meals and had spent the rest of his time finishing her floor while she recovered. *From the injury he had given her*, she reminded herself. It was easy to slip into thinking Kent was a nice guy—when he was so annoyingly helpful—but their long history told her otherwise.

Jess pulled back from the tight embrace and looked around the kitchen. "I'm glad you're feeling better, but are you sure you're well enough to deliver all these cookies today? Shouldn't you still be taking it easy?"

"It's been almost a week, Jess. I'm one hundred percent back to normal."

Jess eyed her as if she might argue, but Noelle was saved by Chloe's return. Jess scurried off to get her daughter settled in the dining room with her snack, leaving Noelle alone with her thoughts.

She felt completely recovered from the concussion—that part wasn't a lie—and yet she wasn't quite her normal self. Around her second batch of gingerbread cookies, it had crossed her mind to set aside some for Kent as a thank-you for his renovation work. It would be easy enough to drop them off at his mother's house, given she lived nearby.

But such an idea was ludicrous.

For starters, bringing *Mister Grinch Incarnate* a plate of cookies associated with Christmas would likely backfire. Kent inexplicably hated the holiday season, though Noelle long suspected it had something to do with her love of all things festive.

And then there was the minor detail of him being her mortal enemy.

"Hey," Jess said, reentering the kitchen with Prince Petey hot on her heels. "I've been meaning to ask how your little project is going. Have you met anyone besides the married Brawny Thor guy?"

"Not yet, but I've only been off *bed arrest* for a few days. I'm going back to the hardware store this weekend to look at paint samples, so who knows? It's all about timing. Mister Right will show up eventually."

"Confident, as always. But how do you know you haven't already met Mister Right?" The way Jess said it, paired with her meddlesome smirk, let Noelle know exactly what, or rather who, she was talking about.

"For the bazillionth time, there is nothing going on between Kent and me, nor will there ever be. What you witnessed was merely an unfortunate tripping incident paired with extremely *bad* timing."

Her sister's grin widened. "Who said anything about Kent? I didn't mention him or the *incident*—if that's what we're calling full-frontal nudity these days—so, clearly, he must be on your mind."

"You're incorrigible," Noelle muttered, frustrated at herself for taking the bait, and even more so since Jess was right.

She had been thinking of him. She'd considered taking him gingerbread cookies, *for North Pole's sake*. And great… now there were visions of his naked body dancing in her head.

Blocking them out, Noelle returned to the topic at hand. "I'm confident, dear sister, because I always have a backup plan. If the hardware store doesn't pan out, then there's always the possibility of an online love connection. I setup a profile last night on this cute Holiday Pines dating site."

"Holiday Pines has its own dating site?"

"Well, it's more like a community networking page, where locals share tips and news. But it's called *Holiday Pines Connections*, and there's an option to list what you're looking for and to privately message other members, so I figure it's the same thing."

"Not quite, but okay," Jess said, drawing out her syllables in typical big-sister fashion.

"Anyway, I didn't include a picture or use my real name, but my profile heading is 'Must Love Christmas.' Cute, right? I'm hoping to strike up an anonymous conversation with a local, who perhaps I'll also meet in town. But of course, we won't realize we've run into each other until we've already fallen madly in love through our messages."

"Aw, sweetie, I know you love *You've Got Mail...* but the chance of that happening in real life is incredibly slim."

"The chance is zero if I don't try! Besides, that's only *one of* the marshmallow skewers in the campfire right now. One way or another, I'll be having a s'more."

"You know I only want the best for you," Jess said, wrapping her in another hug that felt both genuine and annoyingly placating.

After an obligatory three-second squeeze, Noelle broke free. "Okay, new subject. I finally decided on my store's name and filed the fictitious business name statement with the county clerk this morning. Do you wanna hear it?"

"Uh… yeah!"

"Well, I liked the idea of having the word *holiday* somewhere in the title, but I also wanted to make it clear that it's a holiday store and not just a play on the town's name, like Holiday Pies or Holiday Wines are. So, after a lot of votes and suggestions from my followers, it came down to either Merry Holidays or Holiday Joy Shop."

"Ooh, I love them both!" Jess said. "I mean, being *merry* is kind of your thing, but Holiday Joy Shop also has a cute ring to it."

"I thought so too, but then, a very astute follower commented that a joy shop sounded like a good place to buy sex toys. And once I read that, I couldn't *not* picture reindeer-shaped vibrators and peppermint-flavored lube everywhere. So…"

"Merry Holidays?" Jess asked, sounding unsure.

"Merry Holidays," Noelle confirmed.

Jess wiped fake sweat from her brow. "Phew. Good thing you asked for other people's opinions, huh?"

"I usually find that helpful," Noelle agreed.

"Speaking of other people's opinions," Jess said without an ounce of tact, "I'm worried about that online dating option you mentioned."

"We're back to that?"

"You need to be careful, Noelle! There are lots of weirdos out there. It's bad enough you've already moved away from your entire family to a remote mountain town. You don't need an online stalker on top of that. Something really awful could happen to you."

"Please don't worry," Noelle said to the deepening eleven between her sister's brows. "I promise I'll be careful, and I'll keep you updated on anyone I start chatting with."

Before Jess could argue, the sliding glass door to the backyard opened and Lucas came rushing in. "Mom, it's raining outside. Can I play Mario Kart now?"

"Fine," Jess replied, "but only for an hour. I don't want you playing video games all day."

"Yay!" Lucas cheered. "Auntie Elle, do you wanna play with me?"

Noelle glanced around the kitchen, taking in all eight dozen gingerbread cookies resting on various cooling racks. "I don't know, bud. I still have a lot of work to do in here."

Her eight-year-old nephew crossed his arms. "It's okay. I understand if you're afraid to lose to me."

"Oh, I see how it is! I suppose I could spare a little time. After all, these cookies still need to cool, and you can help me decorate them after I beat you."

"Ha, you can't beat me!" Lucas said, powering on the game console.

Noelle wiped her hands on a kitchen towel and then joined him in the adjacent family room. "Watch me."

Kent detested the rain almost as much as the so-called merriest time of year. Traditionalists would at least wait until after Thanksgiving to bedeck their surroundings in profligate displays, but since far too many people lacked such self-restraint, a barrage of colorful lights further obscured his vision as he strained to see through the torrential assault on his windshield. To make matters worse, the festive fervor seemed to commence earlier with each passing year.

And at the forefront of the seasonal charade stood Noelle Serrano.

If her disdain toward him had ever been in doubt, those few days together had confirmed it. All he'd wanted was to alleviate some of the burden she always insisted on carrying alone, and to maybe, just maybe, get on her good side.

Instead, he'd inadvertently injured her, flashed her, and managed to earn an even more prominent position on her "naughty list," despite not knowing what he'd done to land there in the first place. He supposed it might have something to do with his aversion to her favorite holiday, but would Noelle miraculously like him if he were to embrace Christmas with her level of enthusiasm?

Kent quickly dismissed that fanciful notion as he shifted into park. He'd arrived at his destination but couldn't seem to budge from his seat.

He shouldn't be there.

He didn't *want* to be there.

He'd much rather be at home, kicking back with a sudoku puzzle or a good book, even with his mother yelling slurs at the TV. "You call yourself smart? Even I knew that one! Who comes up with these questions? My genius son should be on this show, not these people. Kenny, look into getting onto Jeopardy and make your ma proud!"

In truth, he would have preferred to be anywhere else in the world, but there he was. Duty had called, and it was time for him to answer.

It wasn't like he was doing anything wrong.

After several more reassurances to himself, Kent exited the refuge of his SUV with his windbreaker lifted overhead and hastened toward the building's entrance. He hadn't made it far when his foot encountered a deep puddle, drenching him from the ground up, since the aerial onslaught apparently wasn't enough.

"Shit," he muttered, hopping on one foot while pointlessly shaking his waterlogged loafer.

If a shoe absorbed water equivalent to 150% of its dry weight and rainfall continued at a rate of X inches per hour, at what rate would water need to be expelled to achieve relative dryness? Express in terms of X and list assumptions for unknown variables. *That would be a good one for his AP students.*

Spoiler: The rate would be high. Very high.

On the lookout for more water traps, Kent continued his stride and immediately felt a warm body collide into his chest.

"Are you trying to kill me?" a shrill, yet familiar voice rang out. "Ugh, I'm soaked! You knocked me into a puddle, an actual puddle!"

Kent removed his fogged glasses, and his eyes confirmed what his ears had already deduced. "Noelle? What are you—Sorry, here, let me help you up." He extended his hand, which she reluctantly accepted with a sharp glare.

"I'm starting to think you have a savior complex," Noelle quipped as she rose to her feet. "You knock women out, and then down—and maybe even up, as far as I know—all so you can play the hero who helps them. What are you even doing here, KFC?"

"What are *you* doing here?" he shot back, feeling the added weight of her accusation atop his crushing mountain of guilt.

Noelle shielded her face with her hands. "Do you really want to have this conversation in the pouring rain?"

"You're right. Let's go inside."

"Let's," she mocked. "And no, I just left there. You go inside, and I'll go blast the heat in my car during my hour-long drive home."

"Fine. Where are you parked?"

She gestured toward her forest green car while heading toward it, then yelled over her shoulder. "Why are you following me?"

"If you want to talk about why we're both here, we can do it from the shelter of your vehicle. Plus, it's dark, and I want to make sure you get to your car safely."

"Aren't you chivalrous?" she sneered.

"Just open your car already," he said, once they reached the Volkswagen Beetle she'd of course named Evergreen.

Kent wouldn't have been surprised to see it adorned with twinkling lights, or those obnoxious reindeer antlers some people affixed to their car windows, but all he spied was a single sprig of holly peeking out from behind the steering wheel.

Noelle fumbled with her keyless remote, muttering under her breath as it failed to respond.

"What's wrong?" he asked.

"It's not working. Maybe the battery is dead." *Yet, she continued pressing the unlock button.*

"Let me see it." Kent took the remote from her hand, then extended the manual key tucked on the side. "We can open the door the old-fashioned way."

Noelle grabbed at the key. "Here, gimme."

"I've got it," he said, right as the wet remote slipped from his grip, vanishing into the dark depths of the parking lot's pavement. Kent blew out a curse. "Look what you made me do!"

"No way is this my fault! If you didn't have to be a white knight all the time, this damsel could have opened the door herself." She bent forward, then held out a hand to prevent him from doing the same. "Don't go bonking me with your big, hard head! I don't think I could survive two concussions in a week."

He resisted the urge to defend himself, if out of nothing but urgency to get out of the frigid rain. "You look over there. I'll look under the car. And you really need to stop saying big, hard head."

"Why? Does it make you uncomfortable? I'd think you'd be flattered by that description, since I've seen you naked and all. Got it!" she said, holding up the key in triumph.

"I'm never going to hear the end of that, am I?"

"Not a chance." Noelle moved toward the car as if to unlock it, but then turned and looked up at the sky instead.

"We're drowning out here. What are you waiting for?"

In response, she spread her arms wide and laughed manically into the rain.

"What's so funny?" he demanded.

She only laughed harder.

"It's freezing! Give me that." He reached for the key, but she pulled it close to her chest.

"No. We'll get Evergreen wet. Besides, it's like sixty degrees. I'd hardly call that freezing. We're so soaked."

"Being soaked makes it feel a lot colder than sixty," Kent said, a shiver tearing through him to make his point. "If you don't want to get water in your car, let's go in mine."

"Let's, let's, let's," she chanted, leaning against her car and once again angling her face so the rain hit it dead on.

"Noelle, I think you've lost it," he said, running his hands through his hair the way one might in the shower. *An absurdly cold shower.*

"I don't think I could get any wetter," she said to the angry sky in an apparent daze.

And okay… Enough was enough. All the cold showers in the world couldn't save him from what he was about to do next.

"I bet I could help with that," he said, closing the distance between himself and the insane woman who drove him even crazier.

Her eyes popped open, then narrowed. "Are you messing with me, KFC? Tell me what the F stands for and then maybe…" Noelle wiggled her eyebrows suggestively, but he wasn't falling for that one.

Two could play at her games.

Kent shifted until their bodies brushed, then he craned down to whisper into her ear. "If I told you, I'd have to kill you. And it depends. Is it working?"

"No… Of course not."

"Then, of course not," he said.

Noelle lifted her chin. "*Of course not* to 'are you messing with me?' means you're being serious. So, tell me, KFC, are you being serious?"

"You tell me," he murmured, tucking a strand of dripping, green-tipped hair behind her ear.

Those plump lips of hers parted; any sound that may have escaped, lost to the roaring hiss of the rain beating down around them. Or perhaps it was the drumming of his heart.

With the downpour blurring their surroundings, her brilliant green eyes came into focus like a photo in portrait mode, two heavenly stars cutting through the night sky. The warmth of her presence, the intensity of her gaze—both pulled him in like a gravitational force, and he soon forgot the objective of their game. His head fell at a glacial pace until his mouth hovered mere inches above hers.

"I don't need to," she said, those lush lips tugging into a smirk. "That big, hard head of yours is telling me."

Kent took an uncomfortable step back. So much for cold showers.

"I should probably get going…" Noelle said. "But wait. You never told me what you were doing here."

"You never told me what *you* were doing here," he countered, trying his best not to gawk at her soaked chest. The flesh-toned sweater clinging to her like a second skin wouldn't do any favors for his already precarious predicament.

"I was delivering gingerbread cookies to the residents here. It's something I do to spread holiday cheer as often as I can." Noelle folded her arms, a silent prompt for him to speak, yet he found himself unable to form words amid the din of his internal turmoil.

Her kindness, so freely given to everyone but him, stirred a complex blend of emotions. He was overcome with longing for a meager scrap of her generosity, while simultaneously plagued by the gnawing guilt that he was unworthy.

"Well? Why are you here at the nursing home, KFC?"

The directness of her inquiry cut through his haze. "I'm here for an informational interview," he confessed.

"For your mom?" The shock in her voice struck him like a physical blow, the impact reverberating through the already turbulent waters of his being.

His already tight throat further constricted as he said, "I'm researching options for round-the-clock care."

"I see."

"No, you don't see!" he snapped, needing her to understand. "My leave from work ends in the new year, and I'm afraid she'll need me and I won't be there. My mom gets dizzy sometimes, and because she refuses to believe she can't do everything on her own right now, she's almost fallen a few times. I've already hired a part-time nurse to help, but finding a trustworthy stranger to care for her full-time has been overwhelming. I thought maybe the staff here could recommend a reputable in-home caretaker. I'm not sending her to this place. I'm not!"

And he wasn't.

No nursing homes. It was one of his mother's few requests ever given to him and Brad. She wanted to live out the rest of her days in the same house she'd raised her children, which wasn't too much to ask after all the sacrifices she'd made as a single mother.

"I'm so sorry, Kent. I had no idea." Noelle stepped forward and wrapped her arms around his torso with a loud squish, her warmth a soothing balm to his wounded soul.

Never let them see you cry—the haunting refrain of his father's words—played through his mind as liquid heat filled his eyes. It seemed to bubble up outside of his control, like an artesian spring under a steady flow of pressure.

When the tears spilled down his cheeks, Kent had never felt more grateful for the rain.

Noelle sat on her bed that night, feeling as wrinkled as the prunes in her grandmother's sugar plum recipe. *That's what happens when you almost kiss your archnemesis in the pouring rain*, said the annoying and somewhat sinister voice that she'd long ago dubbed "Jiminy Grinch."

Correction: *he* had almost kissed *her*.

Despite mentally replaying their encounter the entire soggy drive home, Noelle still couldn't believe it. She'd considered stopping to borrow dry clothes from Jess on her way, but that would've required explaining what had happened. And before that would be possible, someone might need to explain it to her first.

After finally making her favorite resident smile—a feat none of the staff had deemed possible—Noelle had been soaring through a moonlit sky on an open sleigh when she'd stepped out of that nursing home. And then, *bam!* She'd ran squarely into Kent Full-Of-Himself Clark.

Besides the swift knockdown—from which Noelle could already feel a bruise forming on her left butt cheek—everything leading up to the almost kiss had happened in slow motion. Kent had crept into her personal space with the clear intention of provoking a reaction from her. But unlike the romantic movie version, where he'd have passionately pressed her up against the car, he merely stood so close that she could feel the firmness of his body without any of its weight.

It had been incredibly annoying.

When Kent had inched down as if he might kiss her—or more like centimetered down (that's how slow it had been)—she'd held her breath the way one would before plunging underwater. He'd stared at her with a dare in his deep blue eyes, which were dark and brooding, like a storm brewing at sea. They could've easily drowned her, and Noelle hated how much she liked that.

Luckily for her, the evidence of his arousal had presented the perfect opportunity to declare victory in their unspoken game of who could make whom more sexually frustrated. Never mind that he'd succeeded in that endeavor as well. A win was a win.

But then Kent had told her about the situation with his mom.

The stress and guilt etched onto Kent's face had left her feeling a lot less victorious and a lot more... *something* toward him. She'd always assumed he'd taken a leave-of-absence to help with things like driving Carole to and from her cancer treatments and maybe some housework. That alone would have been a lot... but a full-time caregiver? How had she not realized everything he'd been going through?

Shaking off the thought, Noelle powered up her laptop. She needed to focus on achieving her goals, which meant wiping San Diego—and everyone in it—out of her mind. Holiday Pines was a place where she could finally set down roots, and there was no time like the present.

A red dot near her inbox indicated she had two messages waiting for her. The first was a boring welcome message, which listed the resources available on the *Holiday Pines Connections* site and gave directions for things like resetting her password. The second one had her squealing like a schoolgirl.

```
To: everyday_merry
From: average_joe

Hi there, I'm intrigued by your headline, "Must
Love Christmas." I assume it pays homage to the
romantic comedy, Must Love Dogs. That would be
a great movie to watch together sometime, after
getting to know each other here first, of
course.
```

I admire how direct you are in your profile
about wanting to find love. Besides a love of
Christmas, what is the number one quality you
seek in a potential partner?

> Hopefully yours,
> Joe

Despite the cool temperature in her loft, Noelle had to fan herself. *Talk about being direct.* This guy got right to the point. She admired that quality, she realized, but wasn't sure she'd consider it number one on her list.

Truth be told, she'd never made a checklist of the traits she desired in a mate. She'd always figured she would "just know" when she met "The One." A list would only limit the possibilities. Then again, maybe not having one was why her dating history could be summed up in a *Who's Who of Human Garbage* publication.

Noelle spent the next hour creating her list of qualities, and another hour ranking them to narrow it down before she replied.

To: average_joe
From: everyday_merry

A man who knows his rom-coms and asks great
questions? If that isn't hot, I don't know what
is. But in all seriousness, it's nice to
(virtually) meet you, Joe.

A number one quality is difficult to choose, so
here are my top five. My ideal partner would be:
honest, family-oriented, kind, witty, and
physically attractive.

I realize that last one makes me sound shallow,
but I think physical chemistry is a crucial
element to a healthy love life. Would you agree?

Also, it's your turn to share what qualities you
look for in a woman.

Maybe yours,
Everyday Merry

P.S. I admire your directness as well.

After re-reading Joe's initial message a few more times, Noelle closed her laptop and beamed. The only thing more satisfying than a competitive win was a plan coming together. Sure, Joe could be a troll for all she knew, but he could also be her Prince Charming. The possibility, even if slim, thrilled her to no end.

And if Joe didn't work out, Screw It had to produce an eligible bachelor at some point. At the thought, Noelle snuggled into bed, excited for the day ahead.

And then she sneezed.

8

"Baby, It's Cold Outside"

Idina Menzel

45 days until Christmas

After two failed attempts at clearing her nose, Noelle groaned into her pillow. *This was not at all how her day was supposed to go.* She felt like a parade of elves had traveled through her throat overnight, with sandpaper attached to their curly-toed slippers, and then set up camp at the pressure point between her eyes.

Rolling onto her back, she glimpsed the outside world through the small window in her loft. Pops of red, orange, and yellow danced in the rosy morning light, as if mocking her for being stuck inside. *Great.* Even the fall foliage she loved had turned against her.

Noelle grabbed her phone. Her followers would need to be kept in the loop if she had to take yet another break. She scrolled her Instagram feed for an undeterminable amount of time, then stuck out her tongue to one side and snapped a selfie. After adding a filter, a caption, and as many hashtags as she could think of to extend her reach, she shared her bleak news with the world: *this boss babe has a head cold.*

Said boss babe then went online to take care of actual business. Her store's grand opening was in two short weeks; only half of the merchandise had arrived so far; the walls needed paint before she could stock the shelves; and the store didn't even have a sign yet. A lesser person would've been freaking out in her position.

But, as always, Noelle had a plan.

Although her move to Holiday Pines had been arguably impulsive, she had been dreaming of (and planning for) her year-round Christmas store for years. In addition to negotiating great contract terms, she had backup suppliers for each of her wholesalers and knew exactly how much she needed to sell in order to turn a profit. Even if that took some time, as she knew was often the case, her savings and passive income would get her through the first year or two.

Soon enough, everyone would see that she was more than *a pretty face*. She was going to prove herself, once and for all, as a successful business owner. The key to getting everything done on time: quick decisions.

She'd planned to go to the hardware store that day to look at paint samples, and to hopefully meet Mr. Right, but the paint would need to come to her instead. Noelle selected a white paint called "snow" and a red shade aptly named "candy cane," added both to her cart, and requested overnight shipping. *A will, a way.*

With that matter out of the way, she pulled up the *Holiday Pines Connections* site on her phone and downloaded the app for ease of access. Her foggy brain struggled to remember her password, but after several guesses, she was in. And she had new messages!

It was exactly the dopamine rush she needed in her sickly state. There were two: a reply from average_joe and a new message from Peater88 (an odd spelling of Peter, she thought.) Curiosity led her to open the new one first, and… *Oh, bad banana with the greasy black peel!*

She threw her phone down, fighting the inclination to check her hand for burn marks. Of course, there were none. Her wounds were only psychological, as the image seared its way through her brain. The urban legends were true. She'd heard plenty of horror stories about unsolicited dick pics, yet even with her constant online presence, this was the first she'd ever received. And from someone in small-town Holiday Pines, no less!

She had half a mind to print the photo and post it around town to shame its owner, but that plan had at least three flaws: one, she'd have to look at it again; two, she'd be subjecting the rest of the town to such vulgarity; and three, Peater88 clearly had no shame. Her next (less voluntary) thought was to compare its subpar size to the Goliath paradigm of maleness imprinted in her memory.

Kent Footlong Clark had a package worthy of professional photography, and yet she knew he would never send such an offensive photo. And why was she now thinking of Kent? *Ugh*. She needed to clear her stuffed-up head.

As soon as she rolled out of bed, the chill of the room penetrated her flannel pjs, skipped right past her skin, and hit solid bone, sending a shiver from her bare feet to the top of her head. She quickly donned her red fuzzy robe and slippers, then headed downstairs to the thermostat. Clutching the robe against her chest, she squinted at the display. Fifty-seven degrees? Why hadn't the heat kicked on?

To save money until the store could open, she'd lowered the heat setting to sixty-five degrees, but her thin, SoCal blood wouldn't allow her to go lower than that. She fiddled with the dial, cranking it as high as seventy-five, but nothing happened. A broken heater on top of a head cold was the last thing she needed, but the way things had been going so far, it seemed about right.

Ten minutes later, Noelle set a steaming mug of Gingerbread Spice tea on the box that doubled as her nightstand, pulled on her thickest socks, and crawled back into bed. Being sick and cold (and all alone) might not be ideal, but Noelle was determined not to let it get her down. At least she had her favorite hot beverage to warm her and some downtime to finish the Christmas rom-com she'd been reading. She reached for her book, but then she remembered something else she had yet to read.

Joe's reply.

She'd nearly forgotten everything that had happened before she'd gone downstairs. Or perhaps her brain had blocked it out.

With trepidation, she fished her phone out of the pile of blankets on her bed and attempted to close the last message without looking at it. No such luck. Her eyes were once again assaulted by the male sex organ she now realized was not only inferior in size, but also slightly crooked and in bad lighting. Her head tilted to straighten the image before closing it. Seriously, what was wrong with men? *If you're going to send a crude photo, at least make it a good one.*

If her congested head didn't feel like it might explode at any minute, she might even laugh at the absurdity of her morning. She could only hope that Joe's good guy vibes would help make everything else feel better. Without further ado, she tapped open his latest message.

> To: everyday_merry
> From: average_joe
>
> Hi again, Merry. I hope you don't mind if I call you Merry, as I assume there is nothing ordinary, or *everyday*, about you. I also assume Merry isn't your real name, which is fine. Joe isn't my real name either, but if I'm being honest, I kind of like this whole anonymity thing we've got going on.
>
> It's exciting when you think about it. We could pass each other in town or bump into each other at the hardware store and not even realize it. Until later, of course, when we've fallen madly in love. At least, that's how I hope the story

will go, and what a great one it will be to tell our future grandchildren! ;)

I sincerely hope I'm not coming on too strong and scaring you. If we end up nothing more than pen pals, I suppose that will be okay too, but I believe in putting what you want out into the universe. Let's see what it sends our way, Merry.

As for your question, I agree that physical chemistry is a key element in a romantic relationship. Sometimes, though, it's easy to get caught up in appearances and not take the time to get to know the real person underneath. That's another reason I'm glad neither of us has shared a picture yet… the whole anonymity thing *and* no preconceived notions based on looks.

I know what you must be thinking now, but I swear I'm not a hideous beast. I stay relatively fit and have often been told I'm easy on the eyes. (Granted, my mother is the one who says it the most, but that still counts, right?) Please excuse my lame attempt at being witty… It was on your list of desired qualities.

As for what I look for in a woman, I liked your list and would also add: someone who challenges me; someone who has a bigger heart than most people realize; and someone who never gives up on her dreams.

Does that sound like you, Merry?

Hopefully Yours,
Joe

Noelle sipped her tea along with Joe's words, both warming her insides as she reread his message several more times. Each sentence nourished her soul the way a hearty soup did the body.

And there was a lot to digest.

She'd already assumed his real name wasn't Joe, as hers wasn't Merry, but she appreciated his honesty on the matter. Quality number one: check.

Most importantly, though, her mystery man shared her excitement over falling in love with an anonymous local. That she could unknowingly meet "Joe" in-person and also fall in love with him online was a dream come true in the making. And his comment about telling the story to their future grandchildren… *Be still, her merry heart.*

Despite feeling as gooey as a chocolate chip cookie straight from the oven, Noelle forced herself to reel in her excitement. She didn't need her worrywart of a sister to tell her there were a lot of weirdos out there; she had the dick pic to prove it. But she also wasn't going to let the risk of trusting a stranger stand in her way.

After another moment of internal debate, Noelle decided she would proceed with caution, while also giving Joe the benefit of the doubt. After all, she was a woman who never gave up on her dreams.

```
To: average_joe
From: everyday_merry

Hi Joe, the same could be said for you not
seeming to be "average" in the least. I woke up
with a head cold this dreary morning, and your
message has filled my day with sunshine. You
sound almost too good to be true… I agree we
should get to know each other better here before
revealing our secret identities. :)

To answer your question: Yes, that definitely
sounds like me.
```

I will happily challenge you. I've been told I can be a handful, especially by my mother, but I consider it a compliment.

My heart is so big it hurts sometimes. It might seriously explode all over Whoville one day… but most people in my life see me as a self-centered brat. I realize that doesn't paint me in the best light, but honesty is the best policy, right?

As for my dreams, I will chase them until the end of time. One such dream includes the love story I also hope to tell my future grandchildren someday. The universe already knows nothing short of an epic romance will do.

On to my questions for you, starting with the basics:

1. What's your favorite color?

2. Are you a cat or dog person?

3. Besides writing amazing messages, what do you do in your free time?

Until next time,
Merry

P.S. My heater may be broken… if you happen to know a repair company in the area, I'd greatly appreciate a recommendation. Thx!

Satisfied with her message, Noelle hit send, blew her nose (finally with some success), and then buried herself deeper under the covers to get some rest. It seemed to be getting colder in her room, but she lacked the energy to do anything about it yet. Besides, Joe might come through with a stellar recommendation, saving her the tedious chore of researching options online. One could only hope.

A loud bang jolted her awake. She glanced outside and noted the darkening sky, unsure if due to nightfall or storm clouds. How long had she been asleep? The banging, which was coming from downstairs, continued.

Groggy as a princess coming out of a sleeping curse, Noelle rolled out of bed in slow motion, wrapping two blankets around herself as she did. "I'm coming. I'm coming."

Only as she muttered the words to herself did she recognize the banging sound as someone knocking on the shop's front door. The hairs on the back of her neck instantly lifted. Her family was miles away, and she hadn't made any new friends in Holiday Pines yet. Who could be at her door?

Noelle crept down the stairs like a child trying to catch Santa on Christmas Eve, which was ridiculous. This was her store-slash-home. She didn't need to sneak around. Once at the bottom step, she readied herself to holler *who's there*, then cursed instead when she saw the tall figure outside the frosted glass door.

She knew exactly who was there.

9

Noelle swung the door outward, hoping to hit him with it. "What are you doing here?"

"Hello to you, too," Kent said, pushing past her without an invitation. "It's freezing outside."

"That's not an answer to my question."

He turned a full rotation as if taking in the store. "It's freezing inside, too. What's going on? You look awful, by the way."

"Nice. Leave it to you to show up unwelcomed, state the obvious, and insult me all within thirty seconds."

"I was worried you might have gotten sick from being drenched yesterday, and it looks like I was right. You're pasty, and there's… stuff… hanging out of your nose. Here, I made you some chicken noodle soup."

Why did he have to bring up their encounter in the rain? And why in the North Pole did he make her soup? Too flustered to ask, Noelle wiped at her nose with one of the plush blankets wrapped around her shoulders before reluctantly taking the container he held out.

"And you're wearing blankets," he continued, walking toward the wall with the thermostat. "Doesn't your heat work?"

"I'm having a repairman come later today." *It was on her to-do list, so not a total lie.* "The heat setting is at sixty-five, but it's not kicking on."

"Have you tried a manual override?"

"There's a manual override?"

"I'll take that as a no. Let's switch this from 'Auto' to 'On' and see if that works." Kent fiddled with the thermostat and then clucked his tongue. "No luck."

"Well, I tried *that* obviously," she lied, grateful such a simple act didn't fix the problem. Saving face beat being warm.

"Do you know if your heater is gas or electric?" he asked, stirring an anger so sudden and fierce she didn't have time to think before she snapped.

"I'm done with this game of twenty questions! I already told you a repairman is coming later today. You don't need to swoop in here with your savior complex and try to fix it, and you didn't need to make me soup." She charged forward and shook the container in his face to make her point. "Also, I wouldn't even be sick if it wasn't for you!"

"Oh, that's right. Everything is my—"

"Yes, KFC, everything *is* your fault. First you hit me with your big, hard head, and somehow, I'm the only one who got a concussion. Then, you knocked me down into a puddle of freezing water and delayed me getting into my car—"

"How did I—"

She held up a hand. "Don't interrupt me. We both got soaked in the rain, and yet I'm once again the only one suffering from it! You're standing there all handsome and healthy-looking, while I feel like something out of a Tim Burton film."

"Noelle—"

"No. Don't Noelle me. My head is congested, my throat is scratchy, my nose is clogged with snot—as you so rudely pointed out—and my n's sound like d's. Meanwhile, you drive up to *my* small town for some undisclosed reason like you're a freaking white knight with your stupid soup and your—"

Without warning, Kent's mouth crashed down on hers, cutting off her words, her thoughts, her oxygen supply. His rough kiss felt almost as angry as she'd been mere moments earlier. It was all lips and teeth—nipping, pressing, sucking. Noelle imagined they looked like actors kissing after a tense or dramatic scene, angling their heads side to side while forming a hermetic seal with their mouths to create the illusion of passion.

And why—*dear Jiminy Grinch, why*—was she suddenly craving Kent Frenchless Clark's tongue in her mouth? She shouldn't want to kiss him. She shouldn't even be allowing whatever *this* was.

The container of soup, still in her hands, wedged between them, and she used it to push herself back.

"What was that for?" she asked, gathering her breath.

"To end your tirade." Kent placed his glasses back on, then raked a hand through his dark hair. "And to catch your cold, I suppose."

"You want my cold?"

"Would that make you happy?" The soup container was once again the only thing separating them as he leaned forward. "Would it?"

It was another one of their dare games; only she didn't understand the rules. Her mind split into fractals of thought, like pine needles on an evergreen with infinite branches. Did Kent want to make her happy? Was her happiness worth him getting sick? Would him being sick even make her happy? She couldn't isolate a single coherent reply.

After time stood still for an eternity, all she could manage was, "I don't like soup."

Kent grinned and tucked a strand of hair behind her ear. "No, you don't like onions, and they're in most soups. But I made this batch without."

She stared up at him in disbelief. It was easy to forget how well he knew her, but in that moment, he felt like the only person in the world who truly did.

And it was terrifying.

"What about the broth?" she asked.

"No onions in that either. It's homemade bone broth. My secret ingredients are fresh ginger and lemon, which makes the broth tastier and adds some nice health benefits as well."

Her mouth stuttered in tune with her heart. "Why would you… go through such… trouble for me?"

"It was no trouble. My mom doesn't like onions either, and I always make extra for freezing. This broth was borrowed from her stash, which I'll replenish later. The rest of the soup was quick to throw together."

Noelle's fluttering heart sank at the mention of his mother. *His immunocompromised mother.* "I'm so sorry," she said, taking a step back. "I wasn't thinking. You need to be healthy to take care of your mom. Who's taking care of her now?"

"Brad, and it's fine. He wanted to spend some time with our mom and said I should take the next few days to myself. So, I thought I'd come get some fresh mountain air, check in on you, and then relax at the Holiday Pines Inn. I hear it has an indoor heated pool," he said with a wink that had her imagining a hot tub. "And more importantly, a working heater. I bet they have two rooms available. Come on, go pack an overnight bag, and you can thaw out while waiting for the repairman."

Her whole body sagged. "Why are you so nice to me when I'm so... not?"

Kent pulled his glasses toward the tip of his nose and looked over them like a sexy male librarian. "Because, Noelle Mary Serrano, you're nicer than you think, deep down."

"Ugh. It's not fair that you know my middle name when I don't know yours. I bet it's something embarrassing, like Franny... or Fabio."

"Deep, deep down," he said.

Despite the cold weather, Kent was sweating buckets by the time they reached the inn.

"Good afternoon, we'd like two rooms for the night, please," he said to the burly older woman at the counter.

She wore a deep scowl and looked oddly familiar—dull brown hair parted all to one side, a square jaw, and broad shoulders that made her look like a mobster or goon from a movie. In fact, if she were wearing a beret, she could pass for the main antagonist from *The Goonies*.

"Unfortunately, we only have one room available tonight," the Mama Fratelli look-alike said in a surprisingly pleasant voice.

Kent glanced at Noelle, only to find her biting back a laugh. She would find this humorous.

"What?" he asked.

Noelle crossed her arms, amusement still radiating off her. "I bet the room only has one bed, too."

Kent returned his gaze to the innkeeper, who smiled at them knowingly. At least her scowl was gone.

"The only room left is our honeymoon suite." She tapped on the keyboard in front of her as if checking them in was a foregone conclusion.

"Are there any other hotels in the area?" Noelle asked.

"I'm afraid not, Miss," the mobster lady said, still smiling, but now in a creepy '*I've got you, my pretties*' type of way.

Her name tag read MARGE. That sounded right.

Kent turned to Noelle. "We can always go back down to San Diego. I'm sure you could stay with your sister or parents until your heater is fixed."

"I'm afraid not," Marge said again. "There's a bad snowstorm coming. It's why we're full tonight. No one can leave."

Noelle harrumphed next to him, as if having proved some point.

"It's okay. I have a four-wheel-drive," he said, feeling increasingly creeped out by the phrase *no one can leave*.

"Doesn't matter," Marge said. "Police have the road blocked off. Emergency vehicles only. The pass is at a higher elevation than town, so it's already been blasted with snow, but it'll reach us later tonight.

They're callin' it a freak blizzard. Climate change and all that. So, would you like to pay with cash or credit card?"

Five minutes later, Kent and Noelle were climbing the stairs to the top floor of the small inn.

"We're room two-oh-three," he said, once they reached the landing.

"You mean the honeymoon suite," Noelle teased, not that her taunts mattered in the grand scheme of how tortured he already was by the entire situation.

A half hour ago, his mouth was on hers. And now, they were checking into a romantic inn together.

With one bed.

He swiped the key card, pushed the door open, then extended his arm. "After you."

"Thank you," she said, heading inside and then spinning in a circle. "Wow! This place is nicer than I expected. Look, cute little pine trees on the bedspread and chocolates on the pillows. Oh Saint Nick!" she yelled from the bathroom. "There's a heart-shaped tub in here! Ooh, and I love when hotels provide comfy bathrobes and slippers."

"I'm glad you like it, but you do realize we're not actually on our honeymoon, right?" he asked, hoping to calm his own nerves by extinguishing her palpable excitement.

Noelle reappeared with a robe in her arms. "Buzzkill. I thought we were married after that passionate kiss."

And there it was: *the new thing she would eternally mock him for.* Frankly, he was surprised she hadn't brought it up until now.

"Go ahead and joke," he said. "I'm sorry about that, though. I was… out of line."

Noelle's features softened for a moment, then she sat on the king-sized torture device and crossed her legs. "I call the bed, since I'm sick. You can take the love seat. Or you can sleep in the heart-shaped tub, if you prefer."

Kent peered across the room at the tiny two-seater and nodded. The pinecone-patterned sofa looked about as comfortable as a littered forest floor, but it would have to suffice. A sound of disgust drew his attention back to Noelle.

"Is everything okay?"

"I guess," she said, scrolling on her phone as she so often did. "But I don't understand how people can be so rude. Someone posted a brutal book review on Insta and tagged the author."

"That seems harsh," Kent said, doing his best not to fixate on the arch of Noelle's back as she slowly reclined onto the bed, or the fact that her little red sweater was creeping up her abdomen with each rise and fall of her chest.

"Right?" she agreed in a nasal tone. "It's like, fine, voice your opinion, but don't intentionally hurt someone else's feelings in the process. I'm sure countless hours and cocktails went into the production of that book. Add to cart," she said, tapping her phone screen.

And damn if her compassion wasn't more than he could bear. Much like her generosity at the nursing home, and so many other acts of kindness before. He might not be a beneficiary, but Noelle Serrano cared—hard and often.

Between that fact and her now completely supine position on the bed, the otherwise spacious room seemed to shrink with each passing second.

"I'm going to head to the store for some blizzard-survival supplies," he said, eager to retreat. "Do you need anything? Cold medicine, maybe?"

Noelle stroked her chin as if thinking, eyes still on her phone. "I have cold medicine, but some cough drops would be nice. The all-natural kind, honey or cherry-flavored, if they have it."

"Got it," he said.

"Oh, and I also need some feminine products."

"Some… what?"

"You know, tampons and pads. That would be great. Thanks!"

"What, um, kind?" he asked, stammering as light sweat dampened his brow.

"Some of each kind. I'm not picky. Oh, and if you could pick up a bottle of Midol and some chocolate, too, that would be *amazing*. You're the best."

"Okay, let me make a list so I don't forget." Head spinning, he pulled up a note on his phone and typed out the items, starting with the cough drops.

He was up to *my doll*, or however it was spelled, when he heard laughter. He lowered his phone and glared at Noelle, who was holding her stomach and convulsing.

"I'm sorry. I thought I could hold it together until you left for the store, but your list is too adorable."

Of course. Hadn't he already acknowledged that her kindness didn't extend to him?

"I take it you don't need any of that stuff, then?"

"Just the cough drops, please. And I would never turn down chocolate," she said, still laughing. "I can't believe you were actually going to buy me tampons. I'm touched, really."

"Happy to be the butt of your jokes, as always," he said, quite accustomed to the blend of self-pity and annoyance stewing within him.

"I'm sorry. I just always wanted a guy to buy that stuff for me, but none of the ones I dated ever stuck around long enough for me to ask."

The room fell silent once that bomb landed. After an awkward minute, she added, "Anyway, it was wrong of me to ask you. It's not even my time of month, so—"

"The room has a microwave," he said, drawn toward it like a sinner to church. "Would you like me to reheat the soup for you before I go?"

Noelle flashed him a grateful smile. "Yes, please. I haven't eaten all day."

Two minutes later, Kent was out the door and headed on foot to the nearby market, which, unlike the other cleverly named businesses along Main Street, had a sign above that simply read, General Store. In the window, another sign, handwritten with a Sharpie, read, "We've Got It All, Y'all."

Yeah, that would do.

10

Forget Lucky Charms. Kent's soup was magically delicious. Noelle felt ninety-two percent better right after eating the enchanted concoction. Her headache and lethargy had dissipated with each spoonful, probably due to her being hungrier than she'd realized. The tasty, onion-less potion had also soothed her scratchy throat, cleared her stuffy nose, and relieved her sinus pressure.

It was the best soup she'd ever had. Not only could she eat it without the fear of triggering her gag reflex to the sometimes-slimy, sometimes-crunchy, body-odor-scented vegetable found in practically everything, but it also had the perfect ratio of *stuff*.

Large pieces of chicken (not the negligible bits found in canned soup) were combined with sliced carrots, celery, and herbs. The wide egg noodles had melted in her mouth, while the right amount of gingery, lemony chicken broth filled her senses. If she'd eaten the soup at a restaurant, she would've written a glowing review.

But Kent had made the soup.

For *her*.

Hence, the other eight percent that felt a whole lot worse.

She had given Kent a hard time for acting like a white knight, but as she looked around the hotel room, warmed by a working heater and the soup in her belly, it was clear she'd needed his help. Not that she couldn't have checked into the inn by herself, but she wouldn't have. Instead, she would've stubbornly hunkered down in the cold, damp loft with a pile of blankets and nothing more than a meager stash of granola bars and snacks for sustenance.

Kent had saved her from herself.

And how had she repaid him? First, by screaming at him so much that he'd felt the need to kiss her to shut her up—an action he clearly regretted. Then, by asking him to buy her feminine hygiene products she didn't even need. But the joke was on her when she'd overshared about her pitiful love life, as she tended to do in his presence.

In need of a distraction, she considered scouring reviews of local heating repair companies (was that a thing?), but then she had a better idea.

"Yes, hello. This is Noelle in room two-oh-three. My heater is broken at home, and I was wondering if you could recommend a repair company," she said into the inn's phone after dialing the front desk.

"What a coincidence," said the cheery voice on the other end. *Marge? Or maybe Madge?*

The older woman's outfit had been too distracting for Noelle to remember what she'd read on the nametag. Marge or Madge had been wearing a charcoal gray shawl that made her broad shoulders look even wider, and underneath, what could only be described as a multi-colored muumuu. However, despite needing a serious makeover, Marge or Madge had been quite pleasant at check-in, and Noelle had taken an instant liking to her. It also didn't hurt that the innkeeper seemed to make Kent uncomfortable.

"Coincidence?" Noelle asked.

"Yeah. Your handsome boyfriend came down here and asked the same thing about ten minutes ago," Marge or Madge said.

"He's not my—" Noelle started, but since there was no point correcting a stranger, she finished with, "Oh, I see."

"I'll tell you the same as I told him. Mack's Heating and Plumbing. He's the only one in that business up here."

"Mack's," Noelle repeated. "Okay. Thank you very much for the information."

"I have the number handy, if you want it."

"That would be great. Thanks!"

Noelle typed the number Marge or Madge relayed into her cell, thanked her again, and hung up the inn's phone. *Well, that was enlightening.*

Having grown up in a city with over a million people, it hadn't dawned on her that there might only be one option to choose from in a small town. If she'd known that before, she wouldn't have put off the task for as long as she had.

But why had Kent asked the same question? She'd told him a repairman was already coming. Had he (correctly) assumed she'd been lying? Or was the recommendation to compare against whoever she had chosen? It would be typical of Kent to think she lacked the capability to select the right option herself.

To quell her rising anger, Noelle dialed the number for Mack's and tried to put Kent out of her mind.

"Mack of Mack's Heating and Plumbing here," a deep, laid-back voice said.

An attractive voice.

It might be a longshot, but maybe this was the plot twist her story needed: *Girl's heater breaks. Girl meets hunky repairman. Girl falls in love and lives happily ever after.*

After scheduling an appointment with Mack, who unfortunately couldn't come out until Monday—three long days away—Noelle padded into the bathroom. The heart-shaped tub in the corner made her smile, and on impulse, she began filling it. She then triple-checked that the bathroom door was locked, undressed, and lowered herself into the hot sudsy water.

As she sank farther into the bubbles, her mind involuntarily slipped to Kent again. He'd come to Holiday Pines to take a break from his caregiver responsibilities and, instead, had gotten stuck taking care of an ungrateful brat with a head cold. No wonder he'd run off to the store like he couldn't get away fast enough.

Kent probably needed a holiday from his holiday.

Or was he mad at her? That "kiss" had certainly felt angry, but it had also felt... nice.

No, nice wasn't the right adjective. It had been naughty, in a *this is so wrong it feels right* type of way. She touched a finger to her lips, remembering the intensity of his mouth on hers and all the feelings it had conjured. The rest of the world had fallen away. Time had stood still. They were the only two people alive, consumed by the intimacy of knowing each other completely. Basically, she'd been sucked into a romance novel.

"Mortal enemy," she muttered to herself. "He is your mortal enemy, Noelle."

Needing a distraction from her sudden and irrational desire, she wiped her wet hands on a nearby towel then reached for her phone. She opened the *Holiday Pines Connections* app and was pleased to find a reply from average_joe:

> Dearest Merry,
>
> I already sensed you were my dream girl, but your answer to my question confirmed it. I'm looking forward to getting to know you, your big heart, and your life dreams even better.
>
> Also, I'm sorry to hear about your head cold. If your heater is broken (what horrible timing!), you'll need to call Mack's Heating and Plumbing. He's the only repair company in town. Please let me know if there's anything I can do to help. As for your great questions to me, below are my answers:
>
> 1. My favorite color is green.
>
> 2. I feel like there's a right answer to the cat vs. dog person question, but my honest answer is this: I like all animals but don't

currently have a pet. I guess if I had a gun to my head and had to choose, I'd take one of each ;)

3. In my free time, I enjoy reading and swimming. I also go for long runs, but not because I enjoy running… I'm told heart disease *runs* in my family (pun intended) so I force myself to do it at least once a week for my cardiovascular health.

I'd like to throw the same three questions back to you and add two more:

A. What do you love most about Christmas?

B. What's one thing that no one else knows about you?

Feel better!
Joe

A lot to analyze, but before Noelle could begin, a knock on the bathroom door startled her. "Noooo!"

"Noelle? Are you okay in there? I'm back from the store."

"No, I'm not okay. You made me drop my phone in the bathtub!" Noelle fished her prized possession out of the soapy water and wrapped it in a towel.

That's one way to cool your loins for your mortal enemy, the annoying Jiminy-Grinch voice said.

"Uh, sorry about that. I can help—help you, um, dry it out," Kent said through the bathroom door. "Besides your phone, is everything else okay?"

Nothing was okay.

"I need to be alone right now," she said.

"Okay. Well, I'll just unload the stuff from the store and then find that heated pool. A swim sounds nice right now anyway."

Noelle wanted to yell that she didn't need the play-by-play, but something he said stopped her.

A swim.

Noelle sat as still as a mannequin, listening to Kent's footsteps shuffle around the room until the front door closed with a click. Since her bath was effectively ruined, she drained the tub, then took a quick shower to rinse away the bathwater, along with her disturbing thoughts.

No, Kent couldn't be Joe.

Swimming and reading were both common pastimes. It didn't make sense that her mind would even jump to such a preposterous conclusion, unless… on some sick and twisted level, *she wanted Kent to be Joe.* And that was beyond absurd. She could not be developing feelings for KFC.

Lust, maybe. But feelings?

Never.

After her aura-cleansing shower, Noelle put on the inn's pinecone-logoed bathrobe and slippers and listened at the door. *Not a creature was stirring.* Confident the coast was clear, she left the sanctuary of the bathroom, managing two steps before freezing in her tracks. Her hand rose to cover her mouth as her disbelieving eyes beheld the spectacle of the bed… piled high with what had to be nearly a year's supply of feminine products.

There were multiple packages of every brand, type, and absorbency. Pads with and without wings. Various pantyliners. Tampons for light, regular, and heavy days. Some with applicators, some without. There was even a reusable menstrual cup, next to a bottle of Midol and a generous stack of chocolate bars.

Tears filled her eyes. Kent *Freaking* Clark had bought her a crapload of period supplies, and it was the most ridiculously romantic thing anyone had ever done for her.

11

Surfacing at the edge of the pool, Kent removed his swim goggles and then regarded the afternoon sky through the large, arched window overlooking Main Street. When Noelle had said that none of her boyfriends ever stuck around long enough, the darkness enshrouding her joy had filled him with an insatiable need to bring light back to the sunniest person he knew.

Idly, Kent wondered if she'd found her requested contraband yet and what her reaction had been. If nothing else, she'd at least get some enjoyment out of having something new to tease him about.

A different type of darkness—cast from the twin sets of tall, ominous clouds within view—pulled him from his musings. Ready or not, he supposed he should head back to the room before the snowstorm arrived. Although the heated pool had been indoors, he hadn't considered that he would have to walk outside (in freezing weather and wet swim trunks) to get back to their room on the second floor. *So much for his genius IQ.*

By the time he reached the door marked 203, his numb, quaking body craved a hot shower more than his lungs needed air. White flurries danced above him as he fumbled for his key card. He shoved the key into the slot, removed it quickly, then hurled himself into the room.

"It's officially freezing outs—" Kent cut himself off when he saw her face. "Hey. Are you okay?"

Noelle stood a few feet in front of him, wearing a bathrobe and a blank expression. Her eyes glistened, and her cheeks appeared to be streaked with tears. *Oh, damn him to hell.* He'd wanted his purchases to make her smile, possibly laugh, not cry.

"I'm sorry if—"

The rest of his words disappeared—from his throat, from his brain, from existence—when Noelle rushed forward and captured his mouth. A combination of urgency and tenderness, her sweet kiss felt like a fever dream. Had he died and gone to Heaven?

As she pressed her soft, warm body against him, her heat not only thawed him, it kicked off a fire near every point of contact. He wanted to wrap his arms around her, to pull her even closer, but he was afraid he'd interrupt the dream if he moved. Because this couldn't be real. Noelle couldn't possibly be kissing him.

Kent would've thought he was in an alternate reality within the multiverse if not for the fact that, for the second time that day, he tasted the sweetness of her lips and felt the warmth of her mouth, heard her soft gasps and smelled her distinct aroma. *Freshly baked cookies.* No dream—and he'd had plenty—had ever engaged his senses so fully.

This was really happening.

Noelle framed his face with her hands, and, of their own volition, his hands slid down the sides of her body and gripped her hips, pulling her flush against him. Their kiss deepened with the motion, her tongue sliding around his in a synchronized dance that could rival an Olympic artistic swimming routine.

They both let out a low moan, and then Noelle broke the kiss, retreating several steps back as quickly as she'd advanced. She brought her hand to her mouth as her eyes darted wildly around the room.

Still catching his breath, Kent gripped the wet towel draped over his bare shoulders. "Noelle…"

"Well, there you go," she blurted, placing her fists on her hips. "That's how you kiss someone. I thought I'd show you, given your embarrassing attempt earlier. You're welcome."

"Uh… Thank you?" His jumbled brain searched for more words, but there were none.

She'd kissed him like that *as what? Some type of tutorial?* Well, point taken. He'd already known his assault on her lips earlier had been horrible—and not at all how he'd imagined their first kiss happening. She'd been upset and yelling at him, and he'd felt overcome with the need to calm her down. In hindsight, it was not his finest moment.

A violent shiver ripped through him as he stood there in his wet swim shorts. All the heat had left his body the second she'd stepped away. There had been a passionate blaze burning inside her. He'd felt it in her kiss, or at least he thought he had, before her fire had turned to ice.

Noelle paced in front of him, her arms crossed over her chest. "You look cold. Why don't you go take a hot shower or something?"

Kent nodded, since words still eluded him. Cold, hot, cold. Yeah, a hot shower sounded nice.

Noelle replayed the kiss over and over as she tossed and turned that night. She hadn't planned on kissing Kent, but between his sweet gesture and him looking sinfully gorgeous—with nothing but a towel over his muscular shoulders, and those damn perfect forearms—she had lost all control.

Given how meticulously she planned everything in her life, the irony of it hit her like a snowball in the face. She could only hope he'd bought the "kissing lesson" lie. But that wasn't even her biggest problem. When Kent's mouth and tongue had moved against hers, teasing and satisfying her all at once, it was clear he already knew how to kiss.

Amazingly well.

So well that, for a brief period of temporary insanity, she'd forgotten all about his unforgivable crime and had allowed herself to feel things she'd only ever read about in the swooniest of swoony romance novels.

Thank Christmas her senses had come back.

Kent had cleared the bed by transporting all of his purchased contraband to Merry Holidays, then he'd spent the rest of the evening lounging on the love seat, reading a thick book (most likely written by Merriam-Webster) and looking obnoxiously hot in basic gray sweat pants. Meanwhile, she'd occupied herself by rereading all of Joe's messages on her laptop—a.k.a. her life force until her submerged phone could be resurrected.

Her fear that Kent could be Joe was squashed when she'd thought of her own answers to the questions she'd posed:

1. Her favorite color was also green.
2. She loved all animals but had neither a cat nor a dog at the moment.
3. She also liked to read and swim, among other things.

Clearly, Joe and Kent having those pastimes in common meant nothing. She shared all three answers in common with Joe, but that didn't mean *she was Joe*. Sometimes two unconnected people liked the same things. It was a coincidence, not a clue.

Unsure how to reply to Joe's additional questions, she'd drafted a partial message without sending and then moved on to some marketing materials for the store. She had lost herself in her work, taking a break only to eat some surprisingly tasty sushi rolls that Kent had brought back from his trip to the general store.

That had all been hours ago.

Now, sleep eluded her no matter how hard she tried to catch it. The wind howled outside as fluffy ice crystals blew past the sliver of uncovered window. An almost full moon and a nearby streetlamp targeted her face like high beams on a backcountry road. Multiple times that night, she'd considered adjusting the curtains to block the light out, but the idea of being in complete darkness with Kent deterred her.

She rolled to her left, which had her facing the general direction of Kent in the dark corner of the room, then back onto her right side, toward the blinding light.

"This is ridiculous," Noelle said, rolling over again.

There was about a thirty-second delay before a groggy sounding Kent asked, "What is?"

He'd been asleep. Of course he had. According to a popular TikToker she followed, there was one person in every relationship who annoyingly conked out as soon as their head hit the pillow. Not that she and Kent were in a relationship… far from it.

"You're tall, and on that short couch, and I'm small on this huge bed. That's what's ridiculous," she said without thinking.

"Are you offering to switch?" he asked.

"No," she replied, unsure where she'd been going with that until her traitorous mouth blurted, "I'm saying there's room for both of us on the bed."

Dead silence followed.

Did she just invite Kent into bed with her? It felt like an out-of-body experience. The real Noelle floated somewhere near the ceiling, pointing down at her while laughing.

"Unless you can't handle it," the shell of her body added to save face. *Smooth.*

More silence from the dark corner of the room. Noelle swore she could feel his stare reach out from the shadows.

She rolled onto her right side again, putting her back to him. "Suit yourself."

A minute passed—maybe fifty-eight seconds—and then there was a barely discernable creak, followed by light footsteps, followed by a dip in the mattress.

"I can handle it," Kent said, his low voice rumbling like distant thunder through her chest.

When Noelle rolled over again, the chiseled edges of his face came into view. And within them, the phrase 'it was a dark and stormy night' took on new meaning.

Thanks to the moon-slash-streetlamp beams pouring in from behind, shadows shielded her features as she perused his at length. Those lips that only hours ago had been on hers. The small scar above his left eyebrow from when he'd fallen off his bike as a kid. The subtle way all the angles of his face—whether formed by his flexed jaw, straight nose, or defined cheekbones—pointed toward his intense eyes, which held hers in what felt like a staring contest.

And she was not one to back down from a challenge.

"I've been thinking a lot about that lesson from earlier," he said, his gaze dipping to her mouth. *Okay, maybe she wasn't as shielded as she'd thought.*

"Have you now?" she asked as coolly as possible.

With the side of his face pressed into the pillow, Kent nodded once. "I think I understand the basics, but, as with most things, it's going to take some practice to master it."

Her mouth went dry and watered all at once. Where in the holly had this man come from? The Kent Clark she knew was mild-mannered and easily flustered, much like his reverse namesake. But take off his glasses, and apparently, he turned into a super smooth talker.

She felt herself lean in. "I bet I could teach you some other things, too."

His breath visibly caught, and she smiled.

"Would you like some more lessons?"

"Yes," he said without hesitation, nodding like an eager child at a candy store.

"Lesson one, whatever happens tonight,"—she motioned between them—"it changes nothing. Do you understand?"

He nodded again, slower that time.

"I need to hear you say it, Kent."

"I understand."

"Good boy. Lesson two, always set boundaries in the bedroom. For tonight, we'll set it right down the middle of this bed." She drew an imaginary line with her finger while maintaining eye contact. "You stay on your side and keep your hands to yourself. Got it?"

Kent rolled over, putting his back to her. "Good night, Noelle."

It should have felt like a win. A little torture was the least Kent Fraud Clark deserved for ruining her life. But as soon as she'd said the words 'keep your hands to yourself,' she couldn't help but imagine his hands all over her.

Noelle desperately wanted to take back her petty words. She wanted him to touch and kiss her, and to not stop there. She wanted Kent Freaking Clark.

An ache formed low in her belly as liquid heat pooled at her core. How had she let this happen? *Don't overthink it*, the voice of Jiminy-Grinch advised. Sex didn't have to be complicated. Two people could take care of each other's needs without any strings attached—like friends with benefits.

Except Kent wasn't her friend. Enemies with benefits? Could that be a thing?

Okay, she was officially overthinking it. She reached her hand out, ready to take action, but then retracted it when her ears detected a rhythmic pattern. A nasally intake followed by a light huff of air at regular intervals. Not quite snoring, but definitely not the normal sounds of someone awake.

Well, great.

She'd intended to punish him and, instead, set herself on fire during a snowstorm. Now all she could do was lie there and try to extinguish the flames by reminding herself—for the millionth time—why she and KFC would never work.

12

Kyle Fisher was the most popular guy at Clairemont High, *and he planned to ask her out.* Noelle had heard so from her friend Marcus, who had heard from Eric Branson, who had heard from his girlfriend, Madeline, who was best friends with Kyle's sister. Given the source, the rumor had to be true.

Only one question remained: When?

Noelle had moved her lunch circle closer to Kyle's over two weeks ago, in hopes he'd come over and ask her out, but nothing had happened yet. Was the problem that all of her friends were guys?

Yeah, no.

Marcus consistently wore high-watered pants, despite being short and chubby. Josh had major acne, braces, and spoke with an occasional lisp. And Ryan—poor, sweet Ryan—wore Coke-bottle glasses and had a phobia of being touched. He carried his trombone case everywhere, using it to create a six-foot radius of personal space around himself. Her oddball crew couldn't possibly intimidate someone as amazing as Kyle.

"Hey, Josh, would you mind walking me to fifth period?" Noelle asked as lunch ended.

"Of courth," Josh lisped, "but you don't have to keep pretending to be my girlfriend juth 'cuz you feel sorry for me."

"I don't feel sorry for you, J-dog. I enjoy tormenting Adam Leeks. You should've seen his face after I told him I would've gone out with him if he wasn't such a bully. *As if.* It's bad enough his last name is related to onions, but him making fun of the way you speak is beyond uncool."

"Well, whyever you do it, thank you. Those jerks haven't meth'd with me since I started walking you to class."

Noelle smiled at Josh, who, she reasoned, would be attractive without the temporary ailments of acne and braces. He had a symmetrical face, spiked blond hair, and pale blue eyes. Though not her type, he'd surely be a catch for some other lucky girl (or boy?) someday. If she could help him out in the meantime, why wouldn't she?

"It's my pleasure," she said, taking Josh's arm as he led her to the Spanish class she shared with Adam Jerkface Leeks.

On the way there, Noelle spotted Kyle Fisher's best friend walking toward them. "Hi, Kent!" she said, plastering on her cheeriest smile as he approached.

Kent, however, passed by without as much as a glance in her direction—ignoring her, as per usual.

"Yiketh. What's his problem?" Josh asked.

Noelle threw her head back. "Thank you! I was starting to think I'd been imagining it, but that guy is seriously rude."

"Isn't he a senior? How do you even know him?"

"My older sister is dating his older brother. I swear, if they get married and we become family, I'll lose my mind. He acts like he'll turn to stone or something if he looks at me. Either that or he thinks he's too cool to acknowledge a lowly freshman."

"That sucks. Sorry, Noelle."

"Whatever. I wouldn't even bother talking to him, but since he's Kyle's best friend, I've been trying to get on his good side... assuming he has one."

"Speaking of good *thides*," Josh lisped, "Marcus said you're helping him get some new clothes to impress Misty."

"Yeah, but I'm only on phase one of the plan, which involved buying a bunch of cute outfits for myself from the thrift store."

"Uh, how does that help Marcus?"

"It's a long game, my friend. First, I flaunt the stylish items I bought, including my outfit today," she said, referring to the green silk blouse that she'd paired with vintage bell-bottomed jeans. "It's part of my *Secondhand is Sexy* campaign, which I'm hoping will make the hand-me-downs Marcus has to wear seem less unattractive. Then, when all the biters on campus are dying to copy my style, I'll move on to phase two: hosting a fashion auction, where I resale my thrift store purchases for more than they cost and use the profits to buy Marcus some new threads."

"That's genius," Josh said, flashing her a metallic smile. "Well, here we are."

Noelle peered through the classroom window to confirm Adam Leeks was watching, then leaned in for a big hug. "Thanks again, Josh. Have a good rest of your day."

"You too."

Oh, she planned on it.

Fifth period came and went, or *vino y se fue*. Since Noelle loved excelling at things, Mrs. González's Spanish class was her favorite. It also explained why she hated her sixth period algebra class. But she got through it, because Wednesdays meant baseball practice after school, and baseball practice meant spying on Kyle in tight white pants.

Careful not to be seen, she crept under the bleachers near the dugout and settled into a cross-legged position on the ground. Book in hand to ward off suspicion, she scanned the area. None of the players had arrived yet, so she occupied herself by reading *Great Expectations* for her English literature class until she heard voices approaching.

"What do you think?"

"About what?"

Noelle looked up to see Kyle and Kent entering the dugout.

"About me asking out Noelle Serrano," Kyle said, his charming smile bright even under the gray October sky.

Noelle covered her mouth to suppress a squeal. *The rumors were true!*

"I don't know," Kent said. "Isn't she dating that blond kid with braces?"

"No way. Everyone knows she only befriends misfits to protect them from bullying. It's sweet."

"Oh, I didn't realize—"

"And she's way too hot for that guy," Kyle added.

"She may be hot," Kent said, slamming a ball into his glove, "but she doesn't have much else going for her. You should steer clear of that one."

"What do you mean?" Kyle asked.

Noelle clenched her fists around the book in her hands. *Yes, Kent, what the hell do you mean?*

"I mean, she has a pretty face and all, but… I don't think the lights are on upstairs."

"The lights aren't on?" Kyle asked, sounding as confused as she felt.

Was Kent seriously calling her stupid?

"Yeah, you know… she's ditzy and superficial, plus way too immature for you."

The pages of her Dickens novel were now tearing.

"Really? How do you know?" Kyle asked.

"I've met her enough times to know that a guy with your potential doesn't mix with someone like that. Plus, you're going off to Harvard next year. You can't be dating some high school chick."

"Dude, that's like light-years away. I was thinking I'd maybe take her to homecoming, see where it goes."

"I'll tell you where it goes," Kent said, slamming the ball into his glove again and again. "You hook up with her at homecoming, then maybe she gets pregnant, and the next thing you know, your hopes of one day being a senator are dashed. Instead, you're stuck with a girl way below your caliber. You're smarter than that, dude."

"Wow. All right, all right. Let's go throw that ball before you destroy it."

The loud *thud, thud, thud* of Kent hitting the ball against his glove stopped. "So, you're not going to ask her out?"

"Nah. I'll steer clear, like you said. What's your batting average these days, anyway?" Kyle asked, as both guys headed toward the field.

Noelle exhaled once it was safe to do so, her blood boiling with rage. She wanted to scream and cry and burn the world down all at the same time. Though not sure how yet, she would make Kent pay for what he'd done.

Kent F. Clark was officially her mortal enemy.

13

Merry vibe:

"Let It Snow! Let It Snow! Let It Snow!"

Dean Martin

44 days until Christmas

A narrow beam of golden light shone in from the window, illuminating a small fraction of the room as Kent struggled to gain his bearings. The blurry image of the uncomfortable love seat brought it all screaming back. He was in the honeymoon suite at the Holiday Pines Inn. In bed. With Noelle.

Unsure what to expect, he rolled over with the speed of a sloth and found the other side of the bed empty.

"Noelle?" he called out, squinting at various obscure objects in the dark.

No reply.

Probably for the best, he thought, looking down at the tent he was pitching under the bedsheet. Given how turned-on Noelle had gotten him before he'd fallen asleep, he wouldn't be surprised if he'd been hard all night.

Her particular brand of torture always involved some form of reeling him in, only to dig the hook in deeper before casting him back out to sea. And yet he took the bait, time and time again. Pathetic didn't feel like a strong enough adjective for what he was. Still, he'd rather be tormented by Noelle than live a peaceful existence without her.

If only he knew *why* she hated him so much. He'd asked her, of course, many times before, and had gotten her standard "If I told you, I'd have to kill you" response.

Kent rose from bed, switched on the lamp, and searched for his glasses. He'd last worn them before he'd gone swimming, which was before Noelle had kissed him.

That kiss. He didn't care if it was merely instructional. It had been the type of kiss poets wrote about; the kind a man could happily die after; better than his best dreams. He sighed, then shook his head to clear the memory... with minimal success.

Digging around in his overnight bag, he found a spare pair of glasses with thick black frames. They weren't as stylish as his rimless pair—a fact Noelle would surely notice and comment on—but at least he'd be able to see clearly again.

As he debated going to look for his other glasses at the pool, he drew back the curtain and gazed in wonder at the white blanket covering literally *everything*. And then he saw it.

A small snowman that had Noelle written all over it. Not only was she the type of person who enjoyed playing with frozen water molecules, but a glint off the snowman's face confirmed it.

With a shake of his head, he threw on his coat and boots and treaded outside. As he did, Noelle approached from down the street with an outrageously cheerful smile on her face and two steaming cups of what he hoped was coffee.

"Hey! You met Frosty Clark," she said, with more enthusiasm than anyone should have on such a frigid morning.

"I was looking for these," he said, removing his rimless glasses from the icy figure.

"Aw, now Frosty can't see. Oh well." She shrugged before holding out a cup to him. "Hot apple cider?"

"Was it made from a poisoned apple?"

"Ha ha. No, it's a peace offering. I never thanked you for the soup and for buying me all those… products. That was really sweet of you. And I'm sorry about last night, and for borrowing these this morning," she said, pointing at his glasses. "Though, to be fair, you'd left them at the pool. Marge brought them out to me when she saw me making Frosty. I was hoping your specs would bring him to life, but no such luck."

He took the cup of cider, unsure how to respond. Her apology seemed sincere, which was disconcerting. And then, as it always did, her radiant presence melted him into a puddle, ready to be stomped.

"Also, for what it's worth, I think those black frames look better on you," she said, motioning to the spare glasses on his face. "They're very mild-mannered news reporter."

Cup in hand, he crossed his arms. "How original."

"Relax. I meant it as a compliment. Clark Kent is hot, especially the Dean Cain and Henry Cavill versions." Noelle fanned herself, and Kent did a double-take of her face. It exuded joy.

"Why are you in such a good mood this morning?"

"Is it that obvious?" she asked, still beaming. "I'm having the best morning ever!"

"The best morning ever," he repeated without her ten implied exclamation points.

"Let's go inside, and I'll tell you all about it. I got muffins, too," she added, tapping her purse.

Kent regarded her skeptically. "Okay… let's."

As they headed back toward their room, Noelle jumped right into storytelling mode. "First, I woke up to this magical winter wonderland. So, obviously, I *had* to build a snowman."

"Obviously," he said.

"Then I headed to the local coffee shop, Holiday Grinds. How cute is that?" Once inside, Noelle threw her bag on the bed and plopped down beside it. "Anyway, I planned to get coffee for you and tea for me, but then I saw that they make fresh apple cider, and I was like, yum! Do you like it? I love mine."

"Are you sure there isn't caffeine in that cup of yours?" he asked, before taking a sip of his drink. *Warm and acidic with the exact right amount of sweetness.* "It's good. Thanks."

"My acupuncturist once told me that an apple in the morning can give you more energy than a cup of coffee. I assume that applies to apple cider as well. Anyway, I haven't gotten to the best part yet." She clasped her hands over her chest, shoulders lifted toward her ears as if holding back any longer might cause her to burst. "When I was waiting for our drinks, the barista called out my name, except it was spelled N-O-E-L on the cup. Since people often misspell my name, I didn't think much of it at first, but then a guy reached for the cup at the exact moment I did. And it was him!"

"Him who?" he asked, sensing the world's worst knock-knock punchline coming.

"Noel Kris Clauson! He's this super-hot guy I met on my first day in Holiday Pines, when his reindeer ran in front of my car, but then he mentioned his wife. Oh, and he runs a Christmas tree farm with his parents. How perfect is that?"

"I'm so confused."

And he was, on multiple levels. Noelle had met some guy with a reindeer, a Christmas tree farm, and a wife? And that was perfect?

"Well, he goes by Kris—with a K—but apparently, the barista went to school with him and insists on calling him by his first name, Noel. We laughed about the whole 'confused name on drink' thing, and then he ran off with his coffee. I assumed he didn't chat with me longer because of the wife he'd mentioned, but then..." Noelle reached into her bag and pulled out two muffins wrapped in plastic. "Blueberry or pumpkin spice?"

"Definitely blueberry."

She tossed it to him. "I figured, but it seemed more polite to ask. The muffin is part of my new *trying to be nice* thing, by the way, but I'll get to that part of the story in a minute."

"Thanks, but I'm pretty sure telling someone you only did something to *try to be nice* negates the niceness of the act."

Noelle snapped her fingers in the universal sign for darn, and Kent lowered onto the love seat across from her.

"Anyway, you were saying?" he prodded, despite the gut punch he sensed coming.

"About what?"

"About Kris *with a K* and his wife."

"Ah, yes. Well, I'd assumed he was married, but then I was chatting with the barista—a lovely woman named Sandy—and she told me his wife died two years ago. It was sudden and tragic, and the whole town mourned her. Her name was Becca, and she used to run a bookstore out of the space I've now leased.

"Sandy also mentioned that Kris is in his early forties, which is older than I'd assumed, but I'm not opposed to an age-gap romance. Oh, and he has a daughter who's six. That's all I know." Noelle took a bite of her muffin, then continued talking while chewing. "Well, that and the fact that Becca was apparently a very nice person. That's why I need to work on that if I'm going to win Kris over."

"Win him over?"

"Yeah, he hasn't dated anyone since Becca's death, which is understandable. But don't you see how perfect this is? I wanted a storybook romance, and the single-dad, widower trope is a classic! I can help him move on from his grief *and* gain an insta-family in the process."

Kent's head spun. *Why was she telling him all this?* Were they friends now? Or was this yet another form of her torture?

"I'm struggling to see how this is all perfect," he said. "His wife is dead. And that's a good thing?"

Noelle sprang from the bed. "Of course not! I'm not a monster. But good to know your opinion of me is as low as ever. And, as always, you're missing the point."

"And what's the point, Noelle?"

"The point is *everyone*, including you, thought I was crazy for moving to a small town to find the type of love found in books and movies. But I'm going to prove you all wrong."

Recognizing the inferno inside him as a raw rage only she could evoke, Kent gripped the cushion beneath him to keep himself grounded. "And that's what matters most to you, isn't it? Proving everyone wrong," he spat, unable to keep the fire from his voice.

"No. Finding love is what matters, but proving *you* wrong will certainly be icing on the gingerbread cookie." She shoved her finger in his chest. "You've always thought you were so much smarter than me."

"What are you talking about?"

"Oh, you act so innocent, Mister Stanford. I may have only attended state college, but I'm smart enough to know when someone is two-faced."

"Seriously, what are you—"

"Do you still talk to Kyle Fisher?"

Her question threw him for a loop. What did his best friend from high school have to do with any of this? "No, we haven't talked since after college. I think he lives in D.C. now. Why?"

"I bet he's some big, important politician. Maybe even a senator," she said, straddling his lap.

His anger quickly lost out to arousal and confusion. "What are you doing?"

"For someone with such a big brain, you can be awfully slow." She removed his glasses, then ran her fingers through his hair. "What does it look like I'm doing?"

In that moment, Kent knew exactly what she was doing. It was the same thing she'd been doing for years: seducing him for the sole purpose of making him want what they both knew he could never have. *Her.* She rejoiced in (and was quite skilled at) getting a literal rise out of him.

Little did she realize that such maneuvers weren't necessary. He'd wanted her from the day they'd first met, and even more after he'd learned she'd befriended all those misfits in high school to protect them from bullying. Her big heart was sexy as hell. The attractive packaging around it… Well, that was *icing on the gingerbread cookie*, as she would say.

Her straddling tactic was new, though. And fuck, it was already working.

He cleared his throat. "Let me rephrase. *Why* are you doing this?"

Her hand trailed along his jaw to his chin, then tilted his face up to meet hers. "Again, it's such a shame that your big brain is so useless. Kinda like the other big organ you have."

"Noelle, I swear I'm gonna…"

"You're gonna what?" she taunted.

What happened next felt out of his control. He closed the small distance between their mouths. The resulting kiss—not nearly as aggressive as the lip smack in her store, but rougher than her "lesson" the previous afternoon—filled him with more need than he thought possible.

Because, astonishingly, Noelle kissed him back… with her full body.

Her hips rocked and ground against him as her teeth nipped at his bottom lip. Her hands again weaved through his hair, and that perfect packaging of hers pressed into his chest. He tugged her even closer, and her thighs tightened around his sides like a vise. When he deepened the kiss, she let out a moan that would have brought him to his knees if he weren't already sitting.

His hands traveled down her back until they cupped her round ass, squeezing and guiding it as she continued to grind on his lap. He hadn't come inside his pants since his preteen years, but the probability of it happening there on the love seat rose with each slight movement of her hips.

Breaking free from her intoxicating mouth, he planted kisses down her neck and slid his hand to the steamy crevasse between her thighs. *And holy fucking shit.* Hot condensation practically beaded on his palm as he cupped her through the thin fabric of her tights, or leggings, or whatever women called these heavenly skin-hugging pants.

Noelle gasped, then shifted more weight into his hand, which he pulsed.

"Do you like this?" he whispered into her ear.

Her head fell back as she breathed out "Kent" like a prayer.

Hearing her say his name unleashed something primal in him. He used the strength of his legs to stand, lifting her with him, one hand still between her thighs and the other supporting her ass. Her legs squeezed even tighter around his hips as he walked them both toward the bed.

When his legs bumped the mattress, he stood there, frozen in space and time. He wanted to throw her down on the bed like a caveman and have his way with her. He imagined stripping her bare and kissing every inch of her flawless body. He wanted to make her moan his name again and again.

But what did Noelle want?

If her body language was any indication, she wanted him too. But he'd been fooled into thinking that many times before. And each time, she'd pulled away, or rather pushed him away, like the gullible fool he was.

Unbridled need coursed through his veins as he held her in his arms, touched her with his hands. It made him feel dangerous, unhinged. What he needed to do next became painfully clear.

As Noelle started kissing his neck, Kent tossed her onto the bed. Then he turned on his heels and marched out the door.

14

Noelle lay there, stunned.

Her revenge plan had been simple: Make Kent want her, but never let him have her. She'd come up with the idea years ago. Kent had been checking her out in her bridesmaid's dress at Jess and Brad's wedding, and even at sixteen-going-on-seventeen, Noelle knew when someone found her attractive.

Patience had been key, especially while Kent was away at college, but her plan kicked off in earnest the summer before her twentieth birthday. Soon after his return from Stanford, Jess and Brad had hosted a graduation party for Kent at his mom's house. Noelle had worn her shortest skirt and flirted with all his friends that night. She'd felt Kent's eyes on her the entire time, and thus began his ongoing sentence of sexual frustration—a fitting punishment for what he'd done.

Until now.

She'd been ready to scrap her revenge plan—to give herself to *Kent Freaking Clark*—and he'd walked away.

Now she was the fool.

The bitter taste of her own medicine left her feeling hollowed out, like a pumpkin ready to be carved. She had wanted Kent, and she'd thought he'd wanted her too. More than thought. She'd tasted the need in his kiss, saw it in his eyes, felt it in his touch.

An electric current raced through her, its warm hum pulsing steadily in all the places he'd touched her—all the places she *still* wanted his touch. It was as if he'd flipped an irreversible switch. Her need for revenge, her pride, her competitiveness—none of it mattered anymore.

The hollowness in her chest filled with heat as she lay there, clenching and unclenching her fists. Kent had broken her, gotten her to the desperate point of no return, and then walked out the door. *How dare he?*

Noelle welcomed her anger like an old friend. It beat the emptiness. When paired with the ache between her legs, she suddenly felt charged and alive. Like laughing into the pouring rain, the sensation was liberating—empowering, even.

She didn't need Kent Frustration Clark. There were other ways to satisfy her... cravings. Slipping a hand under the waistband of her leggings, she soon found a natural rhythm, her slickness making it easy to—

"What are you doing?"

The low, gravelly voice that cut across the room jolted Noelle upright on the bed, her hand caught in the proverbial Christmas cookie jar. She hadn't heard the door open or close, but there Kent stood like a fierce statue—the angles of his face sharper than usual, his jaw set in stone.

Her body burned with mortification, but she played it cool. "What does it look like I'm doing?"

Kent stepped one foot forward, then, as if rethinking the idea, slid it back. "Noelle," he growled.

She batted her lashes at him. "What? I'm just finishing the job you started."

His jaw twitched, and the lines on his usually smooth forehead deepened to a pained expression. He took a step back, and then another, until his back was against the wall. She watched with delight as his fists clenched and unclenched repeatedly, much like hers had earlier.

After a few moments, he shoved his hands into the front pockets of his jeans. "Please, don't stop on my account, then."

If she backed down now, he'd know she'd been embarrassed. Further, the way he was looking at her had the ache growing unbearable.

Noelle locked eyes with him as her fingers resumed their task. "Don't mind if I do."

Drawing small circles around her throbbing sugar plum, she moaned for effect two seconds before an unplanned gasp escaped. The area had grown too sensitive—or, in the language of her beloved romance novels, *engorged*. Hips undulating, she dropped her head back during an impossible surge of pleasure.

"Noelle," Kent growled again, the sound much closer than before. When she opened her eyes, she saw him glaring down at her. "If you're screwing with me, you need to cut it out right now. I can only take so much."

"I'm not. I want you."

In a heartbeat, her back hit the mattress as Kent crawled on top of her, his perfect forearms framing her face as his mouth crashed down on hers. It was a hungry kiss, full of a need that matched her own. Two sets of lips, tongues, and teeth, all taking greedily but never getting enough.

"Touch me," she murmured into his mouth. She might seriously die if he didn't.

He pulled back from the kiss, his firm chest heaving. "Are you sure you want this?"

She brought her fingers to her lips and nodded, already missing the pressure against them.

"I need to hear you say it, Noelle. Because once I touch you again, I won't be able to stop. Tell me exactly what you want."

"You."

He rested his forehead against hers and rocked it side to side. "Not specific enough. Tell me what you want me to do to you."

And holy holly, could consent get any sexier?

She arched into him. "I want you to put your hands and mouth all over my body. And then I want *this*…" Her hand cupped the tree trunk between them. "I want it deep inside me. Is that specific enough for you?"

Kent pushed up to his knees. "I'll give you what you want… under one condition."

An ache formed in the back of her throat. It hadn't occurred to her, until then, that he might be getting her to beg for what she desperately needed, only to leave her hanging again. Even more terrifying was her next thought: she would agree to any condition.

"What is it?" she asked, hoping she didn't sound as frantic as she felt.

Danger flashed in his dark blue irises like lightning in a bottle, contained but eager to be unleashed. It sent a thrill to every inch of her body. She would beg if he wanted her to—pride be damned.

When the silence stretched on far too long, she snapped. "Tell me already!"

Kent took her wrists and lifted them above her head. His woodsy scent filled her lungs as he leaned down close to her ear. "When I make you come, again and again, I want to hear you moan my name."

Every muscle in her body simultaneously contracted and relaxed, anything resembling tension replaced by the electric current from earlier.

"Done," she said.

"And not KFC." He nipped at her bottom lip, sending another bolt of longing straight to her core. "I want to hear my real name from these sweet lips."

She arched her back again, lifting until their hips were flush. "Kent. Please. Whatever you want."

His playful nip transformed into a deep kiss, less ravenous than the last, yet somehow more passionate. With her arms still pinned overhead, Kent shifted both of her wrists into one hand while his other traveled down at a torturously slow pace. Pausing to cup her face, he deepened their kiss, pressing the glorious weight of his rock-hard body against her, before continuing south to her breasts. His teasing thumb stroked the outer curve of one, and then it was gone.

She wanted to scream at him, but with her tongue tied up with his, she could only grunt noises she hoped sounded like, "I'm. Going. To. Kill. You."

He pulled back with a smirk on his face. "Did you want something?"

She glared at him in return.

"How about this?" Kent grabbed the hem of her sweater and, like a tablecloth trick, had it up and over her head in one fluid motion.

When his appraising eyes scrolled over her, Noelle was grateful she'd worn one of her sexy bras—the kind more for show than support. "Like what you see?"

Instead of a reply, he lowered her arms to her sides and then pressed himself up to standing.

"Where are you—"

"Stand up," he ordered.

She grumbled, but obeyed. "Bossy, bossy. I'm not sure I like this side of—"

"Shh," he said, gripping the waistband of her leggings with both hands and dragging them toward the floor. His fingertips grazed the outside of her legs on the way down and then caressed the sensitive skin of her inner thighs on the way back up, igniting every nerve ending along the way.

Tingling with anticipation, she cursed when he stopped short of her center. "I hate you."

His dangerous eyes, scrolling once more, caught on the front clasp of her bra. After unsnapping it, he slid the straps down each of her arms before tossing the lacy undergarment aside.

"I know you do, Gingerbread," he said, pulling down her matching red thong. "But I've yet to figure out why."

"Gingerbread?"

"Your favorite cookies are a lot like you. Sweet and spicy." His hand once again grazed up her inner thigh, and then he took a full step back.

"You're torturing me!" she cried.

"Patience, beautiful. I believe I'm owed an eyeful first, given you've already seen me naked."

At the mention of the word *naked*, Noelle realized that's exactly what she was. He'd stripped her completely bare—and under the harsh spotlight of the mid-morning sun, no less. Though she'd always been comfortable in her own skin, being on display for Kent unnerved her in more ways than one.

"Kick those away," he said, referring to the leggings and underwear around her ankles.

"You're not the boss of me," she said, then did as he instructed. "There, but only because they were a tripping hazard."

"Good girl," he said with a wink.

And damn if the heat from her loins couldn't melt all fourteen inches of snow they'd received overnight.

Kent crossed his arms while scrolling his eyes along her body— up and down, then up again. "Okay, boss. Where do you want me first?"

Her already ragged breath caught in her throat. He was handing back control—something she generally liked, but not with Kent. With him, she'd much rather be told what to do. *What was happening to her?*

"On second thought," she said, "I enjoy this new take-charge attitude you've got going on. Do with me as you please."

A fire lit in his eyes. "*What I please* is to please you."

Her gasp was quickly consumed by his kiss as he made good on that statement. She lost herself in the feel of his warm mouth and hands, found solace in his reverent touch and whispered praise. Never before had she felt so desired and cherished as he inched his way down her body, planting a trail of soft kisses from her temples toward her toes.

"Spread your legs wider for me," he said, his mouth hot against her skin. She happily complied as he dropped to his knees.

To his knees.

Her own knees threatened to buckle as Kent Forbidden Clark kneeled before her. She dared a glance down, and lightning once again flashed in his irises—untethered and stormy in the best possible way. Holding his gaze, she watched with awe and delight as he planted his first kiss between her thighs.

"Kent," she half-gasped, half-moaned.

His vigor intensified at the utterance of his name, and it soon became the only word in the English language her brain could recall. "Kent, Kent, Kent." Time stood still while her pleasure soared, then peaked, his tongue doing things to her body she'd never experienced firsthand before.

And truth be told, simply reading about it was *not* the same thing.

She'd had sex with plenty of men, and yet… How had she never experienced *this* before? His tongue circled, then plunged, then circled some more, diving deeper each time as if unable to get enough.

When he finally came up for air, his hand deftly took over, grabbing the baton in a relay race she sensed would be a marathon.

"Tell me this is only for me."

The feral possessiveness of his words, uttered both as a command and a plea, pushed her over the edge.

"It's only for you," she said between shallow breaths, as his mouth created a whirlpool of suction over her sensitive nerves, his hand still pumping all the while.

Forget pat your head and rub your belly. *This* was the ultimate multitasking test. And Kent Focused Clark had earned an A-plus-plus. The man was a freaking magician.

"Kent, yes, Kent."

When she collapsed onto the mattress, he crawled up her spasming body, watching her come undone like an artist admiring his own work. As far as she was concerned, Kent was Leonardo da Vinci,

Michelangelo, Raphael, Donatello—and a bunch of other skilled artists with non-ninja-turtle names—all rolled into one.

The skilled sculptor of satisfaction then pulled the black T-shirt he wore over his head, and it was her turn to admire a masterpiece. She reached out and traced her fingers down his defined abs, which might as well have been carved from marble, then fumbled with the button on his jeans.

His hand came down on top of hers with a curse. "Sorry, I can't believe this, but I need to run to the store first. Unless you happen to have—"

"I don't, but…"

"But what?"

"I'm on the pill," she said, "and I get tested regularly. I've never had unprotected sex before, but I'm good with it, if you are."

He leaned down close and weaved his fingers through her hair. "I'm definitely good with it."

Many satisfying hours later, Kent was exhausted, hungry, and the happiest he'd ever been. Years of fruitless longing had miraculously blossomed into the best day of his life.

As they made love for the third time—with Noelle holding his gaze while riding him like the sexiest cowgirl to ever live—the reality of what had always seemed an impossible dream settled over him. Noelle Serrano was finally his. She'd said it herself: *only for you.*

The first time they'd been together had been dreamlike. With each thrust, he'd felt the need to pinch himself to prove it wasn't all an elaborate hoax of his subconscious. How else could he be sure he wasn't in a deep state of slumber, going through the motions devoid of true awareness, like sleepwalking, but… sleepfucking? He'd certainly fantasized about being with Noelle before and couldn't fathom its actuality.

The second time—in the heart-shaped tub—had been outright unbelievable. He'd been both the star and director of his own pornographic fantasy. The things she'd done to him, and everything she'd *begged* him to do to her. His brain was still having a hard time sorting fact from fiction.

But this was real.

She was real.

They were real.

That thought alone had him reaching his limit. As the pressure built, he started what had become his favorite game yet: volleying each other's names back and forth until climax like a sexy version of Marco Polo.

"Noelle."

"Kent," she moaned from above, breathy and… *Damn, once was all it took this time.*

His body shuttered as he burst inside her. His brain turned off, but he managed to utter another broken "No…elle" before finishing completely.

Another "Kent" met his ears as Noelle collapsed on top of him, still making those incredible circles with her hips. "Don't leave me," she mumbled into his neck.

His fingertips mapped out the contours of her silky back as he wrapped her in his arms. "I'll never leave you, Gingerbread."

Her body—once a molten mound of movement and perfection—stilled and went as stiff as he'd been only moments earlier.

"What's wrong?" he asked.

"I meant don't pull out yet. It'll be messy."

"Oh, okay," he said, sensing her need to clarify meant much more than her words conveyed.

Sex *was* messy. Hell, life was messy. Yet it seemed improbable that Noelle's post-coitus plea not to leave her had stemmed from a simple concern for hygiene. He wanted to question her further, but the prospect felt akin to rousing a sleeping bear—fraught with danger and uncertainty.

His nerves buzzed with anxious energy as they lay there like that for several more minutes, her tense body eventually relaxing before she rolled off him.

"I need to use the restroom," she said, rushing away without a backward glance.

When she reappeared, composed and radiant, Kent rose from the bed to take his turn washing up. "I'll be right back."

"Take your time," she said, setting him on edge again. *What had he done wrong?*

While brushing his teeth at the sink, Kent wracked his brain to solve for "x" in Noelle's discontentment equation. Was it because he'd called her Gingerbread? She hadn't seemed to mind the first couple of times he'd used the nickname, but he supposed it was possible.

However, Noelle not expressing her candid opinion on such a matter would be grossly out of character, making that theory highly improbable. So why had she tensed up? Had it been something he'd said or did earlier that day?

After exiting the bathroom, Kent stumbled his way through the dark. "Hey, I'm sorry if… Noelle?"

He'd crawled back into bed, only to find it empty.

"Noelle?" he repeated.

Though her lack of a reply was enough, he flicked the lamp on to confirm his solitude. What the hell? He hadn't been gone all that long. How could she have vanished without a word? And where would she go? The world outside was shrouded in snow and clouds.

Concern had him jumping into his pants, tearing through his bag for a fresh shirt, and pulling on his boots. He would search the whole town for her, if that's what it took.

He wrenched opened the door and—

"Hey, perfect timing," Noelle said, stepping inside with two lidded cups in her hands. She looked impossibly gorgeous in an oversized sweatshirt and jeans, her wavy hair loose around her bare yet flawless face. "I went down to the lobby to get an update on the storm, and Marge had made a fresh pot of coffee. I wasn't sure how you like yours, so I got it black with a variety of sweeteners and creamers on the side."

"Thanks," he said, taking the cup she offered. "I was worried you'd been abducted." *Or changed your mind.*

It didn't take a genius IQ to grasp the improbability of a socially awkward nerd like himself ending up with someone as unequivocally out of his league as Noelle. Their math didn't calculate. And yet, her presence in his life was the only theorem that proved true.

"And you know I take my coffee black," Kent continued, adding levity to his tone. "You've been equating it to the color of my soul for years."

Her gaze dropped to the floor. "Yeah, about that…"

"I'm joking," he said. "The past is the past, right?"

Noelle's head jerked up. Her lips parted as if she might argue, but then a mask of calm settled over her face.

"Right," she said unconvincingly.

Kent swallowed down his building anxiety. "Are you hungry? That leftover soup we had hours ago wasn't nearly enough. I thought maybe we could take a quick shower and then—"

"Marge said they're letting vehicles with four-wheel drive or chains through the pass now," she said, pushing past him farther into the room, "so you can head home, if you want, or stay here. Whatever. Either way, I need to get back to the store now. I have a lot to do to get ready for the grand opening."

"Now? I thought the repairman isn't coming to fix your heater until Monday."

"He's not, but I can bundle up in the meantime." She lifted her overnight bag onto the bed and began organizing its contents. "My congestion from earlier is long gone, and I need to prep the walls for fresh paint."

"I'll come help you, then," he said. She was stressed about the store. *That* he could handle.

"No!" she practically yelled before slipping back into her mask of nonchalance. "I appreciate the offer, but I want to do it on my own. It's my store, my business… not your problem to fix."

"It's no—"

"You should go see your mom," she interrupted.

"Brad is with our mom for the weekend, which you already know. Why are you trying to get rid of me?"

"I'm not. I just—"

"Noelle!"

Thunder boomed in his chest, and for a moment, Kent thought himself in the middle of a raging storm. Only he *was* the storm. How did this woman consistently get under his skin like no other?

Noelle sighed dramatically, then said the absolute worst four words. "We need to talk."

With a deep inhale, Kent put on his own mask to match hers. He paired it with an invisible suit of armor, complete with a shield, breastplate, helmet, and greaves. She'd called him a white knight before—it seemed a proper time to wear the metaphorical panoply.

He crossed his arms. "Talk, then."

"It was just sex, Kent. Good sex, but it doesn't change anything between us."

Good was a gross understatement, but he supposed he should take the compliment. Something told him much worse was coming. Noelle headed into the bathroom, and he followed, the storm within threatening to shatter his armor as she tossed her toiletries into a glittery bag.

"And what exactly is between us?" he asked to her reflection in the mirror. "Why won't you tell me what's really bothering you?"

"You!" she said, with a surprising amount of venom. "You are bothering me, Kent! Stop asking questions and just let me go."

"Not until you tell me why you're acting like this!" His arms fell slack at his sides as his whole body trembled. Stepping out of her view, Kent gave himself a moment to stabilize before asking what he most feared. "Do you regret today?"

Her hand stilled on a hairbrush, then, after only the briefest hesitation, she whispered, "Yes."

The monosyllable shot through him like a bullet. As it ricocheted inside his battered breastplate, his father's voice boomed in his head: *Never let them see you cry.*

Kent staggered backward out of the bathroom, then clenched his jaw and steeled his heart. He would not cry. At least his disappointing father had been good for something.

A minute later, Noelle reemerged. "I'm not trying to hurt you, in case that's what you're thinking," she said, voice low. The pity in it felt like another shot—and a cheap one at that.

"Why would I be hurt?" he fired back.

"Kent, someone like you and someone like me… we don't mix. We're oil and water. That's why I regret today. It was fun, but it can't happen again."

Fun? She was calling the passion they shared *fun?*

With a bitter laugh, he grabbed his own overnight bag and stuffed a few loose items into it. "Thanks for the chemistry lesson. I'd say you're more like vinegar than water, though. Oil makes you tolerable."

"You're the intolerable one!" she huffed, hauling her bag toward the door.

"Go ahead. Make your grand exit. You're so competitive, you even have to be the first to leave."

She pulled the door open, then turned to face him. Her cold, green eyes held none of the warmth from earlier. "Let's forget today ever happened."

"Let's," he said, matching her venom.

"Good," she returned.

"Good."

That should have been the end of it. He should have let her go, like she so clearly wanted to. But as she turned to leave, one more question slipped past his lips.

"Why?"

Noelle kept her back to him as she replied, "Because we'll still have to see each—"

"No," he interrupted, "why do you hate me so much?"

Her shoulders lifted, then sagged. "I don't hate you, Kent. I feel nothing for you."

Then she walked away, and his once sturdy armor shattered, leaving behind a broken knight on the battlefield of love.

Part 2 – Strangers & Lovers

"Lovers don't finally meet somewhere. They're in each other all along."

— Rumi

@bookstafashionista

"Hey, merry followers, it's progress report time! Check out the wall behind me… that's right, I painted it myself! This festive shade is called 'candy-cane red,' and I used stencils to spell out my store name in 'polar white.'

"For the other three walls, I started with a base of polar white and then sponged over it with a second shade called 'snow' to create a winter wonderland effect. I think it came out pretty well, though maybe a little boring. What's missing? Drop your thoughts in the comments!

"Also, quick shout-out to the kind owner of Screw It for lending me a hand truck so I could move some bookshelves into storage. You rock, Earl! Now, I can rock around the Christmas trees—all six of them—in the middle of the store here. I still need to decorate them, but it's all coming together!

"Mark your calendars: Merry Holidays will open the day after Thanksgiving. Exactly one week from today!"

15

38 days until Christmas

The storm had taken its toll.

High on the hillside overlooking town, straggling bursts of faded red and orange clung to the skeletons of almost bare trees. Icy puddles glistened on the edges of the road, while scattered clumps of brownish-white slush and pine-needle corpses littered the open fields on either side. It was like driving through a marshmallow world's graveyard—the aftermath of her own personal nightmare before Christmas.

"No means no!" Noelle yelled, as Dean Martin sang the line, "But baby, it's cold outside," for the hundredth time through Evergreen's speakers.

With temperatures peaking in the mid-forties, the infuriating song fit the weather. It *was* cold outside, but—thanks to the repairs to her heater earlier that week—it was at least no longer cold *inside*, she thought, reminding herself to be grateful.

Mack, of Mack's Heating and Plumbing, had showed up as promised on Monday morning. He'd spent about an hour tinkering with the thermostat, then called it "good as good does." Mack

Gump—plagued with advanced male-pattern baldness, a paunch that rivaled Santa's bowl full of jelly, and a stereotypical plumber's crack—had not been her dream man after all, but Noelle couldn't bring herself to care.

Her mind had been elsewhere that day.

It lingered in the same vicinity as she drove west along Main Street. How could she have slept with someone who once called her "ditzy and superficial?" Now he probably thought of her as a "pretty face" *and* a good lay, which somehow felt worse. It didn't matter that it'd been the best sex of her life; it couldn't happen again.

Even six days later, the biggest lie she'd ever told still played on a loop in her head: *I feel nothing for you.*

If only that were true.

Guilt-induced nausea threatened to bring up the quiche she'd had for breakfast at Holiday Grinds. Chatting with Sandy that morning had been a welcome distraction, at least. The bubbly barista had shared photos of her adorable twin boys, as well as the latest town gossip, which included: a scandalous theory about how the mailman's toupee ended up in her neighbor's backyard; heated opposition to a proposed new stop sign on Main Street; and rumors that Earl (from Screw It) had been the one to send anonymous flowers to Marcy at Holiday Wines.

Noelle would have stayed at that coffee shop all day if she had the time to spare. But alas, unlike her thoughts of Kent, Merry Holidays couldn't exist rent-free. She had a new business to launch.

After turning off the main road, Noelle rolled her window down to calm her nerves, letting in the biting cold with the fresh scent of pine. Up ahead, an attendant directed traffic. Following his hand signals, she parked her car between a red pickup truck and a silver minivan, then carefully stepped out in her flat, knee-high boots. Although heels would've technically gone better with her business attire, function *sometimes* prevailed over fashion.

Mindful of the muddy puddles, she navigated her way through the small dirt lot before turning back to figuratively smell the roses. The picturesque red truck backed into the parking space next to hers displayed a large holly-covered wreath on its grill, and the festive spectacle of the three vehicles together—red, green, and silver—tugged the corners of her lips upward for the first time all week. Not quite a full smile, but she'd take it.

A path to happiness could often be found in the appreciation of tiny wonders. It was one of the many reasons Noelle loved the holiday season. Merry music, sparkling lights, packages wrapped in bows—all minor things when taken at face value, but they possessed the power to brighten any mood if embraced for what they truly were: reminders to feel joy.

I feel nothing for you.

Noelle shook off the thought as she walked along a pathway trimmed with giant plastic candy canes and inflatable Santas. People bustled in and out of the large building ahead, many hauling some variety of fir, spruce, or pine. A good sign for business.

And business was all that mattered at the moment. Noelle clutched the folder in her hands, took a deep breath, then entered through the barnyard-style doors of Santa's Village Tree Farm.

Inside, children laughed and played around a red-and-white-striped post marked the "North Pole" in the center of the room, while others rode in a wooden train that circled the perimeter. Wood-paneled walls climbed toward a high ceiling covered in twinkling white lights. Against the right wall sat a large, throne-like chair, where she imagined Santa would soon take pictures with young children eager to share their wish lists.

As Noelle ventured farther into the room, she saw snowflake-shaped signs with directions. *Christmas tree farm, straight ahead. Santa's reindeer and restrooms to the left. Gift shop and snack bar to the right.* She'd hoped to find a front desk or receptionist to speak with, but since there didn't appear to be one, she made her way toward the gift shop.

She would ask to leave some flyers for her store's grand opening at the register. A Christmas tree farm was the perfect business to complement hers. She'd point people to their farm for trees, and they could send customers to her store for the lights and ornaments to deck them. It would be a merry business partnership, a symbiotic relationship, a union of…

Noelle rounded the corner, then stopped short. The gift shop, much larger than she'd imagined, sparkled with lights and ornaments galore. It was the spitting image of her dream Christmas store—and, apparently, a direct competitor to Merry Holidays.

She sank against the wall right as a little girl ran by with an ice cream cone. *Great.* They also had the lure of sugar and fat, an irresistible combination. How could she have been so brainless? Scoping out the competition was Market Research 101, and she had failed miserably—as would her business if she didn't come up with a new plan. And quick.

In the interest of belated research, she entered the gift shop to get a closer look at the merchandise. Competition didn't have to mean failure. Maybe her store would have more affordable prices or better offerings. Surely, she'd find some competitive advantage over this family-run Christmas conglomerate.

Those hopes were dashed almost instantly as she scanned the aisles. Their ornament prices were *lower* than what she'd planned, and in some cases, for identical products. Noelle took out her phone and discreetly snapped a few photos. It felt unprofessional—okay, flat-out wrong—but business was business, right?

"Can I help you?"

Startled by the husky voice, Noelle spun around and blurted, "I'm fine," before taking in the green-and-black checkered flannel, stretched incredibly tight across what was possibly the world's broadest chest. "Brawn… I mean, Kris. Hi! It's nice to see you again."

One corner of his mouth quirked up. "It's nice to see you too, Noelle. Glad you finally made it into our shop."

"Ugh. I can't do this." She dropped her head back in shame, only to notice snowflakes painted on the ceiling. *Why hadn't she thought to do that?*

"Can't do what?" he asked. "Do you need help finding something?"

Noelle straightened to look him in the eye. "I have to confess something. I was taking pictures of your prices, but I'm deleting them right now," she said, opening the photo app on her phone. "I'm sorry. It was a shady thing to do. I was just surprised you sold ornaments here. And lights… and decorations, and… oh, look, you even have a holiday book section."

Noelle didn't know whether the embarrassment or dejection she felt would kill her first.

It must have shown on her face, because Kris put a comforting hand on her shoulder. "I take it your new store offers all the same products?"

She nodded, unable to meet his eyes. "I didn't do enough research. It wasn't my intention to compete with—"

"It's okay," he interrupted. "The gift shop is my mom's pet project, but I'm honestly not sure how much longer we'll keep it open. My parents are getting older, and it isn't our primary business. Besides, a little healthy competition never hurt anyone."

At that, her eyes darted up to his, which she now realized were the vibrant green of a noble fir. The smile reflected in them matched the grin on his full lips. Kris wasn't upset with her. In fact, he seemed to be flirting with her.

Noelle felt herself blush, much like she had when they'd met on the side of the road two weeks prior. So much had happened since her move to Holiday Pines—namely with Kent Forsworn Clark—but she needed to put that behind her in order to get her plan back on track. Never mind that her *number of hours without thinking about Kent* held firmly at zero. Noel Kris Clauson (a.k.a. Brawny Thor) was gorgeous, kind, and—unlike Kent—someone she could see herself with long-term.

Her small-town love story started now.

"Noelle?"

She blinked, and if her dry eyes were any indication, it was for the first time in a while. How long had she been staring blankly at his face? She should say something. Something witty.

"I know about your wife," she blurted instead.

Kris dropped his hand from her shoulder and took a step back. *Good job, Noelle.*

"What I mean is, I know she passed away a couple of years ago, and I'm sorry for your loss."

I'm sorry for your loss? What was wrong with her? She wanted to live out a Hallmark movie, not sound like one of their trite greeting cards.

Noelle looked up at the snowflake-covered ceiling again. "I'm also sorry for saying, 'I'm sorry for your loss.' You're probably sick of hearing that, and I shouldn't have even brought it up. I honestly don't know what's wrong with me."

"Can I be honest with you?" Kris asked.

"Honesty is the best policy," she said, daring to look into those evergreen eyes once more.

"These past two years have been tough, and I'm not sure I'm ready to move on. You moving into Becca's old bookshop is also weird for me. In short, I don't want to like you."

"I understand." She dropped her gaze to the floor—to boring beige tiles. At least her store had the flooring beat. *Ugh, thanks to Kent.*

"But..." Kris said.

Noelle's head shot up so fast she might have given herself whiplash. "But?"

Brawny Thor took a step closer, bringing with him the scent of heavenly pine. "But... you make it darn hard not to. Your blunt honesty is refreshing. Sweet, actually."

"Blunt honesty is a nice way of putting it," she said, heat once again reaching her cheeks.

His crooked grin returned. "I've been meaning to compliment your hair, by the way. I like the colored tips. A bold choice in a small town like this, but the style suits you well."

"Thanks," she said, twirling a strand around her finger. "I usually dye the ends either red or green for the holidays. Last year was red, so…" Noelle finished her sentence with a shrug.

"Well, lucky me, then. Green is my favorite color," he said with a heart-stopping wink.

"Young man, can I get some help with an item on the top shelf?" a gray-haired woman asked from the other end of the aisle.

"Of course, ma'am," Kris replied, before turning back to Noelle. "I gotta go, but you should visit Dasher in the stables before you leave. He misses you."

"Will do," she said, feeling her first genuine smile in days spread across her face.

As Noelle watched Brawny Thor saunter away, everything she'd been obsessing over for days resurfaced, but from a fresh perspective. So what if she'd slept with her mortal enemy? Kent had served a decade-long sentence for his crime, and nothing could erase that. Sleeping with him had merely been the natural progression of their (strictly physical) attraction. *A prison release that had ended with a bang.*

In a way, what had happened between them was a good thing. It wiped the slate clean. Kent was no longer her enemy, nor would he ever be her friend. And with Kent Fiasco Clark finally out of her life, she could devote her energy to the things that mattered, like opening her dream store and snagging her dream man—Noel Kris Clauson.

Later that evening, Noelle chomped on a slice of "Mountain Margherita" from Pizza Pines, eating straight from the box as she powered up her laptop. She needed to check the status of two delayed orders, as well as research apparel wholesalers for her latest idea: a "Styled by Noelle" corner of the store, where she would display and sell outfits selected for fictional characters from holiday rom-com novels.

It was the perfect way to differentiate Merry Holidays from the competition, while also tying together her three biggest passions: fashion, romance, and holiday cheer. Better yet, she could leverage her success on social media to draw in nearby followers to Holiday Pines. Of course, she'd also need to add ecommerce capabilities to her store's website for those too far to travel...

Her mental to-do list grew as she reached for another slice of cheesy deliciousness. It would be a stretch to complete everything before her store's grand opening on Black Friday—one short week away—but her newest vision was one hundred percent achievable. Her business would not fail. She would not fail. Everything was going to be fine.

Because she had a plan.

The next three hours flew by as she scoured wholesale marketplaces, sent requests for quotes to potential vendors, calculated demand estimates, and updated her website to announce the new "Styled by Noelle" section as "coming soon." Satisfied with her progress, she was about to close her laptop when a little red dot in the corner of the *Holiday Pines Connections* app caught her attention.

She had a new message.

The memory of Joe's previous correspondence came screaming back. He'd answered her three basic questions and posed two more of his own. She'd drafted a reply during the snowstorm... while in the honeymoon suite... with Kent.

A scrambled montage of mental images immediately flooded her brain. Kent on his knees. His stormy eyes. Him on top of her, behind her, under her. Everything they'd done in the heart-shaped tub. Kent holding her as he said he'd never leave her. The pain in his eyes as she pushed him away.

Great. There went her record of four blissful hours without thinking of him. Eager to expunge the intrusive memories, Noelle opened the latest message in her inbox.

> To: everyday_merry
> From: average_joe
>
> Hi, Merry, I hope everything is okay. Were you able to get your heater fixed?
>
>   Joe

Her heart was officially three sizes too small. She'd been utterly thoughtless, ghosting poor Joe for almost a week, and yet he seemed worried rather than angry. Determined to set things right, Noelle pulled up her unsent draft, speed-typed an explanation, and hit send before she could second-guess it.

> To: average_joe
> From: everyday_merry
>
> I am so sorry! A lot has happened in the past week, but that's no excuse for not getting back to you sooner. Yes, Mack's Heating and Plumbing fixed my heat. Thanks for the recommendation :)
>
> I have to be honest with you, Joe. I've recently met someone… in person. I'm not sure where it will go, but I thought you should know. That said, I would still like to continue getting to know each other through these messages, if you're open to it. I completely understand if you're not.

Assuming you're still interested, below is the reply I had previously drafted last week but forgot to send. (Sorry if that makes it worse!)

Hi Joe, it sounds like we have a lot in common! My favorite color is also green, and I also love all animals but don't currently have any pets. (Cat vs. dog was a trick question, in hindsight, but you aced the test. One of each, please!)

As for pastimes, I like to read and swim (same as you!), but I'm also into yoga, baking, and long walks on the beach (as cheesy as that sounds.) The beach is something I definitely miss, having moved here from San Diego, but the mountains have their own appeal. I'd like to go on some local hikes once the weather warms.

Also, I'm glad you said you don't actually enjoy running. Being chased (like, by a bear) is the only valid reason to run, in my humble opinion. And before you think it, yes, I know not to run from a bear. It would win. Ergo, no point in running at all. In all seriousness, though, good job taking care of your heart health.

As for what I love most about Christmas, I'd prefer to hear why YOU love Christmas first. But I will tell you something no one else knows:

Someone once said something horrible about me, and my biggest fear is that it's true. To spare myself, I won't share what was said, but you should know I'm doing my absolute best to prove him wrong.

Sincerely,
Merry

Noelle then re-read her previous messages from Joe. The epiphany that followed had her lying back on her bed, blinking up at the antiquated popcorn ceiling.

She couldn't believe she hadn't made the connection sooner. *My favorite color is green.* The memory of Kris Clauson winking at her as he'd said those exact words earlier that day replayed several times in slow motion. Had he dropped that as a hint?

Kris was one of the few people in town who knew she planned to open a year-round Christmas store. Assuming he was on the *Holiday Pines Connections* site—as any business owner in town should be—it wouldn't have been a stretch for him to figure out that she was everyday_merry. And as a widower who hadn't dated in years, it made sense that Kris would prefer to remain anonymous while testing the waters online.

As further evidence, "Joe" had wanted to avoid preconceived notions based on looks, and Brawny Thor would certainly be used to women hitting on him without first getting to know the man underneath those muscles. Heck, she'd been guilty of that herself.

Noelle rolled onto her side, drifting into dreamland before her heavy eyelids had even closed. Kris could be Joe, and Santa's Village Tree Farm was literally the rival to her small Christmas "shop around the corner."

Her *You've Got Mail* fantasy was coming true.

16

37 days until Christmas

The next morning, Noelle woke to the following reply:

> To: everyday_merry
> From: average_joe
>
> No need to apologize. As long as I still have a chance, even a slim one, I'd love the opportunity to continue getting to know you better. One thing you should know about me: I'm not easily deterred by competition.
>
> I suppose I shouldn't ask who the mystery man is, but please tell me it isn't Mack. If I was in any way the matchmaker there, I'll never forgive myself. Great news on the working heater, though!
>
> I'll have to get back to you on the Christmas question, as it's clearly important and therefore requires proper consideration. Right now, I'm honestly stuck on your biggest fear.

Whoever the *him* is in that story, he's a complete asshole (please excuse my language) and dead wrong. I don't need to know what was said to know that. Any slur so horrible couldn't possibly be true. I'm sorry you were ever made to feel anything less than the incredible person you are, Merry.

Since you bravely shared your biggest fear, I'll do the same. As pathetic as it may sound, I'm most afraid of being left all alone in this world. Every day, I wake up and wonder if the few people I care about most in my life will still be around tomorrow, and if I'm even worthy of their love.

Sorry to end on such a low note, but please know that chatting with you is an absolute joy. I will happily do so for as long as you allow me.

All my best,
Joe

Tears stung in Noelle's eyes, her heart breaking for a man she didn't even know. Joe was a stranger, yet her soul felt inextricably connected to his. How was that possible? She re-read his message several times, as usual, then typed her reply.

To: average_joe
From: everyday_merry

Dearest Joe, I'm not sure where to

Noelle stopped typing when her eyes caught on a green bubble next to Joe's username with the words "online now." Clicking on it, a chat window reminiscent of decades past popped up. "Interesting," she said to her empty loft.

> **everyday_merry:** Hi… Are you available to chat? I was about to reply to your last message and saw that this site had IM capabilities. Who would have guessed??

> **average_joe:** What a pleasant surprise! Yes, I'm available, and I know, right? Holiday Pines may revel in its gold rush history, but this app is uncharacteristically advanced.

> **everyday_merry:** Yes, it is. And I didn't mean to insult the town. I love its historic buildings and charm. Did you grow up here? I don't think I ever asked you that.

> **average_joe:** I didn't, but even if I had, I wouldn't be insulted. The graphics on this website scream early 2000s at best.

> **everyday_merry:** Ha, I was thinking mid-90s. Where did you grow up?

> **average_joe:** San Diego, same as you. You were right when you said we seem to have a lot in common. Listen, about what I said in my message last night… I had a rough week and apologize for baring my soul like that. I promise I'm fine.

> **everyday_merry:** You don't need to apologize. I liked seeing your soul. And if by fine you mean "freaked out, insecure, neurotic, and emotional," then I'm fine, too ;)

> **average_joe:** Lol

everyday_merry: But seriously, Joe, everyone deserves lasting love, and from what I know of you so far, you are more than worthy. What made your week rough, if you don't mind me asking?

average_joe: I don't mind, but the answer is long and boring, so I'll spare you the details. Can I ask you a question?

A brief pause, then...

average_joe: Besides that one.

everyday_merry: Lol, I suppose.

average_joe: Have you ever been in love?

Noelle considered the question. She'd certainly been hurt before, but in hindsight, it had been more from ego crush than true heartbreak. Had she ever been in love? Her obstinate mind wandered to Kent.

I feel nothing for you.

In truth, she felt more emotions for him than she could name, most ranging somewhere between love and hate. But in love?

everyday_merry: I'm not sure, which probably means no, because I like to think I'd know if it ever happened. What about you?

average_joe: Yes.

everyday_merry: Um, details please!

average_joe: It's not a great story, trust me.

Noelle pondered Joe's evasiveness, first about his bad week, then regarding his past love. Curiosity urged her to pry for more information, but compassion wouldn't allow it. *Every day, I wake up and wonder if the few people I care about most in my life will still be around tomorrow…*

Clearly, he had lost someone he cared about before. If Kris Clauson was Joe, as she now suspected more than ever, pressing him for details would mean dredging up painful memories of his deceased wife. *Again.* Being insensitive to his loss was a mistake she'd rather not repeat.

> **average_joe:** I have another question. Do you think you might fall in love with the person you met recently?

> **everyday_merry:** It's way too soon to tell. In fact, I feel like I know you much better than I know him yet. And it's not Mack!

> **average_joe:** Thank goodness, on all counts. Please promise to let me know if you ever think you might love him, though. Like I said before, I'm not easily deterred by competition. I will fight for you, Merry. But the last thing I want to do is stand in the way of your happiness, even if that means falling in love with someone else.

> **everyday_merry:** Thank you for that, and I promise. I wouldn't want to lead anyone on, especially someone as kind as you, Joe.

> **average_joe:** I should get going now, but let's chat again soon. Have a nice Saturday!

Joe signed off before she could hit send on her reply of, "Yes, let's." Once again, she couldn't avoid thinking of Kent. *Let's. Let's. Let's.* It had to be her guilty conscience (or damn Jiminy Grinch.)

Even though Kent had tried to deny it, the hurt had shown on his face when she'd told him she regretted their amazing day together.

But that had been a full week ago. It wasn't like Kent Frown-Face Clark was sitting around crying over the "ditzy" girl he slept with. He was probably relieved that she'd spared him the trouble of gently cutting her loose, as a guy like him would surely do. Once he got over the shock of her ending things first, he'd be grateful—happy even.

It was time to stop beating herself up over it.

"One large hot apple cider and a slice of cinnamon crumb cake, please," Noelle said to the teenage girl dressed in all black.

Her outfit seemed to be more of a fashion statement than an employee uniform. It was on theme with her dark eye makeup and revived 1990s-style black choker, as was her maroon-colored hair, which blended almost perfectly with the exposed brick wall behind the counter. Noelle couldn't see the girl's shoes, but a classic pair of Doc Martens would finish off the look.

The girl, who had yet to make eye contact, picked at her purple fingernails. "For here or to go?"

Noelle gazed longingly at the cheerful collection of ceramic mugs hanging beneath the chalkboard menu. *A paper cup wouldn't be the same.* "Uh, do you know if Sandy will be in today?" she asked, hoping her question didn't sound as desperate as she felt.

In truth, she could use some company, and the chatty barista was the closest thing to a friend that Noelle had in Holiday Pines—or that she'd had in a long while, if she were being completely honest.

The girl's head finally lifted. "Um, the owner's not here yet, but she usually comes in around ten on Fridays. Do you want me to give her a message?"

Owner? Sandy *owned* Holiday Grinds? Noelle glanced at the time on her phone. It would be ten o'clock soon enough.

"That won't be necessary. I'll enjoy my order here."

Noelle paid, then selected a small, round table near the door, adjacent to a wall that pleasantly resembled an Easter egg, splattered in soft blues, greens, and purples. She checked her socials, more out of habit than necessity, then scanned her surroundings, admiring the warm buzz and eclectic décor of the cozy café.

Unlike the building's exterior—which she found reminiscent of Snow White's cottage, with its high-pitched gable roofs and old-world charm—the interior was mostly modern with a few quaint European touches, like a fleur-de-lis pattern on the tiled floor and antique-style upholstered chairs. A long table with built-in power outlets accommodated people on laptops, while small round tables with marble tops filled in the center of the room. Several sofas and armchairs—all occupied by seemingly satisfied customers—lined the back wall, which had a solid lavender base with white script that read, "Life's a grind, sit back & unwind."

By the time Noelle's cider and pastry arrived, the growing line of customers had spilled onto the sidewalk, everyone eager for their morning fix from the thriving café. As if on cue, Sandy's endearing laugh—which sounded equal parts amused and startled—filled the room. Had Noelle not heard the same laugh in response to mundane comments about the weather last week, she would've assumed that someone must've said the most unexpectedly hilarious thing that Sandy had ever heard. Yet, therein lay Sandy's charm.

Seconds later, the successful businesswoman behind it all walked through the door, looking chic in a long, cream-colored sweater, patterned leggings, and crimson boots with a faux-fur trim. Her already luminous face brightened as she approached. "Noelle! How lovely to see you here this morning."

Was that a British accent? And if so, how had Noelle not noticed it before?

"Look who I ran into in the queue," Sandy continued, ushering forward a young girl with blond ringlets and a pink puffer jacket. "Miss Daisy, meet Miss Noelle."

"Nice to meet you," the darling girl said with a curtsy.

To mimic the gesture while seated, Noelle leaned forward and then straightened. "It's a pleasure to meet you, Miss Daisy."

"Miss Sandy said I don't have to wait in line for my cake pop. Do you like cake pops?"

"I like cake in all forms. This crumb cake is delicious, too," Noelle said, meeting Sandy's smiling brown eyes.

Sandy walked around the counter and grabbed a round pop with pink icing and sprinkles from a display case. "I'm glad you're enjoying it. And here you go, love," she added, handing the treat to Daisy before continuing in the jaunty lilt of Mary Poppins. "Miss Daisy here is going shopping for new winter clothes today, and I told her I know the perfect fashionista to help her."

"Me?" Noelle asked, picking up on Sandy's not-so-subtle wink and nudge in her direction.

"Miss Noelle picks out entire wardrobes for fictional characters."

"How did you—"

"I looked you up on the Gram," Sandy said with another wink, referring to Noelle's bookstafashionista account.

"Well, I'm flattered and would be happy to help." Noelle stood and directed her attention down at Daisy, who couldn't have been older than six or seven. "Are you here all by yourself, sweetheart?"

Daisy smiled up at Sandy, silent communication bouncing between them like coded messages, before she said, "My daddy's in line for coffee."

17

The blatant setup by Sandy Poppins and her young accomplice should have nettled Noelle, but it was hard to be upset when "daddy" appeared behind Daisy.

Scrolling up to meet his gaze, Noelle's eyes lingered (perhaps longer than was appropriate) on the impossibly broad chest eclipsing everything and everyone around them. The entire line of customers, hidden from view. Goth girl, gone. The child near his legs, cast in shadows. All that remained were his bulging muscles, flexing as if trying to escape their prison of blue and green intersecting bars. The thin yellow lines of the pattern bent—and then broke completely—at the vertical row of buttons threatening to pop.

"Hi there, I see you've met my daughter," said the vision in tightly stretched plaid.

Noelle swallowed the saliva pooling on her tongue before locking eyes with none other than Brawny Thor Clauson. "Kris… Hi… What a surprise, running into you again. Daisy and I were just discussing our shared love of cake pops."

"And shopping," Sandy interjected.

Right, Sandy was still standing there, too.

"Noelle has a keen sense for fashion. I bet she'd be willing to offer her expertise today, if you want," Sandy said to Kris, before turning to point a thumb at him over her shoulder. "Trust me, male Noel here can use all the help he can get."

Noelle felt compelled to defend her namesake while simultaneously wondering if he owned any shirts that weren't tight-fitted flannels. *Not that she was complaining.* "Oh, I'm sure that's not true."

"Sadly, it is," Kris said, pushing his rolled sleeves above his elbows. "But thanks for pointing that out, Sandy. I see you're feeling fake British again today."

"I'll have you know," Sandy huffed, amping up her prim accent by stressing each vowel. "I lived in London for four and a half years when I was at university."

"Ah, that makes sense now," Noelle said, more to herself. Upon catching Sandy's inquisitive expression, she added, "I was confused earlier, because I thought you grew up here, and I hadn't noticed your accent before."

"It comes and goes," Sandy said, dropping the accent, only to pick it right back up again. "All for a spot of fun. Speaking of fun…" She motioned toward the door, a glint of mischief in her eyes. "The three of you have some shopping to do."

"Oh, I wouldn't want to intrude on their father-daughter—"

"Please, you have to come!" Daisy said. Then her pleading eyes darted up to Kris. "Miss Noelle can come with us, right, Daddy?"

"Of course, but only if she wants to. It's not polite to pressure people." His stern eyes bounced between his daughter and Sandy.

"We would never," Sandy said, lifting a hand to her chest as if shocked by the accusation, all the while grinning with the smugness of Santa's favorite elf.

Kris turned to Noelle. "If you don't already have plans today, we'd love to have you join us. No pressure, though."

Noelle considered the invitation. Shopping was always fun, and she technically didn't have any other plans. If she accepted, she could use the opportunity to get to know Kris better, and maybe even suss out whether he was average_joe. It would also please Daisy, who placed second only to her niece for being the most adorable little girl. On the flip side, Kris seemed irritated by the obvious matchmaking and was probably still apprehensive about dating. Would this even count as a date?

"I don't know," Noelle began.

"What's not to know?" Sandy said, making a shooing motion at them. "Go. Get. Some of us have a coffee shop to run."

And that's how Noelle ended up at Main Street Fashions, perusing a wide selection of little girls' apparel.

"Sorry again if you felt pressured to join us," Kris said, as she thumbed through the cutest collection of bell-bottomed pants in a variety of fabrics and colors.

"Not at all. I feel like you were the one who was pressured into letting me tag along."

"No, I'm happy you're here. Trust me," he said.

"Well, I'm happy to be here."

"Good. I'm glad that's settled, then." Kris let out a nervous chuckle while running his fingers through his golden locks.

Noelle smiled at him over her shoulder, then turned her attention downward. "Okay, Miss Daisy, the first rule of shopping is to keep an open mind. Our goal today is to find you a statement piece, but we won't know what that is until we see it."

"Like sparkle leggings?" Daisy asked.

"Maybe…" Noelle hedged. "But I've found that the best way to avoid disappointment is to not look for something quite so specific, like sparkle leggings… or the elusive perfect sweater dress. Instead, see if anything right in front of you stands out as an item you'll want to wear every day."

"Solid life advice, too," Kris whispered, his breath hot against her ear as his hand landed on her lower back.

Noelle nearly jolted at his touch. It was both new and familiar; coy and presumptuous; reassuring and unsettling. Unsure how to feel about it, she side-stepped his advance, moving farther down the clothing rack. "So, um, did you grow up here, Kris?"

She'd asked Joe the same thing only hours ago, and while eager for clues regarding his identity, a small knot formed in the pit of her stomach as soon as the question left her mouth. Noelle found herself on a game show, anticipating the grand reveal behind door number two, but with the added anxiety of not knowing whether she'd rather have the goat or the car.

"It feels like it sometimes." Kris laughed, almost bitterly. "But technically, no. I was already a sophomore in high school when my parents moved us up here from San Diego. They wanted to start the Christmas tree farm, and what better place than Holiday Pines to do that?"

The knot in her gut tightened. *Joe had grown up in San Diego, too.* "That must've been a tough adjustment for you at that age."

"It was. My surfer style didn't exactly fit in here, and I was a lot less swole back then, so I got picked on a bit. Sandy was always nice to me, though. She's a good friend."

"That's right. I forgot you two went to high school together," she said, doing her best to ignore his cringe-worthy use of the word *swole*. "It's why she calls you Noel instead of Kris."

"I think that's more to annoy me, but yeah, we go way back."

Noelle walked over to the next set of racks, needing time—and distance—to process all the thoughts fighting for dominance in her head. "See anything you like yet, Daisy?"

The young shopper-in-training ran her fingers over each piece of clothing, examining it at length before moving on to the next item. "Not yet, but I will."

"You're determined. I like it."

"What's determined mean?" Daisy asked, still hyper-focused on her mission.

"It means you know what you want, and you go after it. Nothing can stop you."

Ironically, Noelle's words stopped the young girl in her tracks. Daisy slowly turned, then struck a superhero pose—fists on hips, small chin tilted high—and declared, "I'm determined."

"Yes, you are, baby girl," Kris said, his hulk frame coming to rest behind Noelle.

Once Daisy resumed her search, moving down the rack and effectively leaving them standing alone, Noelle felt the small hairs on the back of her neck rise. It was as if they could sense the move before he made it. Then, sure as snow, Kris once again palmed her lower back. Something crawled down her spine and settled in her stomach, heavy and lifeless like a lump of coal—the exact opposite of butterfly flutters.

What was wrong with her? Kris was her small-town romance hero in the flesh—a ruggedly handsome, flannel-wearing, single dad who ran a freaking Christmas tree farm. She should've been thrilled by his obvious interest, not put off by it. Similarly, Kris having things in common with Joe—someone she'd quickly come to care for—should've had her doing somersaults of joy, not flipping out.

"I'm determined, too," Kris said, his low, smooth voice transporting her to a bedroom.

Or rather, to a hotel room, where an even smoother voice had coaxed the words *only for you* from her desperate lips, the way a skilled interrogator might force a confession.

Noelle closed her eyes, hoping to dispel her ghost of recent past, but the mental image only intensified. She could both see and feel those stormy blue eyes peering up at her, igniting her body while branding her soul. *Tell me this is only for me.*

"This is cute," she said, stepping out of the hulk's reach once again while pulling a random item from the rack.

"Is that my statement piece?" Daisy asked.

"I don't know. Let's see." Noelle held the pale-yellow sweater up to Daisy's chest, taking in its design. Printed text encircled a fuzzy animal striking a sassy pose. "Llama shop 'til I drop," she read aloud. "It certainly makes a statement, but what do you think? Is this *the one,* or should we keep shopping?"

Daisy tapped her chin. "Hmm, I like it... but I think we should keep shopping."

"Until we drop?" Noelle asked, earning a giggle from Daisy. She then turned to face Kris, who now stood a respectful distance away. "Would it be okay if I get this sweater for Daisy to wear while we keep browsing?"

"Sure thing, but I'll take care of that." Kris took the sweater from her hands and headed toward the register.

Noelle pressed a light fist to her mouth as she watched Brawny Thor walk away. She'd once considered him her dream man, and now...

Her nails dug into the flesh of her palm, her fingers curling gratuitously tighter. *Damn Kent for ruining this for her. Damn him all the way to the South Pole.*

18

"Do They Know It's Christmas?"
Band Aid

36 days until Christmas

"Here you go, Ma. Can I get you anything else?" Kent said, handing his mother a tray with her lunch.

"Absolutely not. If you do one more thing for me, I'm gonna kill you!"

"You can take the girl out of Brooklyn, but you can't take the Brooklyn out of the girl, huh?"

"Don't get fresh with me, sonny boy. I still have friends on seventy-seventh street that'll set you straight."

"Oh, shoot. I forgot the saltines for your soup. Be right back," he said, moving to exit his mother's bedroom.

"Stop right there! This is already more than enough. You hear me?"

"It's impossible not to, Ma."

"Ha! If only that were true! You boys don't listen." She let out a deep sigh. "I know I get tired a lot more these days, but I'm not helpless. You do too much for me. You need to live your life, my darling boy."

"I am living my life. This is my life." Kent motioned around the room at nothing in particular.

"That's about the saddest thing I've ever heard. And I've been told I have cancer, *twice*," she said, holding up two fingers for emphasis.

The headscarf he hardly noticed anymore caught his attention at her mention of cancer. Today's was turquoise with bright pink and purple flowers all over it. Colors better suited to spring or summer than fall, but that was Carole Clark—vibrant in the face of impending winter.

"You know what I mean. You're my mom, and I love you. I don't mind helping."

"I love you, too. And not only because you make the best soup, no saltines needed." Carole shot him a wink as she lifted the spoon from her tray. "Now, pull up a chair. I want to talk about *you* for a minute."

Kent grabbed what was once a desk chair from the corner of the room and took a seat by her side. "What about me?"

"You've been moping around the house all week. Don't think I didn't notice. What's going on?"

"Nothing's going on."

His mother stared at his face the way one would read a book. "It's a girl, isn't it? Did she break your heart? You let me talk to her."

"Ma, no. And if there were a girl involved, why would she have broken *my* heart? I could've broken hers, you know."

She laughed. *Actually laughed.* "Oh, my sweet boy. You never were the heartbreaker type. And that's a good thing! Don't get me started on your brother. I'm still mad at him for what he did to my darling daughter-in-law. I raised you both better than that. We're all invited to Jessica's house for Thanksgiving, by the way."

His decidedly not-broken heart palpitated at the prospect of seeing Noelle again so soon. Her words—*I feel nothing for you*—had been ice daggers to his chest. Once the initial freeze had thawed, however, he adjusted to the cold and saw her words for what they were: a complete lie.

Noelle might not feel the way he did, but she felt *something*. Of that, he was certain. He'd been there, after all. Her moaning his name again and again over the hours they'd spent tangled together had not been nothing. The way she'd gazed into his eyes had not been nothing. And, after the first time they'd made love, the light brush of her lips against his forehead when she'd thought he'd fallen asleep had damn well not been nothing.

Some unknown variable was causing her to push him away, and he was going to solve that equation.

His mother eyed him over a spoonful of soup. "Are we going to talk about this broken heart of yours?"

"It's not broken. It's… punctured but healing," he conceded, seeing no sense in hiding the truth from a human polygraph.

"I see. Well, she'd be lucky to have you. And I'm not saying that because I'm your mother." A few drops of soup flung from her spoon as she spoke fervently with her hands. "You might very well be the most selfless soul on this planet, as much as that pains me. I wish you'd put your own needs first for a change and go after what you want."

"I'm working on it, Ma. I promise. But how have you been feeling this week? I know this is a difficult time of year for you."

"It is, but I'm doing better than expected. I feel almost guilty saying this, but it gets a little easier with each passing year."

"I think that's normal," Kent said, grateful she allowed the subject to change. "Time heals all wounds, or so they say."

His mom nodded, then took a sip of her smoothie, puckering her lips as she did. "What's in here? Grass?"

"No, not grass. Kale, apple, lemon, ginger, carrot, and wheatgrass—Okay, technically, there's grass in it, but it's good for you, Ma."

A knock sounded from down the hall.

"Saved by the door," his mother muttered. "You answer that, and I'll finish my grass juice in peace."

"It'll clog the bathroom sink. At least flush it down the toilet this time," he said, heading down the hall toward the front door.

Answering on the second knock, Kent came eye to eye with a friendly young face. "Bryden, hey. Is everything okay, buddy?"

The gangly teen shuffled his feet side to side, the motion causing his baggy T-shirt to sway on his narrow shoulders. "Hi, Mister C. I hope I'm not bothering you on a Sunday."

"Not at all. Would you like to come in? I made some chicken noodle soup if you're hungry."

"Um, yeah, thanks."

Kent ushered Bryden into the formal dining room off the kitchen. "You can put your backpack on the table and have a seat. I'll be right back with two bowls of the good stuff."

As Kent reheated the soup, he pondered the meaning of Bryden's unexpected visit. Did he have troubles at home? At school? One of Kent's foremost concerns when planning his leave of absence had been the potential for adverse effects on his students. Although he'd extended an open invitation for assistance, Bryden had never taken him up on it—until now.

"Here you go," Kent said, placing a bowl down in front of his favorite student. "Do you have any homework I can help you with, math or otherwise?"

"No… I mean, yes," Bryden said, sounding flustered. "Yes and no. I have a ton of homework, but I think I know how to do it on my own. Thanks for the soup, Mister C."

"Any time."

Taking the seat across from Bryden, Kent tasted his own soup and did his best not to think about the last time he'd enjoyed it—with Noelle. The first hit of steamy broth coated his insides like a much-needed hug. He relished its savory warmth in comfortable silence for a few more spoonfuls, and then the corners of the Rubik's cube clicked into place.

"I'll be reading in the living room, if you need anything." Kent stood to leave, picking his bowl up as he did. "Studying in a noisy house can be tough. It's pretty quiet here if you want to stay and do your homework."

Relief swept over Bryden's face. "Thanks, I'd like that." Kent took several steps away before he heard, "Mister C?"

"Yeah, Bryden?"

"How did you know my house isn't quiet?"

"Lucky guess."

Bryden's head and shoulders sagged, as if he'd been tricked into confessing to a crime. "My parents yell a lot, mostly at each other. It's not that bad, but it makes it hard to concentrate."

"I can imagine," Kent said, reminding himself that a two-parent home wasn't necessarily better than his upbringing. "You can do your homework here whenever you want."

Bryden's face brightened. "Thanks, Mister C."

"Just make sure your parents know you're here, so they won't worry about you."

"They won't," Bryden muttered but dug his cell phone out of his backpack. "I'll text my mom."

Kent nodded and made his way to the living room, his mind applying the algorithm necessary to solve the rest of the puzzle. The nearest library was two blocks closer than the distance between their houses, a fact the astute sophomore would've been well aware of. Given that and Bryden's excessively appreciative demeanor, Kent deduced that his student sought more than a quiet study environment. Like all adolescents, Bryden needed a safe space *and* someone who gave a damn about him.

Kent would be that someone.

Though not his first choice when considering vocations, he'd gone into the same noble profession as his mother to help kids. It didn't matter that he might be breaching school policy by letting a student study at his residence. If he couldn't extend meaningful aid to Bryden, what purpose did his career serve?

Besides, getting fired wouldn't be the worst thing. He still hadn't figured out a caregiver solution for his mom, and Principal Geyser's incessant "reminder" emails about his expected return in the new year—as if his eidetic memory would ever let him forget—only added to his overwhelming stress.

Kent pulled out his phone, but rather than opening his Kindle reading app, his thumb hovered over another application—one that fed his famished soul even more than books did. Lately, it had been his only source of nourishment. He *needed* to talk to her.

His wounded heart skipped a beat when the alert he'd set popped up on the screen: everyday_merry was online.

> **average_joe:** Fancy meeting you here again. It must be my lucky day.

Fancy meeting you here? Where had that level of cheese come from? He might as well have said something like, "Of all the chat rooms in all the world wide web, you had to logon to mine."

> **everyday_merry:** Well, hello again. I probably shouldn't admit this, but I logged on to see if you might be online. Is that lame?

> **average_joe:** Not lame at all, given I did the same.

> **everyday_merry:** That's a relief.

> **average_joe:** Also, I'm not talking to anyone on this site besides you, in case you were wondering. What about you? Any other competition for me to crush, besides Mr. In-Person?

everyday_merry: Competitive, I like that. Let me think…

Kent stared at the "typing…" bubble on the screen, waiting for the metaphorical water to boil.

average_joe: You're killing me…

everyday_merry: Lol. Ok, ok. No, I'm not messaging with anyone else here… if you don't count one extremely unsolicited dick pic received.

average_joe: Are dick pics ever solicited?

everyday_merry: Great question. I believe I speak for all womankind when I say that's a big fat NO.

I mean, even if it were a nice-looking one, what good is a picture? I'd much rather form an ideal image in my head while reading a steamy romance novel, just saying.

average_joe: Ha, good to know.

everyday_merry: You don't strike me as the type of guy who would ever send a dick pic though, unsolicited or otherwise.

average_joe: Is your "or otherwise" a subtle way of asking for one?

everyday_merry: If I asked, would you?

average_joe: Absolutely not.

everyday_merry: See, I was right.

average_joe: Probably not for the reason you think, though. It's less about integrity and more about my lack of photography skills. I assume there's a whole art form to getting the lighting and angles perfect, and I've sadly never had much artistic ability. I'm more of an analytical "left-brain" kind of guy.

And there's nothing worse than a poorly taken dick pic.

everyday_merry: Exactly! Lol.

average_joe: I know my limitations. So, romance novels… Is there a particular reason you enjoy them? Besides the superior phallic imagery, of course.

everyday_merry: That, of course. But also, romance books transport you to a land of hope.

average_joe: Hope?

everyday_merry: Yeah, that's what love is, after all… Hope for a brighter future. You want the best for the people you love, and you hope for their love in return.

average_joe: What if they don't return your love?

everyday_merry: Easy. You love them anyway.

average_joe: And they eventually come around?

everyday_merry: Only if that's what's best for them. Nothing in real life is certain, but that's the beauty of the romance genre: guaranteed happy endings.

A great romance will have you rooting for the characters and their journey toward love, despite how predictable or unrealistic it may be. Because, at the end of the day, we all want to believe in the _possibility_ of happily ever after, even if our experiences have yet to prove its existence.

Sorry if that was a little too deep…

average_joe: I'd say that was the right amount of deep.

everyday_merry: My gutter-mind wants to say "that's what she said," but it's probably just all the phallic imagery speaking.

Can I ask you an annoyingly invasive question?

average_joe: Sure, but I don't have a measuring tape handy.

No reply. No "typing" bubble. Nothing. Had he gone too far with his joke? He was an online "stranger," after all.

average_joe: Sorry! I was going for witty, not sleazy, but that was inappropriate.

everyday_merry: No, it's fine. I was busy wiping up the floor. I'd taken a drink of water and did an actual spit-take. Bravo!

Kent guffawed in relief, unsure of when he'd last laughed. It felt good, really damn good.

"Funny book?" Bryden asked, peaking around the archway of the dining room.

"No, sorry. I was messaging with a friend. How's the homework going?"

"Good. I was just wondering if you have anything to drink."

"Absolutely," Kent said, already en route to the kitchen. "No soda, but we've got ice tea or juice…" He opened the refrigerator to confirm, then added, "Orange and grape."

"Grape juice sounds good. Thanks again, Mister C… for everything."

"No problem." Kent poured the juice and handed it to Bryden before making his way down the hall to check on his mom.

The kale smoothie sat untouched on her nightstand as soft snores poured from her open mouth, her chin dipping lower with each exhale. Her empty soup bowl remained on the tray beside her, and a fleece throw pooled around her lap. Kent pulled the blanket up around her shoulders, grabbed the tray, and then headed back to the kitchen.

When he returned to his phone, a slew of chats awaited him.

> **everyday_merry:** For the record, I don't think you're sleazy. Like, I don't think you have a sleazy bone in your entire body.

> **everyday_merry:** I feel like I know you, even though I don't. Is that weird?

> **everyday_merry:** Anyway, my annoyingly invasive question, which I don't plan to reciprocate an answer to is: why are you still single?

> **everyday_merry:** Or maybe "still" isn't accurate. Either way, please ignore my stupid question. It was rude of me to ask.

> **everyday_merry:** I should get back to my work now. Take care.

She was no longer online. Kent deflated as he sank into his mother's quilted armchair. He knew it was pathetic that his only source of joy came from messaging a woman who thought he was someone else. A woman who wanted nothing to do with the real him.

He'd also known from the start that it was wrong to deceive Noelle... but, like her beloved romance stories, their online chats gave him hope. If Noelle could love Joe, then there was a non-trivial chance that she could love him too.

With a rush of emotion, Kent composed his most candid and vulnerable message yet, though still careful not to include anything that might reveal his identity too soon. As much as he yearned to share that secret with Noelle, he needed the truth behind everything to unfold seamlessly. Above all else, he desperately hoped she'd be happy whenever she found out.

19

Merry vibe:

"The Thanksgiving Song"
Ben Rector

32 days until Christmas

"Is there anything I can help with?" Kent asked, wandering into the kitchen to make himself useful.

Jess pulled a casserole dish from the oven, revealing a delectable display of gooey, toasted marshmallows. "Vegan candied yams are ready," she said with a smile in Avery's direction. "And thanks, Kent, but I think we're good here. The turkey needs to rest before it can be carved, and all that's left is to rewarm a few of the sides once everyone arrives. Noelle called to say she's running a little behind, but she's on her way and apparently bringing a new friend."

Jess regarded him as if assessing the damage after a car crash. Kent was fairly certain she had lingering suspicions surrounding the night of the shower incident, but so much had transpired since. Did sisters divulge such intimate details to each other?

And now Noelle was bringing a *new friend* home for Thanksgiving.

"Can I refill your wineglass at least?" he asked, topping off his own as uncomfortable warmth crept up his neck.

"No, thanks. When you start with mimosas at seven a.m., you've got to pace yourself," Jess said, before leaving the kitchen to holler something at Brad and the kids.

Prince Petey, the family's beloved poodle-mix, trailed closely behind her, leaving Kent alone with Avery.

"Thanks, by the way," he said, "for hosting us all today. I know it must be weird to celebrate Thanksgiving with Jess's ex-husband and in-laws."

"You know, I thought it would be weird," Avery said, extending her glass, which he promptly filled, "but Jess and I are solid, and you guys will always be family. I never want that to change."

Her sentiment resonated with him on an incalculably deep level. For years, Kent couldn't help but feel like the unwanted variable in any familial equation, let alone one so complex.

"To family," he said, gratefully raising his glass.

"To family," she agreed.

"Ooh, I want in on that!" Jess squealed, her exuberant reappearance interrupting their moment of camaraderie.

But rather than toasting their wineglasses, Jess instead wrapped him and Avery into a tight hug. *She hadn't been joking about her champagne consumption.* A throat cleared, and Kent looked over their heads to where the matriarch of the family stood near the kitchen entrance.

"Am I missing out on a group hug?" Deedee Serrano asked, hands on hips in a pose she'd clearly passed down to her youngest daughter.

"It's not too late, Mom. Get over here!" Jess said.

Kent exchanged an apprehensive look with Avery. With the addition of Deedee, the embrace tightened exponentially. The Serrano women were known to be enthusiastic huggers, sometimes to the point of cutting off airways.

With one notable exception. The woman whose arms he would happily die in, if only she would let him into her heart. The same woman who was on her way there with a *new friend.*

WHEN LOVE HOLIDAYS | 175

"I should go check on my mom," Kent said, extricating himself. "But please let me know if you think of anything I can help with."

"The kids might need some entertaining," Deedee offered. "Their grandpa's silly stories can only captivate them for so long."

"Consider it done," he said, already on the move.

"Who's winning?"

Kent looked up to see Noelle smirking at him, and his thumb forgot how to move. Had she somehow gotten even more beautiful in the twelve days they'd been apart?

"I win!" Lucas yelled, pinning Kent's thumb with his much smaller one.

"He won," Kent conceded.

"I won five times, and Uncle Kent won five times," Lucas clarified.

"You know what that means, right?" Noelle asked, before she and Lucas both shouted, "Championship round!"

"You can play the winner, Auntie Elle," Lucas said.

Noelle's eyes darted to Kent. A hint of panic crossed her face before she donned the mask of indifference worn during their last interaction—her apparent weapon of choice.

"Sure, I can beat your aunt, too," Kent said, his gaze fixed on Noelle as he gripped fingertips with his young nephew and once again declared war.

The kid's thumb moved with impressive speed—he had to give him that—but it was no match for Kent's elongated reach.

"Take him down, Lucas," Noelle said, a tinge of wariness betraying her otherwise playful façade.

Kent extended his thumb safely out of reach while briefly entertaining the idea of conceding victory to his nephew. On the one hand, it would make Lucas happy, bring an end to the thumb war, and potentially sidestep an uncomfortable encounter with Noelle. On the other hand, surrendering meant forfeiting an opportunity to challenge Noelle's resolve to *feel nothing* for him.

"Sorry, Kid," Kent said, pressing his thumb down for the winning count. "One, two, three, four. I win the thumb-o-war."

"Man!" Lucas groaned. "Your turn, Auntie Elle."

Noelle twirled a strand of green-tipped hair around her finger as if bored, then rested her elbow on the table. "Ready to lose?"

Matching her confrontational stare, Kent hooked his fingers with hers. "To you? Any time."

Her eyes widened a second before her elbow slipped off the edge of the table, pulling his hand down to its wood surface with a thud. She then proceeded to wipe imaginary crumbs from the spot in front of her while slowly regaining composure, forcing him to bite back a grin. Surely, his words wouldn't have had such an impact if she felt *nothing* for him.

"Something bothering you?" he asked.

With a pinched expression, Noelle leaned forward, signaling for him to do the same. "You couldn't have let the kid win?" she grumbled near his ear.

"Would you have?"

Kent knew he had her there. Noelle would sooner perish than allow another to claim victory.

"Fine," she said, settling back into thumb war position. "Let's get this over with."

"Let's," Kent repeated, his gaze still locked with hers as they each maneuvered their thumbs side-to-side. "One, two, three, four, I declare—"

"Noelle, you're here!" Jess interrupted. "Where's your friend?"

Kent's thumb halted, suspended amidst all the air that had left his lungs. He'd completely forgotten about the *new friend*.

Gathering his wits, he scanned the dining room. His mom sat nearby playing patty cake with Chloe, who was perched on Brad's lap as he scrolled through his phone. Deedee was at the other end of the long table, chatting with Jessica's best friend, Natalie, and her mother, Linda.

The rest of the guests—Natalie's husband, Derek; Avery's brother, Damien; and Noelle's father, Carlos—could be heard laughing about something in the backyard. Was the *new friend* with them? Kent didn't consider himself a jealous person, yet the notion of Noelle's prospective new partner bonding with those he cherished as family hit him like a sucker punch to the gut. *They were his.*

"Ow," Noelle said, tugging her hand back.

"Sorry! Are you okay?" he asked, releasing his clenched fist.

Noelle ignored him, replying to Jess instead. "My friend should be here any minute. Can I help with anything in the meantime?"

"My sous chef, Avery, has everything covered in the kitchen, but thanks for offering. We'll start reheating the sides now that you're here. And Brad," Jess said, turning to Kent's brother, "you can carve the turkey now, if you're ready."

"I'm on it!" Brad helped Chloe off his lap before jumping up and following Jess back into the kitchen.

"Need a hand?" Kent hollered after him.

"Nope. I got it, bro. Enjoy your thumb wars," Brad said, his smirk audible.

"I'm gonna go wait outside," Noelle said, before swiftly fleeing the dining room.

Craving a moment alone with her more than his empty stomach desired the coming feast, Kent ignored the strong *don't follow me* vibe left in her wake and trailed Noelle out the front door.

Once outside, he squinted against the spears of light piercing the blue sky, wishing his eyeglasses were sunglasses, or even those transition lenses his students had deemed *cringe*. Instead, he found himself tintless on a clear day, walking toward Noelle like Icarus nearing the sun.

"I'm sorry you regret what happened—"

"Nothing happened," she snapped, her gaze directed down the long driveway as they stood side-by-side.

Kent crossed his arms to mirror her stance. "Lie to yourself all you want, but I was there. And I know we agreed to forget, but the thing is,"—he leaned closer and lowered his voice—"I wouldn't want to forget, even if I could. That was the best day of my life, despite how poorly it ended, and I want you to know I'm not giving up on you... on us." At the satisfying sound of her breath hitching, he pressed on. "Because whether you admit it or not, Gingerbread, there is an *us*. So, will you please at least tell me why you think we don't mix?"

"This isn't the time or place, KFC. It's Thanksgiving, a happy holiday."

"It's not happy for everyone," he said, kicking a rogue rock back into the landscaping. "And people shouldn't have to pretend just because it's a holiday."

Noelle scoffed, angling her body to face him. "You don't get it. You never have. It's not about pretending to be happy. It's about choosing to focus on the good, rather than the bad. To be grateful for everything we have, rather than sad about what we don't. In a perfect world, we'd feel grateful every day, but since the world is far from perfect, holidays help provide a nice reminder. And Thanksgiving is literally a holiday about giving thanks, so that's what I plan to do today."

Kent opened his mouth to respond—with what he hadn't a clue—but Noelle was already walking away.

"Sandy, you made it!" Noelle gave the woman who approached a hug. "Thanks so much for coming. You didn't need to bring anything, though."

"I wasn't raised to show up empty-handed," the newcomer said, holding up flowers and a bottle of wine. She was maybe a decade older than Noelle and emitted energy the way a freshly brewed cup of coffee woke the senses.

"Well, thanks again. Let's head inside, and you can give those to my sister directly. Oh, and this is my ex-brother-in-law's brother, Kent. Kent, this is my friend Sandy."

"Nice to meet you, Sandy," he said, with a short wave and a tsunami of relief. Her *new friend* was an actual friend… not a flannel-wearing lumberjack. "Let me get the door for you."

Needing a moment to gather his thoughts, Kent hung back after the ladies headed inside. He leaned against his *ex-sister-in-law's* house and closed his eyes, savoring the heat of the autumn sun as it permeated each layer of his being. Was Noelle right? Had his fixation on the negatives in his life overshadowed his ability to recognize the positives?

Besides the temperate climate he was privileged enough to reside in, he had numerous reasons to be thankful. His mother's latest round of cancer treatments seemed to be working. The amicable nature of Jess and Brad's divorce had allowed them to continue gathering as a family. And Noelle. Even if she didn't return his feelings, Kent was beyond grateful for all things related to Noelle. Her presence in his life was enough.

"There you are. Time to eat."

Kent opened his eyes to see Brad studying him, his head at a tilt.

"Is everything okay?" his older brother asked.

"Not everything, but enough things are, so that's actually really good."

Brad stepped outside, letting the door slam shut behind him. "That's *actually really* cryptic, bro. Are you sure you're okay?"

"I'm great… really," he added when Brad looked unconvinced. "I probably don't tell you this enough, but I'm grateful to have you as my big brother. After Dad left us, you played catch with me, and you taught me how to use tools and how to drive. You stood up for me when I get picked on, and you helped me fit in. You've always had my back. I don't think I've ever thanked you for all that before, so... thanks."

Brad blinked at him for a solid minute before clearing his throat. "You made it easy, Kenny. You were the best little brother a guy could ask for. I wish I could've done more for you."

"You did plenty." Kent wrapped his arm around Brad, slapping his back in a literal bro hug. "And stop calling me Kenny, Bradley."

"Let's go eat before we get yelled at, *Kenny*," Brad said with a laugh.

Lightened by the buoyancy of gratitude, Kent couldn't fight the smile that stretched across his lips if he tried. "Let's."

20

An overlapping melody of *yum, please, and thank you* played like background music as all fifteen guests at the long table filled their plates.

"Thanks again for having me," Sandy said while passing the mashed potatoes. "It's my first holiday without my boys, so I'm grateful Noelle was kind enough to invite me."

"Of course, the more the merrier!" Jess replied.

"I'm so glad you came, despite the long drive," Noelle said, still feeling guilty that she hadn't been able to carpool. Her to-do list that morning had been three miles long. "No one should spend the holidays alone."

"Well, at least I get Dane and William for Christmas," Sandy said, upbeat as usual. "If I hadn't come here today, I probably would've spent the day drinking and writing, like I normally do when the boys are with their father."

"Ooh, what do you write?" Jess asked.

"Mostly historical romances," Sandy said, switching to her British lilt, "but with less misogyny."

"Alternative history, then," Kent quipped.

Noelle kept her eyes on Sandy, doing her best to ignore the infuriating man who, of course, had taken the seat directly to Noelle's left. Him and all his *us* talk. "Get out! I didn't realize you were a romance writer! How many books have you written?"

"Only three that are published, but my fourth, fifth, and sixth books are all in various stages of completion. It's hard to find the time and focus while also running the coffee shop, but I love it. One might say I found my *passion writing passion*."

Noelle clasped her hands. "I love that! And I'd love to read them. Do you write under a pen name? Or would I find your books under Sandy... Uh, sorry. I don't know your last name."

"No worries. I've had a few of them," Sandy said with a laugh. "I can tell you I most certainly did *not* publish under my maiden name... Crotchit."

Jess gasped and then yelled, "Your name was Sandy Crotchit?"

Noelle mouthed "rude" across the table at her sister before returning her focus to their guest. "I'm so sorry, Sandy."

"It's okay," Sandy said, sounding unphased. "I like to think all the sandy crotch jokes helped to thicken my skin. Although, the unfortunate nickname was probably why I rushed to get married to my first husband, whose last name was Smith. It didn't get any more basic than that. Sadly, that marriage was about as boring as the name and only lasted a year.

"Then, before the ink had even dried on my divorce papers, I met my next husband at university." Sandy got a far-off look and a twinkle in her dark eyes. "I'd sworn I would never get married again, but our whirlwind romance was insta-love meets opposites attract on steroids. Liam was charming, tall, and British... swept me right off my petite American feet. I was bookish and shy, if you can believe that, and he was the life of every party."

Noelle felt herself lean in, enthralled by Sandy's story. A quick glance around the table told her others were equally captivated.

"Anyway," Sandy continued, "I kept Liam's last name after the divorce last year. It was the least he owed me after nearly two decades together. And since I couldn't think of a better pseudonym, my books are all published under my legal name... Sandra Bullock."

A moment of stunned silence filled the crowded dining room, a remarkable event for Noelle's boisterous family. Even the side conversations at the opposite end of the table—either about the cost of *gas* or *grass* (equally probable given her father's landscaping business)—ceased. A platter of turkey being passed between Derek and Linda skid to a halt in midair.

"Your legal name is Sandra Bullock?" Noelle asked.

"Like the actress?" Jess added, as if necessary.

Sandy raised her hand like a witness on the stand. "I solemnly swear. It's been the name on my driver's license for the last twenty years."

"Wow, I'm totally updating my Facebook status right now," Jessica's bestie said, phone in hand. "*Dining with Sandra Bullock.*"

"Good idea," Noelle said, pulling out her own phone. "Except Facebook is for old people, Nat," she added, earning her a discreet middle finger.

"Noelle, you didn't tell us you were bringing a celebrity to Thanksgiving," her mother hollered from the far end of the long table. She added an exaggerated wink before returning her attention to Chloe, who sat in a booster seat between both grandmas.

"Can someone pass the turkey?" Brad shouted.

"Oh my darlin', oh my darlin', oh my darrrrrlin', Sandy Bee!" Carlos sang from his seat next to Deedee. *Bless her sister for seating their parents as far away as possible.*

Sandy laughed. "I must admit, I get a kick out of introducing myself to new people."

Noelle leaned back in her chair and smiled. Inviting Sandy (a.k.a. Sandra Bullock) had been the absolute best idea. Sandy appeared to be enjoying herself; everyone else seemed entertained; and Noelle hardly noticed the heat radiating off the lean, muscular body too close for comfort.

"That's smart to capitalize on such a well-known name for your books, since it's legally yours too," Avery's lawyer brother said.

Noelle's first impression of Damien had been: hot but extremely uptight. When she'd asked Jess months ago whether he was single, her sister's firm reply had been, "Don't even think about it."

Naturally, it only made her more curious.

"Is that your professional legal opinion?" Noelle asked, using a deliberately flirtatious tone.

Damien's lime-green eyes shot to hers, and his cheeks pinkened to match the salmon-colored tie he wore.

Beside her, Kent started violently coughing. When all eyes turned to him, he held up a hand while gulping down a glass of water. "Wrong tube," he croaked. "I'm okay." Then, a little clearer, he said, "Brad, isn't the Cowboys-Giants game starting soon? Maybe the men should migrate to the family room."

"Because only men like football?" Noelle asked, facing him for the first time since they'd sat down.

Kent pushed his thick-framed glasses up the bridge of his nose and sputtered, "No, it's not... I just meant—"

"I'm with Noelle on this one," Kent's mother hollered from four seats over in her distinctive New York accent. "Your ma didn't raise chauvinists, so you better have a good explanation, sonny boy."

Side conversations at the table once again grew quiet, and Kent audibly gulped. Noelle didn't even try to hide her pleasure at his discomfort. *The genius had put his size-twelve foot in his mouth yet again.* She crossed her arms and waited for him to choke on it.

"Women can like football too, of course," Brad said before his shell-shocked brother could speak. "But Kent already knows that none of the ladies here enjoy watching the games, except maybe our new guest. Are you a football fan, Sandy?"

"I can't say I'm a fan, but I loved *The Blind Side*, mostly because my name-twin won her first well-deserved Oscar for her performance in it."

"Oh, she was great in that movie!" Deedee shouted.

"I concur," Jess said.

"One of Sandra Bullock's best," Avery agreed, while Natalie and Linda both nodded.

"Well, that confirms it. None of the women at this table like football, unless it's in a movie starring one of America's sweethearts,"

Brad said, winking at Kent over Lucas's head. "Shall those of us who enjoy the sport head into the family room now?"

Noelle wished she could pinch the smugness right off Brad's face. She'd never liked her sister's ex. Still, she had to admit his protectiveness over Kent was admirable. Family was important, and despite her justified grudges against both Clark men, she found herself feeling grateful that Kent had an older brother to stick up for him.

"I went to every single one of your games, Bradley!" Carole yelled, even though Brad sat directly next to her.

Brad puffed out his chest. "That's because I'm your son and the greatest high-school football star of all time, Ma. You never watch it on TV."

Noelle shared an instinctive eye roll with Natalie, her long-time anti-Brad ally, before returning her focus to Kent. "You don't even like football. You played baseball in high school."

Kent's blank expression morphed into a self-satisfied grin.

"What? Why are you smiling at me like that?" she asked, the temperature around them rising a thousand degrees.

"I didn't realize you paid such close attention to my interests, Gingerbread," he said, in that smooth, hotel-room voice of his, and damn if her panties didn't spontaneously combust.

Noelle mentally fanned herself as a chorus of sweet nothings—all in that voice—cycled on repeat in her brain.

Tell me this is only for me.

I'll never leave you.

I'm not going to give up on you... on us.

The firehose of thoughts scrambled her senses. What had happened between them had been purely physical. Kent couldn't possibly have real feelings for her, could he?

Deedee pounded her fork on the table, garnering everyone's attention. "No one leaves this table until we go around and each say at least one thing we're grateful for."

I'm grateful for you, Mom, Noelle thought, shutting off the running faucet of her mind.

"Sandy, as our guest of honor, would you care to go first?" Jess asked.

"Sure. Mine is easy. I'm grateful that I get to spend this holiday with such a lovely group of people," Sandy replied.

"To new friends," Damien said, raising his glass in the air.

Everyone repeated the sentiment, then Natalie added, "And no one is allowed to copy anyone else. You have to come up with a unique thing to be grateful for. It's the rules."

"You and all your rules," Derek said, playfully bumping Natalie's shoulder before kissing her, long and deep.

"New rule: No PDA at the dinner table," Noelle said. "Some of us are still single."

This earned her a side-glance and bashful smile from Damien. *Yep, he was definitely single too.*

"My house, my rules, and I say public displays of affection are allowed." Jess then planted a kiss on Avery.

At the same time, Carlos made a dramatic show of standing from the table, side-dipping Deedee in her chair, and kissing her like a sailor on leave.

"Ewww!" Lucas exclaimed from his seat on the other side of Kent.

"Lucas speaks for all of us, Dad. Please never do that again… like ever!" Noelle yelled to be heard over the ruckus.

"Yeah, I retract my rule," Jess said. "No more PDA."

Damien raised his hand like a kid in class. "I'm grateful for the PDA rule. And since that takes care of my turn, I pass the baton to Ems."

"How nice of you, Raldy," Avery replied, using the other half of the nickname that represented their last name: Emerald. "Well, I'm thankful for everyone here today, especially my beautiful girlfriend who went out of her way to make sure I had vegan options on this otherwise carnivorous holiday. You're amazing," she said, looking at Jess.

"I'd argue that saccharine declarations count as PDA, but… To Tofurky!" Damien cheered, lifting his glass again.

As Noelle laughed and raised her glass along with everyone else, several things occurred to her. One: Avery's older brother wasn't as uptight as she'd originally thought. He was actually kind of funny. Two: Toasts were apparently Damien's thing, though he might've been a bit drunk. And three: Damien's wit and general hotness didn't matter, because she couldn't stop thinking about Kent Forget-Me-Not Clark.

And she hated it.

Sure, they'd slept together less than two weeks prior, but it didn't have to *mean* anything. Why then, in the world's worst mistletoe mystery, did Kent's proximity give her heart hunger pangs?

"I'll go next," Carole shouted. "I'm grateful, first and foremost, for my two kind-hearted sons, one of which has gifted me with two even better grandbabies." Kent's mother blew kisses at Chloe and Lucas before directing her gaze down the table, where it ping-ponged between Kent and Noelle. "I'm still waiting for your contribution in that department."

Carole had to be addressing Kent, not both of them, right? That was the only reasonable explanation, unless… *O Holy Night! Did Kent's mother know about their sexcapades?*

Noelle's face flashed hot at the possibility. As incriminating as the move felt, she looked from Carole to Kent, who also turned at that exact moment. Kent's stormy eyes locked onto hers through his glasses, which were far too transparent to shield her from his smolder. But instead of mirroring her mortification, his eyes seemed to be asking: *Whatta ya say? Wanna make a baby?*

What the actual South Pole.

"Mom says if you two have babies, I'll have double cousins," Lucas said, looking down at the turkey in his messy fingers.

Noelle pulled her focus across the table to her backstabbing sister. "She said what?"

"It's a factual statement," Jess said, her large brown eyes feigning innocence.

"Sandy, as a writer, you must have a large vocabulary," Noelle said, not taking her eyes off Jess. "What's the word for murdering a sister?"

"Noelle, shame on you!" Deedee chided. "Besides, I want more grandkids too, and you're not getting any younger, sweetheart."

"It's sororicide," Sandy replied, before adding under her breath, "and matricide is the word for what you're thinking now."

Noelle glared down the table. "Thanks so much for that, Mother. I thought I was aging in reverse."

"A recent study found that ovaries actually age faster than the rest of a female's body. I read it in a scientific journ—" Kent cut himself off when her glare shifted to him.

Needing a subject change, fast, Noelle said, "I'm grateful that my store is ready for its grand opening tomorrow, even though no one in my family cared enough to ask today."

"Hey!" Jess said, clearly insulted. "I asked you how things were coming along yesterday."

"We'll all be there first thing tomorrow morning, honeybee," Carlos yelled. "And I'll have a hammer to bang on the front door until it opens."

Noelle shook her head. "That makes no sense, Dad, but I love you."

"What are ovaries?" Lucas asked, bringing the conversation back into the danger zone.

"I'll let your Uncle Kent explain that one to you, buddy," Noelle said, patting Kent's forearm and then immediately wishing she hadn't. His lean muscles flexed under the heat of his skin, sparking memories that told her it was definitely too soon to be touching him.

"Ovaries produce ova, or eggs, which can turn into babies. They're located inside a female's, uh… belly," Encyclopedia Kent said.

"Are there eggs in your belly, Auntie Elle?"

"Um, I believe so," Noelle answered, hoping her nephew wouldn't yet concern himself with exactly *how* the eggs turn into babies.

"Good, because I want a baby cousin," Lucas said.

"Another grandbaby from you two would be *muy bueno*," her dad piled on in Spanglish.

"*Cómo que* what now?" Noelle shot back, her mouth hanging open in disbelief.

Betrayed by her own father, of all people. She knew her dad always liked Kent, and he'd even hinted before that he thought Noelle should date the younger Clark brother, but encouraging her to make a baby with him? Saying it would be *very nice*? That was—in the words of Vizzini—inconceivable! And frankly, the whole day was quickly becoming too much to bear.

Noelle pushed back from the table. "Excuse me. I need to use the restroom."

Kent reached for her, but she evaded his grasp and rushed from the dining room. He was the absolute last person she wanted comforting her.

21

Sitting on the cold floor of the kids' bathroom, Noelle felt herself bottom-out with grief. And the irony of it all: She was the self-designated *holiday cheer girl*. She hounded others to focus on the good and to be grateful for what they had, yet all she could seem to think about were the gaping holes in her life.

"I'm coming in," Jess said, seconds before pushing through the door that Noelle now wished she'd locked.

"Hey! What if I'd been naked?" She started to lift herself off the ground, but then sank back down. Why bother?

"I'm your big sister. I used to wipe that cute little tush of yours when changing your stinky diapers. Speaking of stinky, did you get sick in here?"

"Yes, and I blame your green bean casserole."

Jess placed her hands on her hips. "You didn't even eat my green bean casserole."

"I couldn't, thanks to the boatload of onions, but it was right in front of me the whole time. Talk about stinky," Noelle said, hoping to deflect her sister's pity stare. They both knew emotional lows often wreaked havoc on Noelle's sensitive stomach.

Jess sat on the floor beside her. "What's really going on? I'm sorry about what Lucas—"

"It's not his fault," Noelle cut in. "It's been... a rough couple of weeks."

"Wanna talk about it?"

"Not really." Noelle rested her head against the wall and stared up at the rubber duckies on the ceiling. "I forgot you painted those."

"It was your idea," Jess said, matching her upward gaze. "And I couldn't have done it without your genius stencil design."

Noelle laughed weakly. "Yeah, I'm a real genius."

"Will you please tell me what's wrong?"

"No offense, but you wouldn't understand."

"Maybe not, but I can still listen. *And offense taken.* You've supported me through all of my emotional drama, and there's been plenty over the years, but you never let me reciprocate. You don't have to suffer alone, you know. I love you and want to help."

"I know, and I love you too. It's just…" Noelle searched for the right way to put it. "You met Brad in high school, got married, and started your family. Even after you two split, you were only single for what? Less than a year before you reconnected with Avery. And don't get me wrong, I'm so happy for you. But I've been pretty much single my whole life.

"My longest relationship lasted six months, and that was only because I'd managed to withhold sex for that long. But once he got what he wanted, he was done with me, same as every other guy." Noelle shook her head. "I never thought I'd say this, but maybe Mom was right all along. No one wants to buy the cow when the milk is free. It's either that or I'm just not marriage material."

"Okay, first off," Jess said, "never say *Mom was right.* If she hears you, neither of us will ever hear the end of it. Secondly, excuse my language, but that is total bull honky!"

"You do realize you didn't actually swear, right?"

"My point is, my beautiful yet crazy sister, you are definitely marriage material—and worth so much more than your *milk.* Did you ever stop to think that maybe you're picking the wrong guys? The meathead jocks in high school, the frat guys, the motorcycle mechanic with the neck tattoo… and don't even get me started on that womanizing bartender from last summer."

"And who should I date instead? Brainy guys with fancy degrees and serious jobs?" Noelle asked, heat rising from her churning belly. "They'd laugh at someone like me, who makes a living telling people how to dress like their favorite rom-com characters. Or do you think they'd be wowed by the fact that I sometimes start businesses doomed to fail? Does that make me marriage material?"

Jess grabbed her by the shoulders. "Is that why you've always dated losers? You don't think you're good enough?"

"Please don't shake me. I might hurl again." As a precaution, Noelle leaned closer to the toilet.

"Noelle, you're gorgeous, kind, and driven. You're the best at practically everything you do, annoying as that is, and you've never been afraid to walk your own path. I've spent most of my life wishing for just an *ounce* of your confidence, and now I'm hearing that you think you're a joke? No way. I don't accept that."

The nausea passed, and Noelle sat upright. "If I could afford a therapist, they'd probably say I overcompensate with my confidence."

"Don't do that," Jess scolded. "Don't make light of this and definitely don't put yourself down. You are a gem. Do you hear me? An absolute gem."

"Thanks, sissy. I know I have a lot going for me. It's just…" *Ditzy and superficial* rang in her head, and she shrugged. "There are different calibers of people—like social classes and whatnot—and I know where I fit in. That's all."

"Obviously you don't! Otherwise, you'd date princes instead of deceptively attractive frogs," Jess said with a playful-yet-painful pinch to Noelle's arm.

Lacking the energy to argue, Noelle forced a smile. "We should probably get back out there."

"Not until you also tell me what's going on between you and Kent."

"Nothing's going on there."

"Come on, Noelle. An electric carving knife couldn't cut the tension between you two. I saw all those side glances at the table, and you flipped out when Lucas made the double-cousin comment. That was *not* nothing."

"I still owe you one sororicide for that, by the way."

Jess crossed her arms. "We're not leaving this bathroom until you tell me."

"Fine," Noelle said, all the fight beaten out of her for the day. It was time to rip off the Band-Aid. "Weekend before last, Kent and I kind of… slept together."

"What?" Jess screamed, framing her face with her hands like Macaulay Culkin in *Home Alone*.

"Sssh! Keep your voice down. It's not a big deal."

"Um, yes, it is! It's huge!"

"As was he," Noelle mumbled, unable to help herself.

Her overly tactile sister once again grabbed her. "You said nothing was going on, you little brat! I can't believe I'm barely hearing about this!"

"I can't believe I'm telling you at all. You're clearly chill about the whole thing."

"I can be chill," Jess said, folding her hands in her lap for two whole seconds before death-gripping Noelle's arm. "Now spill. How did it happen? Who initiated? And how was it? I want every last detail!"

Noelle wrenched her arm free. "Very chill. And no, perv. None of the details matter, anyway, because Kent is not the prince you think he is. He's a frog, like all the rest."

"What do you mean? Was he a jerk to you after?" Jess sucked in a loud breath. "Oh, I will kick his nerdy butt if he hurt you!"

"I love you for that," Noelle said, taking her sister's hand. "But no, it's not like that. If anything, I might've hurt him… or his ego, at least."

"I'm confused. Why is he a frog, then?"

Noelle rubbed at the back of her neck, unsure how to explain. Doing so would require sharing her most embarrassing secret, her deepest fear. She'd already told Jess about sleeping with Kent, though. There seemed to be no going back.

"It's something he said about me in high school," Noelle started. "Basically, he told his best friend I wasn't good enough to date guys like them. He said I had a pretty face, but *nothing going on upstairs.*" Her eyes watered at the memory. "I never should've slept with him, Jess. That's on me. But I couldn't possibly be with him, knowing what I know."

Her sister stayed uncharacteristically quiet as they sat, hand in hand, for a solid minute. When Jess finally spoke, she said, "High school was such a long time ago."

Noelle yanked her hand away. "I knew you wouldn't understand!"

"Hear me out, please. I understand the destructive power of words far better than you know," Jess said, her glassy eyes fixing on a distant point beyond the room. "My first semester of community college, a couple of guys in my theater class were talking about me offstage, not realizing I could hear them. One of them said I was too fat to be playing the lead role, and that stuck with me for years. I never told anyone, but it's a big part of why I didn't pursue an acting career after college."

"Jess, you are not—"

"I'm overweight," Jess interrupted, "especially by Hollywood's standards. I've accepted that, but I don't let it hold me back from doing what makes me happy. *Now.* But back then, I let their words have power over me, over my life, because I believed they were true." Tears rolled down Jess's rosy cheeks. "It breaks my heart to hear that you've believed such a horrible thing about yourself since high school. Please, Noelle. Please learn from my mistakes and stop letting other's opinions control your life."

"But what if…" Noelle bit back a sob, resisting the urge to ugly-cry into her sister's shoulder. "What if it's true?"

"It's not," Jess said without hesitation. "Look at me, Noelle. You are smart, creative, caring, and a bunch of other wonderful things. So what if KFC has a higher IQ? *Whoop-dee-freaking-do!* That doesn't mean you're not worthy of him or anyone else. If anything, *he's* not worthy of you!"

Noelle wiped at her eyes, a smile tugging on her lips. "You've never called him KFC before."

"Well, now I get it. I'm serious, though. You could date a freakin' rocket scientist if you wanted to. Heck, look at me and Avery. She's a physical therapist with a doctorate degree from UCLA. She knows more about the human body than—I don't know—probably most doctors, whereas I do community theater and give out restaurant recommendations at a hotel. Does that mean I'm not good enough for her?"

"Of course not, but—"

"No buts," Jess said, wagging a finger before spreading her arms wide.

Noelle sank into the hug. "Thank you. I promise I'll consider what you said, but can we please keep this all between us?"

"I take it Kent doesn't know that you heard what he said about you?"

"No, and he can't. Please!"

Jess shook her head and sighed. "I think I would've been even more mortified if those theater jerks had known I'd overheard them. I won't say anything."

"Thank you so—"

"But," Jess said, holding up a hand.

"You said no buts."

"Kent is not some random theater guy you'll never see again, Noelle. I really think you should tell him. It doesn't seem fair to hold a grudge this long without the other person knowing what they did wrong."

Noelle crossed her arms. So much for her sister being on her side.

"I better get back out there," Jess said, rising to her feet. "Take as much time as you need in here. I'll tell everyone you ate something bad… earlier, of course. My cooking would never get anyone sick."

Noelle nodded her appreciation, and Jess exited the bathroom, leaving her as she so often felt—all alone.

Kent drummed his fingers on the table. Was Noelle okay? She'd been in there with her sister for a while.

A warm hand landed on his shoulder. "Your brother turned the game on in the family room. Want to join us, *mijo*?"

Kent looked up to see Carlos Serrano, the father he'd always secretly wished he'd had. His use of the Spanish slang for *my son* melted away some of Kent's worry. If Noelle wasn't okay, at least she had the support of a loving family.

"No, thanks. I'm more of a baseball guy. I'll hang back and help clean up," Kent said.

"Ay!" Carlos clutched his chest as if shot. "You make the rest of us look bad!" He then straightened and added, "But you'll make a lucky lady very happy one day."

"Yes, he will!" Kent's mother loudly agreed.

Of course she did. His mom had always been his biggest advocate. His rock. His everything.

Once again, Noelle had been right. He'd spent most of his life dwelling on his lack of a father, instead of being grateful for having the best possible mother. He'd always considered the holidays a reminder of everything his family had lost, but in doing so, he'd lost sight of what mattered most.

His throat constricted as he stood. "I should go check on Noelle," he said to no one in particular.

Carlos had wandered off to the family room, as had all the other males at the table, and Avery was busy collecting a stack of dishes to carry into the kitchen.

"No need," Jess said, reentering the dining room and giving him a glare he'd only ever seen from her sister.

"Is she okay?" he asked.

"She might have eaten something bad, but she'll be fine. I'll take care of these," she said to Avery, taking the stack of plates from her hands.

"Here, let me help," Kent said.

"You've done enough," Jess snapped, then turned on her heels and marched into the kitchen.

Okay… What had he done now?

"You must be the guy," a voice said.

Kent turned to see Noelle's friend, Sandy, looking up at him with a pensive expression. Dark discerning eyes traveled over him before settling back on his face.

He straightened his glasses. "Um, what guy?"

"*The* guy. Mister Complicated. And in my professional opinion, the hero of her story."

"I'm sorry. Did I miss something?"

"They always do. Tell me," Sandy said, coaxing him forward with a curled index finger before whispering, "are your feelings new, or have you always been in love with Noelle?"

Kent stumbled back. How could this woman—this total stranger—know such a thing? Either she was exceptionally astute, or he was miserably transparent.

"I don't know… what you mean," he stammered.

Sandy's lips stretched into a wide smile. "Yes, you do. But it's okay if you want to keep it to yourself for now. Just don't wait too long." She winked, and his gut clenched.

Did Sandy know something he didn't? Was he about to lose Noelle forever, perhaps to Mister Christmas Tree Farm?

Kent gulped at the thought and then busied himself carrying leftover food into the kitchen. He always felt better when contributing, rather than merely taking up space. *Make yourself useful, or make yourself scarce*—another great mantra from Dear Old Dad. And scarce was the last thing Kent wanted to be to the people he cared about.

Several trips to the kitchen later, he noticed Jess scowling at him again. "Hey, did I do something wrong?"

Jess crossed her arms. "I don't know. Did you?"

"Uh… My factoid about ovaries aging faster was—"

Jess cut him off with a headshake. "You know, I've always been on Team Noent—or Koelle, I'm not sure which ship name I like better—but I'm done helping you, KFC. You'll need to use that genius brain of yours to figure it out."

Kent took a step back, mentally slapped. His greatest ally had turned on him, and while he suspected it was warranted, he couldn't for the life of him *solve for why*. What could Noelle have said to Jess? And more importantly, what had gotten Noelle so upset? He knew she wanted a family of her own someday. Was all the pressure to procreate rubbing salt in some hidden wound? And if so, what role had he played in making it worse?

Cheers and jeers from the adjacent family room pulled him from his newest form of torture: the *how have I hurt Noelle* deep-dive.

"A giant would crush a cowboy in the wild. This game will be no different," Brad said, making his allegiance clear.

Their father had been a New York Giants fan, too.

"Because there are so many wild giants roaming around," Damien said with the verbal tone of an eye roll. "The next game is the only one that matters, anyway. The Patriots are going to dominate."

A series of boos erupted from all the non-New Englanders in the room (i.e. everyone except Damien.)

"Hate all you want, but you'll see. You'll all see! Right, Sis?" Damien called into the kitchen when Avery entered.

"I'm staying out of that one," Avery smartly replied.

When Jess leaned in to kiss Avery, Kent used the opportunity to flee the kitchen unnoticed, cutting through the family room, then heading down the long hall toward the bathroom.

Once outside the door, quiet yet unmistakable sobs filtered through, each decibel of sound hitting him squarely in the chest with the force of a missile. Every fiber of his being wanted to bust through the door—Incredible Hulk-style—and take her into his arms. But what if his presence only made things worse?

Everything he said or did lately only seemed to upset Noelle, plus she'd been openly embarrassed the last time he'd seen her cry. That had been the same day he'd learned of her desire to find love—specifically, romance-worthy love. He wanted so badly to fulfill that wish, but would it be enough if offered by him?

His hand rested on the doorknob, immobilized by indecision. Did he hold the key to make all of Noelle's dreams come true, or would he say the wrong thing and be locked out forever?

"There you are," a familiar voice boomed.

Kent winced at having been caught, then swiveled to face his all-knowing mother at the other end of the hall.

"Sorry to interrupt," Carole said, "but I'm feeling a little tired and was wondering if you could drive me home. I'd ask Brad, but he—"

"Of course I'll take you, Ma," Kent said, sprinting away from the bathroom door to avoid being heard.

After saying his farewells, Kent spared one more longing glance down the hall before ushering his mom out the door. It seemed the decision was made for him. Carole needed her rest, and they both needed the dreadful holiday to be over.

22

Merry vibe:

"Santa Tell Me"

Ariana Grande

31 days until Christmas

"The rest will be smooth," Kent told himself.

Whether he'd meant the remainder of the drive or the discussion he needed to have, Kent wasn't sure, but the vague affirmation helped to ease his nerves as he gripped the steering wheel, tugging it left, then right, then left again. He accelerated after each curve, slowing when a line of vehicles came into view.

Ahead, the single-lane highway disappeared beneath bumpers and brake lights, each set crawling forward then lurching to a halt as if caught off guard, only to crawl once more. *Ah, holiday traffic: the only reliable gift of the season.*

It was Black Friday—the consumerism-based pseudo-holiday where retailers' accounting ledgers reportedly turned "black," or profitable, after being "in the red" all year. While Kent found the idea of overspending for alleged deals absurd, he hoped the day had been fruitful for Noelle's new store. She deserved a break after what had clearly been a tough Thanksgiving. And while he didn't plan to bring up overhearing her sobs, he fully intended to get to the bottom of what she had against him, once and for all.

Fifty minutes that should've been *fifteen minutes* later, Kent passed the town limit sign for Holiday Pines (population 1,318) and parallel-parked on Main Street, directly across from Merry Holidays. A rustic, wood sign hung above the door, with the store's name expertly painted in red-and-white block letters resembling candy canes. He admired it while crossing the street. If anyone could pull off doing something at the eleventh hour and having it still be perfect, it was Noelle.

"Your store looks great," he said, stepping inside after noting she'd be closing in ten minutes.

Noelle looked up from behind the register, shock and confusion written on her face. "What are you doing here?"

"You still owe me a thumb war," he deadpanned.

She crossed her arms and glared at him, clearly unamused by his wit. It was worth a try.

"I came to congratulate you on your grand opening and to buy an ornament for my mom. She explicitly requested the 'fanciest' one you have, whatever that means."

Noelle didn't budge at first. Then, after what seemed like an epic internal battle, she straightened and came around the counter.

"I don't know about the fanciest, but I have a couple of handcrafted options I think she'd like." She took an ornament from one of the six artificial trees and handed it to him. "Since your mom used to be a schoolteacher, this little green chalkboard ornament has a retro classroom feel. It comes with a piece of chalk that clips onto the side, so she can write her own messages on the board, like I wrote 'Merry Holidays' here. And this border is sustainable bamboo... hand-wrapped by blind monks in Tibet."

She looked so damn beautiful—more so than usual, which said a lot—and all while talking about a tiny chalkboard. Her entire being glowed with the kind of unadulterated joy he wished he could trap in a bottle and take tiny sips of to get him through each day.

"Nice," he said without thinking, before amending with, "Wait. Really?"

"Yes to everything except the blind monk part. Your eyes glazed over for a minute, so I was just making sure you were still listening."

Heat rushed to his face, and he cleared his throat. "I was listening. Sounds expensive."

"Fancy is code for expensive. This one's actually in the mid-range. I can show you something pricier, if you want," she said.

"That one is perfect. I'll take it, plus your favorite ornament in the store."

She eyed him wearily. "Why my favorite? Who's it for?"

"Do you give all your customers the third degree?"

"Who's it for?" she repeated.

"It's for me. Aren't I allowed to own an ornament?"

"No. You hate Christmas and all things joyful."

Kent let out a heavy sigh. He'd been hoping to ease into the discussion, but there it was. "Is that why we don't mix, Noelle? Because I hate Christmas?"

"What? No," she sputtered. "I mean, I don't understand *why* you hate it so much, but plenty of people don't celebrate Christmas, and that's perfectly fine."

"Yeah, but would we mix better if my middle initial stood for *festive* or *figgy pudding*? Or what if I wore flannel and owned a Christmas tree farm? Would you give me a chance then?" Heart pounding, he leaned in until their faces were mere inches apart. "Because I'll do it, Noelle. I'll legally change my name. I'll buy a damn Christmas tree farm if that's what it takes to be with you! Please, just tell me what it'll take."

Her lips parted, and her eyes became molten emerald pools, the depths of which he could get lost in forever. When her chin angled upward, Kent was ninety percent confident she might kiss him. He'd finally gotten through to her.

A bell jingled from behind him, and Noelle took a step back. "Kris, what a surprise."

Kent whirled around as a bulky, blond man strode into the store. The plaid-patterned fabric across his chest was stretched tighter than a bad face lift, and its owner looked like he spent hours at the gym… or hauling heavy trees all day. Dammit.

The lumberjack prick in the flesh.

"Am I interrupting anything?" he asked.

Hell yes, he was.

"No, not at all," Noelle said, walking past Kent toward the Christmas-themed action figure. "Welcome to Merry Holidays!"

"Sorry to show up so late," Kris *with a K* said. "It took me a while to work up the courage to come in here, but I wanted to congratulate you on your grand opening and to give you these." He held out what appeared to be a bundle of weeds, but, upon closer inspection, were white flowers with yellow centers.

Kent mentally slapped himself. Why didn't he bring flowers? If he had, they would have been something Noelle actually liked, like poinsettias or lilies—not some pathetic roadside daisies.

"Thank you," Noelle said, holding them to her nose.

"Daisy helped pick them from the field behind our farm. She wanted you to know they were from her too."

Well, great. Lumberprick's daughter's name was Daisy. Noelle would love the flower choice. She also loved kids. How could he possibly compete with that? Kent didn't know the answer to that rhetorical question, but he did know one thing: he wouldn't give up.

"Aw, how sweet. Please tell her thank you for me," Noelle said.

"You can tell her yourself tomorrow night, if you want," wannabe Kris Kringle said. "That's part of why I stopped by. Our farm hosts a tree lighting event on the night of Small Business Saturday every year. It'll be a hectic day, so all the local shop owners get together to blow off some steam after closing, and the rest of the town gets a light show out of it. We'd love to see you there."

"That sounds amazing! Thanks, I'll be sure to stop by," Noelle said, sniffing the flowers again.

Kent walked over and stuck out his hand. "I'm Kent, by the way. Nice to meet you… Craig, was it?"

"Kris, and nice to meet you too."

Lumberprick shook the hand Kent offered with more force than necessary. His smug expression—a subtle squint of his eyes paired with a crooked smile—communicated volumes. It said: *Nice job trying to cock-block me.* Kent tightened his handshake and glared back with his own silent warning: *Hurt her and I'll kill you.*

Kris released his hand, dismissing him to address Noelle. "The tree lighting is at nine, but people start gathering as early as six. Come over whenever you can."

"Will do. Thanks again," Noelle said.

After a few nauseating goodbyes, Kent and Noelle were once again alone.

"What the hell was that?" she snapped, flipping over the *we're open* sign to *closed* and locking the door.

"What was what?"

"Don't play innocent. 'I'm Kent, by the way. Craig, was it?'" she mocked. "It was so obvious you were trying to claim me. You might as well have peed on my shoes."

"First off, I would never do that. And that guy? Really?"

"Oh, is there something wrong with an incredibly handsome man who brings me flowers picked by his adorable daughter and invites me to a Christmas tree lighting?"

"You mean the guy who wears his shirt two sizes too small and clearly thinks he's God's gift to women?" he shot back, following Noelle toward the register.

She took the chalkboard ornament from his hand and rang it up, along with what looked like a pine cone. "He rocks that flannel, for your information, not that you would understand."

"See, that goes back to my previous point. You love that he wears flannels and hosts Christmas tree lightings. What if I did those things?"

"It wouldn't matter."

"Why not?" Kent yelled, and then, because curiosity got the better of him, he added, "And what's with the pine cone?"

"It's my favorite ornament in the store. Its pine scent gives the artificial trees a real-tree feel." She then spouted his total as he handed her his credit card.

"Why not buy a real tree, then?" Kent asked, perplexed by her logic. His mother would equate it to putting lipstick on a pig.

"Because, even though real trees look and smell nice, they don't last very long. A quality artificial tree, on the other hand, can last a lifetime."

He signed his receipt, then leaned over the counter to whisper near her ear. "Kris is a real tree, Noelle. I would last a lifetime, if you let me."

At the satisfying sound of her breath hitching once again, Kent pulled back to take in her slack-jawed expression. Those molten eyes once again met his, and he was beyond tempted to race around the counter, lift her onto it, and show her exactly how long a lifetime could last. But first, he needed answers.

"I'll ask again. Why wouldn't it matter?"

Her gaze held his. "I already told you. Your feelings toward Christmas have nothing to do with why it won't work between us."

Kent had a long fuse. He was not the type of guy to lose his temper, and yet… his hand slammed down on the wooden counter. "Then tell me what the problem is already! And don't say *if I told you, I'd have to kill you*, because you're already killing me, Noelle."

Noelle crossed her arms, seemingly unperturbed by his outburst. When she finally spoke, her gaze shifted to the wall behind him. "You called me stupid."

"What?" he asked, truly baffled.

"My freshman year in high school, Kyle Fisher planned to ask me out, and you told him I had a pretty face with nothing going on upstairs. You said I was ditzy and superficial. A girl like me didn't *mix* with someone of his caliber."

"Noelle. I didn't—"

"Don't even try to deny it," she snapped without raising her voice. "It wasn't gossip I overheard. I was sitting under the bleachers while you guys were in the dugout. I heard every word with my own ears."

A dull ache formed behind his sternum, in the cavity where his punctured heart once resided, as the memory of that long-ago conversation slowly came back to him.

"And maybe it's childish or petty to hold a grudge from fifteen years ago," she continued, "but the thing is… that was one of the worst days of my life. Not only because it ruined my chance of dating Kyle, but because that day has made me question myself every day since."

Noelle walked around the counter, putting her back to him as she moved ornaments around on one of the trees. "It was little things, at first. Like I'd miss a few questions on a quiz or get a low grade on a paper, and I'd think: Oh no, what if Kent was right?"

"I wasn't—" he started, but Noelle cut him off high-school-style by holding her palm inches from his face.

"Then, when I lost my virginity to Chris Baker in the backseat of his car after prom, only to have him dump me the next day, I thought: Wow, only someone 'with the lights out upstairs' would have fallen for his lines," she said, now pacing the floor.

So many thoughts inundated his brain, the least of which revolved around wanting to hunt down Chris Baker and pummel him into the ground. Kent wanted to tell her she was wrong and a million other things, but he felt dumb in the true meaning of the word: unable to speak.

"Since my looks were the only thing going for me," she continued, "I started taking a bunch of selfies and posting them online to grow my following and monetize my social media accounts. But as it turns out, my success as an influencer has only reinforced my reputation as *ditzy* and *superficial*. It doesn't prove that I have what it takes to run an actual business."

Noelle moved to another tree, filling in the gap where the chalkboard ornament had been. "And even now, with this store…" She paused, and he thought he heard a sniffle. "Only a handful of people came in for today's grand opening, and besides my parents, you were the only one who actually bought anything. How's that for irony?"

"I'm so sorry," he finally managed to say, an anvil of guilt crushing him. His careless words had hurt her. They were *still* hurting her.

She spun around to face him. "I'm not telling you all this for your pity. You can keep that. I'm telling you so you'll understand why it will never work between us. I may not be as smart as you, but I'm not devoid of self-respect. I will *never* date someone who has ever thought so little of me."

"Noelle…" He reached for her, but she moved toward the door.

"Think of the sex we had like a parting gift," she said, "a reward for putting up with my attempts to torture you for over a decade. I gave you my body—arguably my best attribute—but you'll never get my heart." Her voice cracked on the last few words as she unlocked and opened the door. "Now, please, get out of my store and out of my life. Forever."

Kent took a step forward but shook his head. "Please, can we just—"

"Now!" she yelled, tears filling her brilliant green eyes.

Leaving felt like the worst possible option. He wanted to stay and talk things out. He wanted to make Noelle understand and to comfort her. But since his continued presence was clearly upsetting her, he walked through the door she held open and braced for the rush of cold air as it slammed shut behind him.

With great effort, Kent drew in a breath against the heavy weight in his chest. He'd always wanted to be the man to make Noelle happy, the one to protect her from ever getting hurt. Instead, he'd been the source of her pain all along. How could he possibly fix that?

As if the universe might hold the answer, he looked up at the night sky and immediately spotted Noelle's favorite constellation, Orion— or specifically his belt, because "even the stars needed accessories," she'd once said. The joy on her face when she'd pointed out those three bright stars to Lucas and Chloe had been far more radiant than anything the heavens had to offer. He would do anything to bring that joy back.

Please, Universe, give him a chance to make things right.

In response, a small meteor—inaccurately known as a shooting star—streaked through the earth's atmosphere. A fleeting speck of light against a backdrop of infinite darkness. He hoped the spectacle meant his wish had been received. It had to at least be good luck, right?

Kent looked both ways, then stepped off the sidewalk to cross to where he'd parked his car. But as soon as his foot hit the pavement, it slid forward, putting his center of gravity far behind him. He caught one more glimpse of Orion's Belt right as the back of his head made contact with the curb.

Then everything went as black as his soul.

Noelle heard the commotion before she saw his motionless body on the ground. Pushing her way through the small crowd that had formed, she ran to the edge of the sidewalk and collapsed next to Kent.

"Oh my god! Is he okay?" she cried to the middle-aged man crouched down beside him.

"Not sure. He's unconscious. Went down pretty hard," said the man she now recognized as Earl.

"Kent, wake up! It's Noelle. Please wake up!" She gently tapped his cheek but got no response.

"Ambulance is on its way," an older woman holding a grocery bag said. "I saw the whole thing from across the street and called nine-one-one."

"He slipped on this here patch of black ice," Earl said, pointing to the section of road directly beyond the gutter. "Impossible to see, 'specially at night."

"It could've happened to any of us," another local chimed in.

"So awful," yet another said.

Their voices faded into the background, unintelligible over the rapid thumping of blood pulsing in her ears. Noelle couldn't think. She couldn't breathe. *Kent had to be okay.*

"Please wake up," she begged again.

Nothing.

Sirens blared in the distance, the distinctive shrill growing louder as it approached. Men and women in uniform soon surrounded the area, pushing Noelle back into the crowd of observers on the sidewalk. She stood and watched with dread as they lifted Kent onto a stretcher and wheeled him toward the back of the ambulance.

"Wait, please! I need to stay with him," she pleaded, rushing forward to grab the arm of a female paramedic before she could shut the vehicle's rear doors.

"Sorry, ma'am, we're not supposed to have passengers in the back of the rig and the front seat is already taken," the tall woman said without even looking at her. "You'll have to meet us at the hospital."

Kent was already out of her sight. This couldn't be happening. She wouldn't let it happen.

"But I'm his fiancée," she blurted. "Please!"

The no-nonsense paramedic frowned at her watch, scanned Noelle's tear-soaked face, then waved her inside the large, boxy vehicle.

"Thank you so much!" Noelle took a seat next to Kent's gurney and held his hand. "I'm right here, Kent. I won't leave you."

Kent's previous words reverberated through her soul as the siren once again screamed on the bumpy ride to the hospital. *I'll never leave you.*

23

"Oh my gosh! Is he okay?" Jess exclaimed through the phone.

"I don't know. They took him for a CT and won't let me back there." Noelle bit her quivering lip as she paced the dreary waiting room. Its cracked paint and stained linoleum did little to instill much confidence in the rest of the hospital. "I feel like I'm in a bad episode of *Grey's Anatomy*—minus all the sexy, world-class surgeons—and the doctor is going to come out any minute and tell me he has a subdural hematoma and that they need to operate, and then... and then..."

"Deep breaths, Noelle. I'm sure Kent's going to be fine."

"He has to be! I took your advice. I told him that I overheard what he'd said about me, and then I told him to get out of my life *forever*. Those were my last words to him, Jess." A sob broke free, and she covered her mouth to silence it.

"Oh, honey. I'm so sorry. But listen to me," Jess said, using her motherly tone reserved for pep talks and scoldings. What followed felt like a combination of both. "Those will not be your last words to him, so don't even think that way! We'll all pray for him, and he'll be okay. I know it."

Noelle wished for an ounce of her sister's unshakable faith. Her own experience with prayers hadn't given her as much cause for reassurance. "Can you do me another favor?" she asked.

"Of course. Anything."

"Call Brad to let him know what happened and please ask him to take care of Carole, since Kent normally would be there. She'll need to be informed, too."

"Good thinking. I'll do that right away, and then I'll drive up there to wait with you after I take the kids—"

"No, sissy," Noelle cut in. "Stay put with the kids. I'll be fine, and I'll let you know the second anything changes."

"Are you sure? It's no trouble for me to drive back up there."

"Kent slipped on black ice, Jess, and it's dark. So, yes, I'm sure I don't want you driving up here tonight. It's not safe."

"Got it. Well… I guess I better call Brad. Keep me updated. Love you."

"Love you back." Noelle ended the call and ran her fingers through her hair. No longer vibrant nor merry, the bottom three inches of green looked as faded and sickly as she felt.

Kent had to be okay.

"Oh, Noelle, there you are! I came as soon as I heard," a voice with a British lilt called out from behind.

Noelle turned to see Sandy approaching with her twin boys in tow. Word certainly traveled fast in a small town.

"How are you holding up, lovely? Never mind. That's a stupid question. You must be a wreck! Come here," British Sandy said, wrapping her into a hug. "How is he? Have you heard any news yet?"

"Not yet," Noelle said, glancing at the closed doors beyond the reception area for the millionth time.

Sandy pulled back and held her by the shoulders. "Please let me know if there's anything I can do for you, anything at all, now or later. I'm here whenever you need me."

"That's very kind of you. Thank you."

"And I'm sure your *fiancé*…" Sandy said with a wink, "will be just fine. He seemed pretty hardheaded when I met him."

Despite the worry shredding her insides, Noelle coughed out a laugh. "You have no idea."

"I made this for your friend," one of the young boys said, holding out a piece of paper.

The crayon-colored picture had a stick figure handing a red heart to another stick figure, a rainbow in one corner, the sun in another, and *GET WELL SOON* written across the top.

Noelle's eyes instantly filled with tears. "How sweet."

"These are my boys, Dane and William," Sandy said, pushing them forward one at a time. "Boys, this is Miss Noelle."

"Hi, Miss Noelle," the identical twins said in unison.

"It's so nice to meet you both. You're much taller than you look in the pictures your mom has shown me."

"That's because they've probably sprouted several more inches in the short time we've been here," Sandy said, slipping into her American accent. "I didn't have them until I was thirty-five, you know," she added in a whisper, no doubt due to the emotional meltdown she'd witnessed on Thanksgiving.

Grateful for the crumb of comfort offered, Noelle forced a smile before addressing the twins. "I'll have to introduce you both to my nephew, Lucas. He's about your age."

"We're eight," William said.

"So is Lucas. Well, eight and a third, according to him. His birthday was in July."

Dane giggled. "We'll be nine in April."

"Oh, so you have him beat by a few months."

"Does he like Mario Kart?" William asked.

"Okay, that's enough," British Sandy chided. "Let's not bother Miss Noelle with trivial questions right now."

Let's, let's, let's.

Let us.

Kent's words from the previous day hit her next. *I want you to know I'm not giving up on you… on us. Because, as much as you deny it, Noelle, there is an us.* How could she have been so blind?

Tears once again pricked at her eyes, but she shook them off. "It's okay. I appreciate the distraction, and yes, Lucas loves Mario Kart. I'm pretty good at it myself. Maybe we can race sometime."

"Yeah!" both boys shouted.

"Um, excuse me, Miss? Are you Ken Clark's fiancée?"

Noelle whirled around to see a gray-haired woman in pink scrubs. "It's Kent. How is he? Can I see him? Is he awake?"

To the hospital employee's credit, she seemed completely unphased by the rapid-fire questions. "He's still unconscious, but he's out of CT now. You can follow me back to his room, and his doctors will be in there in a minute to go over the results with you."

"Go on, honey, and remember to call me if you need anything at all," Sandy said, but Noelle only half-heard her.

She was at the door to the patient rooms in three long strides, practically stepping on the heels of the woman in pink. She followed her down a bleak, beige corridor lit by overhead fluorescent lights, turning once before reaching a room with an open door.

"This is it," the nurse said as Noelle rushed past her to Kent's side. "I'll give you some privacy before the doctor gets here."

The door clicked shut as a fresh batch of hot tears rolled down Noelle's cheeks, their heat a sharp contrast to Kent's icy hand and corpse-like body. Only the rhythmic graph on the monitor provided any proof of life—each periodic low beep, a reassuring *he's alive, he's alive.*

"Kent, I don't know if you can hear me, but I'm here, and everything is going to be okay. All you have to do is wake up. Can you do that for me? *Please.*" Her voice cracked on the last word, which she repeated until her throat ran dry. "Please, please, please wake up, Kent."

"That might not be in his best interest."

Noelle craned her neck toward the door, where a stunning woman with long, dark hair stood, wearing olive green scrubs that nicely complemented her warm complexion.

"I'm Doctor Sharma, Head of Neuro," the beautiful woman said in a heavy accent. "Are you a relative of Mister Clark's?"

"I'm his fiancée," Noelle replied, the lie rolling off her tongue easier each time.

The doctor nodded, closing the door behind her. "Mister Clark experienced blunt trauma to the back of his head. The good news is his scan shows only minor edema, with no bleeding detected. Your fiancé seems to have an exceptionally thick skull," she said with a slight upward curve of her lips.

Noelle wiped at her face and coughed out a sound somewhere between a laugh and a sob. "Yeah, he has a big, hard head."

"Yes, well… in trauma cases like these, we'd often medically induce a coma to protect the brain and allow the body to heal," Doctor Sharma continued, "but since Mister Clark is already unconscious and the swelling is minor, we'll let him rest and observe him closely over the next twenty-four hours."

"So, he'll be okay?" Noelle asked, hope sparking in her chest.

"The next twenty-four hours will be critical. There's always a chance of deficits with cerebral edema, but I'm hopeful he'll make a full recovery without needing surgery."

Noelle gulped at the thought of someone drilling into Kent's amazing skull. "And if he does need surgery? Would you be his surgeon?"

"Yes, I'm the neurosurgeon on call here in Holiday Pines, though I'm normally based at Scripps in La Jolla."

The doctor's affiliation with a much larger hospital gave Noelle some relief, but not enough. She hated herself for even thinking it—anti-feminist as it was—but this woman seemed too gorgeous to be a brilliant neurosurgeon. This was real life, after all, not some nighttime drama where all the surgeons were smoking hot *and* at the top of their respective fields. Could someone really be flawless in both appearance and intelligence?

Noelle gazed down at Kent and answered her own question. He was the full package: handsome, kind, funny, family-oriented, and a literal genius. Kent could've been a neurosurgeon. Or a rocket scientist. Or one of those computer guys programming the social media algorithms she'd never understand. Kent could've gone into any profession he wanted, yet he chose to be an underpaid high-school math teacher to help kids.

And she'd been stupid enough to let a comment he'd made fifteen years ago keep her from going for gold. Because that's what Kent was. Pure gold.

"The nurse will be back shortly to adjust his IV, and I'll be back in a couple of hours to check on him myself," Doctor Sharma said.

Noelle thanked the beautiful neurosurgeon, then took a seat next to the hospital bed without releasing Kent's hand. *I'll never let go*, she said internally in the dramatic fashion of Rose to Jack.

Several minutes later, the gray-haired nurse reappeared and removed the near-empty IV bag from its glorified coat rack. "How are you holding up?" she asked.

"I don't know," Noelle replied honestly. "I feel everything at once, but also nothing… like I'm going through the motions while waiting to wake up from a bad dream."

"That's completely normal when something awful happens to someone you love," the nurse said in a soothing, grandmotherly tone. "Will any other family members be joining you?"

"Huh?" Noelle asked, still processing her use of the word *love*.

The nurse rephrased her question. "Will more family be visiting the hospital?"

"Oh. Um. I called, but I'm not sure when they'll be able to get here."

"That's fine, dear. I just wanted to let you know that we're limited to two visitors in the room at a time, so when they arrive, you may have to take turns." After replacing the IV bag, the nurse headed toward the door. "There are guest blankets here on this table, if you plan to spend the night. Try to get some rest. I'll be back in a bit."

The kind woman in pink was gone before Noelle's brain could form words again. Love. Her reaction was normal *for someone you love*. The reference to other family members struck her too. She'd often denied Kent being part of her family, even when Jess and Brad were still together. But as Noelle sat there, stroking his hand with her thumb, there was no more denying anything.

She loved Kent, and he was her family.

"So, apparently, it's a good thing you're not awake yet," she said to him. "Your big, hard head did its job, but your brain needs to heal while you sleep. I'm sure you already knew that, though."

She gave his hand a squeeze and then waited a beat, as if he might squeeze hers back. When the gesture went unacknowledged, fresh tears gathered, blurring her vision.

"You said you'll never leave me, KFC, and I'm gonna hold you to that. I'm also going to find out what that F stands for, because you were right. There is an *us*, and I want to know everything about you. And you know what else?" she asked, smoothing his dark hair back. "I'm done holding grudges. Maybe you made a snap judgment, or maybe you were a jerk in high school. But you're not a jerk now, despite all I've put you through, and that's what matters. You've always been there to help me out, even when I was too ungrateful and stubborn to admit I needed you. But I'm admitting it now. I need you, Kent. Please, please, don't leave me."

Noelle bit back a sob, squeezing his hand once more. With her free hand, she pulled out her phone and sent a quick text to Jess, though there wasn't nearly enough information to share. Selfishly, she felt relieved that Brad and Carole couldn't get to the hospital yet. They had more right to be in the room with Kent than she did, and yet Noelle knew Brad was going to have to pry her cold, dead fingers off Kent's hand before she ever left him willingly.

I'll never leave you.

Her silenced phone vibrated in her hand, and she glanced down to see an incoming call from her sister. "What's up?"

"Hey, I got your text and have an update of my own," Jess said. "I called Brad to let him know what's going on, and he immediately headed over to Carole's. But when he got there, she had fallen in the kitchen. Apparently, the night nurse Kent hired had already left, and

Carole thought she could help herself to a glass of water, but she got dizzy."

"Oh no. Is she okay?"

"Brad thinks she will be, but he took her to the emergency room to get checked out. So, they're still here in San Diego, and Brad hasn't told her about Kent yet. He doesn't want her getting upset or leaving the ER to be with him."

"That makes sense. Honestly, there isn't much they could do if they were here, anyway. Kent is still asleep, which his doctor said is a good thing."

"And how are you doing?" Jess asked.

"I'm okay," Noelle lied. "A little bored. It turns out watching someone sleep is less exciting than scrolling through endless pictures of someone else's lunch."

"Well, it's good that you're there with him. He shouldn't be alone right now."

Noelle's throat constricted. "I gotta go, but please keep me updated on Carole, and I'll do the same."

Afraid she might crumble, Noelle hung up the phone before Jess could say anything else. Kent wouldn't be alone. Not then, and not ever again. She wasn't ready to share such revelations with her sister yet, though. Whether she'd have the courage to bare her soul to Kent once he woke up remained debatable as well.

Talking to him while he slept was infinitely easier. She filled him in on his mom's condition and told him not to worry. Getting better should be his only concern. She then sang a few verses of "Soft Kitty" from Kent's favorite TV show, *Big Bang Theory*, and listed off all the different shrimp dishes she could think of, since *Forrest Gump* was one of his favorite movies. Somewhere after shrimp gumbo, shrimp kabobs, shrimp and potatoes, and coconut shrimp, Noelle fell asleep.

24

"Please Come Home for Christmas"
Eagles

30 days until Christmas

A light rustling sound caused Noelle to bolt to attention. She hoped the movement meant Kent was awake. Instead, a different nurse in pink scrubs stood on the other side of Kent's bed, changing the IV bag.

"Sorry if I startled you," he said in a voice deeper than she expected from such a petite man.

Noelle gauged his height to be about the same as her own, and his narrow bone structure had him on the slimmer side. When not in scrubs, she'd bet he could rock a pair of skinny jeans.

"It's okay. I thought maybe…" Noelle trailed off as she gazed down at Kent.

In the morning light, his face looked more like Frosty Clark than the warm-blooded version, pale with a light sheen of sweat. The drabness of his hospital gown—which she imagined would bring out the color of his eyes, if only they would open—accentuated his sickly appearance, and Noelle feared she might be sick herself if Kent didn't wake up soon.

"Where are his clothes?" she blurted, before considering the triviality of her question.

The man she loved was in a coma. Why in the South Pole did it matter where his clothes were?

"The night staff probably put them…" The man in pink walked around to her side of the bed and opened a drawer on the nightstand. "Yep, here they are." He then handed her a large, clear bag containing Kent's belongings. "His shoes are in a separate bag in here too, if you want them."

"No, this is fine. Thank you," she said, taking the bag that had been ridiculous to ask for.

Once the nurse left, Noelle stared through the plastic at the items on her lap. The distressed blue jeans and black sweater he'd worn the night before were neatly folded, seemingly unscathed. Though basic, the outfit had looked great on him. Come to think of it, he'd been more put together than usual—fitted clothes, a freshly shaved face, the thick-framed glasses she preferred and… was that sweater new?

She reached into the bag with the sudden urge to run her fingers over the fabric, which was feather-light and silky soft. Had Kent been trying to impress her with his fashion choices?

She thought back to the pleading look in his eyes when he'd said he would buy a Christmas tree farm and legally change his middle name to be with her. She also vividly remembered wanting to kiss *Kent Figgy Pudding Clark* before they'd been interrupted. Brawny Thor had looked as gorgeous as ever, and yet she'd felt nothing for him. How long ago, exactly, had she fallen in love with Kent without even realizing it?

While petting his sweater, Noelle noticed several smaller items in the bag: Kent's wallet, keys, and phone. Her fingers traced a hairline crack running from the corner of his phone screen to the center, and she reasoned that he must've been carrying his phone in his front pocket when he fell. If it had been in his back pocket, the damage would've been much worse. She winced, imagining the impact to the back of his head.

His beautiful, brilliant, big, hard head.

As Noelle stared at Kent's cracked screen, her own phone vibrated beside her.

"Okay, so, I have another update," Jess said, skipping all pleasantries when Noelle answered the call. Her sister was rarely all business. *This was not good.* "Carole was seen at the ER last night, and she's okay, but it turns out she didn't just get dizzy. She had a minor stroke."

"Oh no!"

"I know. It's awful." Jess sniffled, clearly crying. "They think she got a blood clot from the chemo port in her arm, and it traveled to her brain. The never-ending aftermath of cancer."

"But she's okay? You said she's okay." Noelle swallowed the salty sting of fresh tears. *Kent couldn't lose his mother,* not after everything he'd already been through.

"She is," Jess confirmed. "They said the stroke was minor, and she doesn't seem to have any deficits."

"Well, that's good at least."

"It is. They admitted her to the hospital, though. Something about salt to keep the swelling at bay. How are things going up where you're at? Is Kent still asleep?"

"No change since last night," Noelle said. *Except that her whole world had changed.*

After promising to keep each other updated, Noelle ended the call and stared at her non-cracked screen, the date on display catching her attention. It was Small Business Saturday, the most important day of the year for a store like hers. But like everything else, that didn't matter anymore. The only thing that mattered was the person next to her getting better.

Noelle swiped up on her phone and navigated to the only Holiday Pines phone number programmed in it.

"Oh my word, Noelle! I'm so glad you called," an exuberant Sandy exclaimed. "How is Kent? Is he awake yet? How are you? Is there anything I can get you?"

"Hi, Sandy. He's still unconscious, but the doctor says that'll help his body heal. There is something you could do for me though, if you don't mind."

"Name it, and it's done. Do you want me to come get your keys to open your shop? I noticed the closed sign this morning and assume that means you don't have any help. We have the full crew here at Holiday Grinds today, so I could easily slip away if needed."

Noelle leaned back in her seat, deeply touched by her friend's kindness. "Wow, that's an incredibly generous offer, but I'm fine with my store staying closed today. I was actually wondering if you're planning to go to the tree lighting at the Clauson's farm tonight."

"Oh, yeah. I take my boys there every year," Sandy said, and then, as if regretting her words, she quickly added, "But I don't need to. What can I do for you instead?"

"No, no, I want you to go. I just don't want Daisy to be disappointed if she was expecting me. Can you please let her know I'm sorry and thanks for the flowers?"

"Goodness, yes! I'll definitely let her know. Don't you worry about that for another second. Peppermint latte for Sal!" Sandy yelled away from the receiver. "Sorry, it's crazy today. Tourists and locals alike supporting small business. You sure you don't want me to open your shop? I don't mind at all."

"I'm sure, but thank you again. You're seriously the best." After a few more parting words, Noelle hung up and sighed.

Her new life in Holiday Pines hadn't gone as planned, but she'd made a quality female friend—something she'd never had before—and she'd also found love. The man of her dreams had been in her life all along.

"Kent? Are you waking up? Can you hear me?" she asked when she thought she saw his closed eyelids flutter.

Nothing.

After several more minutes of unsuccessfully willing him awake with the power of her mind, Noelle gave up and went back to her phone. It had been almost a week since she last chatted with Joe, and since there was nothing else to do, she figured it was as good a time as any to break the news that she was in love with someone else.

Joe had asked for that courtesy, and honesty was the least he deserved. It wouldn't be easy, though. Not only did she risk hurting him—something she desperately wanted to avoid—but she would also miss their chats, which had been oddly therapeutic. He'd been vulnerable with her, and in turn, she'd shared more of her true self than she ever had before.

A flash of light caught Noelle's eye, drawing her attention away from the phone in her hand to the one on her lap. Despite the crack, the screen of Kent's phone had come to life. An illuminated picture of him with his arm around his mom stared up at her.

"Carole must be calling," she thought aloud.

But… It wasn't an incoming call. The photo was his wallpaper, a testament to how much Kent loved his mom. Smiling mother and son were both now in hospital beds, fifty-odd miles apart.

They *both* had to be okay.

Noelle squinted to read the notification banner at the top of his lock screen, then dropped her phone on the ground. "Oh Saint Nick!"

She gawked up at Coma Kent and then back at the notification on his phone: *everyday_merry is now online.*

Noelle almost fell out of her chair as she scrambled to scoop her own phone off the floor. Kent was Joe. Joe was Kent. He'd been the one messaging her all along. A little voice reminiscent of Jiminy Grinch whispered that she should be furious—he'd tricked her, after all—but she was too overjoyed to be mad. It was the fairytale ending she'd secretly wished for.

"I wanted it to be you. I wanted it to be you so badly," she recited to an unconscious Kent, borrowing the words Kathleen Kelly had said to Joe Fox at the end of *You've Got Mail*.

Joe Fox.

Average Joe.

Kent was her Joe Fox, her enemy-turned-lover. She clutched her phone to her chest. Enemies-to-lovers had always been her favorite romance trope. How had she not seen this coming?

Noelle quickly navigated to her inbox. Sure enough, she had an unread message from six days prior.

> To: everyday_merry
> From: average_joe
>
> Sorry, I'd stepped away from our chat for a few minutes, and when I returned, you'd already signed off. I wasn't ignoring your perfectly fine question.
>
> It's fair to say I'm still single, although *why* is complicated. Any effort to explain requires another large dose of honesty: I've been in love with the same girl/woman for as long as I can remember. She's my other half, but I'm not hers. It's as painfully simple and complex as that.
>
> Every relationship I've had has been intentionally short. I didn't want to get serious with anyone I already knew wasn't "the one."
>
> You're different though, Merry. I can't yet tell you how I know this, but you are.
>
> Still hopefully yours,
> Joe

Noelle's eyes filled with tears for the billionth time that day. If everything Kent as "Joe" had said was true, then he'd been fighting for her all along, even before they'd slept together—and more importantly, even after they had. Regret settled into the pit of her stomach and put down roots. He'd been in love with her, and she'd said *she felt nothing for him.*

> I'm most afraid of being left all alone in this world. Every day, I wake up and wonder if the few people I care about most in my life will still be around tomorrow, and if I'm even worthy of their love.

It all made gut-wrenching sense now. Kent had been abandoned by his father as a child, and he'd been living with the fear of losing his mother to cancer for years. And thanks to Noelle's stubbornness, there was now a real possibility that he could die without ever knowing how incredibly worthy he was of long-lasting love.

"Damn you, Kent!" she yelled, gripping his hand with all her strength. "You better wake up right now! You don't get to end things like this. Do you hear me? You fought for me, and now you need to fight for yourself. Because I'm here, and I'm not going anywhere."

Even if Kent were conscious enough to hear her, she doubted he'd be able to make out her sob-slurred words. Her endless supply of tears seemed to flow from a raging river that serpentined through her heart, carving a canyon so vast the opposing sides might be lost to each other forever.

"Please wake up, Kent. Please! I love you."

25

Freshmen year, Kent had been caught watching *The Little Mermaid* on repeat. Brad had threatened to tell everyone at school, until Kent countered with his own threat, thus protecting the secret of his favorite Disney movie. After all, a crush on a redhead in a seashell top was less embarrassing than Brad wetting the bed until age twelve.

It might not have been a mermaid lulling him, but everything sounded garbled, as if underwater. Kent heard the most beautiful voice—not singing exactly, but also not speaking. Crying words, maybe?

He tried to open his eyes, but his eyelids felt weighed down, like the time Brad had buried him deep in the sand. He attempted a back stroke, in case he was in fact underwater, but his legs and arms were completely immobilized. A dull ache throbbed at the back of his head. He concentrated on lifting it, hoping to relieve the crushing pressure, but again, nothing happened when he tried.

To combat the sudden onset of dread, he honed in on the distorted, angelic voice. It sounded far away. Sad, but also frantic, like maybe its owner was drowning and calling out for help. He wanted to rescue her, whoever she was, but he couldn't move a single muscle. All that weight training he'd been doing in the school gym seemed useless now. As the realization of his helplessness sank in, Kent feared he might be the one who required saving.

The voice got closer, and he could make out the words *wake* and *love*. Did the voice belong to his mom? It didn't sound like her, but nothing seemed normal in the underwater nightmare he found himself in. One minute, he felt anchored to the sea floor; the next, he was floating to the surface, still unable to move, but lighter, as if being lifted.

He imagined a beautiful mermaid swimming him up toward the sunlight. Moments later, they were on the shore, his body sprawled on the warm sand. Her seashell top disintegrated, exposing her bare breasts as she leaned over him… because why not? This was his fantasy.

She pressed her lips against his, and a twitch between his legs told him at least one muscle still worked. He couldn't kiss her back, as much as he tried, but he felt warmth where he'd once been cold. And he could feel his hand being squeezed… so intensely it almost hurt.

Wait. This wasn't part of his fantasy. Someone, or something, was latched onto his hand. His eyelids sprang open. And then he saw her.

"Ariel?" he rasped.

His throat seemed to be coated in sand, reinforcing his beach theory. Had he almost drowned?

"You're awake! It's Noelle. I'm here," the beautiful woman said in the same enchanting voice he'd heard earlier, now above water.

As his eyes adjusted to the brightness surrounding her, the soft edges of her face came into focus. And wow, her voice hadn't done her beauty justice. She had plump lips, smooth skin, and those eyes… unnaturally green and sparkling.

"Are you a mermaid?" he asked. "Did you save me?"

Her brow creased, and she reached over him. "I'm just gonna…" She repeatedly pressed a button, and he noticed her sweater. *Why would a mermaid be wearing a sweater?*

He looked around the room, taking in large pieces of equipment, including the bed he was in. Panic officially set in. "Where am I? Where's my mom?"

A short dude in pink rushed into the room.

"Get the doctor. He's awake and confused," the beautiful woman said to the dude, who then turned and left as quickly as he'd came.

The merwoman squeezed his hand again, more gently this time. "It's going to be okay. You're going to be okay."

Moments later, another beautiful woman with darker skin and hair walked in. She looked like a Victoria's Secret runway model but wore hospital scrubs.

"Hi, I'm Doctor Sharma. How are you feeling today?"

Kent lay there, unsure how to answer. Had he landed in some alternate universe where a bunch of hot chicks attended to his needs?

"Can you tell me your full name?" the doctor asked.

He hesitated for a second, then replied, "Kent Franklin Clark."

The hottie sitting next to him sucked in a breath. When he and the doctor both looked at her, she added, "Sorry, go on."

"Very good, Kent," the doctor said. "Do you know where you are?"

"Hospital, I assume, but I don't know how I got here."

"That's okay. Do you know what day it is?"

He tried to shake his head, but it was excruciating. "Not exactly. Sometime in late May, I think. Did I get hit with a baseball or something? My head hurts."

The hot doctor looked at the gorgeous chick sitting next to him again. "Do you know this woman?" she asked.

He strained to study the human he once believed to be a mermaid. Reddish-brown waves framed the most beautiful face he'd ever seen. The tips of her hair faded into the color of seaweed, and he again wondered if she were a mythical creature as her glistening green eyes—mesmerizing enough to sink a battleship—bore into him.

"I don't think so. I assumed maybe she saved me. Can someone please tell me what's going on?"

"You slipped on ice and hit your head," the doctor said. "It's normal to have some lapses in memory. Can you tell me the last thing you remember?"

"I slipped on ice?" he repeated in disbelief. "In San Diego?"

"You're not in San Diego, Kent. You're in Holiday Pines. Do you know where Holiday Pines is?"

The doctor's nonsensical question grated his patience. "No, I don't know where Holiday Pines is. What the heck is going on? How did I get here, and where are my mom and brother?"

The woman in the chair beside him tapped buttons on what appeared to be a fancy calculator. When she looked up at him, her eyes glistened with tears. "Carole and Brad can't be here right now, Kent, but they'll come as soon as possible. I'm Noelle. You don't remember me?"

Kent stared at her, certain they'd never met before. He wanted to ask how she knew his mom's and brother's names, but his desire to avoid making her cry again outweighed his curiosity. "I'm sorry," he mumbled.

"It's okay, Kent," the doctor said. "Please tell us the last thing you remember before you woke up here."

It hurt to even think, but he racked his brain. "I was with my mom and brother in the car. Brad was driving." The machine next to him beeped, his heart rate skyrocketing as everything went blank after that memory. "Did we get into a car accident? Are they hurt?"

The doctor and the woman calling herself Noelle exchanged worried glances.

"Where are they?" he cried, adrenaline allowing him to lift his body up several inches before it collapsed back onto the bed.

"Your family is fine," the doctor said. "There wasn't a car accident. You slipped on ice, remember?"

But he didn't remember. He had no recollection of anything they were claiming happened. Hot or not, these women were strangers, and he was in a strange place. All he wanted was his mom, but since crying for her like a five-year-old felt out of the question, he buried the feeling and nodded as much as his aching head would allow.

"Do you remember anything after riding in the car?" the doctor asked, continuing her interrogation. "Do you know where you were headed?"

"Yeah. My brother was driving us to his girlfriend's house. Her parents invited our whole family over for dinner so we could meet, because Brad and Jess are getting pretty serious. I think Brad might propose soon." At least he still remembered his family.

Noelle looked at the doctor and whispered something he couldn't hear.

"Can you tell me your age, Kent?" the doctor asked, as if he were three and would need to hold up his fingers to say, *I'm this many.*

Despite the pain it inflicted, he rolled his eyes. "Seventeen. I'll be a senior in the fall. You don't have to treat me like I'm a little kid."

An empty shell of Noelle's body followed Doctor Sharma into the hall at the neurosurgeon's request. She'd been transported out of her *Grey's Anatomy* episode and straight into one of the poorly scripted telenovelas that her Tia Rosa loved so much. This couldn't be happening.

"Reverting to youth is rare with retrograde amnesia, but it does happen. Do you recall the event he last remembers?" Doctor Sharma asked.

Noelle slowly nodded, the word *amnesia* echoing in her head. "It was the day we first met. But that was over fifteen years ago."

"The point of memory lapse is usually significant. Often, it's right before the injury, but it could also be the last time he felt safe or a pivotal life moment. Since you're his fiancée, it makes sense he'd remember the first time you met."

Noelle continued nodding, sick to her stomach. She wasn't Kent's fiancée, nor did he remember actually meeting her. When faced with two alternatives, his brain had protected him by assuming he'd gotten into a car accident on the way over to her house. The last time Kent had felt safe was apparently *before* he'd met her. His words as Joe hit with new meaning: *It's as painfully simple and complex as that.*

"I'm going to order an MRI now that he's awake," Doctor Sharma continued. "Retrograde amnesia often self-resolves, but it helps if a loved one can fill in the gaps sooner. When we go back in there, I'd like you to explain your relationship to the patient, how much time has passed, and any other important events from the last fifteen years. It'll be hard for him to hear at first, but I promise it will help his healing process. Do you think you can do that?"

Um, no. How could she lie to a man who she'd already done more than enough to hurt?

"I need to make a phone call," she said instead, delaying the inevitable.

"No problem. We'll take Mister Clark for his scan now, and you can talk to him when you're ready."

Once Doctor Sharma disappeared behind the nurse's station, Noelle slumped against the wall. She had finally embraced her feelings for Kent, only to discover he subconsciously wished he'd never met her. If she didn't already feel like death, she could've curled into a ball and died.

Cowardly as it was, she waited until the nurses wheeled Kent down a different hallway before making her way back to his room. Floral arrangements flanked the empty hospital bed, causing her to double-check that she indeed had the correct room. Had those been there all along?

When she walked over to where she'd left her phone, two missed calls and multiple texts from Jess greeted her on the screen, the last of which read, "Call me!"

At least the excuse she'd given Doctor Sharma hadn't been a total lie.

"Hey, what's up?" she asked once Jess answered.

"Brad is on his way up to Holiday Pines, FYI, and I'm at the hospital with Carole, who is freaking out about Kent," Jess said. "We told her what happened as soon as you texted me that he was awake. Thank the Lord for that! How's he doing?"

"Um. He's technically okay, but he's suffered some memory loss."

"What do you mean by memory loss? Is it like in the movies? Does he not remember who he is?" Her sister's voice escalated with each question.

"He remembers who he is… but he thinks he's seventeen. He doesn't remember me, or Holiday Pines, or anything that's happened in the last fifteen years."

"Are you serious?"

"No, Jess. I thought this would be an appropriate time to make a joke." When her sister didn't respond, Noelle gritted her teeth and continued. "Yes, I'm serious. And before he gets back from his scan, there's something you should know. Everyone at the hospital thinks I'm his fiancée," she whispered, glancing at the open door.

Jess did the opposite of whispering. "What? Why would they think that?"

Noelle held her ear away from the receiver, lowering her voice once more. "I told the paramedic I was, so I could ride in the ambulance, and then I kind of let it run forward since only family members are allowed to visit."

"Oh my!" Jess said, sounding amused. "I'll be sure to let Brad know before he gets there so he doesn't blow your cover."

"Thanks, but that's the least of my worries right now." Noelle walked over and closed the door to ensure privacy. "Kent will be back with his doctor any minute, and she wants me to tell him about our *relationship* and to help fill in the last fifteen years for him. I'm freaking out! What do I do? Do I come clean, or do I tell Kent I'm his fiancée?"

Braying laughter, complete with a snort, erupted from the other end of the line.

"This is not funny, Jess! I'm thinking I should tell the truth, but I'm worried they'll kick me out, not to mention the scandal it'll become in such a small town. My friend Sandy already heard the fake news, so half the town probably has, too."

At the thought, Noelle walked over to the table lined with flowers and read a few of the cards:

```
All of us at Screw It are rooting for your
fiancé. -Earl

So sorry about your fiancé! Hang in there. -Your
friends at Main Street Fashions

Black ice is the worst. Hope your fiancé
recovers well. -Mack, Mack's Heating and
Plumbing
```

"Correction, they definitely heard and have sent flowers. Everyone is rooting for my fiancé."

"Well, you wanted your small-town life to play out like a rom-com," Jess said, still laughing, "and now you have a fake fiancé with amnesia. It's very *While You Were Sleeping*."

Noelle groaned, both loving and hating that. "Except I'm not secretly in love with Kent's brother," she corrected.

Just secretly in love with Kent himself, the voice of Jiminy Grinch returned.

A knock on the door proceeded the man in question being wheeled in.

"Kent's back. I gotta go," Noelle said into the phone, silently adding *thanks for nothing* as she hung up. She then paced the room as the nurse helped Kent back into bed. "Will Doctor Sharma be back soon as well? And I'm sorry... I never caught your name."

"I'm Javier," the nurse said. "Doctor Sharma had to check on a few other patients, but she said his scans looked good, and she'll be back shortly."

Noelle thanked Javier, waited for him to leave, then continued pacing while admiring the flowers to avoid eye contact with seventeen-year-old Kent.

"Do I have amnesia or something?" he asked, as simply as one might ask whether their shoes matched their outfit.

She pulled the chair closer to the bed and sat, afraid she might pace herself into the ground otherwise. "It seems so. Why? Are more memories coming back?"

Hope flooded her chest until Kent said, "No, but I overheard a nurse say my age is thirty-two, and she called you my fiancée."

Noelle reached for his hand. "About that—"

"Kenny! I'm sorry it took me so long to get here," Brad said, barreling into the room.

Kent's eyes widened. "Dad?"

"What? No, I'm not—"

"Brad, did Jess get ahold of you on your drive here?" Noelle interrupted.

"No. I didn't have reception on the pass and haven't checked my phone since I got here. Why? Is there an update on our mom?"

"Brad? You're so old," Kent muttered. "It must be true."

"What's true? What's going on?" Brad asked.

"Maybe we should speak outside for a minute," she suggested.

"No need. I can help explain," Doctor Sharma said, walking past them to stand by Kent's bedside. "You must be Kent's brother. I'm Doctor Sharma, Head of Neuro here at Holiday Pines Hospital."

Brad shook the hand she offered, looking very much transfixed by the runway surgeon's beauty. "Hi, Doctor. Good to see my little brother is in excellent hands. I'm Brad."

"He's not as little as he thinks," Noelle mumbled under her breath.

The neurosurgeon kept her eyes on Brad as she said, "Kent, you have mild cerebral edema, which is—"

"Slight swelling in the brain caused by an excess accumulation of fluid," Encyclopedia Kent finished. *At least some things hadn't changed.*

"Yes, very good," Doctor Sharma said.

"Sorry, my brother's a bit of a know-it-all." Brad flashed a toothy smile, which—if Noelle didn't know better—would have been charming. *Gross.*

"You don't seem to have any deficits in intellectual processing," Doctor Sharma said to Kent. "You are, however, experiencing what we call retrograde amnesia."

Kent nodded and then winced.

Concern filled the empty pit in Noelle's stomach. "Are you in pain?"

"It hurts when I move my head," Kent confirmed.

Noelle turned to the doctor. "Is that normal?"

"Wait. My brother has amnesia?" Brad asked at the same time.

"Yes, and yes," the doctor replied, before returning her attention to the patient. "Kent, can you please tell us again the last thing you remember before waking up in the hospital, especially if there's anything new?"

"Um, nothing new. Like I said, I was in the car with my mom and brother. Brad was driving us to meet his girlfriend's family at their house for dinner." Kent's dark-blue eyes darted to Brad. "Hey, did you ever propose to Jessica?"

Brad stumbled back a step. "Uh, yeah, bro. Jess and I got married a long time ago. You were my best man. But we're getting divorced now," he added, looking at Doctor Sharma. *Hitting on his injured brother's doctor, really?*

"They also have two kids," Noelle added for Kent's benefit. "Our niece Chloe, who's five, and our nephew Lucas, who's eight."

Kent furrowed his brow. "Our?"

"Jess is my sister. Sorry, I don't think I said my last name before. I'm Noelle Serrano."

"Noelle Serrano. Noelle Serrano," Kent repeated, staring toward the foot of the bed. After a moment, he looked up at her. "I remember the dinner now! Your mom made chicken tortilla soup and rice pudding for dessert."

"Yes!" Noelle cheered.

She remembered that dinner well. Kent had been cute—in a teenage heartthrob before the makeover type of way—with his thick-rimmed glasses and lengthy limbs. At three years her senior, his voice had been deeper than those of the boys in middle school, and he'd seemed even more mature than Brad. (Another thing that never changed.) But Kent had hardly made eye contact with her that night, and that trend had continued when she'd started high school in the fall.

"Wait. I'm still confused," Brad said.

"Kent's last memory is from when he was seventeen," Noelle explained.

"But him recalling a later memory is promising," Doctor Sharma added. "I'll have the results of your MRI in a few hours, Kent. In the meantime, your loved ones can help you fill in the missing pieces while your brain continues to heal. I'm going to leave you with your brother and Noelle for now. Ask them whatever questions you may have about your life and see if anything sparks more memories. I'll be back in a little while to check on you."

Doctor Sharma left, and Noelle, Kent, and Brad all exchanged uncomfortable glances. The steady *tick, tick, tick* of a wall clock filled the room.

Finally, Kent spoke. "Do either of you have a mirror?"

"I do," Noelle said, reaching for the purse she soon realized she didn't have. She'd jumped into the ambulance with nothing more than her phone and the keys in her hand. "Actually, I don't, but I'm sure I can find you one. Do you mind coming with me for a second, Brad?"

The pungent odor of disinfectant assaulted Noelle's nose as she closed the bathroom door behind them. She then spilled the tea in one long exhale, explaining her predicament for the second time in the last hour.

"Obviously, I need to clear up the truth for him," she added at the end.

"Maybe not," Brad said, using the same tone a villain stroking his jaw might.

"What do you mean, *maybe not?* I can't lie to him."

Brad held up his hands. "Hear me out. Kent doesn't remember that he gave up his dreams by dropping out of Stanford when our mom got sick, or that she's been battling cancer for almost a decade."

Kent gave up his dreams? What dreams?

"I'll also have to let him know our mom is back in the hospital at some point," Brad continued. "There's about to be a lot of bad news flying at him, but maybe him thinking you two are engaged can be a bright spot for a little while."

"How is having a fake fiancée he hardly remembers a bright spot?" she asked, still trying to wrap her mind around the mystery dreams he'd given up when Carole got sick.

"Because it's you, and I know my brother. He's been crazy about you ever since that first dinner. He wouldn't shut up about you the whole ride home. Noelle's so pretty. Noelle's so clever. Noelle, Noelle, Noelle. I told him you were way too young for him and to not even think about it. But once you both grew up, I could tell he had it bad."

"I… He…"

Brad crossed his arms. "Don't act like you didn't know. I've seen the way you've toyed with his emotions over the years. I told him again and again to move on, but he wouldn't listen. Please, just let him think he got one thing he wanted in his life, at least for a little while."

Noelle opened her mouth, but zero words of protest came out. *I've been in love with the same girl/woman for as long as I can remember.* The "for as long as I can remember" part felt like a cruel joke now. Brad was right. This was the least she owed Kent.

"Fine. Let's go, fake future-brother-in-law who's also my soon-to-be ex-brother-in-law."

The telenovelas couldn't beat that if they tried.

26

"How's your burger?" Noelle asked Kent, pushing soggy lettuce around on her plate.

"It's not In-N-Out, but it's good. I'm just happy to be out of the hospital," Kent said, taking another bite.

Doctor Sharma had released him after reviewing his MRI results. She'd said the swelling had gone down and that everything seemed fine—everything except the minor detail of Kent still not remembering the last fifteen years. Being back in his usual routine was supposed to help with that.

"Yeah, sorry, Holiday Pines doesn't have any fast-food chains." *How had she not realized that before?*

"And people can live like that?" Kent asked.

"I guess so. There's a bigger town with chain restaurants and big-box stores about thirty minutes away, though. It's not the total boondocks here," she said, more to reassure herself.

Life in Holiday Pines was far from Kent's normal routine. She'd tried to make Brad see that, but he'd insisted Kent was better off staying with her, at least for a couple of days. Brad needed to get back to Carole in the hospital, a fact he neglected to share with Kent. As far as Kent knew, his mother hadn't come to visit him in the hospital because no one had wanted to worry her with the news of his accident. A partial truth that Kent accepted far too readily.

And it wasn't like Noelle could refuse to bring her fake fiancé home.

"The pie here is supposed to be a big deal," she said, giving up on her salad completely.

"I kinda figured, since the restaurant's called Holiday Pies."

She swiped a fry from his plate. "Funny. I guess you were a smart-ass even at seventeen." Kent's eyes grew wide, and she laughed. "Actually, I didn't know you very well back then. This is a nice opportunity to get to know teenage you."

"What do you want to know?" Kent asked.

"Hmm, let me think." Noelle stole another crispy piece of heaven and tapped it against her lips. "Ooh! Brad mentioned you have big dreams for what you want to do after Stanford. Why don't you tell me about them?"

"That's an easy one," he said. "I plan to get my PhD in Mathematics and stay in academia, most likely as a researcher, developing new principles and practical models. My mom thinks I should be a teacher, like her, but I'd much rather be the guy writing the textbooks, you know?"

Noelle hadn't known. Kent never obtained his PhD. Instead, he'd given up on his dream when his mom got sick and took a job he'd never wanted. No wonder Brad didn't want to tell him the truth.

"What else you got?" he asked, oblivious to her soul-crushing epiphany.

"Um… Why don't you like using your middle name, Franklin?"

Kent glanced around the dimly lit diner-slash-bakery before meeting her eyes. "I think it upsets my mom. So, I don't like to say it out loud, especially not around her." Her confusion must have shown, because Kent continued. "Franklin was my older brother who died before I was born."

Before Noelle could react, an older woman in an apron that read *Pie or Die* walked up with their orders.

"Apple pumpkin for you," she said, setting down a heaping slice in front of Noelle, "and classic apple à la mode for the handsome young man. Can I get you two anything else?"

"No, thank you," Kent said, the words more than Noelle could manage.

"How—how did I not know this before?" she finally asked, long after the thuds of the server walking away had faded.

"It's not something my family ever talks about. After my dad left us, we kind of stopped talking about... everything." Kent looked down at his plate, and Noelle caught a glimpse of a much younger boy, broken-hearted but forced to put on a brave face.

"I understand if you don't want to talk about it, but I'd love to hear more, if you don't mind."

Kent shoveled a proportionate amount of pie and ice cream onto his spoon. "I don't mind. It's harder *not* to talk about it, to be honest. At home—or when I used to live at home, I guess—it felt like walking on eggshells most days. I was always worried I'd mess up and say something that would make my mom cry, which was the last thing I wanted."

His words squeezed both halves of her broken heart. Telling Kent he technically still lived with his mom was a discussion for a later time, but it made Noelle wonder. Did he still have to tread carefully all these years later?

"Anyway, my parents both took Franklin's death pretty hard," Kent continued. "He was born with a rare condition and needed a bunch of surgeries as a baby. Before he was born, the doctors had told my parents he wouldn't survive, but my dad had been convinced they were wrong. So, they put Franklin through surgery after surgery, racking up medical bills along the way. And then, a month after he was born, he died on Christmas Day."

Noelle gasped. "I'm so sorry. That's awful."

"Needless to say, the holidays weren't a fun time in our household," he said. "I came along a little over a year later. *The replacement kid.* Since Franklin was my middle name, I thought that meant it was my job to help them remember him."

Kent paused to take another bite of his pie, his demeanor surprisingly stoic. Had suppressing his feelings been another way he'd learned to walk on eggshells? To avoid staring at him with what would surely come through as pity, Noelle took her first bite of the town's claim to fame.

What followed was otherworldly. The delicious combination of crisp apples, sweet pumpkin filling, and cinnamon-crumb goodness tasted like sunshine on a cool autumn day. Pleasure permeated her senses, and before she could stop it, a sensual groan ripped through the crowded—but suddenly quiet—diner. Several patrons craned their necks at her, one holding his fork midair.

"Great pie," Noelle said to them all, before returning her attention to Kent, whose gaze dropped to her mouth. She wiped at its corners, in case of residual pie crumbs, then straightened in her seat. "Sorry about that, but this pie might be the best thing I've ever put in my mouth."

A slow grin spread across Kent's face.

"I meant food, the best food. Not that I'm in the habit of putting non-food... You know what?" She swiped at the air to erase the last sixty seconds. "Wait. Do you remember?"

"Do I remember what?" His grin grew into a teasing smile.

"Don't mess with me, Kent. Have your memories returned?"

"No, I still don't remember anything after meeting you at your parents' house. But since we're engaged, I assume that means we've done *stuff*. Trust me, I wish I could remember."

Thoughts of the *stuff* caused her to squirm in her seat. "Actually, we're saving ourselves for marriage, so there's no *stuff* to remember," she lied.

They were definitely not talking about anything even tangent to sex until he remembered being at least old enough to vote. Old enough to qualify for the U.S. Senate would be ideal.

The grin fell flat off his face. "Are you serious?"

"Yes, so please get your dirty teenage mind out of the gutter."

"Man, I thought I grew up and suddenly had game. Turns out, not too much has changed." Kent touched the sides of his face. "At least I don't wear nerdy glasses anymore."

"I hadn't noticed they were missing, but yes, you still wear glasses. And they're not nerdy. They look good on you. The ones you were wearing must've gotten lost when you… fell." She pushed away the painful image of Kent lying unconscious on the road. It made her want to wrap her arms around him and never let go, but she couldn't yet. Not when she was hardly more than a stranger to him. "Hey, does that mean you can't see right now? How many fingers am I holding up?"

"Three," he answered correctly. "I can still see. I just can't read things that are far away, and I get a headache if I watch TV for too long without them. Things like that."

"Interesting," she said, drawing out each syllable. "I'm learning so much about you tonight. Speaking of which, I'm sorry for interrupting the story of your childhood. Please, continue."

Kent took a sip of the root beer he'd ordered, then said, "It's kind of ironic that I don't remember the last fifteen years. I think I would've rather forgotten the first fifteen."

"I'm so sorry, Kent." She reached across the table and squeezed his hand.

He shrugged, but his apathetic façade cracked. "The earliest memory I have is of Brad and our father picking me up from preschool one day. Brad was around seven at the time, so I have no idea why he wasn't at school himself, but they'd spent the day fishing together and reeked of it. It was almost Thanksgiving, and I'd made one of those turkey drawings, where you trace your hand on the paper." He held up his palm at a sideways angle to demonstrate.

"As we all have," she said in solidarity.

"Yeah, well, per my teacher's instructions, I'd labeled each family member. Mom was the head, or thumb. Then, on the four fingers, I wrote: Dad, Brad, Franklin, and Kent. My dad ripped the artwork out of my hand and tore it up the second he saw it. He made me promise to never show such a thing to my mom. He said it would make her cry and that I should be ashamed of myself. I was only four, so I didn't understand what I'd done wrong. I thought maybe the drawing was bad, but Brad later explained it was because Franklin was on there.

"So, after that, I never said or wrote his name on anything again, especially if there was a chance my parents might see it. I don't understand why they named me after Franklin if his name upsets them, but not saying it for all these years kind of feels wrong, like I've erased the memory of him." Kent let out a mirthless laugh and stabbed his spoon into the pie. "Like I said, ironic."

"Kent, that's so…" The words eluded her.

He shrugged again. "Enough about me. Tell me something I should know about you, or would know, if I remembered."

Noelle took a deep breath, grateful she'd delayed bringing him back to her place. "Well, since the holidays are understandably not your favorite time of year, you should probably know that I run a year-round Christmas store called Merry Holidays. And I'm temporarily living in a loft above the store. There's only one bed, but—" She held up a finger at the return of his smirk. "I have an air mattress you can sleep on tonight."

Kent's shoulders deflated. "Figures. I still can't believe a nerd like me scored the most amazing chick on the planet. How did we get together?"

His words shook her like a snow globe, rendering her speechless until the glitter settled. "I'm not… and you're not… Why do you keep calling yourself a nerd?"

"Uh, because I am. I spend my weekends at Mathlete tournaments, or I did."

"That's because you're a freaking genius, Kent. You took an IQ test after high school that proved it. Plus, you weren't just a Mathlete… You played baseball, too," she offered, hoping to boost his depressingly low self-esteem.

"I only joined baseball because I was sick of getting beat up, and Brad said playing sports was the best way." Kent looked down at his pie again. "So, you started dating me because of baseball?"

"No. We didn't date in high school. You wouldn't even look at me." Noelle bit down on her trembling lip, hoping he hadn't noticed.

As much as she wanted Kent to regain his memory, she was equally grateful that he'd forgotten what he'd thought of her back then.

They spent the rest of the meal sharing less painful childhood stories as Noelle devised a new plan: Operation Fresh Start.

The next few days consisted of board games, movies, and a lot more sharing. Noelle was surprised by how little she actually knew about Kent... or teenaged Kent, at least.

For instance, his favorite ice cream flavor was vanilla, and the chilly winter weather posed no deterrent to his consumption of it in heaping bowlfuls. His favorite number was two, due to it being the first prime number and the only even one. (Why that mattered was beyond her understanding, but she found it endearing.) And he was born left-handed, like his dad, but had taught himself to do everything with his right hand as a kid to avoid seeming different.

Noelle thought that last one might've also had something to do with Kent not wanting to be like the man who had deserted his entire family, but who was she to psychoanalyze him? It seemed Kent had been a stranger to her all along.

"Why vanilla?" she had asked one night, after he'd devoured nearly a quart of the bland ice cream during their viewing of *Die Hard* on her laptop.

Action movie for him. Christmas rom-com for her. Win-win.

"Why not?" he returned.

"Come on. There are *so* many flavors. Rocky road, mint chip, black cherry, strawberry, chocolate, cookies and cream, butter pecan, pistachio, peanut butter cup, chocolate chip cookie dough,

Neapolitan… I could go on and on. How can vanilla be your absolute favorite?"

In what was becoming his signature move, Grown-Teen Kent shrugged. "Vanilla is a lot of people's favorite. It goes with everything, tastes delicious, and if it gets boring, that's what toppings are for."

He had her there. Wasn't that one of her long-held tenets of fashion? Find a versatile item to mix and match, then add accessories. Vanilla was his cozy white sweater.

"Okay. What's your favorite topping, then?"

"Probably cinnamon," he said without hesitation.

She hadn't been expecting that. Sprinkles or hot fudge, sure. Peanuts, maybe. But cinnamon?

"That's more of an ingredient than a topping."

Kent once again shrugged. "True, but I put it on top, then I swirl it around until the ice cream gets silky smooth, like soft serve." He paused, as if tasting it in his mind. "Yeah… the combination of vanilla and cinnamon is definitely my favorite."

The next night, Noelle joined Kent on their makeshift sofa of pillows on the ground with a giant bowl of vanilla ice cream and a bottle of cinnamon.

"Let's do this," she said, sprinkling a generous amount into her bowl and stirring. One bite of creamy, spicy sweetness later and she was a convert. "Mmm! Where in the holly has this been my whole life?"

Kent laughed. "Stick with me, kid, and I'll share all my secrets."

Though delivered in a lighthearted manner, his words evoked a heaviness that even Santa's sleigh couldn't lift. She wanted all of Kent's secrets and more. She wanted to 'stick with him' through naughty and nice, in sickness and in health, and never let go.

But Kent didn't remember all that she'd put him through. And even though he'd apparently been in love with her—for reasons that remained a mystery—she couldn't imagine him wanting to stick around once his memories came back.

Noelle cleared the lump forming in her throat. "What should we watch tonight? How about…" She scrolled through the options on her laptop until spotting one that felt destined for the moment.

"*How to Lose a Guy in 10 Days*?" she asked.

It could only help her case, right? Nothing she'd done to Kent had been nearly as diabolical as the tactics in that movie.

"Don't take this the wrong way," Kent said, "but I've sort of been wondering why you don't own a real TV… or a couch," he added, motioning to the pile of pillows beneath them—the only mildly comfortable seating arrangement available.

It was bad enough that the air mattress had gotten a leak after Kent's first night there, causing them to have to sleep in the same bed. She couldn't handle the idea of spending their waking hours there as well. Not when he was still mentally under the legal age of consent in California. And especially not when it was taking every ounce of her self-control to remind herself of that.

"Well, I *sort of* need this store to start making money before I can afford such luxuries." Laughing off her embarrassing confession, she added, "Besides, this pillow fort is cool, right?"

"Very cool," Kent said with a warm smile. "So, is this where we'll both live, you know, once we're married?"

Noelle followed his gaze as it scanned her loft, which had enough room for her double bed, a tall dresser, the antique vanity she'd scored at a yard sale, several stacks of unpacked boxes, one awkward shower stall in the corner, and not much else.

"Uh…" The truth was on the tip of her tongue. Surely, Kent would understand her reason for lying about their fake engagement. But then Brad's annoying voice filled her head: Let him think he got *one* thing he wanted in his life. The heartbreaking sentiment of that statement had her instead saying, "I know this place is cozy, but it's only temporary."

"Until the store makes money," he said, restating her earlier admission.

"Yeah, that."

"So, let's get the store ready to reopen, then. I'd love to help."

"That's really sweet, but you're still recovering from a head injury, Kent. The store isn't my priority right now. You are."

"And you're mine," he said, his voice barely above a whisper. "I can't let you sacrifice your store's success because of me. Please, let me help."

Lightning gathered in his steely irises as he spoke, and she had to resist the urge to lean in. She could get lost forever in the storm clouds holding her gaze with such intense sincerity. And for perhaps the millionth time over the last seventy-two hours, Noelle wondered how she had never seen it before. The raw emotion that practically oozed out of this man, loving and kind.

"O—Okay," she stuttered. "We should probably go to bed, then. To sleep… since it'll be an early morning."

"Sounds good." Kent rose and offered his hand to help her off the floor. "Let's go to bed."

27

"Somewhere In My Memory"

John Williams

23 days until Christmas

Kent couldn't believe his luck, getting to spend quality time with Noelle without the overarching presence of her contempt. The past week had been amazing. They'd ran her store together, bonded over their shared love of Scrabble, eaten tons of pie with cinnamon ice cream, and traded childhood stories—like the time six-year-old Noelle had been dared to kiss a frog.

Even at that age, she'd been unwilling to back down from a challenge.

"Well, how was your first kiss?" he'd asked.

"Slimy… and disappointing," she'd said.

"Disappointing?"

"Yeah, I'd secretly hoped the frog would transform into a prince."

They'd both laughed over that, but it had also given him an idea. One he'd been waiting for the right moment to act on.

"Hey, good morning." Noelle gazed up at him with sleepy eyes. *Damn, she was beautiful.*

Her head rested near his shoulder, while her hand gripped his forearm like a security blanket. Fortunately for him, the air mattress had deflated after the first night, and there was no logical reason why two engaged people couldn't share a bed.

"Good morning to you, too. How'd you sleep?" he asked, as if he hadn't spent the last ten hours admiring her peaceful slumber.

Once his memories had trickled back, Kent couldn't fathom wasting a single second on sleep. He'd much preferred absorbing Noelle—the rise and fall of her chest, the curve of her face, the soft sound of her breath. He was a sponge that couldn't get enough.

"Too long, I think. It's already bright in here," she said, reaching for her phone on the nightstand. "We need to get ready to open the store."

Noelle and her comforting warmth left the bed, leaving Kent desperate to test his theory. "I've been thinking, since you're my fiancée and all—"

"Stop right there." Noelle held out a palm. "I'm not going anywhere near that thing until you remember being an adult."

Kent followed her gaze down to the tent he was pitching under the comforter. All the blood not otherwise occupied *there* shot to his cheeks as Noelle giggled into her hands.

"Can we be mature about this, please?" he asked, his hand instinctively moving to cover his morning wood.

"Mature? You're the one still mentally stuck in high school."

Noelle was right. He needed to act like a seventeen-year-old boy. A horny seventeen-year-old virgin, in his case. This felt like the fresh start he'd wished for before slipping on that ice. He wasn't about to ruin it by letting on that his memory had returned. Not yet, at least.

He removed his hand and let his eyes drop to Noelle's ample chest, covered only by a thin cotton top. Her arms had returned to her sides and *the girls*, as she called them, were on full display.

"You're not wearing a bra," he said, allowing himself full immaturity rights.

"Most women don't sleep in one," she said, crossing her arms to cover herself. "They're about as comfortable as a jockstrap, I assume."

Kent held up his hands in mock surrender. "I'm not complaining. In fact, I don't think you should ever wear a bra."

"Yeah, but then I'd have pervs like you staring at them all day." Flashing him her signature smirk, Noelle snatched a pillow off the bed and tossed it on his lap. "You might want to take care of that, by the way. The bathroom is downstairs."

His earlier embarrassment rushed back. Pretending to be an awkward teenage boy proved not to be much of a stretch for him.

Noelle grabbed an oversized sweatshirt off a clothing rack and pulled it over her head. It had a black-and-white sketch of Belle from *Beauty and the Beast*, surrounded by cartoon dogs and cats, and a caption that read: Read a book. Save a beast.

Kent recognized it as the sweatshirt she'd worn when they'd both volunteered for the same rescue event at the animal shelter several years prior.

"You still haven't heard my idea," he said, a second before his brain finally caught up with the conversation. "Wait a minute…"

"What?" she asked.

"You said you weren't going near this thing *until I remember being an adult*. Does that mean you would if I had my memory back?" He couldn't help the boyish grin that tugged on his lips.

"That's not what I… I wasn't saying… I already told you we're saving ourselves for marriage," she huffed, obviously flustered.

Empowered by the reddening of her cheeks, Kent rolled out of bed in the men's Christmas pajamas Noelle had given him to wear. "I'm just messing with you. Do you want to hear my actual idea?"

"Sure. Whatever. And you can keep those, by the way," she said, pointing at his borrowed red-and-black flannel bottoms while looking everywhere but at him.

He'd gone commando because of his lack of clean underwear and had to admit it felt a bit scandalous, especially since Noelle had purchased the pajamas as a gift for her father. *Sorry, Mr. Serrano.*

"I'll replace them," he said, acutely aware of the soft fabric's caress against his bare flesh. "Back to my idea…" With two careful steps, Kent closed the distance between them. "I think we should kiss."

"What? Why?" Noelle asked, eyes wide.

"Well, we're engaged, right?"

"Right," she said, dropping her voice along with her gaze.

Kent clamped his lips together to stifle a smile. Even though he wouldn't mind if she held to that story until death do them part, he found it comforting that Noelle couldn't seem to lie to his face.

"So, that means we're in love," he continued. "And if anything can bring my memories back, wouldn't it be true love's kiss?"

Noelle's narrowed eyes returned to his. "You believe in things like true love's kiss?"

"All the Disney movies can't be wrong," he quipped, motioning to the example on her sweatshirt.

"First off, you're not cursed. You have amnesia," she said, her hands moving to those curvy hips of hers. *If she only knew.* Not remembering Noelle was far worse than any curse imaginable. "Secondly, have you even seen a Disney movie?" she asked.

"Of course I have. Until Brad and I were teenagers, Disney movies were the only ones our mom allowed in our house."

Noelle threw her head back. "Oh Saint Nick, that's right! Brad mentioned that a long time ago. He also said *The Little Mermaid* was your all-time favorite."

"Yeah, well, Brad was a bedwetter through middle school." If Kent was going down, he was taking his big-mouthed brother with him.

"That explains so much! Not about Brad, although I'm totally going to find an opportunity to use that against him, but about you!

When you first woke up in the hospital, you asked me if I was a mermaid."

"I did?" Maybe his memory wasn't as fully restored as he'd thought.

"Yeah, I think you mumbled 'Ariel' first, but it didn't make any sense at the time." Noelle looked down at her empty hands, her tone going flat as her eyes grew watery. "I was just grateful to hear your voice. At one point, I didn't think you'd ever wake up."

Kent brushed aside the solitary tear that ran down her face. "It's okay. I'm okay now."

"How are you okay, Kent? You can't remember the last fifteen years!" Noelle's voice broke, splitting Kent's heart right along with it.

He knew he should ease her worry by telling her his memories had returned. But if he did, would she still allow him in her life? Their charade of being engaged would end, and then what? As selfish as it was, he couldn't lose her yet.

Rather than lying, Kent did the only thing he could think of. The only thing he wanted with both halves of his broken heart. He kissed her.

Noelle had forgotten how good they were together. How effortless. How perfect. She melted into their kiss like a snowman on a hot summer day. *Some people really were worth melting for.*

Great. Now she had Disney references on the brain.

As his tongue parted her lips, it was a wonder her brain could function at all. Luckily for her, there was no thinking required, no worrying about technique or intensity. Like a dancer to music, her whole body responded to his touch, her mouth moving in harmony with his as if being led through a well-rehearsed routine.

Savoring their long-overdue contact, Noelle weaved her fingers through his hair. She'd wanted to kiss him as soon as he'd opened his eyes in the hospital. She'd also planned to tell him how much he meant to her and that the past was the past. But then Kent hadn't remembered her. His genius brain, knowing best, had protected him from the trauma of ever loving her.

She pulled back from the kiss. "This is wrong."

"What's wrong?" Kent asked, reaching for her.

"Everything," she said. "Everything is wrong. For starters, I lied. I'm not your fiancée."

"I know."

"And I know I owe you an explanation, but... Wait, *you know*?"

Kent fidgeted with the hem of his shirt, waiting a beat before saying, "I remember."

"Really? That's amazing!" Noelle couldn't keep the excitement from her voice if she tried. *True love's kiss had worked.* "Why don't you seem happier?"

As soon as she voiced the question, icy fear replaced her bliss. Was Kent upset now that he remembered her harsh words? Or worse, had their last argument reminded him that he belonged with someone of his own caliber?

Noelle gasped when his guilt-ridden expression presented yet another possibility. "Oh, seasick crocodile! Have you been faking it this entire time?"

"No, I swear! In the beginning, I didn't remember anything. But a few days ago, my memories all started coming back, little by little."

"A few *days* ago?" she exclaimed, unsure how to feel. Angry that he'd kept the truth from her? Or relieved that he'd gotten his memory back and had still wanted to kiss her?

"I'm sorry. I should've told you right away, and it was wrong to kiss you under false pretenses. It's just..." Kent moved closer, and the heat of his body sent an ache through her core that pushed any anger she might've clutched onto out of her grasp. "Once I remembered how I'd hurt you, I couldn't bear the thought of losing you again. I know it's not a great excuse, but we've been getting along so well, and—"

Noelle cut him off by resuming their interrupted kiss. Relief had won out. True love's kiss or not, she loved the man in front of her. And with his memory restored, Kent Full-Grown Clark was, in fact, *a man* again.

Her palms itched to feel his skin against hers as she clawed at his shirt. She'd deal with his deceit later, well-intentioned as it was. Right now, they had some lost time to make up for.

"Wait," he said, catching her by the wrists. "There's something that's been bothering me."

Oh no, here it came. Noelle closed her eyes. She should've known there would be repercussions for how poorly she'd treated him.

"Before my fall, you called your body your best attribute and declared your heart off-limits to me."

"Kent, we don't have to—"

"Please, I need to get this out," he said. "Your body, while incredible, is *not* your best attribute, Noelle. Your heart is, and you have no idea how badly I want it. Even a fraction would do. Plus, you have a plethora of other qualities that are more impressive than your looks. Your courage, creativity, and sharp wit, for starters. Then there's the fact that you excel at everything you do, because you're absolutely brilliant, Gingerbread. You always have been."

Noelle blinked up at him, unsure if she'd heard all of that correctly. *Kent thought she was brilliant?* "But what you said to Kyle—"

"Was bullshit," he cut in. "When Kyle told me he wanted to ask you out, I panicked. I know it was selfish and wrong of me to interfere, but I couldn't handle the thought of you two together. Kyle was my best friend, so if he dated you, I figured I never could. Plus, Kyle was… commitment adverse. I knew you'd be crushed when he left for college and didn't look back."

Her mouth fell open, but his revelation had her speechless. *All this time...*

"I should have explained all of this before," Kent continued. "Brad had made it painfully clear that, as his girlfriend's much younger sister, you were off-limits to me in high school. That's why I couldn't even look at you back then, because whenever I did, I felt things I knew I shouldn't. So, I did my best to ignore you, impossible as it was. But then..."

"I saw you sharing your sandwich with that kid, Marcus, whose family was too poor to send him to school with lunch money, and I fell hopelessly in love with your beautiful heart. I couldn't help it. It's not an excuse for what I did, and I don't know if you'll ever be able to forgive me. All I do know is, when Kyle asked me what I thought of you, I lied my ass off. I scrambled to think of the worst thing I could say, hoping he'd lose interest in asking you out, and I was relieved as hell when he did."

Kent laced his fingers with hers, slowly waking her from her shock-induced stupor. "But then last week, when you told me you'd overheard my horrible lies—and worse, actually believed them—I felt like the smallest person on Earth. Hurting you is the last thing I ever wanted to do, Noelle. I can't begin to express how sorry—"

"Shut up," Noelle interrupted, her eyes burning with tears. "Just shut up. You had me at bullshit."

Kent gaped at her. "Did you just *Jerry Maguire* me?"

"Yes. Yes, I did." She threw her arms around his neck and pulled him down until their foreheads rested against each other. "But if I'm being honest, you had me even sooner than that. I love you, Kent Franklin Clark, so, so much. You and your big, hard head."

After running the store all day together, they'd made a quick run to the general store for deli sandwiches and some more clothes for him—fresh boxers, gray jogger sweats, and a regrettable "Holiday Pines" hoodie that Noelle had insisted looked great on him.

"How do you always smell so good?" Kent asked into her cookie-scented hair when they returned to the Christmas shop that was quickly starting to feel like home.

Or maybe it was Noelle who'd become his home.

"How do you always say all the right things? Thanks again for your help with the store today."

She then rewarded him with a deep kiss, a wonderful contrast to the chaste ones they'd been sneaking in throughout the day. Was this really his life now? Kissing Noelle whenever he wanted?

He still couldn't believe it. Noelle loved him back. Her declaration had felt like closure and a new beginning all at once.

"Tell me again," he mumbled against her lips.

When her emerald eyes locked with his, the emotion behind them conveyed tender understanding. "I love you, Kent."

The absolute best four-word phrase.

And that fourth word mattered. Hearing his name from her sweet mouth did indescribable wonders to his body and soul. As he stared wordlessly into her eyes, he didn't need to speculate as to what Heaven might be like. He was already there.

Noelle made a loud "ahem" noise, then crossed her arms expectantly.

"What?" *Had he ruined things already?*

"Aren't you going to say it back?" she asked.

The breath he didn't realize he'd been holding released when she laughed. Whoa, that romantic cliché made total sense now.

"Say what back?" he teased, only because it felt so damn good to tease *her* for a change.

She pinched his forearm. "Don't make me hurt you."

"Violence is never the answer, Gingerbread. Besides, saying 'I love you' wouldn't be completely truthful."

Her playful expression fell, and all ability to jest left his body. Kent took both of her hands in his.

He'd never been more serious as he said, "Love isn't a strong enough emotion for what I feel for you, Noelle. Without you, I'm a fraction of myself. A tiny decimal, full of insignificant digits." He brushed his nose against hers. "You make me a whole number."

She pulled back, her face shining up at him brighter than the Christmas trees around them. "Who's Jerry Maguire now? You basically said 'you complete me' in math terms."

He laughed. "I guess I did. But you like rom-com references, so that's okay, right?"

"More than okay, and I especially love your cheesy twist on them," she said, beaming with joy so tangible it reverberated in his chest.

"In that case, I've got another one." He sucked in a breath for dramatic effect, then delivered the line he'd always hoped he'd one day be able to say to her. "I'm just a boy, about to kiss a girl, who should know she's my wholemate."

Noelle cocked her head. "Wholemate?"

"Good one, right?"

"Eh," she said, her smile betraying the indifference in her tone. "A little derivative, if you ask me."

Kent scoffed. "I'll show you derivative."

He then planted the aforementioned kiss, dipping her to lightly brush her lips with his before leaning into the gentle rhythm of their mouths. It was an unspoken love language, he realized, the way she seemed to soften at his touch, going molten in his arms.

She had an opposite but equally gratifying effect on him. His blood pulsed faster. His muscles grew stronger. He'd never felt more alive and powerful than he did with her heart beating in tandem with his. This was *love, finally*.

28

Merry vibe:

"You Make It Feel Like Christmas"

Gwen Stefani

22 days until Christmas

Intense gratitude mixed with pure bliss. For Noelle, that summed up being in love. The following evening, she had never felt more grateful and merry in her entire life. There had been a steady stream of customers all day, and she'd enjoyed every second of it with Kent by her side. She'd finally found *the one*, the person she could no longer imagine her life without, and he'd been in it all along.

"Two slices of apple à la mode for my favorite couple," their matronly server said, setting down the plates in front of them. Today's apron read: *In Pie We Crust*.

"Thank you, Greta," Noelle and Kent replied in unison before she thudded away.

Noelle smiled. She'd never been part of a couple before. She'd also never been a regular anywhere, but Greta had placed their pie orders from memory when they'd sat down at their usual table. It was a day of firsts. Kent had insisted on taking her out that evening for their "first real date" now that they were "officially together." His words.

"I totally blame you for getting me hooked on à la mode, by the way," Noelle said, digging into the creamy mound atop her pie. "I don't think I'll ever be able to eat pie plain again."

"You're welcome," Kent said, shoveling a spoonful into his mouth.

In an unexpected new first, Noelle found herself envious of an inanimate object as she watched the smooth metal of the spoon drag across his bottom lip. The slow and sensual movement as he pulled it out had her recalling everywhere those lips had been before… everywhere she wanted them that very minute.

Fearing she might get them banned from Holiday Pies if she acted on her desires, Noelle fanned herself then quickly took another bite of her cinnamon ice cream. She'd been starving after running the store all day, but with her belly now sated, her hunger for him only grew.

"I have a confession," they both said at the same time.

Noelle laughed. "Jinx. You go first."

"No, ladies first. I insist."

"Okay, well… I *may* have posted some shirtless photos of you fixing the shelving unit the other day to draw more customers into the store. But, in my defense, it worked."

Kent laughed that time, his cheeks turning an adorable shade of pink. "Not sure success counts as a defense, but I'm happy to have helped. That also explains some interesting looks I got in the store today."

"You're welcome," she said with a wink.

"My confession is bigger than that," Kent said, his tone turning alarmingly serious.

It was enough to cool her boiling loins… temporarily, at least. She took another bite and waited for him to continue.

"There's no subtle way to put this, but I can only hope you'll be happy rather than upset with me."

"Okay, now you're making me nervous," she said, gripping her spoon like a weapon.

"It's not bad… or I hope not, at least."

"Out with it, KFC."

"Okay, okay." Kent placed both of his palms on the Formica tabletop as if bracing for impact. "I'm Average Joe."

"Oh, that," she said, feeling all the tension in her shoulders instantly relax. "A notification on your phone already gave that little secret away when you were in the hospital."

Kent released the breath he'd clearly been holding. "So, you're not mad?"

"I probably should be, but no. How could I be mad at the Joe Fox to my Shop Girl?" When he blinked at her in obvious confusion, she added, "*You've Got Mail?*"

"I've got what?"

"Seriously? Well, I guess I know which movie we'll be watching later. The name Joe was a coincidence, then?"

"Um, apparently? *Average* Joe was a play on *Everyday* Merry. You're still not mad, though, right?" Kent asked, reaching across the table to take her hand.

He was cute when he was worried, but since it would be cruel to let those worries linger, she gave his hand a gentle squeeze. "Not mad, but I have questions. For starters, how did you even learn about the *Holiday Pines Connections* site?"

"Um… Jess told me."

"I should've figured! That meddling—"

"Your sister loves you, Noelle. She called me after you told her you set up a profile, and we both agreed it would be safer if you were talking to me, as Average Joe, rather than to some random stranger."

"That's worse than I thought!" Noelle said, pulling her hand away. "I assumed she was playing matchmaker. Instead, you two were joining forces to protect me from myself."

"It started that way, yes, but—"

"But what, Kent? You didn't think I was smart enough to stay away from online weirdos, so you stepped in to save the day?"

"No, it wasn't like that. Please…" He grabbed her hand again. "You're smart, Noelle."

"Kent, you don't have to—"

"You. Are. Smart. Period. I should've told you that a long time ago, because I've never thought otherwise. Not for a second. You know what else I've always admired about you?"

"My boobs?"

"Those for sure," he said, dropping his gaze with a smirk before resuming intense eye contact. "But also, your decisiveness. You get input when it makes sense, which is insanely smart, and then you make quick, educated decisions to move your plan forward. When you combine that with your determination and entrepreneurial spirit, you're an unstoppable force."

Holy holly. This man made it impossible to stay mad at him.

"Thank you for that," she said, eyes prickling with unshed tears, "but that still doesn't explain why you didn't trust me enough to protect myself online."

"I trusted you, Noelle. It's the amateur penis photographers of the world I didn't trust."

The snort-laugh that erupted had her covering her mouth. If she wasn't already head-over-kitten-heels in love with Kent, that might have clenched it.

"And it wasn't just your safety I was worried about," he continued. "I didn't want you to meet anyone else, because I wanted you for myself."

"Well, it's hard to argue with that." She laced her fingers with his, appreciating the warmth that spread throughout her entire body. "So, everything you said as Joe…"

"Was all true," he finished. "Besides the whole secret identity thing, I never lied to you; I swear. I always hoped you'd find out eventually and be happy it was me."

Noelle let out a wistful sigh. "Like the ending in *You've Got Mail*."

"Sure, like that," Kent said with a wink that cranked the heat back on.

"So, what you said about wanting a good story to tell our grandkids someday," she said, waggling her eyebrows. "Does that mean you want to have babies with me?"

"Gingerbread, you're the only person I'd ever want to make babies with." He squeezed her hand and grinned before adding, "We can get started whenever you want."

"Whenever I want?" she croaked, her mouth suddenly dry.

"Whenever you want," he repeated.

Her uterus would've skipped a beat if such a thing were possible. Leave it to the perfect man she'd stupidly resisted for so long to offer to impregnate her *whenever she wanted*.

"And you're being serious? You really want to start a family with me?" she asked, still in disbelief.

"Of course. What man wouldn't want to?"

Noelle could think of quite a few, but it didn't feel like the time to recount her dating history.

"I'm ready whenever you are," Kent confirmed.

"Wow, that's... comforting," she said, as a sensation a trillion times more soothing than the best hug washed over her. "I'm not sure if I'm ready yet, but it's good to know that we'll be on the same page once I am."

"And in the meantime..." Kent leaned forward with an arched brow that definitely did things to her lady parts. "We can still practice, right?"

Loins officially ablaze, she rubbed her boot up the inseam of his pants. "How do you feel about skipping ahead to the 'let's go back to my place' portion of this date?"

Kent signaled to Greta across the diner. "Check, please."

As soon as the door to Merry Holidays closed behind them, it was like a gun had fired at the start of a race. Their mouths locked. Their hands became ravenous beasts, tearing at each other's clothes like flesh from bones. Only the twinkling glow from the Christmas trees lit the path as they stumbled their way toward the back of the store.

"Bedroom," Kent said, the word coming out halfway between an order and a plea.

"No time. Counter," Noelle replied.

As they continued stumbling backward, groping and moaning like sex-crazed teenagers, Kent took pleasure in knowing Noelle was as affected as he was. He'd been dying to make love to her again, but he also hadn't wanted her to think that was all he cared about. She deserved so much better than that, and falling asleep in each other's arms the night before had been equally gratifying.

Well, almost.

When his bare back hit cool granite—*when had his shirt come off?*—he spun Noelle around and lifted her onto the countertop. "Are you sure you want to christen your shop this way?"

"As sure as I am that I need you right now." Noelle wiggled her pants down and kicked them onto the floor. Then, in one swift motion, she lifted and discarded her sweater.

He gaped at the sight of her. "You're not wearing a bra."

"I thought we moved past you being seventeen," she teased, reaching for his shoulders while using her feet to slide his jeans down his legs.

Kent stepped out of them, then gripped her hips. "I mean, you weren't wearing one all day… while running the store."

"And you weren't wearing any panties yesterday," she said, wrapping her legs around him. "I guess our ability to function isn't tied to our undergarments after all."

"Noelle," he groaned, his mind involuntarily traveling back to earlier that day.

He'd had a line several customers deep when *Kris with a K* had come into the store. Noelle had chatted with him briefly before the blond paper towel mascot had left without making a purchase. Kent had done his best to brush it off at the time, but now the thought of the neanderthal standing so close to Noelle with only a Christmas-themed sweater between them had him seeing red.

"Inside me. Now," she ordered.

As much as it pained him, he shook his head. "Not until you tell me you're mine."

"I'll tell you when you're inside me," she argued.

The woman drove him mad, and yet everything he'd said to her had been true. He was a shell of himself without her, the scantest fraction of a man. She made him whole.

But he needed more.

He needed to make *her* whole too, even if she was already perfectly complete to begin with. He needed to add value to her life in a way no one else could. Naked and breathless, Kent placed his hands on the counter when they began to shake.

"What's wrong?" she asked.

He couldn't believe he was going to bring it up now, at the worst of times. But he also knew he couldn't move forward if he didn't.

"I saw you talking to that Kris guy today. And I swear I'm not normally the jealous type, but you wanted rom-com love, and he's your small-town, flannel-wearing dream man who has a daughter *and* a Christmas tree farm. I need to know I'm not the guy standing between you and that dream, Noelle. Because as much as I want you to be mine, I'll never forgive myself if someone else could make you happier."

Noelle slowly shook her head. "Kent, no one could make me happier. I love you. Earlier today, I told Kris I'm not interested in him, and I'm not. Yes, on paper, he checks the boxes. But even before I realized my feelings for you, I knew Kris and I didn't have a deeper connection."

"Are you sure?" he asked, his frazzled nerves relaxing.

Noelle took his face in her hands. "Yes. You're my wholemate, dummy."

And then… action.

"Finally!" Noelle exclaimed as Kent slid into home base. *Look at her using baseball metaphors now.*

She felt like a new woman. Maybe that's what being in love did to a person. The old her would have equated the act to something like sliding down a snow-covered hill on a sled. Oh, how fun would it be to go sledding together? Nothing was more iconic when it came to a holiday romance.

Okay, maybe she hadn't changed *entirely*.

"Admit it," Kent said, plowing pleasantly deeper. "Wholemates is a great line."

Noelle nipped at his sexy lower lip in response, successfully resisting the urge to yell "never!" (Some would call that growth, thank you very much.) And okay, it was a great line—especially since he made her feel more whole than she could begin to describe.

Besides the amazing things he was currently doing to her body, Kent filled the void in her heart, a feat she'd once thought would require all of her dreams coming true. *A fairy-tale romance. A successful business. A marriage with lots of babies.* Noelle still wanted it all, but she no longer needed any of it. She only needed him.

Like a cowgirl desperate to stay on a raging bull, she arched her back and squeezed his hips until her thigh muscles quaked. Clearly understanding the assignment, Kent increased his pace, hammering into her with animalistic might.

"Yes, harder!" she cried, not caring that he'd likely buck her off the counter if he obeyed.

His smooth, hotel-room voice caressed her neck as he growled into it. "Tell me."

As with everything about Kent, she loved this side of him. Unabashedly needy, loving, and fierce. She didn't doubt for a second that he'd burn the world down for her like the alpha males in her dark romance novels, if that's what she wanted, or that he'd spout poetry and write love letters like the heroes of historical romances. He was the best of all the fictional men she'd ever read about combined, but even better.

Because he was real. And he was hers.

"I'm yours," she whispered to the perfect man tangled in her limbs.

Kent groaned and gripped her hips, thrusting even harder—half obedient puppy, half wild stallion—as she dug her fingers into his back to hang on for the best ride of her life. He did not disappoint, sliding his hands under her ass to mash their bodies together.

"Kent," she moaned, so close to climax already.

The depth and force of him would've probably hurt if it didn't feel so unbelievably good. Was that where the saying *hurts so good* came from? Noelle pondered that for a second before her mind went blank, gripped with pleasure. She wasn't sure if his body moved against hers or vice versa, but they ground on each other as if their lives depended upon it.

"You feel so good," he said, echoing her thoughts. "I love how wet you get for me."

"Only for you," she managed.

He replied with what could best be described as a snarl, before he lifted her off the counter and took several backward steps.

"Where are we going?" she asked, gripping his strong shoulders.

"To your bed, so I can make love to you properly."

Her heart thumped in her throat at his words, and she suddenly felt like a virgin—emotionally touched for the very first time. She'd had plenty of sex, but no one had ever *made love* to her before. The enormity of that settled in with the weight of an avalanche as Kent carried her up the stairs.

On top of that, she was still processing their love declarations from earlier that day—and the fact that Kent hadn't actually thought the horrible things she'd believed about herself for far too long. If it was possible to have positive anxiety, to be wonderfully overwhelmed, then it was happening to her now.

Noelle could hardly contain herself. Was this the beginning of their happily ever after? While she didn't know the answer to that, at least one thing was clear: she was about to have her lovemaking cherry popped.

29

14 days until Christmas

They'd spent the entire next week running Merry Holidays together, sneaking kisses while the store was open, and getting tangled in the sheets every moment it was closed. Besides breaks for meals and one unfortunate laundry trip to Clean It, the sister company to Screw It—literally owned by the hardware store guy's sister—neither of them had seen the light of day outside of Noelle's candy-cane-colored walls for days. And Kent was perfectly content with that.

"Mmm. I love and hate you right now," Noelle said, nuzzling his chest. "All that teasing was torture."

"The payoff at the end was worth it, though, right?" he asked, still basking in the glow of his own grand finale.

She replied with another sleepy "mmm" he took as a yes.

"Stopping right before the point of orgasm and then starting again not only prolongs enjoyment, but it's also supposed to intensify the experience," he explained. "It's called edging."

Noelle jerked up onto her elbows and stared down at him with wide, questioning eyes. "How do you know about edging?"

"Um… I read about it… in a book."

Her eyes narrowed to slits. "What kind of book?"

"A steamy rom-com novel," he said as nonchalantly as possible.

"*You* read romance books?"

"I read all kinds of books. Why does that surprise you?"

"Because," she said, "I always imagined you reading boring stuff, like *War and Peace*... and, I don't know. ... encyclopedias."

It was his turn to narrow his eyes. "Encyclopedias? For your information, the best way to learn something is often through genre fiction. Our brains absorb and retain facts better when they're part of a story. Also, there's nothing wrong with loving Tolstoy."

"Mm-hmm. So, you've always read rom-coms, then?"

"It's more of a recent endeavor," he admitted. "I know you love them, so I thought I'd see what all the hype was about."

"And?" she asked.

"And... I find them enjoyable, as well as educational."

Noelle collapsed atop him, her whole body shaking as she buried her face in his chest. "Oh Saint Nick!" she cackled.

"Me reading romance is not *that* funny, but I'm happy it amuses you."

Noelle wiped tears from her eyes. "Sorry, but that reminds me of one of my favorite rom-com series, *The Bromance Book Club* by Lyssa Kay Adams, which I totally recommend for you, by the way," she said, still laughing. "Anyway, the men in that series call romance books *instruction manuals*, and the way you said *educational*..." Her words trailed off into another fit of raucous laughter.

"Okay, okay. Laugh all you want, but you benefited from that education."

Then, as if a switch had been flipped, her laughter halted, her eyes darkened, and her mouth somehow grew fuller. Okay, wow... maybe he'd been reading too many romance novels.

"Yeah, I did," she said, nipping at his bottom lip. All traces of mirth had left her voice, which was low and sultry as she kissed her way to his ear. "Does Hyperion want to come out and play again?"

"Yes," he said without hesitation.

This woman would be the death of him, and he had zero fucks to give about that. He'd much rather give them all to her.

Her plump lips curved into a smirk. "I never explained how I came up with his name. Do you wanna know?"

Did he? Kent couldn't think clearly with her warm hand gently squeezing and tugging at his erection. She shifted to straddle his thighs, still pumping her fist, and he had to fight the urge to let his eyes roll back into his head. Holding her gaze, he managed a nod.

"The first time I saw him, pointing up at my ceiling, I thought he looked like a tree I wanted to climb," she said, teasing his tip with her thumb. "My mind immediately went to the world's tallest Christmas tree, because… well, you know me. But since you're not a fan of the holidays, I generalized it. Turns out, the world's largest living tree is a coast redwood named Hyperion."

"I love that… and you," he rasped, growing unbearably stiffer by the second. "You really know how to stoke a guy's ego, among other things."

"And you know how to turn a girl on by reading romance novels," she said, shooting him a seductive smirk before kissing her way down his chest.

"Noelle… Baby…" Kent sucked in a sharp breath when her hand moved to cup his balls, her hot, wet mouth taking in the rest of him. "I'll read every romance ever written if you keep doing that."

She licked him from base to tip several times before mumbling, "Mmm, next you'll start saying things like, 'Shut up and take it like a good girl.'"

Kent's jaw hinged open, first from her words, then from the sensation of his cock hitting the back of her throat.

"I'd never tell you to shut up, Gingerbread," he groaned, "but you're doing the rest of that statement perfectly."

He could feel her smile around him as her lips glided up and down his throbbing shaft. She moaned, and he nearly lost it right then and there. Kent blew out a curse that was incoherent even to his own ears.

"You like this?" she asked.

Was that a serious question? "Yes, but let me have a turn now. Apple pie's got nothing on that juicy peach of yours."

Noelle gasped as she slid up his body. "Kent Figgy Pudding Clark, did those educational romance novels of yours teach you how to talk dirty to me?"

He playfully spanked her ass and then flipped her onto her back. "I don't know. Let's hear what they've taught you."

"Let's," Noelle teased, biting his lip.

In response, he captured her mouth with his and deepened their kiss, drinking in her erotic moans. She tasted like sunshine and cinnamon.

Once he found the strength to break away, he said, "Sorry, I forgot I'm not supposed to use that contraction. Should I say *let us* instead?"

"No, let's has grown on me. Plus, *let us* sounds like lettuce."

He dragged his mouth down the silky flesh of her neck, nipping gently along the way. "Hmm, a safe word, then?"

"Lettuce?"

"Sure," he said, thoroughly distracted by the nipple reeling him in like a fish on a hook.

"Romaine!" she shouted with a giggle when he squeezed it between his lips.

"That's not it," he murmured, continuing south.

"Frisée?"

"Nope." He nestled into the space between her thighs. "I'm not coming up for air until I hear the magic word."

She gasped again as his mouth made contact. And then, "Your mom!"

His head shot up. "Okay, we really need to work on your dirty talk."

"No, I'm so sorry, Kent! I meant to tell you as soon as your memory came back, but then I got… distracted."

The remorse written on Noelle's face as she sat up in bed had him instantly flaccid. Distracted, indeed. How had he forgotten about taking care of his mother all week?

"What about my mom? Is she—"

"She's okay," Noelle said, answering before he could finish his question, "but she had a minor stroke the same night as your fall. Brad and Jess took turns staying with her at the hospital."

"A stroke?" *This couldn't be happening.*

"They think the chemo port in her arm might've caused a blood clot that traveled to her brain, but they're not sure. She's on a blood thinner and resting at home now, so that's good news."

"And what about…" he started, voice wobbling.

"There wasn't any damage, from what they can tell. Your mom is talking and acting fine, and Brad said she seems even more mobile and energetic than before the stroke." Noelle placed a comforting hand on his arm. "There's no need to worry, but you should go see your mom… like now."

30

"Why didn't you tell me about mom?" Kent punched Brad in the arm and immediately regretted it. "Damn, did you get injected with adamantium since the last time I saw you?"

"I hope you don't say nerdy comic book stuff like that to girls, and you had amnesia," Brad said. "You didn't remember mom had cancer. How was I supposed to tell you the treatment might've caused a stroke?"

"You could've told me everything, instead of lying to my face!"

Kent had sped like a madman toward San Diego. Noelle had offered to go with him, but he'd needed to deal with family matters on his own. It was bad enough that she'd lost out on Small Business Saturday revenue while he was in the hospital and several days of business after. He couldn't inconvenience her like that again.

Still, it had killed him to leave her—especially since she would have to clean the entire store without his help. *Some boyfriend he was already turning out to be.*

Brad straightened his broad shoulders, posturing like a peacock spreading his feathers. "Did you give Noelle shit, too? She could've told you sooner."

"No, it should've come from you. Don't put your cowardice on her."

"That's enough," Carole said, entering the kitchen. "Stop bickering like a couple of teenage boys and give your mother a hug."

Kent did as instructed, wrapping his arms around her too frail shoulders. "Ma, you should be resting."

"Oh, hush. That's what death's for, Kid. How's your head?"

"It's fine. I'm more worried about you," he said, pulling back to check her face. "Your color looks good, at least."

"Of course it does. I'm not dead yet."

"Ma, that's not funny."

"I agree with Kent for a change," Brad said. "Don't even joke about that."

"And here I thought I raised two sturdy boys with a sense of humor." Carole ran her hand over the brightly colored scarf on her head. "Look, I know you both worry about me, but that's the problem. I'm the parent; let me do the worrying."

"But mom—"

"No but mom," she said, cutting Kent off. "Cancer may have kicked my wide behind, but it can't keep me down. In fact, I have some good news."

Kent pulled out one of the kitchen chairs, hoping his mother would take the hint and sit down. She, of course, waved him off.

"Stop fussing over me. I'm not made of glass." Carole motioned to the living room. "Let's go sit on the couch. We need to have an overdue conversation."

Kent locked eyes with Brad as their mother waltzed out through the arched doorway, using neither the walker nor cane he'd bought for her. Though her improved mobility was a positive, sitting on the couch to talk always meant trouble.

"After you," Brad said.

"Age before beauty," Kent replied.

"Well, in that case, you should definitely go first. I'm far better looking."

Kent rolled his eyes, then willed his legs to carry him into the living room, where his mom sat on their worn-down, rose-colored couch with her arms crossed.

"I'll start with the good news first," she said. "My PET scans came back yesterday, and I'm officially cancer-free again."

"That's great news, Ma!" Kent rushed forward to hug her but was blocked by her raised hand.

"It is, but I also have some news you might not be so happy about."

Her tone had a *you-better-sit-down* quality to it, so he took the seat next to her. "Okay… I'm listening."

"You need to move out," Carole said, in her typical sugar-coatless fashion. "I'm moving up north to Washington and selling the house. I probably won't list it until spring, though, so take all the time you need."

"Washington? The state?" Kent looked to Brad. "Did you know about this?"

"I found out yesterday," Brad said. "Ma, since I already know the rest of this story, can I go now?"

Her stare said, *sit your butt down*, so Brad did.

Kent gripped the couch cushion. "Ma, how are we going to—"

"Don't you dare finish that sentence," she said. "You don't need to take care of me anymore. That's what I want you to get through your—thankfully—thick skull! I appreciate everything you and your brother have done for me over these past few months… over your whole lives, truly, I do. But enough is enough."

Kent wanted to protest. Didn't she realize she would only need their help more, not less, as she got older? How could he make sure she was okay if she was out of state?

"Why Washington?" he asked instead.

"The San Juan Islands, to be precise. I'll be living on a boat, spending my days on the water like I've always dreamed, and watching the most magical sunsets every night in the warm arms of my lover."

"Lover?" Kent blurted, at the precise moment Brad cough-choked.

"Seriously, Ma, please don't make me hear this part again. Can I be excused?"

"Fine," she said to Brad. "Come kiss your mother goodbye and then kiss those grandbabies of mine when you see them."

The room spun as Kent processed it all. His mother was cancer-free (a huge relief), but she'd apparently met someone (How? When?) and was moving to the opposite latitude of the country. (The San Juan Islands were practically Canada!) And she was selling his childhood home—the dwelling where they'd shared quality time during home improvement projects, family dinners, and game nights; the walls where their past heights were still marked; the house where he'd assumed his mom would live forever.

"How could you leave Lucas and Chloe?" Kent asked. "And what about when I have kids?"

"It's not like I won't visit," Carole said. "And Mel and I would love to host guests on the boat. It sleeps eight comfortably."

Brad zoomed past him in a cartoon-worthy exit. "Bye, bro," he said, the door slamming behind him.

Though fairly certain he didn't want to hear the answer, Kent had to ask. "Mel?"

"Yes, Mel is a wonderful man I met during chemo. His sister, Hope, was on the same treatment schedule as me, and Mel would come in with her for every appointment." Carole lowered her voice and dipped her head. "Hope's cancer was unfortunately late stage, though, and she was eventually put on hospice."

"I'm sorry, Ma."

"Me too. Mel was devastated, but he kept showing up during my treatments. He said it was to keep me company, but I like to think it helped him through his grief as well. When Hope passed, I attended the funeral with him to pay my respects and—"

"Wait," Kent interrupted. "When was that? How did I not know any of this was going on?"

His mother's expression turned sheepish. "I may have told you that Brad was picking me up for the day, but it was actually Mel. As morbid as it sounds, Hope's funeral was our first date outside the hospital. It drew us much closer, emotionally and physically."

Kent closed his eyes and pinched the bridge of his nose under his glasses, trying (and failing) to block the mental image of their mother getting *physical*. No wonder Brad had exited with Flash-like speed.

"Anyway, between my own ordeal with cancer and Hope's passing, the whole experience reminded me that life's too short to not follow your heart."

"And your heart is leading you to Washington? To live on a boat? You hate camping, Ma." He'd never known his mother to be quixotic. And now she was planning to literally sail off into the sunset with a man she just met?

"Have you ever been in love?" she asked, taking him by surprise.

His brain immediately conjured thoughts of Noelle. Her smile. Her snark. The way the world felt right with her in his arms.

"Never mind," his mother said, "I know you have. Unfortunately, it's been with a girl who doesn't seem to deserve you."

"What are you talking about?" Kent asked, his defenses immediately on high alert.

He rarely argued with his mom, but World War Three was going to break out in their living room if she was about to put down the woman he loved.

"Relax," she said. "Noelle is a lovely girl. What I'm saying is, I've watched you be a lovesick puppy over her for years, and she doesn't deserve your love if she's not going to return it. I don't want to see you get hurt like your…" His sagacious mother's eyes glazed over as she trailed off.

Since there was no point questioning how she knew about his feelings for Noelle, he instead asked, "Hurt like who? Brad? His marriage with Jess didn't work out in the end, but I don't think he'd say the love they shared all those years wasn't worth it. Besides, Noelle and I are together now."

Carole's penciled-in eyebrows raised. "Oh?"

"Yeah, there was a misunderstanding between us, back from our high school years," he explained. "It caused her to hold a very justifiable grudge against me, but we've cleared things up and we're good now. She loves me back, Ma. You can stop worrying about me."

"I see."

"No, no, don't 'I see' me." Kent wagged his finger at her before thinking better of it. "That's what you say when you're skeptical, but it's true. Also, how'd we even get on this subject? We were talking about you thinking it's a good idea to live on a boat all of a sudden."

"We got on the subject because love changes you. It makes you see possibilities for your life that you never thought possible before, like leaving the home you've been rooted to forever to go on an extended holiday. It makes you want to live life to the fullest, dive in headfirst, seize the day… Basically, you turn into an inspirational Pinterest board."

"Okay," he said slowly, still unsure of her point. "So, if I'm understanding you correctly, staying in San Diego, where your sons and grandchildren all reside, is not living your best life."

"Don't be obtuse! Moving away from you all will be incredibly difficult for me, but that's just it… Sometimes, you have to stray from the easy path to explore everything life has to offer. Take the road less traveled and whatnot."

"Wow, you really have become a motivational screen saver."

"And I have love to thank for it." She rested her hand on his knee, giving it a gentle squeeze. "Look, I'm sorry if this is all coming as a shock to you. Raising you boys has been the most rewarding and fulfilling experience of my life. Being a mother was always enough for me. I didn't need romantic love to feel whole. But frankly, I also never knew what I'd been missing. When I fell in love with Mel, everything changed."

"Ma, I didn't mean to guilt trip you about being in love. You deserve that and so much more. If you're happy, I'm happy for you, always. I only wish you could stay *here* and be happy… with Mel," he added begrudgingly, "but if you want to live on a boat, who am I to stand in your way?"

"I know it's wild, and perhaps even foolish. Maybe I'll hate boat life, or Mel and I won't work out, and I'll be back before you know it. But *maybe* this is the adventure I've been waiting for my entire life. It's like love has given me wings. I can't let the risk of falling stop me from soaring."

"Nor should you." Kent shook his head. "Wow, Ma. You're practically glowing. I've never seen you like this before."

"I've never been in love before, kiddo."

"But you were married… to Dad."

Carole sighed and took his hand. "This is the overdue part of the conversation."

31

Noelle stared blankly out the large window of Merry Holidays, which didn't feel as merry without Kent. The sky had recently transitioned from its orange-pink gradient to the shadowy blues that proceeded total darkness. It reminded her of the nights she'd spent at the beach as a child, watching the thin line between sky and sea become indistinguishable. *Maybe it wasn't too late*, she thought as she walked over to close the blinds. She could hop in Evergreen and drive down to see him right now.

Though Kent had been adamant that he needed some one-on-one time with his mom, Noelle knew he'd only said that because her store had been such a mess after the weekend frenzy. In fact, knowing him, Kent was probably beating himself up over not being there to help *her*, when he was the one in need of support. *Ugh*, why hadn't she fought harder before letting him leave? She hated not being there for him.

With the ocean feeling worlds away, Noelle squinted to make out the mountain ridges that marked the horizon instead. Only… the window pane was fogged, and the scene beyond it looked like the static of a TV tuned into the wrong channel. She wiped at the glass with the sleeve of her favorite faux-fur sweater while blinking to clear her eyes, but the white specks blurring her vision didn't budge.

Because they were outside.

Snow flurries—a welcome, wondrous sight… any other time but tonight. She scoffed at the poetic irony. Her long-time love of all things Christmassy, including winter white weather, suddenly felt like a mean joke. Call her a Grinch, but she now hated the snow… Every. Last. Inch.

Given the dangers of driving in any kind of precipitation, let alone icy conditions on a dark, mountain road, she wouldn't be able to go see Kent that night—nor would he be able to drive safely back to her. That last thought had her pulling out her phone. After five dreadfully long, unanswered rings, Noelle hung up on his voicemail and tried again.

And again.

After the third failed attempt to reach him, her heart and mind both raced. She was mentally listing all the people she could try calling next (his mom, Jessica, Brad, local hospitals, the police…) when her phone buzzed with a text message.

> **Kent:** Hey, sorry I didn't get back to you sooner. My mom is doing fine, but there are some things I need to work out before returning to Holiday Pines. I'm going to stay at Brad's place tonight, and maybe a few more days, but I'll be back to help you with the store before the weekend rush. I hope you'll be fine managing on your own in the meantime. Sorry again.

What in Santa's little sweatshop? Kent obviously had his phone, but rather than answering her desperate calls, he'd merely texted her? The idea to send him back a question that only he could answer—to ensure he wasn't being held by kidnappers—flitted past her like a rapidly falling snowflake before crashing into the ground and melting into oblivion when she read his words a second time, and then a third.

The text was definitely from Kent, and yet it wasn't. There was neither an "I miss you" nor an "I love you" even vaguely implied. Worse, the message's tone was that of every other guy who'd blown her off after getting what he'd wanted, usually before ghosting her entirely.

But Kent wouldn't do that. Not to her, not to anyone. Of that Noelle was certain. So, *what in the flocked Christmas tree* was going on?

Noelle: Help with the store is the least of my worries. Is everything okay?

She waited a beat, and then another. Her earlier texts throughout the day asking Kent how things were going with his mom had also gone unanswered. She hadn't read too much into it at the time, but it gnawed at her now. Whatever was wrong, he clearly didn't want to talk about it with her. She sent another text.

Noelle: It's snowing here tonight, otherwise I'd drive down to see you. I'm glad you're safe, at least, and not on the road. I love you (heart emoji)

Noelle stared at her phone with bated breath for what felt like forever. Whenever she blinked, she worried she might have missed those hopeful dots dancing on the screen, but as with a watched pot, nothing happened. No typing dots danced. No reply came.

A deep, weary ache settled in her bones as she crawled into bed (alone) later that night, and with it, sudden clarity. Noelle couldn't explain how she knew, and although she didn't understand *the why*, her body felt *the what*.

Kent Faltering Clark planned to break up with her.

Kent picked up his Stephen King novel and opened it to where he'd left off. Though he'd never admit it aloud, horror was his comfort genre. His life might be complete shit, but at least he wasn't tied to a bed in a deranged woman's cabin, about to get his foot chopped off with an axe. No, his misery ran much deeper.

Not only had he learned that his mother had never been in love with his father—that previously undisclosed fact being the real reason Caleb Clark had abandoned his entire family on Christmas Eve—but his parents' tragic story also contained parallels to Kent's own relationship that couldn't be ignored.

"One more chapter," he mumbled to himself.

Before long, golden light shone in from the window, casting its glow on the soothing cream pages inked with an assortment of letters that, when arranged in the right configuration, were a security blanket for the soul. He'd happily get lost in a book forever if it meant he didn't have to deal with reality.

As the chilling story neared its denouement, a deep, guttural sound jolted him. "Son of a …!" Kent yelled, fumbling the book in his hands until it hit the ground with a resounding thud.

"You're lucky you didn't finish that sentence. If you had, I'd be obligated to kick your ass," Brad said with a laugh. "Scary book?"

"More like scary brother," Kent replied. "You snuck up on me out of nowhere."

Brad sipped from the mug in his hand, his bright eyes twinkling in apparent amusement. "I've been standing here for like five minutes. Ran the coffeemaker and everything. How long have you been awake?"

"Uh, an hour or two." Did it count as being awake if he'd never gone to sleep? "Thanks again for letting me crash on your couch last night. I should be out of your hair soon. I'm planning to tour a few apartments later this afternoon."

"No problem," Brad said, plopping down beside him.

"What are you doing? Don't you have work today?"

"One of the foremen I hired is supervising the site this morning. I'll get there when I get there. It seems time for a little brotherly heart-to-heart first."

"I don't think that's—"

"Oh, but it is," Brad interrupted. "Look, the news about Dad hit me pretty hard too, but I also kind of understand why Ma didn't tell us."

"You would." Kent stood, needing some distance. All the outrage he'd been doing his best to quell rushed to the surface with a vengeance.

Brad placed his hands on his knees, as if he might spring off the couch. "What's that supposed to mean?"

"It means you always avoid tough conversations. You didn't tell me when you first found out about Mom's cancer returning. Then you lied to me when I had amnesia, placing the burden of breaking the news on Noelle instead." Kent threw his hands in the air. "Hell, when you got caught cheating on Jess, you made her best friend tell her rather than coming clean yourself. It's what you do, Brad. You keep the hard truths to yourself. Like mother, like son, I guess."

"Are you done?" Brad said with a calmness that was more jarring than if he'd yelled.

Kent stopped pacing, only mildly aware that he'd been doing it, then he crossed his arms and said, "For now."

"Good, because I have some hard truths to deliver to you, little brother. If you don't get your oversized head out of your ass, you're going to lose the best thing that's ever happened to you."

Kent gritted his teeth. He'd already lost everything. He didn't need his brother rubbing salt in the wound.

"And yes, I may be a lot like our mother," Brad continued, "which is probably why I can sympathize with how difficult keeping a secret like that for all those years must've been for her. I'm sure she already feels like shit. You not talking to her is piling it on."

"How can I—"

"I'm not done. I may be like Mom, but you're acting like Dad, shutting down when things get too emotional for you to handle."

"Dad died!" Kent exclaimed. "And Mom let us think he didn't love us enough to ever come around again. How can you forgive that so easily?"

Brad sat back on the couch, his skin blanching to match the ivory walls. "Dad died? What does that mean exactly?"

Well, shit. Kent dragged a hand down his face. "I take it Mom never got to that part of the story with you." A pained laugh escaped him as his next words left a bitter taste in his mouth. "Of course she didn't. She left it for me to tell you, like you would."

"When did he die?" Brad asked, still alarmingly calm.

Kent took a deep breath, then rejoined Brad on the couch. "Six months after he left. Heart attack."

"Shit," Brad muttered.

"Exactly. He'd been served their divorce papers right before it happened. Mom claims she never told us because she felt responsible. Her guilt kept the truth from us."

Brad nodded, as if that made all the sense in the world to him.

"Are you seriously still not pissed at her?" Kent asked.

"I think I'm still processing, but no. To be honest, I'm kind of glad she never told me."

"Glad? How can you be glad?"

"I know it sounds weird, but Dad was my hero when we were kids. I wasn't even mad at him when he left, not really, because I figured he couldn't help it." Brad shook his head. "But now, knowing the man I idolized was alive for those six months when we needed him, and he couldn't even bother to give us a phone call... Yeah, I'm glad I didn't know that."

"Hold up." Kent held up a hand, the synapses of his brain firing on all cylinders. "All this time, you thought Dad had..."

He couldn't finish the sentence. The mere idea... It was an unprovable theorem. An infinite limit. The square root of impossible.

"I've never said it out loud before," Brad said, "but Dad's 'I can't do this anymore' message read like a suicide note, and Ma never talked about it, so yeah, I thought that's what happened. I knew Dad loved us, so I figured his grief over Franklin had taken him from us. It was hard to be mad at him for that, even though what I assumed was awful."

Only the low hum of the refrigerator and occasional muffled sounds from neighbors in adjacent apartments could be heard during the silence that fell over them. Kent wasn't sure how long they sat like that, together but in separate worlds with their thoughts. Then, at the speed of the last remaining glacier melting, the profoundness of the entire situation hit him all at once.

Kent straightened in his seat. "For the last twenty-five years, I'd assumed our dad was alive and well but didn't care enough to show up, or call, or even send us birthday cards. I'd searched for him in the crowd at every one of my games and graduations, feeling disappointed and angry each time he didn't show. Meanwhile, you believed he'd loved us all along but had taken his own life. You'd found your own peace with that and moved on."

"It seems we were both wrong," Brad said.

"No, I was wrong. Dad loved us, like you thought. And he probably would've shown up for us eventually, if he hadn't passed away."

Brad nodded along. "Yeah, I'd like to think he would have."

"Me too," Kent said. "Wait, if Mom didn't tell you about Dad's heart attack, what did she tell you?"

"Just that she'd never been in love with him, and that he knew. I didn't ask any more questions after that, because I figured she felt responsible for what I'd thought he'd done. I didn't want to make her feel worse." Brad went quiet for a long moment, touching his steepled fingers to his lips as if gathering his thoughts. "So, in all these years, you really never considered the possibility that the reason Dad didn't show up for us was because he wasn't alive?"

"Never," Kent admitted. Then, with another pained laugh at his own naivety, he added, "And that's probably a good thing, because I used to think it was my fault that he'd left us."

Brad contorted his face into an expression that would likely contain an expletive if said aloud.

"His 'I can't do this anymore' note had been written on the back of my wish list," Kent explained. "I'd asked Santa for a bike that year, and when I got old enough to understand the financial stress our parents had been under from all the hospital bills, I figured my request was the final straw that drove him away. Thinking about it now, your suicide theory would've been a much more logical conclusion based on the facts I had, but I guess my guilt wouldn't let my mind even go there. It was less painful to assume he'd just stopped loving us."

"Damn, bro, that's awful. Now I understand why you're mad at Mom for not telling you the truth a lot sooner."

Kent shook his head. "No. It's not fair to blame her for my misguided beliefs. I'd never shared how I'd felt with anyone."

Brad grunted what sounded like his agreement before saying, "That brings me back to what I wanted to talk to you about. Why are you sulking on my couch, instead of in the arms of the woman we both know you've been in love with forever?"

Kent dragged his gaze out the window. Two birds (doves, maybe) sat huddled on a tree branch; the sunny, blue sky behind them—all a sharp contrast to his inner turmoil. "It's complicated."

"Of course it is! Love is complicated as hell," Brad exclaimed. "And look, I know I'm probably the worst person to give anyone romantic advice, but whatever's weighing on that big brain of yours, you need to talk to Noelle about it. You said so yourself… It's not fair to pin your misguided beliefs on someone else, especially if you never share how you feel."

Kent wanted to argue that his beliefs weren't misguided, not in this case, but Brad was right. He owed it to Noelle to at least tell her how he was feeling.

"I ignored her calls and texts yesterday," Kent said, deflating along with his lungs. "She probably hates me again now, and I don't blame her."

"You know, for a genius, you can be pretty dense at times." Brad clapped him on the back. "That's even more reason to go talk to her!"

32

13 days until Christmas

When Noelle stirred awake that morning, there was a coldness along the side of her body where Kent's warmth should've been. She reached out to pat the mattress beside her, opening her eyes when she felt nothing. Then she remembered.

Kent wasn't there.

He'd said—or texted, rather—that he might not come back for days. *Well, not if she had anything to say about it.*

She popped out of bed faster than a kid on Christmas morning and rushed downstairs to ready herself. The thin blanket of snow outside was already beginning to melt under the cloudless sky. A second, bigger storm was expected later that evening, if one could trust the forecast, but Noelle wasn't planning on waiting around to find out.

If Kent wasn't coming to her, she was going to him.

She'd tossed and turned most of the night while mulling over the pros and cons of her action plan. If Kent didn't want to talk to her, he most likely didn't want to see her, either. Showing up at his brother's apartment uninvited and unannounced might even constitute "crazy girlfriend" behavior. Noelle couldn't be sure, but she also didn't care.

It had struck her as odd that Kent would be staying with Brad, rather than at his mom's house. Something was definitely amiss, and she was going to get to the bottom of it.

After getting ready in record time, Noelle pulled on her mid-length puffer coat as she walked out the door. That was, perhaps, why she didn't see the tree of a man standing outside her store.

"Oof!" she yelped, as the side of her face hit what felt like a fabric-covered brick wall.

For a hopeful second, Noelle's heart dared to believe the wall was Kent, there to apologize for his previous radio silence. But a strong waft of pine and the distinct feel of flannel against her cheek told her otherwise.

"Kris," she said, taking a step back. "I didn't see you standing there."

"I'm so sorry! Are you okay?" Kris asked, gripping her shoulders.

"Yeah, I'm fine. Just… What are you doing here?"

His hands dropped awkwardly to his sides, then he hooked his thumbs through his belt loops and looked side-to-side like a cowboy in an old western.

"Dasher. He's gone missing again. I stopped by to ask if maybe you'd seen him."

"Sorry, I haven't, but I'm heading out right now, so I'll be sure to keep an eye out for him along the road."

"Good. Thanks. Good." Kris rocked on his heels. "Listen, I don't want things to be weird between us," he continued.

"It's not weird. We're good," Noelle said with a smile she hoped was convincing.

"Good," he repeated, taking her hand in what she hoped was a friendly gesture. "Because I know you said you weren't interested the last time we spoke, but if things don't work out with that other guy—"

"I'm gonna stop you right there," Noelle said, pulling her hand back as politely as possible. The rest of her response was on the tip of her tongue, but her trembling jaw had her clamping her mouth shut instead.

If things don't work out with that other guy.

No, things *had* to work out with "that other guy."

That other guy was her entire world.

That other guy was her freaking wholemate.

That other guy was... standing across the street, next to a reindeer, looking as if he'd been sucker-punched in the face.

"It's not what you think," Noelle was saying for the third time after ushering him into her store.

"And what do I think?" Kent asked, feeling even more numb than he had when watching his worst nightmare play out in the frigid air. *Noelle smiling at her flannel-clad dream man. Kris holding her hand. The two of them looking like they belonged on the set of a damn Hallmark Christmas movie.*

Not that it mattered, he reminded himself. It only reinforced what he already knew.

"That there's something between Kris and me," she said, "and I promise you there's not. I was on my way to come see you when I ran into him." Noelle squeezed his hand. "What happened with your mom, Kent? I can tell something's wrong."

A laugh escaped, weak as it was. *Something's wrong* felt like the understatement of the century. "I don't know where to start."

"Why don't we go upstairs, and you can start from the beginning."

Why don't we? Yet another phrase that would forever remind him of her. The long version of *let's*.

As soon as Kent sat on the edge of Noelle's bed, he knew following her upstairs had been a mistake. He wanted to hold her, to be comforted by her, but allowing himself that indulgence would only make what he needed to do that much harder.

"I learned a lot of… stuff… when I talked with my mom," he began, ignoring the slight dip in the mattress and the warmth of Noelle's shoulder grazing his when she took a seat beside him. "For starters, she's selling my childhood home and moving to the San Juan Islands to live on a boat with a guy named Mel, who she's apparently in love with."

"Wow. Is she… healthy enough to be doing that?" Noelle asked.

"That was my first concern, too, but she claims she's cancer-free now and has never felt better."

"That's good news then, right? I mean, it sucks about your childhood home, but everything else is a positive. Your mom sounds happy and healthy."

Kent sprung from the bed. "You don't understand!"

"Sorry," Noelle murmured, and he immediately hated himself.

"No, I'm sorry," he said.

It wasn't her fault that he hadn't explained the parts that mattered yet, the parts that Kent wasn't even sure he could say aloud. Like how, on the day before his family fell apart, his dad had pleaded with his mom to tell him what he could do differently to get her to fall in love with him. Or how his mother's response had been: You can't make someone love you. They either do, or they don't. And if you have to jump through hoops to win them over, it probably won't last anyway.

Carole had looked meaningfully at Kent when she'd repeated the words. *You can't make someone love you.* Her pity-stare during the silence that followed had told him the rest. It wasn't just the response she'd given to his father all those years ago; it was a motherly warning. What he had with Noelle wouldn't last.

But maybe he could prolong things. "We don't have to talk about my discussion with my mom right now. How was your day today? I mean, yesterday," he amended, remembering the early morning hour.

"Well, it sucked not being with you, but I was productive. I got all the shelves and trees restocked, mopped the floor, cleaned the bathroom, filled the register with coins to make change… Boring stuff like that." She picked at her bedspread, avoiding his gaze. "I was worried when you wouldn't take my calls last night… or respond to my texts."

So much for delaying the inevitable. "Yeah, I'm sorry about that. I was afraid I'd say the wrong thing."

Her green eyes jumped up to meet his. "You could never say the wrong thing to me, not if it's the truth. Please, promise me you won't walk on eggshells in this relationship. If I get upset or cry over something you say, that's on me. Do you understand?"

"But I never want to make you—"

"Promise me, Kent."

He nodded, even though he didn't agree. He'd hurt her once before with his careless words, and he'd rather die than witness a repeat of that. The problem, however, was that the truth seemed inescapable.

"I feel like I love you more than you love me," he said carefully, before correcting himself with a headshake. "No, that's not the full truth. I don't think you love me at all, not really."

"That's crazy!" Noelle exclaimed. "Of course I love you. I wouldn't say so if I didn't mean it."

"I believe that you believe that," Kent said, the way he imagined one might deescalate a hostage situation. "Or at least you *want* to, since this all feels like a fairy tale."

Noelle couldn't believe her ears. She'd known he'd had some insecurities about their new romance, as evidenced by his frequent need for reassurance, but to flat out deny her love for him was unconscionable.

"Look, I know things have moved fast for us," she said, "but we're already at a point where we're discussing starting a family together. If that's not being sure about someone, I don't know what is."

"That's just it, Noelle. You're sure about wanting a family, not about me." He shook his head. "I can't believe I didn't see it sooner."

"What do you mean? Wait, where are you going?" she asked when Kent shrugged on his coat.

"I mean, you love the idea of having a baby, regardless of who it's with. I'm just the guy who came along at the right time for your 'fall in love and start a family by Christmas' plan."

"That is so not fair! You're the one who offered to impregnate me *whenever I want*, like a soap opera character or something, but I'm fine with waiting. I'm not on a pre-Christmas timeline, Kent, and none of this"—she motioned between them—"was part of my plan."

"Wasn't it, though?" Kent slid his thick-framed glasses up his nose and paced in front of the bed. "You hated me, then I hit my head, became your fake fiancé with amnesia, and *bam*, you suddenly love me? Sounds like a rom-com to me. And let's not forget the 'dream-ending of a movie' part when you found out I was Average Joe. Was that what sealed the deal for you?"

"Don't use *let's* like that. You're ruining it. You're ruining everything." Her lip quivered as she spoke, despite her best efforts to steady it.

Kent let out a strangled groan and placed his hands on top of his head. "I know I'm ruining it! I've always wanted to be with you, Noelle, but not this way. I don't want to be some guy you settled for because I fit your plan. Or one that you pitied, because I was in a coma when you found out I'd been secretly in love with you. Or worse, nothing more than a sperm donor to you."

"You think I want you for *your sperm*? What the hell, Kent! This isn't you."

The Kent she knew would never be intentionally cruel. There had to be more going on with him, something he wasn't telling her.

"You're right. I'm sorry," he said, head hung low. "I'm gonna take off now. I need some more time to think."

"No," Noelle declared, rising from the bed to literally and figuratively stand her ground.

"No?" he asked, gawking at her.

"That's right. No, I'm not going to let you walk out of here to 'think things over' or whatever." Noelle made air quotes as she spoke. "You said you'd never leave me, and I'm going to hold you to that. You're not going to *third-act breakup* us because you're scared."

"I'm not—"

"I get it. Trust me. It's scary that you could love someone more than they might love you back. And it's scary that you can lose people and be left all alone in this world. Anyone who chooses to love *anyone* takes that risk. I'm taking it with you, and I'm scared too, because regardless of what your big, hard head thinks right now, you're wrong about how I feel about you."

Fueled by nervous energy, Noelle paced in circles around the Kent statue in her loft. This was not how their story ended. "Yes, I realized that I loved you after your fall, but it wasn't out of pity or guilt. It was from the gaping hole that the mere possibility of your absence left in my heart. And yes, I love that our story has elements from some of my favorite rom-coms—like us being enemies who became lovers at an inn with only one bed; and me falling in love with your secret identity online; and even you getting amnesia and becoming my fake fiancé for a hot minute—but none of that means that I don't love you for *you*, Kent.

"You're a handsome, smart, kind, *sometimes* witty, family-oriented man with questionable fashion sense and an amazing heart. You're the type of man that reads romance novels because I love them and, more importantly, the type of man that fights for what he wants. You never gave up on me, even when I pushed you away for years, so I'm not going to give up on you now. Because, my hard-headed wholemate, when you love someone, you fight for them."

"Can I speak now?" Kent asked.

She crossed her arms over her heaving chest. "No one's stopping you."

"Good, because you had me at no."

Unable to hold back her squeal if she tried, Noelle rose on tipped-toes and threw her arms around his neck. "Ooh, I love that! For the record, though, the full line is, 'Shut up. Just shut up. You had me at no.'"

Kent's lips curved up into the first smile she'd seen on his face that day. "I would never tell you to shut up, Gingerbread."

That earned him a kiss.

"Kent Franklin Figgy Pudding Clark, I'd rather fight with you than make love with anyone else." She held up a hand. "Yes, that's borrowed from *The Wedding Date*—a Dermot Mulroney classic—and no, that doesn't make it any less true."

"Are we still fighting, then?" Kent asked with a sexy arched brow.

"Yes. We're not done until we discuss why you ever thought I'd use you for your Olympic swimmers. Because I wouldn't, not even if they were gold medalists." Satisfied by the contrite expression on his face, Noelle lowered herself onto the bed and patted the spot next to her. "Now, sit down and tell me everything that happened when you went to see your mom."

33

0 days until Christmas

Kent couldn't wait for Noelle to come downstairs to open her gifts. Frankly, he was surprised she hadn't yet. Despite all her talk of being too excited to sleep, she'd been out colder than a hibernating polar bear when he'd rolled out of their warm bed hours ago.

To be fair, it had been a long Christmas Eve, starting with a morning visit to the nursing home to distribute Noelle's famous gingerbread cookies, and concluding with a midnight mass with the Serrano family. In between those events, there'd been a surprise thirtieth birthday party for Noelle at an ice-skating rink—his sore ankles were worth the smile on Noelle's face as he'd twirled her on the ice—and before that, they'd had brunch at his mom's house.

Though the wounds of Carole's secret would still take considerable time to heal, Kent had reconciled with his mother soon after sharing the full story of his parents' history with Noelle. Luckily for him, Noelle had been incredibly forgiving of what she now called his "third-act meltdown." With her help, Kent had also acknowledged the no-longer-avoidable truth: his biggest fear wasn't ending up all alone; it was ending up like his father.

Caleb Clark had fallen madly in love with Carole when they were both in high school—much like Kent had with Noelle—and then he'd pursued her for years, despite Carole making it clear she didn't feel the same. Their parents had been next-door neighbors, so whenever Carole returned home for family visits, Caleb would offer his help with random tasks for the sole purpose of spending time with her. He'd even once told her that simply being in her life was enough for him—another painful similarity to how Kent had often felt.

Out of pity, Carole would let him fix things from time to time, like a leaky faucet when her landlord was out of town or a flat tire on the side of the road. Then one day, after he'd asked her out yet again, she'd been feeling lonely and had decided to give "Nice Guy Caleb" a chance. Two months later, Carole was pregnant with Brad. They got married, moved to California, and the rest was history.

Carole had grown to love Caleb over time, but it was never the same intense feeling she knew he'd felt for her. That divide only deepened after they'd lost Franklin, as Caleb clung to her for support, while Carole withdrew into her grief, reserving what love she had left exclusively for her sons. Hence the 'I can't do this anymore' after ten years of marriage.

Kent could still picture the shock on Noelle's face when he'd recounted the whole tragic story to her, all the way through to Caleb's untimely heart attack. She'd mumbled something he didn't quite understand about an "accidental pregnancy trope gone wrong" and then proceeded to assure him they weren't like his parents. With each day that passed, he was allowing himself to believe that more and more.

Further, Kent realized that the things he'd done for Noelle over the years—and would continue to do—did not constitute "jumping through hoops to earn her love," as his mother had inaccurately implied. Everything he did was to bring joy to the woman he loved. Noelle deciding to love him back… well, that was merely icing on the gingerbread cookie.

A creak from the staircase drew Kent's attention up to the best Christmas present he could ever imagine. Curves wrapped snuggly in a snowman-themed onesie; a mass of chestnut curls sticking up in every direction; and a smile that could power the world.

"Good afternoon, sleepyhead. Merry birthday!"

Noelle's half-closed eyes scanned the room. "Where's that Christmas music coming from?"

"That would be your store's new wireless sound system, or present number one," he said. "I installed it this morning."

Her sparkling green eyes, fully open now, nearly popped out of their sockets, cartoon-character style. She crossed the room to where he stood and wrapped him in the best hug of his life. *The true joy of Christmas.* He could definitely get onboard with this holiday.

"Thank you! You shouldn't have spent so much on a gift for me, but... I love it, I love it, I love it!" she exclaimed, bouncing in his arms, up and down with each *I love it.* "I also love the sound of present number one, but the sound system is more than enough."

 "One combined present for your birthday *and* Christmas?" He scoffed in mock offense. "I wouldn't dream of it! We both know how you feel about that."

"Past-me may have been a *teeny, tiny* bit obsessed with gifts... and gift-giving... and all things gift-related, but..." She gripped him by the shoulders and leveled him with her stare. "Kent Franklin Clark, the only present I want this year is standing right in front of me."

The sincerity in her voice as she full-named him had hot springs forming in the depths of his eye sockets. Was he about to cry? *Pull it together, KFC,* he scolded himself in the manner he assumed Noelle might.

Except... Noelle wouldn't want him to hide his feelings from her. She would be okay with him crying. And so, as sudden as a craving for apple pie à la mode, Kent was okay with it too.

"Same. All I want for Christmas is you," he said, before wiping his cheeks dry and adding, "But you've got three more gifts to open, so let's get to it."

Noelle grabbed his arm when he reached for the larger of the two boxes under the tree. "Hold on there, Mariah. You know you've already got me, right? I'm yours."

Kent nodded, fearing his mouth would fail him. *I'm yours.* While he'd never get sick of hearing those two blissful words—well, one contraction plus one word—he also felt slightly ashamed of how badly he needed to hear them.

As if sensing his thoughts, Noelle ran her hands down his arms, lingering on the exposed flesh of his forearms before taking his hands. She gave them each a little squeeze as she said, "We all have insecurities—in fact, I'm convinced the human body is just an elaborate handbag designed to hold them—and that's okay, as long as we don't let our insecurities stand in the way of our happiness. For far too long, I let myself believe I wasn't smart enough or impressive enough for a certain type of guy, and that kept me from the best thing that's ever happened in my life. You!"

"That was my fault, because of what I'd—"

"No," she said, cutting him off, "Believing the lie falls on me. To be honest, I don't think your words from high school would have mattered at all if I didn't already have that insecurity, deep down, telling me I wasn't good enough. It's the lies we tell ourselves on repeat that hurt us the most."

He nodded again, because *damn if that wasn't the truth.*

"Anyway," she continued, "I feel like that's the perfect segue into me giving you *your* gift."

"You didn't have to get me anything."

"Yes, I did, but don't get too excited. The store's not making any money yet, and I know you're not big into material things anyway, so your gift is more… conceptual." She looked up at him with an *I hope that's okay* expression, and he laughed.

"Conceptual gifts are my favorite! Hit me with it," he said, puckering his lips.

She granted his wish with a soft peck before saying, "Check your phone."

"My phone?"

"Yeah, check it already."

"Okay, okay."

Kent looked around the store, spotted his phone on the counter next to his toolbox, and dutifully walked over to retrieve it. The notification banner on his lock screen had him squinting to make sure he'd read it right.

"What's this?"

"Open it and see," she said.

And so, he did.

```
To: average_joe
From: everyday_merry

1. I hate that you catfished me; it was a really
   shady thing to do. But I couldn't feel an
   ounce of anger, only joy that it was you.

2. I hate that you're a literal genius, but not
   a know-it-all. You never use your big brain
   to make others feel small.
```

"It rhymes and everything," he said.

Noelle stuck out her tongue in response as he continued reading to himself.

```
3. I hate how much you love me and the selfless
   way you care. Like how you made me soup
   without onions, or that time you held back
   my hair.

4. I hate how good you look in glasses, and the
   stormy eyes they hide. If you were an X-Men,
```

> you'd be Cyclops with a dash of Wolverine on
> the side.

Kent guffawed so hard that liquid would've squirted from his nose if he'd been mid-drink. "I have no idea what that's supposed to mean, but I appreciate the nerdy superhero reference for my benefit."

"They're both hot," Noelle said. "Read on."

> 5. I hate that you think you're a nerd, when
> you're the coolest person alive. You're
> passionate about the things that count (math
> pun!), like helping your students thrive.

> 6. I hate that you bought me feminine products,
> since nothing else can compare. You're like
> that Sinéad O'Connor song or All-4-One's
> greatest hit, "I Swear."

> 7. I hate your perfect forearms and the sexy way
> they flex. They're almost as hot as Hyperion,
> when we're… conversing over text. (Get your
> dirty mind out of the gutter. Tsk, tsk.)

Heat crept up his neck as he allowed his gutter mind to recall the passionate love they'd made earlier that morning, before she'd fallen asleep in his arms at the crack of dawn.

"You got to the Hyperion part, didn't you?" Noelle asked, a sultry dip in her voice. "Keep going. It gets better."

> 8. I hate that you always say exactly the right
> thing, like how I'm yours and you're mine.
> I've never met a man with a butt so fine.

"You mean this thing?" he asked, sticking his backside in her direction.

Noelle shook her head. "I've created a monster, and you're kind of proving my next point."

9. I hate your cheesy sense of humor, and the loving uncle that you are. Because I'd be lying not to admit… those qualities are my favorites by far.

10. But most of all, I hate that you feel unloved, when the opposite is true. All the babies in the world won't make me whole, not if I can't have you.

Forever Yours,
Noelle

P.S. You're my wholemate, dummy.

Kent removed his glasses, not bothering to fight the dam bursting behind them. This woman… How could he be so lucky?

"Happy tears?" Noelle asked, stroking his cheek.

"Extremely," he said. "Your *Ten Things I Hate About You* poem is the best gift I've ever received."

"Way cooler than a boring list of things I love about you," she said with a smirk, "but in either case, I'm hoping it's something you can refer back to whenever you have any pesky doubts."

"I'll never doubt your hate again," he joked, before sobering from the weight of her gesture. "Thank you, truly. You have no idea what this means to me."

"I have some idea," she said, leaning in for another kiss. "Ten points for knowing the movie reference, by the way."

"Oh yeah? What does ten points get me?"

"It depends," she said, short-circuiting his brain by playing with the drawstring of his pajama bottoms. "Do you promise to never again accuse me of wanting you only for your baby batter?"

Kent dropped his head in shame. "I'm never going to live that down, am I?"

"Not in this lifetime," she confirmed, "but you're forgiven, nonetheless. You know why?"

"Because you love me?"

"Well, that, yes. But also…"

"My five hundred apologies?" he guessed. "Because I can keep expressing my remorse."

"Those helped, but no." Noelle playfully pinched his chin. "What I'm trying to say is, I think it's because I'm growing as a person. It's like love has banished all of my petty, grudge-holding tendencies. Does that make any sense?"

Kent thought of his mother's words, about how love changes you, and it made all the sense in the world. More importantly, it validated what Noelle had been telling him all along: she really did love him.

"It does," he said, his heart inundated with joy. "Now, can I please give you the rest of your gifts?"

Ten minutes later, Noelle had relieved her bladder, brewed some Gingerbread Spice tea to refill it, and settled onto the luxurious pillow fort that Kent had created under her favorite tree in the store. She'd also torn open the wrapping paper of her next gift with all the fervor of a young child on… well, Christmas. Warm lights twinkled all around them as she gaped at present number two in action.

"This is officially the best birthmas ever! And it's totally going in the book."

The best part? She'd get to spend the rest of her favorite day with her favorite person, just the two of them. Normally, she would've spent Christmas at her sister's house, inserting herself as an extraneous wheel (third, fifth, ninth, etc.) while her niece and nephew opened their presents from Santa. As heartwarming as watching the joy on their little faces was, it paled in comparison to this.

"What book?" Kent asked.

"Oh, I didn't tell you? When I went to lunch with Sandy last week, she offered to co-author a romance novel with me! We, as in she and I, are going to write the story of us, as in you and me! It'll be mostly true, with some fictional liberties taken, of course."

"Uh-oh. Should I be scared?"

"Don't worry, I'll change our names to protect the guilty," she said with a wink. "Anyway, I'm gonna need you to stand up and strut toward me now, so I can get the full effect of my gift."

"Don't press your luck," he warned.

"I'm told I'm very lucky, and I finally agree. Seriously, let me get a better look at you."

Kent rolled his eyes but stood.

"Take two steps back," she directed. "Perfect. Now, smile," she said, raising her phone to snap a quick photo before he could object.

"Hey, pictures weren't part of the present!"

"I'm going to look at you every day," Noelle said to the dreamy man in the photo, temporarily ignoring the life-size version in front of her.

"Stop, you can't possibly like it that much," real Kent said, playfully grabbing at her phone.

"We all have our fetishes. Don't judge mine." She looked up to scan her gift, top to bottom, losing herself in the repeating pattern of squares and miles of lean, manly muscles. On a satisfied exhale, she said, "Mmm, you sure know how to rock a flannel. Losing the pajama bottoms was a nice touch."

The color of his cheeks deepened to match the red-and-black buffalo plaid shirt hugging his chest. The fit was neither too tight, nor too loose—the goldilocks of flannels—and, *thank the toymaker*, he'd rolled the sleeves up to his elbows.

"They would've clashed with the shirt," he said, looking around as if they weren't the only two people in the room.

As far as she was concerned, they were the only two people on the planet in that moment.

"I one hundred percent agree," she said. "A plaid-on-plaid mountain-man tuxedo would not have been a good look for your first flannel experience. In fact, you should always pair that shirt with those black boxer briefs."

Kent Flannel Clark crossed those magnificent forearms of his. "I can't tell if you're teasing me or being serious."

"I never kid about fashion." Noelle stood and straightened his collar. "Best. Present. Ever."

Kent's gaze dropped to her mouth, a wide smile on his as he closed the small distance between them. She parted her lips, more than ready for his kiss, but he merely brushed his nose against hers once he got into position.

"Let's get to the next one, then," he said, his words warm on her skin.

Then, *poof*—a small box appeared in his hand. Kent took a step back and held it up for her to take. The simple square, topped with a large red bow and crudely wrapped in the same green-and-red paper used for the shirt, was… exactly the size of a ring box.

Noelle's breath caught in her throat. "Kent, I… I…"

"Go ahead and open it," he urged. "But I should warn you, this present is more for me."

She took the tiny package with trembling hands, its weight even lighter than she'd expected. Through a stroke of kismet, "This Christmas" by Donny Hathaway started playing through the sound system. *A very special Christmas, indeed.*

On a deep inhale, she took in the ambiance of her festive store, the coziness of their spot amongst the decked evergreens, the soft glow of the lights, which had recently transitioned to their steady phase—a metaphor for the next stage of her life, maybe?

"Why aren't you opening it?" Kent asked.

"Well…" she started, then paused to find the right phrasing. "I guess I'm waiting because this feels like a moment that shouldn't be rushed. Like, maybe one I'm going to want to remember forever?"

She'd posed her last statement as a question, hoping he'd either confirm or deny her suspicions, and yet his stupid, handsome face gave away nothing. Since when was Kent Forthright Clark a poker player? Ugh. The suspense was officially killing her. There was nothing left to do but open the box.

Each tear of the wrapping paper took ten years. Seriously, how much tape was needed for such a small package? *Good things come in small packages*, the voice of Jiminy Grinch sing-songed in her head.

When Noelle had finally removed enough gift-blocker to pry the lid open, she did so with the haste of a Black Friday shopper at a doorbuster sale. The lid dropped from her hand as she stared into the box, her disbelieving eyes promptly welling with tears.

"Is this some kind of joke?" she croaked. "Because if you gave me an empty box to mess with me, then—"

"No, no, no," Kent said. "Look closer. The box isn't empty. I swear."

Noelle took a deep breath and leaned in closer, feeling as if she were about to enter a magical realm by diving into the box headfirst. She angled her head left, then right, and then she saw it. A small piece of folded paper. Was that his proposal? Would there be four life-changing words scribbled on that scrap of tree pulp? She reached in to find out.

Using her index and middle fingers like a pair of tweezers, she extricated the paper fragment without touching the edges of the box—a feat easily worth three hundred dollars in the game of Operation. *Score!* And why did this suddenly all feel like a game or puzzle she needed to solve? Did Kent know her so ridiculously well that he knew she'd enjoy this? Or was she simply jumping to hopeful conclusions?

She unfolded the paper and was even more perplexed by what she saw. A random series of numbers: 5-5-7-3-1. Was it some type of math riddle? A clue that would lead her to her next clue, like in an escape room? And what would be on the other end of that door?

"Five, five, seven, three, one," she said, hoping hearing it aloud might jog her brain into recognition.

"Yeah," Kent said slowly, "you must be wondering what that means. Sorry, this gift probably isn't as exciting as I'd hoped it would be. You see, I wanted to wrap a shiny key in there—kind of like Derek did for Natalie when he bought her dream home—but the modern convenience of keyless entry prevented such a gesture."

"A key? To a home?" Noelle felt her eyes widening with each question.

"Yes, kind of. Five, five, seven, three, one is the security code that unlocks the cabin I rented in Holiday Pines… for us, if you'll move in with me," he said.

There were no words, so she continued to stare at him, her mouth opening and closing like a goldfish.

"The rental is lease-to-own," Kent continued, "so we'll have the option to buy later, if you love it there, or we can keep looking for your dream home. There's no pressure, of course, if you're not ready to live together. Either way, I wanted to move closer to you. The cabin is only a few blocks from here, and it has a full kitchen and a laundry room—meaning no more trips to Clean It, the place where whites go to die pink." He paused, most likely waiting for the laugh that felt stuck somewhere between her heart and her mouth. "Noelle, please say something. Was this overly presumptuous of me?"

"It's perfect," she finally managed to say, a single tear streaming down her face.

"That's a happy tear, then?" he asked, sounding optimistically skeptical.

She nodded, jostling a few more tears loose.

"So, is that a yes to a shared address?"

Leave it to this man to make a pun out of her favorite reality TV show. She threw her arms around his neck and freed her laugh. "Yes! A million times, yes!"

His gift might not have been what she'd been expecting, but it was perfect. Kent was moving to Holiday Pines to be with her, and he'd leased a cabin that sounded great. The lack of a marriage proposal didn't mean that Kent was any less committed to her... Did it?

No, of course not. They'd barely started dating, and living together was a gigantic step forward. Hadn't she just given Kent a lecture on insecurities? She needed to get her own in check. Besides, her burning desire to get married surely stemmed from a lifetime of societal conditioning. And by society, she of course meant her mother.

Noelle knew Kent loved her. She didn't need proof in the form of a ring and some silly piece of... paper. She stared once again at the note in her hand, as if it might hold the answers to the universe.

5-5-7-3-1.

"Hey, where'd you go?" Kent asked, slowly waving a hand in front of her eyes.

"Oh, I was wondering about... your life in San Diego, your job?"

"Well, I can commute when school starts back up in the new year. The hour drive isn't ideal, but it's completely doable, and I've already started looking into opportunities at Holiday Pines High for a transfer next fall. My mom is moving out of state in a few months anyway, and as for the rest of my life... I'm looking at her, right here."

Well, Blitzen. He really did always say exactly the right thing.

"Have I told you lately how much I love you?" she asked, never feeling those three little words more.

"Not exactly, but you gave me a pretty kickass list of reasons you hate me." His smile grew three sizes, and so did her heart.

"It was pretty kickass," she agreed. "Thank you so much for finding us a place. When can I see it?"

"We can go over there whenever you want. That is, if you're sure about living together. You don't think it's too soon, right?"

"No, not at all. Not unless you do," she hedged.

"I definitely don't," he said.

"But?" she prompted, sensing its presence in the nervous energy radiating between them.

"But," he repeated, a bit shakily, "I can't stop thinking about how disappointed you looked when you opened that box. Was it because you were hoping for this?" Kent asked, dropping out of her line of sight.

When Noelle's gaze followed him down, her hands flew to cover her mouth. Because, kneeling before her, on a single bent knee, was the man of her dreams, wearing a flannel and holding up a stunning ring. It had a pear-shaped diamond in the center, with alternating rubies and emeralds around the band... just like her grandmother's wedding ring. No, wait. It *was* her grandmother's wedding ring.

"What is this?" she asked, hardly believing her eyes.

"This is present number four, which, like the last one, is really for me. Noelle Mary Serrano, will you make me the *merriest* man alive by becoming my non-fake fiancée and soon-to-be wife?"

Tears rained down her face as she dropped to her knees beside him on the pillow fort. "Yes, yes, yes! I will happily *merry* you and marry you."

After a much-needed, slow-melt kiss—reminiscent of spring beginnings, summer nights, fall treats, and winter holidays all rolled into one delectable feeling—Noelle pulled back to admire her soon-to-be husband. His slightly tousled hair; the dark stubble visible beneath the smooth skin of his jaw; those stormy blue eyes piercing through straight to her soul, as Kent Fiancé Clark slid the ring onto her finger.

She'd been right before. She wanted to remember this moment forever.

"I have to know," she said. "How did you get this ring?"

"I got it from your dad when I asked his permission to marry you... a few years ago."

Noelle nearly choked on her tongue. "*Years* ago? We weren't even... I didn't even... You were my mortal enemy!"

Kent shrugged, his cheeks once again matching his flannel. "I'd overheard you saying it was the ring you wanted to be proposed to with someday, and I knew right then that I had to have it. I tried to buy it off him, but your dad wouldn't take my money."

Of course he wouldn't. Not only was Carlos Serrano a man of pride, but he already loved Kent like a son. All the "gentle" nudges her dad made in Kent's direction over the years made total sense now.

"So, we made a deal," Kent continued. "If you fell in love with someone else, I'd give the ring back. Otherwise, I'd spend the rest of my life doing whatever it takes to make you happy. It was a great deal, if you ask me."

"Years ago," she repeated, shaking her head in awe. "And here I thought you might not have been ready for such a big commitment."

"No, I've been ready all along," he said, lightly stroking her ring finger. "Sorry if my tactics today created any doubt. I only asked you to move in first in case you needed some time to catch up to my feelings. If living together had felt too soon for you, then I wouldn't have risked freaking you out with a marriage proposal until you were ready. You've been worth the wait, Gingerbread, and I'd wait for you as long as you needed me to."

"We've both waited long enough," she said, running her hands up his fleshy forearms (*yum,*) to his flannel-covered biceps (*double yum,*) and then resting them on his strong shoulders. "Let's start our forever now."

@bookstafashionista

Photo caption:

We're engaged!!! Check out my new bling! (Heart emoji, ring emoji)
I know it's been a while since I've provided an update on my top-secret project—because, life—but here's the high-level recap:

Two months ago, I moved to the small town of Holiday Pines with a plan to find love before Christmas. Given my in-depth knowledge of the common romance tropes found in books and movies, I'd figured it would be easy to recreate some of those conditions in real life. As luck would have it, I immediately met the cookie-cutter definition of a small-town heartthrob, and, to cover my bases, I anonymously chatted with another prospect online. My plan (a.k.a. top-secret project) seemed to be progressing exactly according to… well, plan.

That was, of course, until my world got turned upside-down by the man I'd long ago sworn off. And that's when I learned a valuable lesson: Love cannot be planned.

Sometimes, you find love when and where you least expect it. Other times, love has been there staring you in the face all along, waiting for you to get out of your own way to see it. In either case, when love comes along, be prepared to be *unprepared*… and then hold on to it with everything you've got.

Until next time, dear followers, stay merry!
#Imgettingmerried #loveunplanned #whenloveholidays

Epilogue

"Santa Baby"
Eartha Kitt

2 years and 51 weeks later

They'd gotten married exactly one year after Kent's proposal—because why not celebrate one's birthday, Christmas, and wedding all on the same day?

It had been a small ceremony (with close family and friends, plus half of Main Street) in a surprisingly grand room within Holiday Pines Inn. Noelle had asked Marge to officiate, mostly to creep Kent out, and the lovely innkeeper had thrown in a free night in the honeymoon suite—the same magical place where her enemy-turned-lover had taken up permanent residence within her heart.

On their first wedding anniversary, they'd once again rented the honeymoon suite—because, heart-shaped tub—and it was there that their "conceptual gifts only" tradition began. Despite the non-material nature of their gifts, Kent had outdone her once again when he'd handed her a document signed by a judge. It was a certified copy of his legal name change… to Kent Franklin Figgy Pudding Serrano-Clark.

Yes, you read that correctly. She was now legally married to Kent Franklin Figgy Pudding Serrano-Clark!

Impossible to top as that was, Noelle had researched the best online PhD programs for mathematics and printed out admission forms as a symbolic gesture. Kent had helped to make her dreams come true, and she wanted to encourage him to pursue his own as well. He'd resisted at first, saying that his dream had already come true the day he married her—*be still, her romantic heart*—but the irrefutable fact remained that he deserved more than a single dream.

"The saying, 'When one door closes, another opens,' is used after a loss or unfortunate ending," she'd said, "but what about after a dream has been realized? Are there no doors left to open?" She'd let him stew on that a moment before continuing. "Here's what I think. Dreams don't require doors, or windows, or structures of any kind; they're boundless. Yes, sometimes you need to narrow your focus to achieve one, but that doesn't mean your other dreams have to go away, or that a new dream can't be born every single day. After all, what is a life without dreams?"

A few months later, Kent had applied (and was subsequently accepted) to a prestigious PhD program with online classes that started in the fall. To celebrate his acceptance, they'd decided to start trying for a baby, and… as it turned out, Kent *did* have Olympic gold medalist swimmers.

Yes, once upon a time he'd knocked her out with his big, hard head. Then he'd knocked her down into a puddle. And now he'd knocked her up as well… times three.

According to the soon-to-be PhD (Perfectly Hot Dad *and* Doctor of Philosophy,) the occurrence of natural triplets was about once in 8,000 conceptions, or 0.013%. But when had the odds ever stood in their way before?

Noelle stood outside the master bathroom of the cozy cabin they now owned, their cat, Jingle, in her arms and their dog, Bells, napping near her feet. *One of each, please.* "Come on out, Big Guy, you can't hide in there forever. We need to get going soon."

"Yeah, no," Kent said through the door. "I don't think I can do this."

"Yes, you can. I know you can." Noelle wiggled the door handle, discouraged to find it locked. "At least let me in. I have to pee," she said, only half lying.

Her compressed bladder could squeeze out more than a few drops on command at this point. The real trick was holding it in.

"Nice try. There's another bathroom down the hall."

"That's too far. Are you really going to make your triply pregnant wife wet herself?"

Noelle waited one second, then two. A muffled grumble could be heard through the door, and on the count of three, it swung inward.

She rushed in, and—"Oh Saint Nick!"—her hands flew to her mouth as she took in the sight of her man sporting more red than Rudolph's nose. "You are one tall peppermint milkshake."

"I know I said I'd do anything for you, Noelle, but I think this is what that Meat Loaf guy was talking about when he said 'but I won't do that.' Even love has limits."

She pressed her lips together. "I don't know what you're talking about. You look perfectly normal."

Kent raised a bushy, white eyebrow, and the giggle she'd been trying to suppress snuck out.

He peered over his rimless glasses at her. "I don't know if I should be upset that you're making fun of me or relieved you don't have a weird Santa fetish."

"No Santa fetish, oddly enough." She stepped closer and tugged down on the scruffy white beard until it revealed his pouty bottom lip. "But I do have a 'Kent wearing something to make me happy' fetish. I promise I'll make it worth your while."

"Well, when you put it like that." His mouth quirked into a smile as he leaned forward, his soft *bowl full of jelly* pressing into her ultra-protruding belly.

Then Kent Claus kissed her, deep and slow. She had half a mind to cancel the event and stay home all day, exploring every inch of the firm muscles beneath his padded suit, but the children of Holiday Pines and beyond were counting on them.

"Thanks again for doing this," she said, the extent of her gratitude swelling in her chest. "None of this would've been possible without you, and I'm glad we can celebrate the store's success together with an event for the entire community."

After three years in business, Merry Holidays had finally recorded four consecutive profitable quarters. There had been a lot of ups and downs—from launching an ecommerce market and trying to attract customers during the off-season, to dealing with supply disruptions and inflation—but Kent had always believed in her, and his support meant more than he could possibly know.

"Willing participant or not," she continued, "it'll mean a lot for the kids. By the way, Lucas and Chloe already know you're Santa today. Jess didn't want them to get confused if they figured it out, so she told them the real Santa handpicked you as his special helper to collect everyone's Christmas wishes, since he's too busy loading the sleigh—something about there being an unforeseen number of children on the nice list this year."

"Wow, Santa selected me himself?"

"Yeah, you two go way back. North Pole nursery school. Ready to go?"

Kent straightened his faux-fur-trimmed Santa hat. "As ready as I'll ever be."

"All right then… From the bathroom to the hall," she sang in the melody of "Get Low" by Lil John, while ushering her man out the door. "Now dash away, dash away, dash away all!"

'Twas the week before Christmas, and all through the store, the event was going better than any before. The custom Holiday Pines keepsake ornament she'd ordered for the occasion sold out within hours. Owners and employees from all the local businesses stopped by with their families. And loved ones came up from San Diego, including Carole and Mel, who were still living the boat life, only now from the relative closeness of Shelter Cove Marina in Mission Bay.

After their nautical-themed nuptials (on land for Noelle's benefit), Kent's mother and her new husband had decided to stay local for the upcoming birth of their new grandchildren, and to spend more time with Chloe and Lucas—both of whom were also excited to meet their three new double-cousins.

Noelle's favorite part of the day, though, had been Santa Clark patiently listening to young children's wish lists for hours and bouncing all the babies on his knee, as she envisioned him soon doing with theirs. He was going to be an amazing father.

"This Santa gig may have to become an annual thing," she whispered in his ear when the line died down.

Much to her surprise, he replied with, "I was thinking the same thing."

"Are you saying you actually had fun today?"

"More than I thought I would. Although…" Kent Claus pulled her onto his lap. "Yeah, this is much better. And what would you like from Santa this year, young lady?"

Heat rushed to her cheeks as she leaned in to avoid being overheard by the few patrons left in the store. "If I told you, I'd end up on the naughty list."

"Ho, ho, ho," he said with a deep rumble that traveled to her toes. "I've checked my lists twice, Gingerbread, and your name is already on both. You're perfectly naughty and nice."

A throat cleared and they both jolted to attention. Noelle turned to find five sets of eyes on them.

"Sandy, you're back! I'm so glad you all could make it!" She climbed off Kent's lap and embraced her friend, next directing her attention to Dane, William, and Daisy. "I was asking Santa for... a pony."

"Is that what they're calling it these days?" Sandy mumbled for her ears alone.

"Good to see you both again," the man beside her said. That man being none other than Noel Kris Clauson (a.k.a. Brawny Thor; a.k.a. Sandy's new husband.)

In an epic friends-to-lovers romance worthy of their own book, Sandy and Kris had recently discovered their deeper feelings for each other. They'd gotten married on the Clauson family's tree farm in October and had spent the past month in London on an extended honeymoon. As happy as Noelle was for them, it was great to see her dear friends back in the States.

"Both?" Sandy Poppins asked Kris, no doubt for Daisy's sake. Of the three children, she was the only true believer left. "Have you met Santa before, love?"

"Definitely," Kris said, not missing a beat. "Santa used to hang out at our place all the time. Remember, kiddo?"

Daisy nodded, and Kris tousled her blond curls before adding, "But now that Pops and Nana are retired and the farm is only open part-time, it makes more sense for Old Saint Nick to come visit the town at Merry Holidays instead."

Kris shot a wink in Kent's direction, and the two men shared a discreet smile. Astonishingly enough, they were good friends now. Kent had gotten over the whole *former-dream-man thing* soon after he'd "put a ring on it."

It's a wonder what an "I do" can do for one's self-confidence, but in all honesty, Kent deserved full credit for his personal growth. He'd put in the work by going to therapy after the revelations about his parents, and thankfully he now understood that his false beliefs about not being worthy of love were precisely that—false. She couldn't have been prouder of him.

Once the kids were settled with Santa, Mrs. Sandy Clauson pulled Noelle aside to catch up. "I have an early birthday present for you, straight off the printing press," she said in her British accent, handing Noelle a padded manila envelope.

Noelle sucked in a breath. "Is this what I think it is?"

At Sandy's nod, Noelle popped the envelope open like a bag of chips. She couldn't care less about preserving the packaging. Its contents were all that mattered.

And there it was. Almost three years of self-doubt and sleepless nights. Countless hours of writing and rewriting. The editing process had been a *literary* nightmare before Christmas (pun intended), but all of that was worth it as she held the labor of love in her hands.

"I figured you'd want to be the first one to hold your book baby," Sandy said.

"Our book baby," Noelle corrected.

"No, no. This one belongs to you. I contributed the way a man impregnates a woman, but you nurtured and birthed it. Speaking of which, how are you feeling today?"

"I assume you mean about this," Noelle said, rubbing her enormous belly with one hand while still gawking at the book in her other. *Was this overwhelming feeling of pride what motherhood would feel like?*

"Yes, ma'am," American Sandy said with a slight drawl. "You're due any day now, right?"

"Almost. My C-section is planned for New Year's Day, unless little Nicholas, Holly, and Joy decide to grace us with their presence sooner. Kent and I have a running joke that I'll probably go into labor on Christmas… which is both incredibly exciting and terrifying. This present is doing a great job of taking my mind off of it, though."

"I can still remember holding my first book baby," Sandy said, switching to a wistful British lilt. "I'd never admit this to anyone else, but it felt even better than holding my human babies for the first time."

"I can see that," Noelle said, not taking her eyes off the gorgeous paperback in her hand.

"Not that I don't love my boys," Sandy amended. "It's simply a matter of level of effort. I carried Dane and William for less than nine months, whereas my first book took almost five years to write."

Noelle nodded her understanding while reading the cover of *her* book baby.

Love, Unplanned
Written by Noelle Serrano-Clark and Sandra Bullock

It really existed. Their book wouldn't be published for another week—on Christmas Day, of course—but it existed. If not for the physical evidence in her hands, Noelle wouldn't have believed it. Soon, all of her fellow romance and rom-com book lovers could experience the (mostly) true story of a young woman whose life was forever changed when love unexpectedly "holidayed" with her in Holiday Pines.

Side note: Even though Sandy had gotten remarried, her pen name remained unchanged. Not only was she an established author with a brand to maintain, but Sandra Bullock was pure marketing gold.

Noelle admired the beautiful, matte cover—complete with a heart made from evergreen boughs—a while longer before thumbing through the crisp pages, landing on her favorite line at the very end of the book.

And they lived happily ever after.

And they did, for the most part.

Marriage, as Noelle would learn, wasn't always easy. Kent and she still bickered from time to time, especially over differences in their parenting styles (Who gives their five-year-old triplets ice cream for breakfast to avoid hearing them cry? Kent, that's who.) And don't get her started on the amount of noise from her dear husband's nightly oral hygiene routine (the electric toothbrush, the Waterpik flosser, the gargling... so much gargling, *ugh*.) And okay, she probably did a few things that bothered him, too.

But despite their squabbles over the years, neither of them would have changed a thing. Because each and every day, they made one simple decision—to love one another—and they were merrier for it.

In **the end**, that's all that ever mattered.

Thanks for reading! If you enjoyed this book, please consider leaving **a review on Amazon** (even if purchased elsewhere or borrowed.) Even short ones help! Please & thank you!

Also, for those on Instagram, be sure to follow Noelle **@bookstafashionista**... That's right. It's a real account!

Lastly, you can find all of my links and subscribe to my infrequent blog at: **SJGREENEBOOKS.COM**

Noelle's Playlist

1. "Run Run Rudolph"
   Kelly Clarkson

2. "It's Beginning to Look a Lot Like Christmas"
   Michael Bublé

3. "You're a Mean One, Mr. Grinch"
   Thurl Ravenscroft

4. "My Only Wish (This Year)"
   Brittney Spears

5. "Dance of the Sugar Plum Fairy"
   Pentatonix

6. "Baby, It's Cold Outside"
   Idina Menzel feat. Michael Bublé

7. "Let It Snow! Let It Snow! Let It Snow!"
   Dean Martin

8. "Christmas Tree Farm"
   Taylor Swift

9. "Where Are You, Christmas?"
   Faith Hill

10. "Do They Know It's Christmas?"
    Band Aid

11. "The Thanksgiving Song"
    Ben Rector

12. "Santa Tell Me"
    Ariana Grande

13. "Please Come Home for Christmas"
    Eagles

14. "Somewhere in My Memory" (From *Home Alone*)
John Williams

15. "You Make It Feel Like Christmas"
Gwen Stefani

16. "Like It's Christmas"
Jonas Brothers

17. "Last Christmas"
Wham!

18. "All I Want for Christmas Is You"
Mariah Carey

19. "Santa Baby"
Eartha Kitt

Bonus "vibe" tracks:

19. "We Need a Little Christmas"
Pentatonix

20. "This Christmas"
Donny Hathaway

21. "The Nutcracker: March"
Tchaikovsky

Acknowledgments

This book would not have been possible without:

- ❖ Love and support from my husband and all of my dear friends throughout my author journey.
- ❖ My amazing first-reader and romance book bestie, Sarah, who can read through an entire draft freakishly fast while still also providing comments.
- ❖ All of my other advanced readers (and readers in general) who gave this book a chance. Thank you!
- ❖ Lots of Christmas music, Gingerbread Spice tea, and occasional espresso cocktails.
- ❖ A healthy obsession with rom-coms—movies and books—carefully developed over many decades.
- ❖ Em dash—the queen of all punctuation—followed by an ellipsis in close second…
- ❖ Did I mention espresso cocktails? It's currently 2am, and I may have had one of those.
- ❖ A lot of people I'm probably forgetting at the moment, so if you're one of those people, please know that I heart you.
- ❖ And last but not least: me. That's right. I would like to thank myself for not giving up, even when that meant rewriting this book multiple times to get it just right. You're welcome, Future Me.

About the Author

Born and raised in Southern California, S. J. Greene currently lives in San Diego with her husband and adorable rescue dog, both of whom are the loves of her life. She enjoys spending time in nature… and reading books! As an author, she strives to help readers imagine a better world—full of happy endings—one book at a time.

Though romance is at the heart of all her stories, S. J. Greene likes to color outside the lines when it comes to genres. In her Fresh Start series, **When Love Hurts** is a romantic suspense novel with crime elements, whereas **When Love Heals** falls under contemporary emotional fiction with LGBTQ themes. **When Love Holidays** is a romantic comedy. She also has plans for another rom-com, a psychological thriller, and a fantasy series…

Be sure to follow her on social media and subscribe to her blog at SJGREENEBOOKS.COM to stay updated on what comes next!

Links to all can be found here: https://linktr.ee/author.sjgreene